I0451061

THE
VILLAINOUS VISCOUNT

— OR —

THE CURSE OF THE VENN'S

AN HISTORICAL
PARANORMAL ROMANCE SATIRE

LUCINDA ELLIOT

The Villainous Viscount
Copyright © 2016 by Lucinda Elliot All rights reserved.
First Print Edition: August 2016

ISBN: 0-9927361-5-3
ISBN-13:978-0-9927361-5-6

Cover and Formatting: Streetlight Graphics

Inca formatted Template Version 5.0
www.incaproject.co.uk

No part of this book may be reproduced, scanned, or distributed in any printed or electronic form without permission. Please do not participate in or encourage piracy of copyrighted materials in violation of the author's rights. Thank you for respecting the hard work of this author.

This is a work of fiction. Names, characters, places, and incidents either are the product of the author's imagination or are used fictitiously, and any resemblance to locales, events, business establishments, or actual persons—living or dead—is entirely coincidental.

To Jayne
and
To Rebecca
With love

I would like to thank all my patient and obliging writer friends who have helped me so much with this work. Robert Wingfield, Jo Danilo, Christina Merlyn, Anne Carlisle, Rebecca Lochlann, Robert Gregson, Jenn Roseton and many others. Heartfelt thanks to all.

1.
Grotesque News

March 1821
Berkshire

"MY DEARS: BOTH GOOD AND bad news," James Greendale, flushed with excitement, looked round the door of his wife's sitting room, where she sat with his two younger sisters. "Poor Uncle Greendale is dead. A bolt of lightning toppled a wall on him over in France, squashing him flat."

His wife dropped her embroidery: "Merciful heavens!"

His youngest sister squealed.

"How horrible," Clarinda patted her hand. "I hope he didn't suffer?"

"Probably not," said James, "It all happened so quickly. Poor old Uncle Greendale! I wish we had rubbed along better together. I'm sure that talk about his being involved in the black arts was only malicious gossip."

"Of course, my love," said his wife, "Such a shocking end; but his misfortune is somebody else's gain. He was so wealthy; I wish he'd left us just the tenth of his money."

As Clarinda hoped that the outrageous old sinner was already forgiven, James face split into the smile he had been keeping back since he opened the lawyer's letter. "He's gone one better than that, dear. He's left every penny to Clarinda."

The others stared, speechless a moment, then spoke at once: "That's absurd!" his wife frowned, while, "I cannot possibly accept it," said Clarinda, "It was so generous of my uncle that I don't care to speak against him, but really…"

"Don't be ridiculous, girl! It was only the other night that I was regretting how few offers you've had. Now, you'll be able to pick and choose."

His youngest sister's eyes lit up. Clarinda frowned. "If through coming into my uncle's money I am to be hounded by fortune hunters, then that is no great benefit."

"Don't be coy. We'll take a smart house in Town for the season, and see what we can do for you." He broke off, flushing. "But obviously, now is not the time to think of such things. We must order our mourning clothes."

"Whatever can have possessed your uncle to leave his wealth to a girl of twenty-one rather than to you?" His wife asked sourly. Still, the look she turned on Clarinda had in it some awe; she was no longer a plain looking unmarried burden with an unsuitable name, but an heiress.

James shook his head. "It is bizarre. But things might have been worse; before now, the reprobate threatened to leave his fortune to his horse."

Foyle's Fatal Accident
May 1821
London

George Foyle, lean from debauchery and impeccably dressed, was in the middle of the group of revellers who surged towards the high, winding staircase leading down to the doors of the Coconut Club. Most were unsteady on their legs and breaking into snatches of song.

One suggested they give a Charley's kennel[1] a sound shaking. Lord

---

1   Charley's kennel: Before the introduction of a London police force in 1829, night

Venn[2] objected, saying the poor old fellows weren't worth plaguing, but tricking a constable with a false alarm might be fun. With howls of laughter and talk about where the nearest could be found, the front of the group surged towards the front doors.

Foyle was at the head of the stairway, with the fair and handsome Lord Venn close behind, when they were stunned by a flash and a roar.

A figure appeared in the doorway opposite, unnaturally tall, its face disguised in a hooded cloak, stretching out a cadaver's arms. Foyle started, lurched forwards and lunged over the low rail, head first down the stairwell.

Mercifully for his fellow revellers, the crack as he hit the stairs two turns below was drowned in the echoes of the thunder. The rest of the group froze. Those at the front had already burst singing out into the night looking for that constable.

Lord Venn yelled, "Get that doctor!" and vaulted over three sets of rails to drop by Foyle. His friend Molyneux rushed to where the figure had disappeared. Venn's less athletic cohorts came downstairs the normal way.

Venn pulled off his jacket to cover the victim's twisted body and the pool of blood spreading under him, saying heartily, "Trust you to take the short way, Foyle."

Foyle wheezed through bloody lips, "Too late for a doctor. Don't make my mistake, Venn… Damn this darkness! Venn, marry the sweet girl who'll come your way."

"I don't know any who'd talk to me," said Harley Venn. "Come, Foyle, you're rambling; you knocked yourself about nicely with that dive, and all for a stupid conjuring trick. You don't know what you say. Lie quiet: the doctor's on his way."

But Foyle would not be silenced. One hand, already devoid of strength, clutched at Harley Venn's. "Must say I repent. I do, for most

---

watchmen, known as 'Charley's and reporting to a constable, were responsible for law and order. They sheltered in wooden box like huts, easily toppled.

2   Lord Venn: Many of Harley Venn's characteristics, including being a heavy drinking socially outcast viscount and a pugilistic musician with a liking for dressing as a costermonger, are taken from the 1894 romantic melodrama 'The Outcast of the Family' by Charles Garvice.

of it... She'll make things right for me. Venn, marry the one with the good eyes... You're worth saving... You too, Molyneux," he added, as Molyneux joined them, shaking his head at Venn to indicate that his chase had been useless. "I should have acted when I saw that thing first... Put it off... "

Molyneux swore, and Harley Venn flinched under the clammy touch.

They made way as the doctor came up. Brisk and dapper, he knelt to feel Foyle's pulse. "Went over the rails, you say?" This, and the blood bubbling at his lips and seeping from under Venn's coat, decided him. "Make your peace with Heaven, Sir."

Foyle rasped, "She did that for me. Beware, Venn; promise you'll marry that sweet girl and reform." His fingers scratched spasmodically at his friend's palms. "Promise me!"

Harley Venn found himself saying, "All right, I promise. Now, lie quiet."

"The Crone... hooded figure... curse... It's my old Flossie!" His lips twisted into a ghastly smile, the breath gargled in his throat, and his eyes went out.

Only the doctor, Venn and Molyneux heard Foyle's last few words. While Venn defied eternity, Molyneux delayed thinking about it, and the doctor was too busy increasing his practice for metaphysics.

Venn and Molyneux swore. The doctor closed Foyle's eyes, and drew the Viscount's ruined coat over his head.

Callow young Carstairs' face was flushed with unshed tears. "I saw something in the middle of that flash." He rounded on the silent group: "Damn it all, you saw the figure. So did Venn, though he laughs such things to scorn."

It was impossible to tell from the evasive looks of the others, if they had seen what he had, and did not care to admit to it, or had not seen it, and wished not to tell him so.

Harley Venn snorted. "Yes, youngster, I saw a damned conjuring trick. Our unlucky friend here was unsteady on his legs, and that was it."

The doctor protested: "My Lord: Sirs: please remember we are in the presence of the dead."

"Then let's move him." Venn scowled, rolling up cuffs already spattered with Foyle's blood. "Take his heels, Molyneux, and I'll take his shoulders, and we'll put him in a side room."

This done, their clothes were so soiled, that calling on Foyle's widow was out of the question, though neither would have admitted to being drunk. Besides, if they went home first to change, even at midnight, she somehow might hear of his accident through some other source, especially as she was known to wait up for him.

Both recalled wordlessly that she had greeted them before now with a jug of cold water thrown from an upper window. Even half in their cups, they could see that was not the best way in which to begin such an interview. Reluctantly, they took up the doctor's offer to break the news to Mistress Foyle.

Shortly afterwards, they were out on the street, on foot. Both, being athletes, took to exercise naturally when disturbed.

They walked swiftly through the quiet streets to the west of the city, made less squalid at this hour by the gloom masking the piles of nameless rubbish and pools of stagnant water, urine, or both.

"If it was a man, he vanished quick as that lightning," said Molyneux. "What a way to go, eh? Poor fellow! And ten to one that cold dog of a doctor will charge the widow for his services."

Harley Venn glanced at a group of figures standing at the corner, but dismissed them as harmless vagrants. "Better to go quickly than slowly. Better still to go without deathbed terrors and mumbled repentances. Would that sawbones dare to put 'deathbed attendance' on the bill?"

"I wouldn't doubt it," said Molyneux bitterly.

"I'll pay the bill," said Lord Venn.

This was a rash promise in one who hadn't paid his own for some while. Venn would, naturally, put off paying the doctor indefinitely. He classified doctors and apothecaries along with tradesman as unreasonable if they expected payment within months. Partly, this was due to his dire financial situation. He had enough difficulty in paying his servants their wages.

"Cursed miserable end for a good fellow." Molyneux sprang over one of the puddles, "Speaking plain, what do you make of that figure's appearance?"

"I think it the footling stage trick I said," returned Venn. "Foyle lost his nerve at a piece of trickery, Jack, and it cost him his life. I'd love to get my hands on whoever did it, but that's all it was."

Their eyes met a moment. Molyneux came to an abrupt stop, nearly tripping his friend, who jumped round him, swearing.

Molyneux said, "Did you ever known him to lose his nerve before? No, Harley, too many co-incidental deaths have built up now, involving thunderbolts and falls down steps. Before it was the old fellows: now with Foyle, it's on to us younger ones. And if you or I lose our nerve likewise, and tip ourselves down some stairs, mark you, Harley, that same fate awaits us, make no doubt about it."

Harley Venn said, "Why do you loiter? I don't like being rooted, when I'm strung up tight as a bow. I need movement to think. Same as in the ring, eh?"

They moved on in silence until Molyneux said, "These coincidences: with your uncle –"

Venn said flatly, "Dead of an apoplexy, at the foot of those steps to the sunken garden in the centre of the supposedly cursed maze at Stoke Castle. They said he 'wore a terrible look' whatever they meant by that. He did as much whenever I cheeked him as lad. Poor old rascal, a painful end's a sure way for a corpse to pull a face. There was a bizarre, local thunder storm that day, concentrating about the castle, and my uncle would walk out into it."

He strode on, as impossible to stop as one of his racehorses. "Your father's death was ten years back."

This made it easier for his friend to say, "'He was frenzied two months before his death, smashing mirrors with his cane. They found him at the bottom of the stairs, with his neck snapped, and this family ring I wear now still clutched between his fingers. Some staff reported hearing one clap of thunder in the night. I was away."

"Not nice," said Venn, in a flash of empathy, starting back to place a hand on his friend's arm. "Yet, their closest fellow rake, young Carstairs' own uncle, is still alive, Jack."

"He is, and poor Foyle's father, too. Old Foyle doesn't drink these days; too busy repenting and doing good works."

"Besides praying the *bejasus* out of himself, as my man would say." Lord Venn jumped over a dead cat, oddly flattened, which lay by the gutter, clearly a victim to a carriage. "Squashed Sir Puss there makes me think of the grotesque death of my uncle's former steward, that Greendale fellow."

He grinned. "As neither of us cared two damns for the old rascal, the lurid account of the *Abbé* and local peasants can serve as light relief.

'Squashed flat when a thunderbolt toppled a wall on him over in France, eh? The locals would have it that bolt of lightning struck from nowhere as he came up to the churchyard, hitting a high wall and piling down on him most tidily, avoiding the gawping peasants and infants nearby.

'Supposedly, the flash lit the grave of some local girl in the churchyard, who local legend connected with him and my uncle. Fine fanciful imaginings, Jack." Venn laughed.

Molyneux did not. "I laughed myself when I heard that nonsense. It's a sure sign my nerves are near as shaken as young Carstairs', for I begin to wonder if Greendale's end is connected with these other deaths, when it has nothing to do with cloaked figures or falls down stairs."

Venn shook his head. "Foyle died through a miserable conjuring trick. We'll thrash this out further tomorrow, but for now we need to drain a bottle between us."

Molyneux was happy to change the topic for the moment, though they must return to it soon enough. His eyes twinkled. "You gave your word to Foyle you'd marry a good girl and reform."

Venn shrugged. "Damn me, I did. I've sworn I'd never marry, though under the terms of my uncle's will that would mean foregoing half of the fortune he left me. Still, now I've run through the half he left me unconditionally, I'm tempted to change my mind. But I've got to get my hands on a wife with plenty of tin, or I'll soon enough get through the other half, and it will be a life spent rusticating in the Castle of Doom fending off duns[3] for me.

'For now, let's get the blood off ourselves, Jack, and open a bottle. We'll put our minds to my marital hopes tomorrow."

"And the reformation?" Molyneux glanced down at Foyle's blood on his coat sleeve. He could not joke, looking at that.

---

3   Duns: Debt collectors.

"I'll leave that to her. I'll pick some virtuous maid. I wouldn't have anyone who's been knocking about too long, and like as not, had half the Town between her thighs on the quiet. It's happened to better men than me."

"Don't talk like that, with Foyle's blood still on you," said Molyneux.

"Why not? It's how he talked himself. Here's my house."

2.
𝔑𝔬𝔟𝔩𝔢 𝔥𝔬𝔲𝔰𝔢𝔥𝔬𝔩𝔡

The house which Harley Venn had taken for this season was north of Russell Square, in an area favoured by wealthy tradesmen. This season, he had let out his own town house in Wimpole Street in a last attempt to mend his finances.

O'Hare, wiry, dark, and exuding a ruffianly air, opened the door as Venn and Molyneux came up the steps. "Sure Your Honour's been milling[4] again."

"Not this time," said Venn regretfully. "Foyle had a fatal accident. Get us a change of clothes, and quick about it. Then we'll have a drink in my study."

"There'll be no fire in your study…Your Honour," drawled the man, who never called Venn either 'My Lord' or 'Lord Venn', almost as if he suspected him of being an impostor, while he often paused before saying 'Your Honour'. "My lad followed the girl in there when she was banking it up, and was after hurling a jug of water over it before she could stop him. Practising for them bloody duns, he was." A look of pride softened his face.

"Curse you, I've told you to keep the little brutes out of there," Venn sounded resigned rather than angry. "No matter, it's not a cold night. Come on upstairs, Molyneux; let's get out of these clothes." He

4   Milling: Fighting

suited his action to the word, unbuttoning his bloodstained waistcoat as he mounted the stairs, with O'Hare at the rear, lighting them with upraised candle.

"Pestilential brats," Venn observed to Molyneux, "At least they come in useful for scaring away creditors. The gunsmith had the insolence to call a week since, whining about payments due, when he ought to be grateful for my patronage. He soon cleared out when I set 'em on him. Else I'd have been tempted to turn one of his own pistols on him – by way of showing my appreciation of their fine balance and the excellent service he's given me, of course."

He hurled the waistcoat back to O'Hare, who caught it with his free hand, while the candle in his other made plunging shadows.

Amongst them, Molyneux thought for a second he saw a figure in a hooded cloak, the eyes dark as empty sockets in a skull. Then it was gone. The vision had been so fleeting that he thought it a trick of the eyes conjured up for him by that visitation earlier.

Now Venn threw back his shirt to his man, narrowly missing extinguishing the candle with it or setting it alight. Once again, the shadows plunged, but conjured up no more sinister a figure to Molyneux's eyes than a naked, statuesque woman at the head of the next stairs. O'Hare leered, raising the candle so that the light shone full on the figure.

It was a strapping servant maid, her hair loose. Molyneux saw that hefty as she was, she had a fine shape, with high breasts and the hips of a goddess.

She seemed half asleep, unaware that Venn had company, which might explain her tone: "Sir, I heard a voice on the stairs, as wasn't none of O'Hare's lot, and I thought was you on your way up to make free with my privates as is your habit, but there weren't nothing there. Fair gave me a turn, it did."

"Your conversation's not fit for mixed company, my dear." Harley Venn laughed. "You were dreaming. Go and get warm for Mr Harley." He winked at both the girl and Molyneux.

But when they'd had their laugh out, Molyneux sobered. What might it have been on those stairs up to the loft bedrooms which Venn, by the girl's account, so often climbed?

Venn and Molyneux drank late, putting off going to bed, and

agreeing that Molyneux would stay the night. By tacit consent, they kept away from their earlier discussion until they were making their unsteady way to the door.

Then Molyneux said, "Remember my warning, Harley. Those were no idle words. I admit there are a couple of rational explanations for what caused our elders to lose their nerve. It could be a trick as you say, or even some mass illusion that took hold of their minds."

Venn paused, candle in hand. "Damn it, your father and my Uncle Toby weren't nervous types, any more than our unlucky friend Foyle."

"Poor young Carstairs is losing his nerve already. We must try and reassure him, or he'll be the next to start at shadows by some flight of stairs, and the youth's only eighteen."

"So, Jack, have you any plans about how to tackle these jolly party tricks, apart from our mutual longing to seize the trickster and beat the daylights out of him?"

Molyneux nodded. "Yes; let's start with rational explanations, dismissing superstition out of hand. Then we must for now – though my instincts say otherwise, I'll ignore 'em – put the drama involving our seniors' fatal falls down to ill luck, bad weather and the excesses of decades catching up with them, all leading to damned fool gossip from the ignorant."

He poked one finger into the soft wax pooling in the candle holder's base. "We'll even say that the ex-steward Greendale's flattening over in France has nothing to do with it, despite the thunderbolt. Then from what we saw of poor Foyle's accident, that trick might even have been a prank that misfired. Still, from Foyle's last words, I doubt it. He said he had seen the thing before."

"He could have been raving, but I grant you, it didn't seem like it," Harley Venn agreed.

"So, it could be some deranged enemy making use of stage effects. He may even have done the same with our relatives, with those co-incidental thunder storms. It might even be mass mesmerism.[5] I've heard of that. "

Lord Venn grinned, "If so, we've enough contacts on the stage, after

---

5   Mesmerism: Franz Mesmer developed an early form of hypnotism in the eighteenth century.

all. Let's call in backstage sometime in the next couple of days to find out how they produce these effects."

"Harley, you rascal, beware those steep steps. I'd rather not lose you; you're the only man I can think of under thirty who's got a worse character than me."

Instead of continuing to his own room, Venn, in line with the servant girl's predictions, placed one foot on the attic staircase, then turned.

"And tomorrow we must find a good young girl with a pile of tin who'll take me. That won't be easy."

Molyneux shook his head. "I feel sorry for the girl. Besides, many would hold that a promise made like that don't have to be binding."

Venn shook his head. "No, I gave my word. After all, I can't think of any eligible girl who talks to me, let alone would have me in marriage."

The next morning, Harley Venn and Jack Molyneux rose jaded and sour. As fighters, they realised that what had made Foyle's death easier for them last night was that same rush of excitement of the ring or the duel. This morning it was gone.

Neither, however, would speak of their trouble. An attitude of contempt seemed the best thing for dealing with episodes straight from a Gothic novel.

Before breakfast, both scribbled a note to their friend's widow, offering any services that they could give. If she hadn't been a plain and virtuous woman, she might have had reason to suspect the nature of those services. As it was, these were as disinterested as any a libertine could make to a woman.

As the maid, Betsy, served breakfast, she looked sour too, perhaps tired after her disturbed night. O'Hare was out on some disreputable errand for his master. Unperturbed at Molyneux's seeing and hearing her last night, Betsy gave him a knowing look.

Last night, in the candlelight, she had seemed to Molyneux to have the attributes of a Venus, but this morning, with her fine hips concealed in her working clothes, her hair shoved up carelessly under a mob cap and a sallow tinge to her skin, that allure had flown for him. Still, that might be because none of the temptations of the flesh had much allure for either libertine this morning. They chewed their ham and hot rolls without enjoyment.

Betsy was pouring a slosh of brandy into their coffee, when loud knocking and shouting came from the back of the house.

"That'll be the butcher again." Betsy made for the door. "I'll get the youngsters."

"Damned insolence!" muttered Harley Venn, "If he acts rough, call me."

Someone was already being fairly rough. Thuds and shouted curses added to the din.

"Good, O'Hare's back. Now I don't need to exert myself," said Lord Venn.

"This is no better than a household of thieves!" shouted the butcher. "Tell your master he has no more honesty than a common footpad!"

"Probably, less." Venn calmly drained his coffee dish. Now they heard the children's footfalls scampering across the floor above, a window opening, falling water, a roar from the victim, triumphant hoots from the infants, and laughter from O'Hare and Betsy.

"I'll have a constable to the lot of you!" The creditor retreated, followed by a chorus of jeers.

"You see, those brats have their uses," said Lord Venn. "They were with their aunt since their mother's death, but she wearied of 'em, and I can't say I blame her: they're troublesome enough... Now, Jack, for a list of likely females. Our Earldom's no mushroom one, that's one thing, going back to Restoration times. Aylesbury House and old Toby's castle and most of the houses are entailed, so I can't do away with 'em."

"You've got through that first half of that inheritance in under five years," said Molyneux, shrugging off his scruples over Venn's future bride. "Let's see if we can find a sweet heiress who'll have you. Not easy, unless you marry into trade.[6] Near all the good families have barred their doors against you. It's this way you have of keeping company with the lower orders and going about dressed like a costermonger, and brawling in the street that's made you a social outcast. They'd overlook a fair bit of drunkenness and debauchery, so long as it was discreet. That killing

---

6   Marry into trade: To have made money through trade was thought vulgar by the aristocracy at this time.

in the duel wasn't your fault, after all. They abhor me, but I don't shock them so much as you. "

"They might unbar their doors, if they know I'm after their daughters for their money, not their bodies," said Venn.

As the girl came in to clear the table, he said, "Give this to the brats for a job well done." He felt in his pockets for some change, although he was short enough of ready money.

"Your Lordship was ever open handed, but now the flow of money's drying up you must change your ways." She turned away with a toss of her head and a flounce of her ample rump.

Venn slapped it. "You've ever found me so... Come, Molyneux. A list of likely chits: it's all of Lombard street to a china orange near all of them won't have me, so we need a good few, so I can call on them in turn."

Their work on the list went slowly, as both felt vague after the last night's excesses.

"Social outcast as I am, I must compromise about this wife," said Venn. "I don't care a hang about pedigree – unlike my venerable father – but I don't want some vulgar huckster's daughter on her promotion, who I have to hide away from my friends. That's another thing! She'll have to be as virtuous as dammit to withstand that crew of rascals. Of course, she'll have to look away from my own peccadilloes."

"You want a wife you can esteem." Molyneux gave some serious thought to the subject of marriage for the first time in his twenty-six years.

Harley Venn grinned. "I want her to have a body I esteem."

"You're too used to choosing mistresses, Venn. They say you have to choose a wife for different qualities. Moral men disapprove of sex after marriage."

"It's the only good thing I can think of about taking a wife. I want one I'll enjoy making heirs with. It's all right for these *sapskulls* who fall in love with some chit on the marriage market," complained Venn. "Then the physical part's all well enough at first, though that can't last. But I never have been looby enough to fall in love since I was a youth, when I learned my lesson about what to expect for a female if she sees the power she has over you.'"

"It's a shame my cousin don't know any suitable chits. She's in Town this season, and most obliging."

"She may have her eye on you, Jack." Venn winked. "I've seen her look soft on you, for all her sharp tongue."

"That's not funny, Venn. She's an admirable woman, with too much sense to think of remarriage, and least of all to a wretch like me. She must be thirty. Wait! Are you and old Trollope still speaking?"

Venn frowned. "That old villain of a magistrate? He was speaking to me a month since, but that was before I gave that fellow a thrashing at the opera. He was there, and takes that sort of thing personally."

"He's got a daughter out on the marriage market this year, with a tidy sum. Pretty girl. But there are some young bucks after her already, so you'll have to move fast."

"If it's less than thirty thousand, it won't do," said Venn. "Besides, I'm wary of that name. I don't want to share my wife with half the Town, and I want my heirs to be mine."

"Then there's the Middleton's daughter."

"Not a damned chance: the whole crew of 'em cut me on my way into church."

Jack Molyneux stared: "What were you doing there?"

"Winning a bet," smiled Venn.

He remembered entering that church behind a merchant's family, the youngest female of whom had an enticing swing to her hips as she walked, and a full, prominent rear. He had settled at the back near the door so as to sneak out early.

When they stood up to sing the hymn, he had fixed his gaze on the girl's rear again. Usually, he liked longer legs, the better to set off a fine rump, but he liked this girl's rump anyway, and the relevant part of him – which he always referred to as 'Mr Harley' stood up likewise, refusing to go down. This was highly uncomfortable in his tight pantaloons.

As if sensing his gaze, the young woman had turned about. Her face, neither pretty nor plain, round nor was oval, with unremarkable features, disappointed him. Still, he had given her a vulgar wink. Looking shocked, she had returned to her prayer book, while he longed to get back to lay hands on Betsy.

Now he realised, "If I had my wits about me, I'd have thought before. My sister will deal with this, and find a few likely runners. Let's go round there now. We can call in at The Pugilists after that."

3.

Spectre at a Ball

May 1821

"STILL, MISS, GOING TO BALLS and visiting these fine places must be exciting," Abigail, the girl her sister-in-law was training as lady's maid, laced Clarinda into her stays.

Clarinda thought that it was sad that this girl had been given the name used for maidservants. It was as if her mother had abandoned any dreams of the better life she must have wanted for her baby within days of her birth. Perhaps she hadn't known of that use.

As the stays tightened over her waist, Clarinda wheezed, "Ow! You will never make a sylph of me, Abbey. Not so tight."

"You need them this tight for this dress, Miss, and you've a neat enough waist. You'll get used to it in a minute: breathe shallow."

Clarinda gasped the question she had been meaning to ask. "Abbey, are you content in your place?" As the girl hesitated, she added hastily, "Don't be alarmed, I shan't run tales to your mistress. But I do fear that staff is overworked."

"I'm well enough here. A working girl's lot is never easy; but we're used to it. If I could just work for you always, that would be a happy thing."

"When I return to Berkshire – having disappointed my family by rejecting these supposed admirers – I'll ask my sister[7] to let you come to me when I set up in my own house."

"That would be fine, Miss." the girl's eyes glowed. Seeing the mischief sparkling in Clarinda's, she risked asking, "Pardon my forwardness, Miss, but you cannot wish to be an old maid?"

"I would prefer that, to marrying some venal gentleman – so called – who wants this new fortune of mine. Why, it has so enhanced my attractions that I've had three of James' acquaintance declare themselves lately. I could be content as spinster buried in Berkshire, if I could have a parrot and a cat. Perhaps I could have a monkey, too. After all, I might find its company just as agreeable as some ladies do their husbands."

As the girl tittered, Clarinda went on, "But this fortune attracts all the wrong people, Abbey, and I'm sorry to say that I can't believe my poor late uncle came by it reputably. If I didn't wish to use it for good purposes, I would give it to my brother and sister."

Abigail could read well, and many of her opinions came from the novels on her mistress' bookshelves. "Ah, Miss! Like the heroine in 'Count *Ulf, Or The Unwilling Bride*', as didn't want anyone who cared only for her fortune, but was forced to take wicked Count Ulf anyway?"

She slipped the new, lilac coloured ball-gown over Clarinda's head and began to fasten it. "Why, you look lovely, Miss Clarinda! It's a beautiful dress, and just the colour to set off the tawny in your hair."

Clarinda's mane of hazel brown hair with its tints of gold had always been admired, unlike her other features. With this new hairstyle, she thought that it looked nearly as striking as the new ball gown, while the rest of her remained unremarkable.

"Your work on my hair will impress even Nancy. Now, don't wait up for me; but I'll make sure to bring back some tasty morsels from the ball. After all, they will hardly miss it."

She brooded. "It's shocking to think of all those overfed people gorging on tables loaded with refreshments, while people starve in the streets. I never imagined so many beggars as there are London! I must think of some way of helping them. When I mentioned it to the Vicar here, he cleared his throat and suggested a donation to the benevolent

---

7   Sisters-in-law were called 'sisters' at this time.

fund, but there must be more done. When I get back to Berkshire after this season is over, I must turn my mind to it properly."

Abigail bent down to straighten the gown's skirts over the petticoats. Proud of her six months' longer experience of the Town, she murmured, "They say, Miss, the high prices since the wars with France[8] have beggared many. Still, half of them beggars is tricksters, posing as maimed soldiers, and even borrowing babies, and deserves no charity at all."

"I sometimes wonder if any of us do," said Clarinda.

Nancy Greendale giggled as James handed the women down from their carriage. Clarinda had never known her so good humoured as since this invitation to Sir Hugh and Lady Barbara[9] Davenport's ball. This made worthwhile the rushed fitting for another ball gown – Clarinda was concerned about the overworked seamstresses – and being made to practice her curtsy all over again.

They were at the side of the mansion. The area to the front was crowded with coaches and shouting footmen waving flaming torches. Their own coachman only managed to get this space by cutting out by a few feet another carriage, which had in it a stout, vulgar-looking woman and a young man who seemed to be asleep.

James thought it as well to make a placating bow to her. Though she looked like a retired actress, she might be a friend of Lady Barbara's.

Meanwhile, the rival coachmen claimed private, disgusting knowledge about each other. James shouted at them to be quiet, and an athletic, fair young man jumped out of the other carriage, calling thanks to the woman. Clarinda recognised him as the man whose gaze she had felt piercing her petticoats in church a while ago. She thought she saw recognition in his look.

---

8   The war with France: The French Revolutionary Wars and the Napoleonic Wars ran between 1793-1815, with brief periods of peace. A coalition including Great Britain invaded France to restore monarchical power in 1793.

9   Lady Barbara: As an earl's daughter, the title as 'Lady Barbara' takes precedence over the one as a baronet's wife.

He shouted over the obscene exchanges, "Hold your noise, you rascals, or I'll make you; ladies present!"

The other coachman whipped up his horses. James bowed and the fair young man murmured something, then, noticing a rowdy group of young bucks across the street, roared a greeting and strode away to join them.

"That was Lord Venn," said James. "And civil. From all I've heard, I'm surprised."

Nancy clicked her tongue. "I didn't realise he would be a guest tonight."

"He's Lady Barbara's brother, after all. I knew him at once from a cartoon which showed him brawling in the street on his way to a prize fight, dressed like a common fellow, with kerchief about his throat. It didn't mention him by name, of course, but didn't need to. He's fond of that. He keeps the lowest company – seems to like it. He's a rough, a toper and a libertine, besides having killed his man in some duel. That seems to be essential with rakehells. That wretch who was killed falling downstairs drunk at a gaming hell less not long since was one of his set. You recall my reading it out over breakfast."

"What was that man's name, again?" Clarinda was eager to add him to the list of souls, living or dead, for whom she prayed.

These included the Devil himself. She had never admitted this to anyone since she had made Nancy scream and the vicar back home choke on his tea by saying so.

"Doyle – Foyle, that was it. A depraved wretch, it seems. Clarinda, it looks as if Lord Venn has wandered away with those ruffians over the road. If he should return, avoid him without being impolite. Now, skip over this puddle, girls!"

As they were announced, Sir Hugh Davenport stepped forward to greet them as suavely as if they met every week. Clarinda was sure he had no idea who they were and cared still less. She wondered again why they had been invited.

Nancy was sure that it had less to do with Clarinda's inheritance than James's reputation as a businessman. She refused to credit that titled people thought business beneath their notice.

A flunkey offered them wine. Clarinda hoped he helped himself to some.

This was the most splendid London ball she had yet attended. Being hauled to Town by James and Nancy for a season on the marriage mart did have compensations in such scenes as this magnificent ballroom lit by dozens of chandeliers. It might be unusually chill for the season outside, but in here, the heat of the candles and the bodies made it very warm.

The musicians were playing a piece from Mozart, and the sight of the dancers moving in sets, with clicking heels and whirling gowns and coat tails, set Clarinda's feet tapping.

She longed to dance. Still, as they knew nobody here, any partner would have to introduce himself to James. With so many appealing girls on the floor, she doubted that many would bother.

Now Lady Barbara came up smiling. Like her brother, she was tall, fair, and finely dressed. Unlike him, she was not particularly good-looking. One of Harley Venn's less bloody duels had been fought with a wag who had likened her to his mare.

She kept them talking, seemingly eager to hear all about life in rural Berkshire. Soon, their group was joined by members of her set, who were introduced. "Mr Carstairs, who leads my poor brother astray," Lady Barbara said of a callow, light haired youth who would be nice looking when he had outgrown his pimples.

The youth beamed. "Lady Barbara, you know it's the other way about. Miss Greendale, would you honour me with this dance?"

He bounced about the dance floor with Clarinda like an eager half grown puppy, making Clarinda smile, until she was caught by a pulling and tearing. They dropped out of the set as soon as they could.

The youth flushed to the roots of his hair – Clarinda had never before seen anyone do that in real life – and burst into apologies.

Clarinda tried to sooth him, "Such things happen at balls. The maid in the cloakroom will mend it in a trice."

"I'm mortified, Miss Greendale: you will never dance with me again."

Murmuring reassurance, Clarinda left him and the ballroom, holding up her torn hem. The lobby off the cloakroom was empty, save for a man lounging against the wall, absently holding up a watch. Clarinda recognised Lord Venn.

She was about to hurry by him with a quick curtsey, when she saw his melancholy look. He missed her approach, surely a rare thing in him as a pugilist. This gave her time to notice again how handsome he was. He could have stepped out from one of Abbey's novels.

His proportions were classical, his sculpted features unmarked by the brawling, his eyelashes and eyebrows dark in contrast to his bright fair hair and glowing side whiskers, the eyebrows slanting upwards. She had heard such eyebrows termed 'Devil's brows', and he might have been a depiction of an athletic fallen archangel.

Remembering James's account of his friend's end, she said without thinking, "Lord Venn, I'd like to outrage convention by saying that I was sorry to hear of your friend Mr Foyle's tragic accident."

Of course, she should not speak to any man not introduced, let alone this one. Still, they had met when he had silenced the coachmen's obscenities.

His bright blue eyes, startlingly clear for a toper's, came back to the present, focusing on her in surprise and resentment. Close to, she could see the faint lines of debauchery about his eyes and mouth.

"What did you say?" was his astounded and uncivil response. She repeated her remark. It sounded even more banal to her now.

What she would have liked to say, was that she was sure that George Foyle would meet with eventual forgiveness from an infinitely merciful Creator. When she had learnt this creed of universal salvation, she had been delighted to adopt it.

But that would sound priggish to Harley Venn, who must be near godless, if his behaviour in church was anything to go by. Besides, the cleric who had taught it to her had advised her not to spread it about, for fear that the wicked, relieved of the fear of hellfire, would be still worse.

Lord Venn went on staring. Clarinda blundered on, "He was too young to die. That always seems wrong, and –"

"But why, Ma'am? He died drunk, and that is probably the best way to go," Lord Venn thrust his watch back into his pocket. "You see my conversation is unsuitable for respectable young ladies, which is all the return you get for taking your charity far enough to condole with me." For all his words, his voice was melodious.

Clarinda was dismayed to react like of the heroines in one of Abbey's novels: her spirits rallied under his ironic tone. "From that return, I assume my speech sounded smug or sententious, for which I am sorry."

Harley Venn now fixed his full attention on her. "I take it that you are a devout young lady. No doubt you go twice every Sunday, and once during the week. I was wondering where I had seen you before: of course - I saw you in church recently."

Then, you must remember my rear rather better than my face.

"I believe you did, Sir," Clarinda felt her lips twitch.

"You have the advantage of me, Ma'am." Now he reminded her of James at chess, moving in on someone else's queen.

"Miss Greendale," she made her curtsey.

"Miss Clarinda Greendale?" He suddenly gave a conspiratorial smile that made her draw back. "I'm happy to meet you, Ma'am. And I thank you for saying a kind word about poor old Foyle. My response was ungracious, when that is more than anyone else has done, and he wasn't the worst fellow about. Now we are introduced, I hope you will give me a dance, later on? I wouldn't ask it of a more conventional young lady, given my reputation – or lack of it." He grinned, clearly expecting her to join in the joke.

She mumbled something about having torn her dress, blushing, losing the small assurance that had carried her into the talk. Conventional people were being proved right: a respectable female who broke their rules risked trouble.

Meanwhile, Harley Venn smiled as roguishly as could be expected. "Come, Miss Greendale, that won't do. I know a maid does the mending. You are with your brother? I'll introduce myself."

She muttered something else, and he bowed, said something about 'Molyneux' and sauntered out of a side door at the end of the corridor.

Clarinda found his way of attending a ball – which seemed to consist of skirting round its edges – eccentric. Probably he was half drunk. *I hope he forgets to come back!* She hurried to the cloakroom.

Here, a little seamstress was repairing torn gowns. There was a long, jagged rip at the hem of Clarinda's, and she assured the girl that she was in no hurry. With any luck, the Villainous Viscount would have been and gone before she returned.

The gown mended, she went back to the ballroom, smiling at the music and the patter of dancing feet, her own slippers making a swishing noise as she walked past heavy framed pictures of ancient battles and Venn ancestors.

She entered through the side door as the announcement came: 'Lord Venn and Mr John Molyneux'.

As the two athletic young men strode into the ballroom, even this sophisticated company, where only a couple of parties belonged to the narrowly respectable, hushed.

The young men would have made a fine entrance without the ripple of excitement made by those names. As an artist, Clarinda had to admire the renegade duo. Both dashingly turned out, and spare and muscular, seemingly without an ounce of fat, with the bouncing walk of athletes. Unlike the fair, extravagantly handsome Harley Venn, his dark-haired friend Molyneux was striking rather than good looking.

Although the guests had been expecting this, the announcement still turned heads, stiffened backs, and straightened mouths. Dowagers raised eye glasses, mothers looked for their daughters, and men drew nearer the women in their groups. But nobody who was prepared to cut even the outrageous Lord Venn had come. Although the crowd parted as water before the prow of a boat as the two young men advanced, people greeted them.

The rumour had already got about, that both were at last eager to marry a woman for her money. Why Molyneux was thought to join his friend in looking for an heiress was unexplained. Unaware of the rumour, he made no effort to deny it. Now, less scrupulous matrons with daughters smiled on them.

They reached Lady Barbara's group just as Clarinda came from the opposite direction, to be stopped by young Mr Carstairs. Lady Barbara came up. "Miss Greendale, these wretches are shockingly late, but they're eager to make your acquaintance."

Nancy, about to scold Clarinda for disappearing, had to smile on Lord Venn while trying to look disapproving. Clarinda thought she did it well.

"We met earlier, when the coachman were at each other's throats." Harley Venn said easily. "Miss Greendale, I hope you forgive that villain's foul mouth and honour me with this dance?"

Young Carstairs' face fell. "The lady promised this dance to me, to show I'm forgiven for trampling on her gown."

"No lady with any sense dances with you, Carstairs. You'll have to wait." Harley Venn took Clarinda's arm to lead her onto the floor.

Why do women have to be led onto the floor like horses, as if they can't make their own way?

Clarinda forgot about rebellious questions as she realised how many people watched them. She put on a smile, concentrating on her steps as they moved through the set.

Harley Venn was as sprightly a dancer as young Carstairs, but skillful. The hem of her gown was safe.

When the movements of the dance brought them together, he was amusing company; he seemed to have cast off the gloom of earlier like a garment. He teased her about young Carstairs, whose gaze on her he likened to that of a puppy.

The hollow cheeked, moustached man in the set next to them was clearly of the military, perhaps the cavalry. He danced with his torso as upright as if he still sat his horse, his movements putting Clarinda in mind of a cantering one, his jaw tense and eyes bulging. "Looks as if he'd swallowed his stick," Venn grinned.

Clarinda had to laugh. The man glared at Venn. Though she doubted that he could have heard over the music, he seemed to hate him anyway. As they moved down the set, he glowered back at them, while Venn glanced at him with detached interest.

"Major Pyke shares a lot of my vices," he told Clarinda as they joined hands and whirled about. "But don't even enjoy 'em. He looks a real skeleton at a feast, eh? Yet, I wouldn't have you think I don't weary of my own vices. I do. It's time to change, before I meet a face like that in my own mirror. But you don't want serious talk at a ball, Miss Greendale, and it's not like me go in for it."

As they joined hands again, he said, "That maid did a fine job of mending your gown, so I'd better keep my feet off it, eh, as I'm hoping you'll give me another two dances later on, if Carstairs leaves you with one free."

"I'm honoured, Sir," she tried to think of a way of escaping him.

It would not do to be seen too much with such a libertine, and would annoy James. Venn might well be falling in love with her fortune. Perhaps, low-born though the Greendales were, Lady Barbara even intended Clarinda's inheritance for her brother; hence the invitation.

The second dance ended and they made their bows, Major Pyke sending Venn another venomous glance.

As they moved back to Lady Barbara's group, Clarinda felt an icy draught from the open doors nearby.

A hooded, robed figure stood there. It vanished at once, but not before she had sensed a gaze far more malevolent than Major Pyke's.

4.

The Kiss, Dear Maid

"**E**XCUSE ME, MA'AM!" HARLEY VENN dashed from the ballroom. People stared. Clarinda picked up her skirts and rushed out into the hall after him.

There was nothing out in the flagged passageway but a great picture of the late king, looking more plebeian than usual. A side door stood open, and she rushed out into a cobbled courtyard, to find Lord Venn striding about and swearing.

"You thought you saw something, Lord Venn, as did I."

His eyes sparked as he said evenly, "Nothing worth mentioning. A sorry parlour trick."

"But it angers you, Sir?"

"This trickster coolly repeats the performance that cost George Foyle his life. Yes, Ma'am, that does provoke me a trifle. But the coward has escaped, and as you are here, maybe it is as well, as I could not have kept my hands off him."

They turned at brisk footfalls. Major Pyke came through the side door, cigar in hand, his eyebrows shooting up in hostility as he saw Harley Venn. "You here, Venn? Servant, ma'am."

"The lady and I came to investigate a trickster, muffled in a cloak as if this was a masque," Harley Venn said, his look matching his jeering tone. "A sorry prank by some fool who'll I'll unmask soon enough."

"Yes?" said the Major, without any interest. "Forgive me, Ma'am. I would have a word with Venn."

"I wouldn't, Pyke, so it must keep," Venn spoke almost amiably, taking Clarinda's arm.

Pyke's eyes lit: "Then I must speak before the lady."

Venn tensed. Clarinda thought they were both as foolish as a pair of tomcats. "Please, gentlemen: be calm. I'll gladly wait in the hall, Lord Venn."

"You won't," Venn kept hold of Clarinda's arm, leading her away.

Pyke called after them, choking with rage: "You won't get away with it this time, Venn! Not twice!" Clarinda, glancing back, saw his face blanched with fury.

Venn ignored him as he handed Clarinda up the steps back into the ballroom. "I apologise for that vulgar wrangle, and about pugilism, too. Not the thing before a lady, I know."

Clarinda was curious. "May I ask, Sir? Why is he so hostile?"

Harley Venn grinned. "I beat his champion on the level – sorry, fairly. But he had betted heavily on it, and now raves about it to such friends as he has. If he was a gentleman, I'd regard myself as insulted; as he's a *parvenu*, I'll lay him out at the next opportunity. Beg pardon, Miss Greendale – that is no talk for ladies either."

"You could overlook his foolishness, as the unhappy man looks near desperate," suggested Clarinda.

"Do you bid me to, Miss Greendale?" he asked, flirtatiously. "I might keep from the pleasure of giving him the thrashing he deserves, to please you."

"I am in no position to bid you, Sir. I hope that Lady Barbara will. – On that strange figure which led us out there –"

They were interrupted by the approach of a siren like woman who had been holding court over the way. Clarinda had already admired how her cerulean coloured gown set off the bright chestnut of her hair, and the lush curves of her tall figure. She swayed and swished up to them in a cloud of perfume.

With a sign of acknowledgement to Clarinda, she addressed the Viscount archly, "I saw you and our friend the Major going outside, and was coming to intervene."

"No need, Lady Hogg, I kept myself in check through my partner's presence," Harley Venn made no effort to introduce them. Lady Hogg tinkled like a musical box, staring into Clarinda's face.

Meanwhile, Lord Venn's gaze had strayed down to the woman's cleavage, and Clarinda couldn't blame him. Lady Hogg had breasts like opulent grapefruits. Her own, though nearly as good a feature as her hair, being high and round, and exposed as never before in this low cut gown, were insignificant in comparison.

With the lady's bright hair and sparkling eyes as near as blue as Venn's, they were easily the best looking man and woman in this room. The artist in Clarinda longed to paint them both, wondering how she could capture the delicate coral pink of the woman's cheeks contrasting with her creamy complexion. Could that be rouge? Now, how could she capture the mischievous sparkle in Venn's eyes?

The woman tapped him with her fan. "You ruffian, Sir!" She rustled on her way, swinging her full rear and leaving a trail of perfume in her wake.

"Lady Hogg," said Harley Venn in a neutral tone. Clarinda thought her surname unfortunate; she supposed that her husband was either rich, or she had been fond of him when they married. If so, then that had changed, for Clarinda sensed intimacy between the two. Perhaps they were lovers.

Harley Venn took Clarinda through to the splendid pillared room, set out with a variety of hanging plants, where refreshments were being served.

Here, the seating was informal. Young Fredrick Carstairs sat with James and Nancy. He jumped up on seeing them. "Do take this seat, Miss Greendale. Your sister wants to speak to you, Venn, and it won't wait."

"Firstly, please mark me down for that other dance, Miss Greendale?"

Clarinda had to assent, despite James and Nancy's warning looks. None of the conduct books covered: -'How to avoid dancing with your hostesses' titled social outcast of a brother without giving offence.'

Nancy leaned over to hiss in Clarinda's ear, "Lady Barbara is a charming creature. But do avoid being thought to encourage her brother. Make sure you get another dance with Carstairs. He's interested, and a much better bet. A baronet's cousin is a fine catch."

Clarinda, hoping that nobody had overheard, hastily said something admiring about a great painting nearby. This showed a group of young men and woman in the clothes of the last century, gathered at the entrance of a maze. A great castle loomed in the background, and behind it, a lowering sky, though none of the light hearted party seemed trouble by the thought of a downpour.

"*The Maze, Stoke Castle,*" James read. "That's Lord Venn's pile. I should like to try out that maze; I've yet to meet one that's defeated me. We don't want to alarm the ladies, but don't they say it's haunted?"

Nancy gave one of her squeals, and young Carstairs tried not to wince. Perhaps it was ringing ears alone that made him look uncomfortable as he said, "Never fear, Ma'am, I've got lost in there at dusk, and never met any ghosts, for all the absurd legend about a Lady Venn's murdered – ahem, gallant – walking there."

Suddenly, music struck up from the temporary stage on which the musicians had been playing, erected in an ante room off the ballroom. The double doors between this ante room and the one where refreshments were being served now stood open, and the musicians had left the stage for refreshments themselves.

Clarinda saw that Harley Venn played the pianoforte, while Jack Molyneux accompanied him on the violin. They must be performing on a whim, their music the more enticing for the improvisation. They were gifted musicians. When they had tried out their instruments by going through the introduction twice, Lord Venn began to sing the song made by Beethoven from Byron's poem, *On Parting*[10].

> '*The kiss, dear maid! thy lip has left*
> *Shall never part from mine,*
> *Till happier hours restore the gift*
> *Untainted back to thine.*
>
> *Thy parting glance, which fondly beams,*
> *An equal love may see:*
> *The tear that from thy eyelid streams*
> *Can weep no change in me...*'

---

10   'On Parting': Lord Byron's 1811 poem was set to music by Ludwig Van Beethoven at some time between 1817-1820.

The buzz of various conversations dwindled into a hush. The least cultured guest was caught by the spell of the song.

Clarinda was enchanted. Such was the beauty of the voice and the music, she could forget the debauched singer. She remembered now, the powerful and melodious voice which had transformed the singing from the back of the church that Sunday.

Such was Venn's assurance as a player, that in between verses and without missing a note, he downed the glass he had balanced by one of the candles atop the instrument, returning to the song even more beguilingly. Clarinda wondered if it was only mermaids who could enchant with singing, or mermen too. If so, he might have been one.

Once Molyneux, still playing, turned a hot gaze on a voluptuous woman passing through the hall, and Clarinda made out the wink he and Venn exchanged. Then she wrinkled her nose, scorning herself for being so moved by their song.

After all, the words had been written by the most fickle of libertines, so soon contemptuous of those conquests to whom he wrote so many of his poems.

The laughing rake, Venn, played the last few notes, grinning outright, while Molyneux's violin entranced with those final tender strokes. As the song ended, the listeners came to themselves, and Clarinda collected some treats for Abigail.

For the rest of the ball, both Lord Venn and Frederick Carstairs pursued Clarinda with their attentions. She escaped several times to the cloakroom to fuss over her hair, gown, or slippers. If they thought she had a problem with her bladder, she didn't care.

"Don't get your hopes up too much about that young dog, Carstairs," warned James in the carriage on the way home, "Very likely, his family have had a match lined up for him since he was in his cradle. That's how these landed people do things."

"I thank you for the warning, brother," Clarinda smiled, "He's sweet, so I'm sorry he has fallen in with such a set as Lord Venn's, but I'd as soon think of marrying Nancy's spaniel pup."

Nancy tossed her head. "Those sour grapes will sweeten soon enough if you can draw him in."

James laughed, "I'll warrant then she'll speak differently. Yet, be wary of Lord Venn. Do you know, he surprised me by saying he'd taken a house near to us – not in Russell Square, but in some street I'd never heard of – and he said he'd call too, but again, don't set too much store by that, Clarinda."

"There is no danger of my 'getting my hopes up' about either. Before we came to Town, didn't I say that I'd rather be an old maid with a parrot to love than a sad matron with a husband who married her for money?" Clarinda's voice was drowned in the jeers from the others.

5.
Prize

O'HARE SHOWED MOLYNEUX INTO HARLEY Venn's drawing room, where prints of prize fighters and scantily clad dancing girls adorned the walls along with paintings in heavy frames. A long portrait of his uncle Toby Venn hung on one wall, though there was none of his father, the Earl of Aylesbury. Antique pieces of furniture were scattered about, including a low seventeenth century table defaced by scratches where Venn rested his boots.

Venn was – as so often – vulgarly dressed, wearing a kerchief knotted about his throat rather than a cravat. Molyneux, unmoved by that, raised his brows to see Venn collecting spare coins from the drawers.

He broke off to say, "Molyneux, it's good to see you. There's time for a drink before we go to the fight. Wine, O'Hare."

"There ain't none," O'Hare turned to say.

"Then go and get some, fellow. Damn me, it's not a civilised house without wine. Still, with you in it, it wouldn't be one anyway."

"No ready money. The pie man wouldn't give me credit last night."

"Insolent dog, eh? Did you tell him you belong to my household?"

"He said that was exactly the trouble…Your Honour. So I seized one of his pies and bit into it. Burnt my lip horrible, so it did."

Harley Venn thrust on him some of the coins he had collected. "Cease that infernal blather, and go for some wine."

O'Hare left, sighing as if put upon.

Molyneux said, "As you like to drink with the costermongers and street hawkers, Harley, you ought to pay him what you owe out of fellow feeling."

He handed Molyneux the glass. "So I would have, if the fellow had been reasonable about it. Take some brandy instead of wine. That villain will be away for hours, coming back with some taradiddle by way of excuse. My apologies for involving you in these household cares, Jack, but you see how my finances become impossible. "

"As a viscount, you'll have no trouble drawing in some girl. I only pity the one you choose. I hope she isn't Miss Greendale. Even from our short acquaintance, I can see she's too good for you with your empty promises of this reformation which you say your future wife must do for you, while you go on as usual."

Harley Venn grinned. "Jack, you haven't even got round to talking of mending your ways. I like the Greendale girl. She surprised me by… No, I won't talk of that. If it wasn't for her relatives, I'd think seriously of her."

"You don't have to live with her relatives. Still, I'm glad she's not your choice." Molyneux laughed. "Young Carstairs has a fine case of calf love already, and is all set to cut you out if his Mama lets him. He and I went to Vauxhall Gardens the other evening, and who should we bump into but those Greendales and their city friends. Carstairs sped her away fast, leaving us all behind, landing me with a fellow who wanted to know the name of my tailor and a young lady who gurgled, 'La!' I cursed him heartily. "

Venn laughed. "Jack, I'll have to find myself this heiress – who must also be a sweet girl, to keep my word to poor Foyle – or I'll have my own tailor chasing me down the street for the coat on my back."

He wandered over to take up a note from the sideboard. "Sister Babs is doing her best for me. As part of my rehabilitation she wants me to turn up unexpected at one of her cursed musical evenings, and win over some respectable young ladies with song. I'm relying on you to come with me to make an evening of damned squalling and strumming bearable. She's inviting Miss Greendale, Miss Trollope and a couple of other chits. Another brandy?"

As he handed Molyneux his drink, he said, casually, "Jack, speaking of Clarinda Greendale, we saw the Hooded Cadaver at Babs' ball."

"What?" Molyneux nearly spilt some of the brandy. "You were in fine spirits, afterwards."

"I felt like some light relief." Venn told the story of the apparition at the ball, only the spark in his eyes betraying his anger.

"Numbskull that I was, to let the coward get away with his tricks a second time. True, that ground floor of Babs' town house is a warren of antechambers, though if he fled anywhere, he went outside, as I was in the corridor before he could have reached the nearest door."

He grimaced comically. "Then, who but our old friend Major Pyke should appear, demanding a word. I was getting the girl away from the whoreson when he yelled after us that I wouldn't win this time. He looked like to have a seizure, had he more flesh on him. Come to think of it, he's like a cadaver himself."

Molyneux nodded. "He's been wild since his last big loss at the races. He's no earldom and entailed properties coming his way, let alone half of a fortune awaiting collection on his marriage. He's never accepted that you beat him and his champion both in a fair fight, though he can't get anyone in the Fancy[11] to listen, save a couple of those punch drunk old style sluggers. He hated Foyle, too, for laughing at him. Even so, dressing up as a skeletal spectre in a cloak doesn't seem his style."

"It doesn't." Harley Venn drained his second glass, "It needs imagination, and I'd say he had less than his horse. And how could he vanish in front of me and the Greendale girl, only to come on us from behind?"

"He'd need an accomplice. But you know how since Foyle's death, none of the others will admit to seeing the figure, with some of 'em denying they saw or heard the lightning bolt? Yet she saw it. Why?"

Lord Venn shook his head. "I couldn't say. Maybe ladies don't mind admitting to such things. One way or another, this damnable prankster can't escape me forever." He grinned. "Our visit to the theatre for advice on stage tricks went happily for us both, eh? That full lipped *senora*

---

11   The Fancy: Pugilism enthusiasts.

knew tricks enough herself. Pity, though, we couldn't find anyone who knew how to do this prankster's party tricks."

Molyneux laughed. "Your reform progresses well, Venn. If you're disgusted by Clarinda Greendale's relatives, you must evade your creditors – pie men and tailors included – until Lady Babs persuades some more families to unbar their doors to you."

"Sure you don't want to pull your man out, Venn?" For all Major Pyke's arrogant air, his eyes glinted with desperation.

"Don't put your shirt on yours," Lord Venn replied. "I'm warning you, for all your damned blather about how I'm supposed to have pulled some stunt against Broughton's rules[12] with both you and the Butterman."

"Good bluff, Venn. Your man will go in five; they always do with the Tottenham Terror." Major Pyke turned to thrust his way through the crowd to his champion's side, while Harley Venn and Jack Molyneux went to meet their own.

Half of the crowd were drunk and many secreted clubs about them. As they passed a young woman who had set up a stall selling gin, Venn said, "Take care, little one. This lot will go up like a powder keg. Get to the edge of the crowd."

She glanced about, "I think you speak true, Sir. Gin?" she turned to Molyneux, who smilingly refused. Another young woman raised her skirts to the knees for them.

"And you too, my girl," said Molyneux.

"Will you come too, Sir?" she pouted.

"Like to, but I've serious matters on hand. The hopeful's my lad."

An hour later, Venn and Molyneux lounged at the side of the ring by their man's backers amongst an uproar of cheers, whistles and catcalls as the contenders, now slowing and clumsy, their clothes spattered in gore, fought on.

Venn and Molyneux had been joined by their fellow rake and

12   Broughton's rules: Following the death of an opponent in the prize ring, these minimal rules were imposed by the champion Jack Broughton in his amphitheatre in 1743.

member of the Fancy, Richard Welch, as heavily muscled as a bull, with a piercing dark stare and wild look.

If the Tottenham Terror was dismayed that the challenger had not fallen in fifteen – let alone five – his savage face showed nothing but concentration and the marks of the fight. His opponent, deaf to the uproar, saw only the Terror. They had thrown, choked, kicked and head butted each other, and both were still up.

Willing up speed, the Tottenham Terror unleashed on the St Gilles Slasher a couple of body blows that rocked him, rousing the crowd to frenzy. Venn, striving to roar his advice above the tumult, caught sight of Major Pyke opposite, mouth gaping and dark as cave, skull-like face contorted, punching the air in an agony of glee, and was reminded again of the skeletal apparition.

Molyneux's sudden, "Filthy damned business," startled Venn, but he was too carried away to trouble about it.

Now the Terror gave a blow to the kidneys that sent the St Gilles' Slasher to one knee, taking the full count of thirty.

Venn roared, "Come on! Watch for that opening!" He acted out his champion's prize move. The Slasher had tried it twice; each time, the Terror had grabbed his leg and aimed a blow to his groin. Venn, foreseeing this, had taught him how to swivel and block it.

The St Gilles Slasher retreated, while the Tottenham Terror stalked him. The uproar rose to a crescendo, blows were struck opposite, and a hat rose like a bird taking flight. "It's off." Venn turned his reckless grin on his friends.

The St Gilles Slasher summoned a kick to the Terror's solar plexus that hurled him back into the arms of one of his seconds, wheezing. The crowd roared like a storm. The Tottenham Terror lay prone. The fight was over.

A general battle broke out all about the ring. Clubs came down on heads, fists smashed into faces, yells and grunts and the thuds of bone on flesh filled the air, while the heavy scent of blood joined the stench of sweat.

Harley Venn saw Major Pyke, stony among the rolling sea of the Fancy, jaw fallen, eyes goggling, unable to register his defeat.

A heavy blow landed on Venn's shoulder, and he turned to face a stocky man attacking him as unthinkingly as a predator. Venn was happy to retaliate. Someone fell on Molyneux, who hit him so hard that his feet left the ground.

As Venn felled his first opponent, another attacked him. Possibly this was an ally of the first man, more likely a stranger, who struggled to bring a knobbly club down on Venn's head. At the edge of the other side of the crowd, he saw the girl he had warned earlier, escaping with her wares. "That's one good thing," he muttered.

Then he glimpsed a flicker, as of distant lightning. An image of a cloaked, hooded figure appeared in the midst of the sea of fighters, seemingly invisible to them. It raised skeletal arms, quivering, as if drawing in power from the brutality all about. Then it was gone.

Venn was fighting too hard to give it further thought. Having floored his opponent, whose club vanished under the surging feet, he saw that Molyneux was surrounded by a team of three, wielding clubs. He put up a savage and skilful fight, but Venn muttered, "One too many," and fought his way towards him.

Welch, who was picking up and throwing one opponent after another into the crowd – resembling, with his workmanlike air, a drayman hurling barrels – was too busy to notice.

Another battle-crazed man leapt at Venn, mouth open to bite. Venn side-stepped, helping him on his way with a kick. Landing on Venn's former opponent, the man sank his teeth into him like a fighting dog.

Venn disposed of the third member of the group surrounding Jack Molyneux with a jab to the back of the head just as Molyneux sent the head of the first crashing back. "Careless, Jack, getting cornered!"

Laughing wildly, he caught sight of Major Pyke only feet away. The Major didn't notice him. Eyes glazed and staring, face distorted, seemingly oblivious of the battle raging round him, he stumped along, a beaten man.

"It is outrageous of you to come here straight from what you would term a mill," the naked Gabrielle Hogg told Harley Venn, who dozed next to her. They lay with the covers down past their waists. She lounged on the pillows with her arms under her head, her waving chestnut hair falling about her magnificent breasts. Despite her two children, they were still high and firm, and the skin on her firm belly was unmarked.

With the same improbable good luck, the philandering Lord Venn had also escaped 'A Disease', though he put that down to using skin sheaths.[13] He had been as lucky in escaping from the riot today with his scalp and features intact, his only injuries some bruises and a cut above the right eye.

He made as fine as sight as she as he lay by her side, with his spare, muscular build, bright hair, and classic proportions. His sculpted features were unmarked by fighting, the only signs of his life of excess the faint lines about his eyes and forehead.

They were both sated. As Sir Maurice was out at his club, Lady Hogg's confidential maid had shown him up the back stairs.

Harley Venn grunted. His cornflower blue eyes opened lazily. "You know I please you best in savage form. Besides, I couldn't resist calling in on my way back... With that boy's win today, I may stave off ruin a month. I've debts of honour to pay, and they'll take up most of the winnings. That fool Major Pyke's ruined. As I saw him stagger by, I near felt sorry for the crazed fool."

He ran his fingers down over her shoulder, caressing one breast, and stroking over her waist and one round hip, moving them further down to caress her thighs.

"When is this reform you boast of to begin?"

"Such fine, pouting lips you have, my beauty." He kissed them. "What? My reform's on course. Barbara seeks a suitable wife, who can do it for me. I'm not eager to saddle myself with one, but there's no help for it. This win today makes no difference in the long run. I can't afford not to marry an heiress, as I can't sell off any of my other houses; they're all part of the entail."

"Surely, that insipid girl I met at the ball isn't to be the one to change your course? Do you fool yourself you could be faithful to a chit like her, complete with dumpy figure? Does Barbara not think it demeaning to marry you off to the niece of your poor Uncle Toby's late steward?"

"I like her figure," Venn said. "I saw her first in church, as befits a

---

13   Skin sheaths: Condoms made from animal bladders were sometimes used by rich philanderers to avoid sexually transmitted diseases.

young innocent. Her behind kept Mr Harley upright for the whole of a confoundedly dull sermon." He drew her hand down to his member.

She squeezed it gently, and turned over. "You wicked creature. You can kiss mine."

"With pleasure, Ma'am," he ran his lips down her long and lovely back to the dimples above her tail bone, and then gently began alternately to kiss and to nibble her full bottom.

"Careful, no bruises!" she reminded him. "Though these days it's once a month with Hogg, you never know; he might come to me tonight."

Later, she turned to rouse him by running a hand down his hard belly. "Whatever will the Earl say at your marrying some city heiress?"

He scowled. "The governor's cast me off anyway. He'd disinherit me as quick as dammit if he could get round the entail, so serve him right. We nobles giving ourselves airs about coming over in the Norman Conquest is cant anyway. There's probably a fellow sweeping the gutter who's descended from the Anglo-Saxon nobles we displaced."

She smiled. "You should try and placate the old gentleman rather than provoke him further."

He merely swore, and retreated into silence, gazing at the ceiling. He was not, however, thinking of his estrangement from his father or his marriage plans. Suddenly, he demanded: "Remember Lodovico Sharman doing a display of magic for your daughter a while back?"

She gave him a thoughtful look, and then her low, throaty laugh. "How, my dear, could I forget? Such a showman. He gave us some fine entertainment, unintentional though half of it was."

"Where could I get hold of the fellow? I want to use him myself."

She raised her eyebrows. His look, while inscrutable, seemed unlike that of one who plans entertainment. "Do you plot a wicked practical joke on someone?"

He rose. "I must be on my way."

The rumours about the indoor lightning flash which had sent George Foyle to his death down the winding stairs of the Coconut Club had reached Gabrielle, and she frowned. "Dear me; poor George Foyle."

He turned, pulling on his shirt. "Why do you say that now?"

"Because there is talk, my dear, that some conjuring trick shocked Mr Foyle into his fall. So, it was unhappy I joked about such matters."

"Ah. Sharman's address?"

"I don't remember. That was the first time I used him in years. I'll have to ask our steward."

He came over to kiss her lips. "Do that and let me know. Don't forget."

"Then it's serious?"

He shook his head.

She ran her eyes over him. "Talking of Sharman, he was a splendid creature, before the demon drink did for him. Rather like you, save he was broader built, and had Roman nose. Haven't you had that portrait done yet? You ought to hurry, if you must keep overdoing it, or you'll have ruined your looks first."

6.
Prospective Brides

Lord Venn kept his promise to call at the Greendale's. Spying him from an upper window the day after Lady Barbara's ball, Nancy pouted that he came on foot, rather than in a carriage with his family's crest.

Flying into action, she scolded the maid Abigail into lacing Clarinda so tightly that she wheezed as she clung to the bed post. Then, rushing Clarinda into her primrose coloured silk, she sent Abigail scurrying for her own rouge pot. Clarinda, seeing how it made her complexion glow like Lady Hogg's, resolved to get some too.

When Clarinda entered the drawing room, the gracious Lord Venn, the picture of athletic health and casual elegance in his tightly fitted coat, was promising to call in at James' club. As he pressed his lips to Clarinda's hand, he glanced down her cleavage. She was tempted to regret in a polite tone how her own breasts, round though they were, must be disappointing after Lady Hogg's.

A couple of days later, in company with young Carstairs, Lord Venn called in on James's club, amiable among the bourgeois. James said later that after all, they were genteel company compared to many of Lord Venn's normal cronies, who included costermongers and roughs of all sorts.

He told Nancy and Clarinda how he had outwitted Carstairs and

Venn at chess, so that the Viscount exclaimed, "Damn me, Greendale, you men of business know about strategy."

After that, the Greendales had cards and invitations from several of Lady Barbara's set, and met Venn, Molyneux, Carstairs, and sometimes the savage looking Welch at several of these great houses.

Meanwhile, young Carstairs' passion for Clarinda heated from simmering to boiling point. Whether this was his following his mentor Lord Venn in everything, including attraction to women, Clarinda couldn't tell. Yet however this infatuation started, while Lord Venn was beguiling and evasive, Carstairs was openly besotted.

After the meeting at Vauxhall Gardens with the Greendales and their city friends that had so bored Molyneux, Nancy's circle loved teasing Clarinda about Carstairs as her 'Titled Young Admirer'.

"Yes, he's much struck," admitted Clarinda, "And no thanks to my charms. At eighteen, infatuation comes and goes overnight. I think his Mama has other plans for him. A few sighs will do away with his disappointment, and a cup of tea shall with mine."

"It's a strange thing that so debauched a fellow should have so musical a voice," said Nancy. Her own betrayed how she had been moved by the song Lord Venn had just finished.

They were at Lady Barbara's musical evening. Clarinda had been even more caught by his rendition of Handel's '*Verdi, Pratti*'[14].

Now, she was disgusted with herself for being piqued that the Viscount stopped on his way through the applause to smile on a simpering dark haired girl, when, earlier that evening, he had distinguished Clarinda herself. As she had no respect for him, this could only be bruised vanity. Vanity must be a comic fault in a girl of moderate attractions, and a dangerous one for an heiress.

"There's no reason why a musical talent should be limited to the virtuous, any more than beauty or charm."

"That dark girl is Miss Trollope, who has a pretty pile," said Nancy. As Clarinda's lips twitched at the name, she went on, "Humph! Such

---

14   'Verdi, Pratti': Aria from Handel's 1728 opera, 'Alcina'.

thick ankles she's got, for all her genteel birth. Word's got out His Lordship's after a rich wife. Look how that old dragon of a chaperone smiles on him, when two weeks since, I'll warrant their doors were barred fast against him. They all copy us."

It was true that the Clarinda, *nouveau riche* tradesman's daughter though she was, seemed almost to have started a fashion in speaking to the Viscount. Still, Lady Barbara had been doing her best to spread word of her outcast brother's wish to make a good match. Respectable families, freed of the fear that the Viscount might want their daughter's bodies rather than their money, had started speaking to him. After all, the rascal could not be disinherited.

Some of these girls were lured by the sparkle in his eyes. Now, Miss Trollope gazed at him as at a creature both dangerous and magnificent.

Clarinda said, "Miss Trollope is scarcely to blame for her ankles, and she does have lovely hair. Poor girl, if her family sacrifices her happiness for the sake of the title."

James nodded, "Not everyone has such indulgent relatives as you, my dear, forever putting your happiness first."

Nancy enquired, "Are those grapes sour again, Clarinda? You were happy to encourage him yourself at Lady Barbara's ball."

Young Carstairs, arriving late at the musical evening, pimples aflame, rushed over to Clarinda. On the way, he spilt some wine down the back of another guest's coat and knocked over a chair. Nancy and James, ignoring these gaffes, greeted him with smiles. He was next in line to a baronetcy; that was nothing like an earldom, but better than no title at all.

"Sir, Ma'am, Miss Greendale! May I introduce my uncle, Sir Timothy Carstairs?"

This relative looked as if he had devoted every minute of the last forty years to debauchery. Clarinda winced as he smiled on her; his teeth were appalling. Though he must have ogled down countless bosoms in those years, he leered down hers as eagerly as if it was the first, drawling, "Charmed, Miss Greendale; servant."

They jumped at a screech from the other side of the room. A hefty girl with a garland of flowers in her hair had begun her song.

Harley Venn, making his way over from Miss Trollope, winced. By an unlucky fluke, Clarinda caught his eye. He gave her a knowing wink, and recalling how he had done that in church, she returned the same blank look to him which she had given him then.

Since that ball, she had been treating him with placid civility. There had been no chance to discuss that shared hallucination – or whatever it was. Naturally, they were never alone together. In a way, Clarinda was glad of that; not only had it been sinister, she wanted no bond of shared secrets with him.

She had been unable to keep from hearing even worse of him than James had told at the ball. She was dismayed at these stories of empty excess. She could only hope for his sake that they were exaggerated. Besides, while some might say that considering a number of possible brides to see who best suited him was sensible, Clarinda thought it sordid. She had no wish to seem to compete with Miss Trollope and the others for such a dubious prize.

Naturally, James and Nancy thought that she was disappointed that she was no longer the only heiress who the once outcast – now semi-outcast – smiled upon.

Clarinda even wondered a little herself.

"What ails you, fellow?" Harley Venn asked as O'Hare knotted his cravat. "Betsy has got wind of my going to propose to the first on my list today, and sulks. Now you're wearing a funeral face."

"When the wife comes in the front door, it is the man goes out the back," O'Hare nodded solemnly. "I ain't made to fit into an orderly household."

"No more am I, and no wife shall rule over any household of mine," grinned Venn.

O'Hare shook his head forebodingly. "Does she go to church?"

"Which heiress? I've got three lined up, but they all have the damnable habit of attending church regular. Respectable people do, you know, while we are at our cards. You've forgotten, you rascal."

"She'll be having us trooping there twice on foot on the holy day, and the brats too – who I had christened good Catholics as befits a careful parent – and my poor shanks never the same since I fell downstairs."

Venn turned his startlingly clear blue eyes on O'Hare. "I mind that was a fortnight since. Were you in your altitudes[15]?"

"No… Your Honour. I was late in slacking my thirst that day. I heard footsteps behind me, and nothing there."

"Don't blather. You've been listening to too many blasted tales about Foyle and my uncle. "

"No, saving Your Honour, and I ain't listened to none about falling walls flattening stewards, neither."

Their eyes met, and Harley Venn let out a shout of laughter. "O'Hare, I never know when you're joking. I can't get rid of you: I'd never get another man who makes me laugh like you. So no more talk of going out the back door when I carry my virtuous bride in at the front. Anyway, the first chit mightn't have me. She finds me shocking wicked, though it may be that she likes me the better for it. Thank the Lord for the circulating libraries[16] putting romantic notions about us wicked rakehells into sheltered girls' heads."

It took some time for Harley Venn to be dressed to his satisfaction and to that of O'Hare. His valet – though careless about his own dress, sure that his charm would win him admirers even in rags – was careful about his master's. At last he was ready.

O'Hare's children peeped round the door from the back of the house, sniggering, as he went out, complete with hat and stick, to swagger into his hired carriage, the sunlight shining on his light golden hair and side whiskers.

Some time later, Harley Venn paced in the drawing room at the Trollope house, having forced himself to speak to the elderly magistrate – as unlikely a father-in-law to the lawless Venn as could be imagined.

Men waiting for their intended bride should dread refusal. He

---

15   In your altitudes: Cant slang for drunk.

16   Circulating libraries: These were private libraries with a middle class readership.

dreaded acceptance. He fought the urge to turn tail as he had never had before any of his most savage prize fights.

"It's true that as a peer, I wouldn't be left to rot in a debtor's prison," he muttered. "But why the fuss? She's a pretty girl, and good natured. Mr Harley likes her well enough. She's a well born heiress."

He didn't feel comforted. Mr Harley was now – for once – inert. Perhaps his member recalled that he had liked the low born and less pretty Miss Greendale far better. That organ's supposed master muttered again, "Yes, but those vulgarian relatives. No: the niece of my uncle's ex-steward has to be last on my list."

The door opened. He drew himself up. Miss Trollope stood before him, looking even less intelligent than usual, eyes round and lips parted.

He shot a look at her fine high bosom, down which he had sneaked glances at the musical evening. She had seen those looks then, and seemed undismayed. Now, she drew back, looking displeased. But he was already speaking.

"Miss Trollope, I cannot deny that I have a sad reputation. You can have heard little good of me. But I wish to change: for that I need a domestic angel to be my guide. You –"

She gave a skittish scream.

"Forgive me, I express myself too hastily. I am not used to dealing with delicate nurtured young ladies. I hope that wretch as I am, you –"

She gasped, bosom heaving: "You cannot be proposing, Lord Venn?"

He smiled. "I know this is sudden, but I am carried away by the warmth of my feelings for you. Your father said that I might hope."

He was wondering if he was obliged to go down on his knees, when she gave a louder shriek. With a quick glance over her shoulder, she fainted, falling backwards on to the *chaise longue*, catching up her skirt as she fell, and showing much of the hefty ankles that Nancy had mocked.

Lord Venn, starting forwards as she began to sway, stopped, allowing himself a bitter smile. He rang the bell pull. At once, a maid opened the door, followed by the Sir and Lady Trollope.

"How now, Sir?" the father exclaimed, while the mother hurried to the girl who lay still, her eyes tightly closed.

"I regret that the young lady fainted before I could finish my addresses, Sir. Truly, I had hardly begun."

One of Miss Trollope's eyelids flickered, and she gave another scream, as if eager to make her point. "Mama, he proposed to me. It was horrible."

Harley Venn drew himself up: "Horrible?"

"Surely, my dear," exclaimed her mother, "Lord Venn said nothing improper?"

"He looked at me…"

He interrupted, before she could specify where his gaze had wandered. "I must go. Clearly, my addresses were unwelcome to the young lady, and I shan't distress her further. Servant, Ma'am, Miss Trollope, Sir."

He hurried past the staring maidservant to the door. As he gained the hallway, he heard Miss Trollope sob, "And I don't like his whiskers. There's something improper about them."

"Foolish, jittery chit! They're magnificent whiskers. She gave me enough encouragement before, with all that eye batting and pouting. These damned illogical women!"

Undaunted, Venn set off on foot for the second on his list.

Arriving at the Wilkins' house, where he had yawned through the tamest evening of cards on his calling only days before, Harley Venn paused on the pavement. "Come on, it's only for life," he murmured. Eyes watched him keenly from the upper windows, a drape moved, and the casement opened. He threw off his hesitation to smile up amiably.

He leapt back: "Dammit!"

Only his fighter's instincts had saved him from a dousing in the contents of a chamber pot.

Miss Wilkins' great grandmother's face appeared at the open window, all smiling malevolence. "I do apologise, My Lord." She spoke as calmly as if emptying jordans onto her front doorstep was part of her normal lot.

Harley Venn bowed, turned on his heel and went briskly on his way on foot. Walking always stimulated his brain.

"Some would say that's fate tipping me the wink," he murmured aloud. "I've crossed Miss Wilkins from my list, fearing for Mr Harley in her hands after I saw her fingers break that fan. Even with tuition, that don't bode well. As the Middleton's don't relent towards me, that leaves Clarinda Greendale. It's a comedown, but Mr Harley likes her best, for all she's no beauty. She's no fool either, innocent though she may be, so I'd best not go and propose without first devoting my attentions solely to her."

He swaggered along towards The Pugilists, looking for a brawl to work out his spite on the way. Finding no excuse for one, he took it into the club and some sparring.

Major Pyke had not been in often lately, and was absent today. A couple of his associates were in. Catching their gaze on him, Venn laughed outright, and they looked away.

"Supposedly, Miss was so shocked at receiving a proposal from such a man, she screamed and fainted before he had properly begun," Nancy told Clarinda over breakfast a couple of days later.

Sir and Lady Trollope had been assiduous in spreading the tale of the Viscount's proposal and their daughter's delicacy. They were annoyed by her behaviour, which they thought had to do with an untitled army man. Still, if they couldn't have an earldom in the family, at least they could pretend to have risen above the wish for one.

Nancy was the unlucky gossip who always hears the latest scandal last. "What do you make of that?" she asked Clarinda, James being engrossed in his paper.

"That she has more sense than I thought," returned Clarinda, pouring tea. "This London milk doesn't taste the same as the milk at home. Still, this jam is nice."

"Don't make yourself sound so provincial, dear. James doesn't complain of how he must neglect the local part of his business while we take you through this season. Only see the opportunities that come your way. You've got three fine catches after you now, besides cockney dandies we'll not trouble about. Who'd have thought it a year ago? But then, dear, with these fine new clothes, you begin to look quite pretty."

"I rather think it is the money that beautifies me, as far as these suitors go. Who are these three fine catches, Nancy?"

"Why, Sir Timothy and young Carstairs. And now the Trollope girl with those big legs has rejected Lord Venn, and for some reason he's lost interest in that Miss Wilkins, if you play your cards cleverly, dear, you'll be a Countess in a few years when old Venn goes."

"It doesn't matter that I was Venn's third or fourth choice as moneyed victim. In being pursued by a brawling ruffian, an old lecher and a callow youth, I have reason to preen myself."

Nancy adjusted a curl, "Yes, Venn's a shocking character, and his excesses must catch up on his looks in time, but till then he is a magnificent creature, you'll allow. It's a shame that if you do draw him in, Lady Barbara couldn't take you for a presentation at court,[17] seeing he's not received generally. There's no need to pull that prissy face, Miss. If you can like him as a man, you can endure his wildness well enough, knowing you've raised our family and done wonders for little Bella's prospects."

Clarinda's mouth being full of bread, "Humph!" was all she could manage.

Nancy was less delicate. Chewing heartily, she went on, "Suppose you don't manage to draw him in, old Sir Timothy won't last long – with the right settlement you could make a fine match there."

Clarinda groaned wordlessly.

"If you really won't have the old wretch, that youth will be fine young man when he's got over those spots. I will say one thing for this dreadful pugilism, it does give a trim waist, just the thing for this new tight cut of coats."

"The poor boy's too young to think of marrying, while the only one of his family who treats us warmly is the old *roué* of an uncle. I suppose they think I set my cap at both the callow youth and the old man. It's provoking."

Here, James lowered his copy of *'The Gentleman's Magazine'*. He must have been following their conversation more than they realised, for he said, "If Clarinda has sense, she'll keep the lot of 'em dangling until she's sure of one. Then it's time enough for her to make her choice. Remember that coal merchant's nephew, Nan?"

"La, I'd quite forgot!" Nancy – always florid – went a shade pinker

---

17   Presented at court: Normally, a viscount's fiancée could expect to be presented at court, if she hadn't been already.

with pleasure, while Clarinda threw up her hands. "You've got to smile more though, dear. The way you scowled at Lord Venn when he singled you out the other evening made you look near ugly."

"I am happy to hear that." Clarinda poured herself more tea.

"When you play, Sir, it makes me feel like giving up music altogether." Clarinda spoke briskly to hide her admiration as Lord Venn came to the end of a series of Scottish and Irish airs on the violin.

Whenever he sang or played, she always forgot her vows to be cool towards him. The man had the music of a male merman at his command.

Lord Venn put down his instrument. "I swear, Miss Greendale, if you give up music, so shall I. You've natural ability, but I had the best tutor. I'd be delighted to show you some of what he taught me, if you'd allow me."

Clarinda fidgeted. Now the Viscount distinguished her alone. Had her vanity been greater, she could have deluded herself that he had come to prefer her. As it was, the thought of Miss Trollope screaming and fainting set her lip curling.

"No, really, Lord Venn –" she began, but broke off, flinching. Nancy, back from searching through a bureau in the room opposite, trod hard on her toes, saying through a tight smile, "You are too kind, Lord Venn. Clarinda would be delighted, only she's too shy to admit it."

Harley Venn's dark, slanting eyebrows were up in the curling pale gold locks that tumbled over his forehead, and Clarinda wondered if he had seen that assault. She hoped he had. It would make her family appear even more vulgar than Nancy's talk of money.

"It would be a pleasure; might I call tomorrow as your music tutor? Call me, 'Mr Harley'." His lips turned up, as at a private joke. Clarinda, irritably sorting out the music, caught his gaze dwelling on her ample behind, and made a point of sitting down on it.

As Nancy thanked Venn some more, Clarinda drew her feet away from her.

Lord Venn smiled, "But you can easily repay me, Ma'am. I would like to see Miss Greendale's sketch book. She won't show me. You could persuade her to oblige me."

Nancy rang for a servant to fetch Clarinda's sketch book. This was soon handed over to him.

One was missing from it, removed by Nancy as 'nasty and odd'.

Clarinda agreed that it was. She had no idea what made her paint a view of the young male and female figures on the roof of a castle, hair and clothing whipped by wind, a livid sky behind them, horror on their shadowed faces as they gazed towards something outside the picture.

Harley Venn was full of admiration. "You have a strong style, unusual in a young lady," he murmured, turning over the pages. "Here's a sunset glowing on the backs of grazing sheep which I can only call evocative. Done, I think, Miss Greendale, from your window?"

She returned his smile with a stolid look. "Yes, Sir. I am no romantic, to work outside then, among the biting insects."

Grinning, he turned the page. "What have we here? Two figures in the centre of a maze…" His eyes dilated. "No, three," he added.

Now the bright blue gaze meeting hers was no longer laughing. He had seen the cloaked, hooded figure painted from behind, which blocked the sole way out of the maze for the couple.

"That is an unlucky daub for you to come across, Sir, and I am sorry for it," Clarinda murmured. "When I painted it, I only saw it as an anonymous messenger."

"It is a common Gothic image, after all," he said lightly. "Do you like mazes, Miss Greendale? We have a notable one at Stoke Castle."

Clarinda remembered hearing something about Tobias Venn being found dead in a maze, and was relieved for them both as he turned over to one of her favourite paintings, a rose garden.

7.

Specious Speeches

June 1821

"Lord Venn's here. You know why." James closed the door to Clarinda's room. "I beg, sister, you give the matter more thought before rejecting him outright as you did Sir Timothy. As I said then, you must have turned the old fellow down at speed, without any show of regret."

Clarinda frowned. "I couldn't hide my dismay at a proposal from such an old *roué*, who'd worn out two wives and their fortunes already. I shall try to be more gracious with Lord Venn, but the answer must still be no. "

James shook his head. "Don't count on the youth. He's three years short of his majority, and that calf love will burn itself out long ere then, even supposing he holds out against his family."

Nancy huffed, alarmingly red. "I can't get the stubborn little fool to see sense. I could box her ears!"

"That would at least make a change from stamping on my feet," said Clarinda. "I don't want the old lecher, the younger lecher, the callow youth, or a title at the price of marrying a fortune hunter."

As Nancy turned redder, Clarinda felt concerned for her health.

James sighed. "I could scarce believe that you would be so willful.

I would never have thought you a reader of novels, sister, holding out for a love match. Lord Venn is bad enough, but given to good works as you are, here is the chance of a lifetime to do good in saving him from himself."

"I don't flatter myself that I am equal to such a task. Still, I am sorry to disappoint you both of joining our family with the nobility."

Nancy wheezed, deprived of speech, and James shook his head.

In the drawing room, Harley Venn drummed long fingers against the mantelshelf, so handsome and vigorous in the morning sunshine that Clarinda's eyes widened.

She longed, as so often since they had met, to paint him as an object of beauty in much the same way as a particularly fine horse. Of course, horses had better morals.

He smiled and bowed. "Ma'am. Your brother has told you of the purpose of my visit?"

She nodded. "Yes, My Lord, and while I –"

"Stop!" he said, "You will say that my character is too bad for you to consider such a match. Yet isn't that uncharitable, Miss Greendale – Clarinda. May I call you Clarinda?"

"No, Sir," she said, but he went down on his knees.

"I have only known you a short while, but I see what a fine person you are. You are everything that I am not. I know that I am unworthy to address you[18], unworthy even to touch the hem of your robe. Yet, if you would consider linking your fate to that of a man who is an outcast from much of decent society, to be my good angel, and try and love me a little, I would be eternally in your debt and your slave. I would spare no effort to make you as happy as I must be myself, were you to be mine."

Were my fortune to be yours, you mean.

He gazed up at her imploringly. Still, she sensed mischief lurking at the back of what a novelist might call his 'cerulean gaze', as if he found these words as laughable as she did. She suspected that he had

---

18   Lord Venn's speech is largely taken from a novel from a later age, Lord Fayne's intended proposal in Charles Garvice's 1894 'The Outcast of the Family'.

borrowed that speech from a novel. She was torn between laughter and indignation that he should take her for such a fool as to be duped by it.

"I cannot accept your flattering proposal, Sir." Tempted to add, '*I cannot even believe that I was second or even third on your list,*' she said instead in a friendly tone, "I am far from angelic, and the idea that a girl of twenty-one could be the guiding light for a man of the world several years her senior is preposterous to me."

As he stared, lost for words, she went on, "Surely, it makes more sense that you must have an influence over me, especially given the roles of the sexes? However, I am sure that many other young ladies would be honoured to assume the role that you offer to me."

Here, she saw Lord Venn's prize fighter's ability to think on his feet, or in this case, on his knees. He spoke in a resigned tone. "I am justly served. I was too hasty in my anxiety not to lose such a jewel to another man. When I heard that old baronet had asked for you, then I felt I must speak. Clarinda, if only we were to become better acquainted you might see how sincere I am."

I certainly would.

Perhaps he misunderstood the sparkle of repressed laughter which warmed her eyes, for his tone was once more assured as he went on, "Don't think I assume because of my title; I can guess how little distinctions of rank mean to you, and what a presumption it is in such an outcast as myself to aspire to you. I approach you with more humility than any untitled man without my disgraceful past. Yet, with a longer acquaintance, you must come to know how I want to change my path."

"No, Sir," she began to tap one foot, as she had at Sir Timothy's spluttered love vows. At least Lord Venn, though surely he had been at the brandy again, didn't have rotting teeth and bad breath. She had cowered back from Sir Timothy's.

He tried his beguiling smile again, a blend of mischief and melancholy. "You underestimate the influence you could have on me. Bad as I am, and young as you are, I know that you could be my saving angel."

"No, Sir. But I am happy to hear of your aim to change your way of life, and I wish you all happiness with the young lady who does feel herself equal to the role you honour me by offering."

She could sense that though was dizzy with humiliation, he refused to let her fortune slip though his fingers so easily. Now, he called on another quality necessary for a pugilist – self-control. Rising from his knees, he took her hands before she could retreat, caressing them. "Clarinda, you remember that you were the only respectable young lady who spoke kindly about poor Foyle's death. You were not cold and implacable, then."

Her lips thinned. "I am only so now in refusing your offer of marriage."

He dropped her hands. "So be it, Ma'am." Too outraged to make the normal civilities, he turned away.

A flash of lightning outlined the window, where a hooded, cloaked figure appeared, suspended on the air. It extended one skeletal hand as if reaching towards them and vanished even as the thunderclap came.

Swearing, Harley Venn dashed to the window. As the thunder echoed away, Clarinda came up behind him. "We saw that oddity before." She gazed about the empty street below. "This time it has appeared at a first floor window. That is extraordinary."

He turned a taut smile on her. "Don't concern yourself, Ma'am, it was a trumpery conjuring trick by an illusionist or mesmerist."

They looked at each other, he defiant, and she curious rather than frightened. She saw the admiration in his eyes at her strong nerve.

"Do not concern yourself about that laughable party trick. I'm not sure how it's done, but it's getting to be a cursed nuisance. You have just seen another good reason to reject me. Please accept my wishes for your future health and happiness." He said this automatically, bent over her hand, and turned away.

He was at the door when she said softly, "Do wait a moment, Sir." He paused, eyebrows raised. She saw that he thought she relented.

"I wanted to say, Sir, that I make no doubt the details surrounding my own late relative's death have become wildly distorted in the telling."

Venn's face fell as he realised that this was no attempt to withdraw her rejection. She went on calmly, "I hope his shocking end can be set aside as irrelevant. Yet, if the story is true, and such a figure as we saw even now appeared to Mr Foyle on his fall to his death, if it was indeed the conjuring trick you say, then it seems to be one with a sinister purpose. Do take care, Lord Venn, especially near stairs."

He drew himself up. "As to me, Ma'am, I find these parlour tricks laughable. As you have rejected my offer so decidedly, there is surely no need to concern yourself with my welfare." He paused and then added coldly, "I believe that these illusions are meant for me, and you have only seen them by default. But should you ever feel yourself threatened by such visitations, do let me know of it." He bowed and flung out of the room.

Clarinda shook her head. "I can easily be concerned about the rascal's future welfare, so long as I don't have to marry him or any of these dismal fortune hunters. But how could any parlour trick create a vision such as that?"

To Harley Venn's fury, he was stopped by James Greendale in the hallway. "My Lord, I fear from your look my sister allowed her maidenly fears to overcome her."

"I don't know about maidenly fears," Venn looked about for his hat and stick. "She gave me a brisk refusal, showing a determination quite contrary to the encouragement you gave me the other night at your club. There is an end of it. No doubt we will meet again, Mr Greendale, and thank you for the chess games." Suddenly he asked, "Did you by any chance hear thunder?"

James stared. "Yes, Lord Venn; I heard distant thunder."

"Distant?" Harley Venn put on his hat. "It may be as well that your sister refuses me. After all, I take about with me my own private weather."

James blinked and his nostrils twitched, as if he was sampling the Viscount's breath. Then he bowed and the footman ran forward to fling open the door. Venn stalked out. James, going over to the window, saw him loitering about at the front of the house, seemingly examining the steps down to the basement.

James muttered, "What is the fellow about, and what did he mean by that wild talk? Perhaps he is – as he would say himself – 'fuddled', and this early in the day. There was brandy on his breath, but there often is. Sour grapes or not, the man is truly an abandoned wretch."

Nancy rushed down the stairs. "I know from your look your sister refused him! Thankless, selfish hussy: we'll never get another chance for a peerage. They'll say she can't be satisfied, and those city gents will back off, thinking that if she won't take a viscount or a baronet, they won't be in with a chance. We shouldn't have bothered taking her to Town at all."

She let out a sob, while he patted her shoulder. "It's hard, dear. Never mind; if Clarinda's ruined her chances this season with this nonsense, we can have a try next year. There's always young Bella due out now her elder sister's had a season."

He didn't add that he wondered if she might prove equally awkward, if not more so.

Upstairs, Clarinda was met by Abbey. "Miss Clarinda: such a handsome gentleman, and so open handed with his tips! You never stuck to your resolve in rejecting the noble rake?"

She would have known the speech which Lord Venn had addressed to Clarinda on his knees. He had lifted it word for word from Lady Barbara's copy of, 'The Demonic Duke Or The Manor of Menace', one of Abbey's favourite stories.

"I had no choice, my dear. I hope you will do the same by any unprincipled man who pays court to you."

"Surely, Miss." Abbey wondered if the youth from the pastry cook's who had offered her a free pie last week, and who made lip sucking noises whenever she flounced by, counted as paying his addresses.

She ignored him. Now she wondered if that might be because she had guessed that he lacked principle. Before, she would have said was because he was too stout.

Clarinda snorted with laughter. "Gracious, I did sound priggish then. I don't like to seem judgmental. Yet my dear, he talked such specious nonsense there was no bearing it except by finding it amusing."

The both turned at the sound of a heavy shower coming on.

Abbey nodded solemnly, wondering what 'specious' meant. "I feel sorry for the poor rejected suitor, though, Miss Clarinda, going home in the rain. Perhaps his heart burns with mortification. Don't you feel at all sorry for him?"

"Not really," said Clarinda, "Firstly, he lives in a street five minutes' walk away, so he should be home by now. Secondly, he wished to swap my fortune for a title, and cloaked the agreement with absurd vows of reform and protestations of regard. Having failed with me, he will soon move on to the next on his list."

"Does he have one? Fancy that, then, Miss, that's shocking. Look at it rain! Well, I hope them poor kittens isn't getting damp in the rain."

Clarinda broke off from laughing at the first part of the sentence to frown at the second. "What kittens?"

"A cat's had a litter in a box in the back yard by the coal hole, Miss, but I'm thinking it's a poor shelter in such weather as this."

"Heavens, Abigail, we must bring them inside! Let's go down at once!" Clarinda pushed her feet back into her shoes.

"But Miss, the cat may scratch, so we'll need a pair of gloves each – Now, Miss, you is never going to use them fine gloves and go out in that downpour... I see you are. Whatever will Mistress Greendale say if we take in a stray cat and its litter?"

She followed Clarinda down the back staircase just as Nancy charged up the front one.

Harley Venn went home on foot, swearing at every step. Once again, he was spoiling for a fight. Disappointed in this – though he glared at the possible candidates he passed on his walk down the road – he arrived home as furious as when he had flung out of the Greendale's house. The rain coming on, he hammered on the door.

Betsy answered. Seeing his scowl, she tried to hide her smile.

"No need to pull a discreet face, my girl, you won't need to flee the house yet awhile."

"Mr Carstairs is in the drawing room, Sir."

Now Venn noticed someone repeatedly picking out the first few notes of '*The Kiss, Dear Maid*' on the piano in the drawing room. He swore some more, hurled his coat, hat and stick on to a chair in the hallway before Betsy could take them, and strode upstairs.

Carstairs turned from the piano as the door opened. His look was anguished. "Venn, I hear you went to ask for Miss Greendale."

Harley Venn marched over to the sideboard to pick up some letters.

"There's no need to look so anxious, my lad. She rejected me out of hand, just as she did your uncle."

Carstairs relaxed. "I can't say I'm sorry, Venn. Neither of you was attached to her." He reddened. "My uncle asking for her was enough to disgust her with all the males in our family, and it's ages till I can do as I please."

Harley Venn grinned. "I remember calf love myself, Carstairs. But it doesn't last."

Carstairs glowered. "That's insulting, Venn."

Venn smiled more kindly. "Come, I didn't mean to ruffle your temper, so don't ask me to name my friends. Miss Greendale's a couple of years too old for you, though. I'm betting you'll wed a girl who's not yet out of the schoolroom."

Carstairs still looked ruffled. "Did you really have a list of eligible young ladies?"

"If I have, at this rate, I'll have a list of failed proposals as long as *Don Giovanni's* list of successful seductions[19]. Pathetic for a libertine, eh?"

He resolved to change into his working man's clothes to go out on one of his wildest sprees tonight in the roughest company. Having worked his way through his list, he had no need to restrain himself. That was one comfort, anyway. Yet, if he didn't find a bride, financial ruin fast came on him. Marriage was the only way to get hold of the other half of Uncle Toby's legacy, and just in case he squandered that, he needed his wife to have some money of her own. Perhaps Babs would find some more heiresses.

---

19   Don Giovanni's list: In Mozart's 1787 opera, Don Giovanni's servant relates an absurd list of his conquests.

8.
Attack

TWENTY-FOUR HOURS AFTER CLARINDA'S REJECTION of Lord Venn, she lost count of the times that Nancy said, "I despair of you. I've got no more to say on the matter." Then she said a great deal, with none of it flattering to Clarinda.

She would have been in a bad temper anyway. Her son was teething, and his nurse unable to keep him quiet either at night or day.

James clicked his tongue and looked at Clarinda for sympathy. "Poor Nan is quite worn out with young Jem, sister. She put herself out a good deal coming up to Town to chaperone you for this season, what with bringing him too. Obviously, she's disappointed in how things have turned out. Two rejected proposals within days! I must be disappointed myself."

Clarinda kept her tone even. "But surely, brother, you would not have had me marry either the old or the young libertine, who, having squandered their own fortunes, are eager to do the same with mine?"

"If you had kept them dangling, as I urged, that would draw others in, and you could have had your choice. As it is, if you haven't got yourself a reputation as impossible to please, I'm a Dutchman."

"Impossible to please, James, because I wouldn't have either of those two prizes? Excuse me; I'll see if I can finish making that toy for Jem." Clarinda escaped, biting her lips and breathing heavily.

Upstairs, Abigail was putting away some newly laundered clothes.

"How do those kittens fare?" Clarinda asked. "Do they like their new quarters in the storeroom? I hope Cook is feeding them and mother cat as I asked and knows she is forbidden to drown them?"

"Yes, Miss, and she says, at least they may grow up to be ratters. The number of rats here in Town is disgusting, Miss, near as many as fortune hunters."

The girl went on folding clothes, but as Clarinda took up her sewing things, she felt her gaze on her. She asked, "What is it, Abbey?"

"I don't like to ask, Miss Clarinda, but what with you being so kind about them kittens, I thought... You see, it's about a friend of mine, who's ill and not happy in her place..."

Half an hour later, they set out via the back door to call in at the house where Abigail's unlucky friend, Sally, was a maidservant. In a basket, they carried fruit and other delicacies. They escaped without Nancy seeing them. She was busy scolding first James for having such an impossible sister, and then the nursemaid for the baby's teething.

It was a brighter day than many this summer, and Clarinda felt a surge of excitement at escaping out onto the streets, instead of riding with either James or Nancy in the carriage.

Nancy had a horror of walking, sure that the London streets were dangerous. Certainly, street vendors and beggars harassed pedestrians, and there was much refuse strewn about, while servants sometimes emptied chamber pots from upper windows. Still, Clarinda thought the chances of meeting with any real danger wildly exaggerated by Nancy and her friends.

She loved exercise, missing the walks she took in the country. Sometimes she ventured out in Town, the footman pacing behind.

She saw the little maid as more of a charge than a chaperone. She knew going out like this would be seen as improper, even though she was visiting a house less than seven minutes' walk from their own.

Their route led past the road where Lord Venn rented a house. As they approached, Clarinda tried to ignore Abigail's glances. Finally the girl said, "Only think, Miss Clarinda, if you had accepted the Viscount, soon we'd have been calling you 'My Lady.'"

Clarinda laughed at her wistful tone. "I think you should rather have been calling me a fool, and later, a wronged wife – and possibly worse, given the risks a libertine takes with his health – but that is no fit topic for the street."

Still, she was annoyed to find herself blushing as they passed opposite Lord Venn's house. All was still.

Abigail stared at it. "They say they treat any tradesman who comes with his bill shockingly."

"Very likely, in so barbaric a household," said Clarinda, "Let's not talk about them, dear. You know, I've always wanted to peep in at the little shop down that side street, where they sell gloves and even snuff. We must look in on the way back."

Across the road, they passed a small group of men idling and chatting, roughly dressed and incongruous in an area of respectable households. Clarinda saw one of their number furtively take out, and handle, a club. She started. Seeing her glance, he stared back insolently, but said nothing.

At the house where Abigail's friend lay ill, there was any number of difficulties, beginning with the door. Clarinda insisted on going with Abigail to the back door. The maid who answered it gawped, recognising her as one of the quality.

The housekeeper, as florid and overbearing as an older Nancy, caught Clarinda on the back stairs. She sent Abigail up alone to Sally with the delicacies, tonics and money from Clarinda, while she bid Clarinda step into her sitting room.

Here, staring as if she thought Clarinda deranged, she insisted that the girl was receiving the best of care, and that the apothecary had been. "The family is out, or I would have you announced."

"I hope I don't seem forward in calling like this, stranger as I am," soothed Clarinda. "I know in a busy household, it is difficult to spare attention for sick staff. I so value the skills of my own apothecary that I would be only too happy –"

"You are all generosity, Ma'am. But I assure you, that our own is satisfied with her progress."

Clarinda felt anything but satisfied, but also, stymied. She could hardly force her way up the back stairs. Abigail now returned and they left.

Going up the back alley, they passed a stout youth with a tray of pastries. He made sucking noises with his teeth, while Abigail flounced by him, eyes downcast.

"You can tell he's Not a Man of Principle," she told Clarinda as they hurried away.

Clarinda laughed, "Probably not. Now, how is your friend Sally?"

"On the mend, and –" they both turned at a disturbance across the street.

The four men she had seen loitering earlier were surrounding and attacking a single young man, half hiding him from view. He fought back savagely, but now they drew bludgeons.

Clarinda pulled away from Abigail's grasp, rushing towards them. She shouted, both for help and with disgust at the unfairness of the fight. Abbey rushed after her: "No, Miss!"

Now Clarinda recognised the young man as Harley Venn, fighting like a demon, but hopelessly outnumbered.

She saw the fight as a series of disjointed moves. A tall young man, with the great chest and arms of a boatman, attacked Venn from the front, swinging at his head. Venn blocked the move and sent him staggering backwards with a lighting punch from the left, trying to wrench the cudgel from him.

He had to let go to deflect the attack from a second man, sturdy and bull-like, who also swung at his head. Venn whirled to parry the blow, elbow the man in the face and kick him in the belly. The man fell away from the struggling group to roll on the ground.

Clarinda saw, incredibly, that Venn was grinning as if he was enjoying himself.

The third man, tall and broad, swung at Venn as he grappled with the second, catching him on the side, half-winding him and rocking him on his feet.

Clarinda reached the group, smashing her parasol down on the fourth man's upper back as he raised his cudgel. It landed with such force that it bent and cracked.

He howled, turning to swing his club at her. She amazed herself by blocking and deflecting the blow with the damaged parasol. Parts of it flew off. He paused, astounded at a female attack.

The staggering Harley Venn, clearly able to think on his feet rather better than his opponents, yelled hoarsely to her, "Get back!" He grabbed the man by the hair and sank his fist into his face with horrible effect; blood sprayed from his nose.

The man stumbled backwards out of the fight, clutching his face. Now Venn recognised Clarinda with a look of amazement. But now, the heavily muscled man who had attacked first, seemingly the leader, closed in on him, flailing his club and yelling orders to the third man who rushed in too, one each side aiming blows to Venn's head.

Though he covered up, Clarinda thought murder done before her eyes. She rushed forward, slipping in her impractical shoes and beating at them with her wobbly parasol: "Cowardly brutes!"

The first man got a savage blow to the crown through Venn's guard, bringing him to his knees, blood welling through his hair. Clarinda shrieked; one of the men hit out at her, catching her on the side and sending her reeling backwards.

A piercing whistle sounded across the street. The injured second man was back on his feet, shambling away. The fourth man lurched away holding his nose, his hands spattered in blood, and the third man followed.

The leader turned from the fallen Venn, then back again to kick him in the ribs. Venn, though half-conscious, still tried to grab his leg. For a moment, the leader's eyes, nearly as cold as a reptile's, rested on Clarinda, looking at her as though she were a thing rather than a person.

"Poxy whore!" he aimed a half-hearted cuff at her as he passed, speeding up after his gang.

She jumped back to avoid the blow, then rushed over to kneel beside Harley Venn. Expecting to find him dying, she was startled to see him struggling to rise, and swearing volubly: "That bastard hit you."

"I fear they hit you rather more, Sir," Clarinda was relieved that he could talk.

Now Abbey was with them. "Is the gentleman much hurt? I sent a boy for the constable. That whistling must have been the ruffians' look-out, giving the alarm."

"Go for Dr Spencer," urged Clarinda, "He lives in the square opposite us. Number twenty, I think. Do ask." Abbey trotted away. Suddenly, people came up on all sides, asking questions.

"You must be badly hurt," Clarinda drew out her handkerchief to mop at Venn's head, but the blood came too fast for her to tell the extent of the wound. Besides, his skull might be damaged.

"I'll be well enough," he muttered, his voice slurred, still struggling to rise.

"Stay there: I've sent for the doctor," she pleaded, but as he staggered to his feet, she took his arm. He leaned against her, swaying dizzily. Using all her strength, she could only just steady him. "Do sit down, Sir!"

"There's lots of blood," remarked one of two small boys happily.

"Can I help, Ma'am?" a man in servant's livery moved forward, but Venn, though wobbly on his feet and leaning against Clarinda, waved him away angrily. "Leave me be. My house is near."

"You're in no state to walk," she pleaded, but a dazed and injured Harley Venn was no more controllable than one in full health, and he took an unsteady step. "If you'll help me," he slurred. Blood dripped down on to his clothes and his face was ghastly pale.

Clarinda doubted they could get to his house, short as the distance was, but she asked the man in livery, "Could you send my maid and the doctor to Lord Venn's down the road?"

"I must thank you," Venn muttered as they staggered away from the onlookers.

"You must put your arm about my shoulders; I can't keep you upright, otherwise," she said, and he did so. To her dismay, this felt natural to her, as if they ought to have been doing it since they met and should go on doing it for the rest of their days. At present, this was the least pressing of her concerns.

He was in no state to joke about her suggesting that embrace – but still, the situation was embarrassing. They stumbled along, and he became paler and dizzier, so that she feared he would collapse.

They came up to his door. Some neighbours, alighting from a carriage, stopped, staring with looks anything but sympathetic. Now his pallor had a greenish tinge, and he muttered, "Go now: I'll be well enough," but had to break off to retch, and the ladies screamed as vomit splashed down Clarinda's dress, splattering on one of her shoes.

"Drunken, brawling ruffian," said the man, glaring at the still heaving Harley Venn, "Come inside." The group hurried up their front steps.

Clarinda's indignation at their lack of charity was fuelled by her vomit-stained dress and right shoe; there was a stench of brandy. "Hypocrites!" she spoke, more loudly than she intended. The stout matron stared at her before going in, holding up her skirts as if they too were in danger of Venn's vomiting upon them.

Clarinda had an uneasy feeling that she had been in company with her before.

She mopped at his face with her bloodstained handkerchief, wishing that she was a hundred miles away. Now that he could talk once more, he used some astounding language, adding, "Sorry... Be on your way..."

"If there is someone at home," she said. "Hold on to the rails, Sir, and I'll ring the bell." There was no answer. Now she felt like swearing herself.

"My key," he slurred, handing it to her, holding on to one railing and swaying alarmingly. As Clarinda helped him up the steps, she caught a glance of the matron next door watching them from her front window.

From the outside, Clarinda had been too preoccupied to notice if the house still had that air of emptiness it had exuded as when she and Abbey passed earlier. As she helped Harley Venn into his vestibule, she sensed this from the lonely tick of the grandfather clock in the hallway and the echoes of her voice as she called: 'Hello! We need help!'

There was no reply. Blood from his head dropped onto the floorboards. Motes of dust sparkled in the sunlight. She had an uneasy sense of premonition, of this moment being pivotal.

"My man will be back soon," he muttered.

She saw that she ought to leave at once. It was risking her reputation to be alone in a house with any man, least of all, this one. Yet, she could hardly leave him alone in such a state. What if she left and he died before help arrived?

Her conscience triumphed over her of being compromised. She decided, "I can't leave you until my maid brings the doctor."

"Damn the doctor," he muttered.

After all, she had left the front door ajar. Surely that must show anyone who had seen them come in that nothing covert was taking place, even if his bleeding and sick appearance did not.

"In there," he slurred, indicating a room further down. His head was lolling on her shoulder, and he seemed about to collapse. Now she was concerned enough to forget her alarm for what she had heard called her 'fair fame'.

They stumbled to his study, a long room with the blinds half down. She helped him to drop onto a long couch, which she recognised as a sort of day bed. Her eyes roved over the prints of pugilists, scantily dressed dancers and racehorses on the walls, combined with antique paintings and a violin on the table along with a bottle and glasses.

"Give me a nip of that brandy and I'll do," he muttered. "And thank you for this."

"I don't think you should," she glanced at him dubiously. He still looked very sick, and she would rather he didn't vomit any more in her immediate vicinity. "I'll fetch you cordial or some such thing."

He closed his eyes and made no reply. She ran along the corridor and down a flight of stairs to the kitchens, which had a banked up fire in the stove, a dripping pump, and was deserted save for a tabby cat. It spat and arched its back at her. "Nice puss." She advanced into the room gingerly, and it hissed again and dashed out through the door.

She sought about for a bowl and clean cloth, finding some dirty floor rags, but no clean ones. Her handkerchief was soiled with a mixture of vomit and blood, but in the end she had to struggle to work the pump and rinse it out under that. She was too anxious about her patient to do anything now about the mess on her dress and shoe.

Back in the study, she found him sitting with his head in his hands.

He roused as she came in, and gazed at her startled. That blue gaze, usually so careless and laughing, was now dazed. That upset her.

"You are still here?" He focused dizzily on her.

"I hardly can leave you so, until the doctor comes. Let me bathe that wound on your head." She knelt in front of him and began to mop at the matted hair. "Do you have a handkerchief, Sir? I could find no rags in the kitchen."

He seemed about to speak again, but now paused. It seemed to her that the dazed look in his eyes changed. He reached for her hand, wincing at the movement. She let him take it. "Clarinda, I thank you." He gave a bemused smile. "You fought 'em, too."

Their eyes met. She drew back. "I didn't do much good, and I would have done as much for anyone I saw set on in so cowardly an ambush."

At last, she heard approaching voices and the tramp of boots on the steps. With infinite relief, she recognised the testy, professional tones of Dr Spencer. She ran to the door.

Seeing her, the doctor's eyebrows almost vanished in the brim of his hat. Surely Abigail must have told him that she was helping Lord Venn? Now, Clarinda saw that the doctor would never have expected her to accompany him inside his house.

In that look of a respectable citizen, she saw that she was truly compromised. Never mind that the rake was injured, perhaps even dying; she had been alone in his house with him. This was the sort of thing that happened to the heroines in Abbey's novels, not to her.

"Miss Greendale!" the doctor removed his hat automatically. "But – where are the servants?"

"They are out," she felt like a naughty child questioned by an authority figure.

"Out, Ma'am?" he glanced into the study, clearly at a loss for words.

Harley Venn appeared in the doorway, leaning on the frame, looking ghastly, with his face turning greenish again. "Miss Greendale was so concerned for me – being her fiancé, you know – she clean forget –" he broke off, swaying, and the doctor seized his arm to hold him up.

"But we're not engaged!" Clarinda exclaimed. She felt trapped, and it seemed to her the hallway, wide for a town house, was suddenly so small that she could not breathe properly.

"Come, My Lord, you must lie down," the doctor said stonily.

Abbey gave a squeal as the Viscount began to retch again, staggering back into the room out of sight.

The doctor shook his head and addressed Abbey, perhaps seeing her as the most rational member of the group. "Take your mistress home, my girl."

9.
The Devil and the Deep...

O N THE WAY BACK HOME, it seemed to Clarinda that all the neighbours were out on the street to take in the sight of her in blood and vomit stained gown, with Abigail hurrying after her, still clutching the parasol as damaged as her mistress' reputation.

"Excuse my disgusting state. I soiled my clothes in helping a man set upon by armed ruffians," Clarinda told those she knew. Their jaws dropped still more.

Clarinda's ill luck that day meant that Nancy intercepted her and Abigail in the upstairs lobby as Clarinda sneaked through from the back stairs. She screamed.

"It isn't my blood - it's Harley Venn's," Clarinda tried to reassure her, while James and the footman came running up the stairs. Stony faced, James ushered Clarinda and Nancy into the drawing room.

Clarinda knew there was no point in trying to keep from them that she had gone into the den of iniquity with its debauched owner. The matron whose name she couldn't remember would spread it the more eagerly as Clarinda had been reckless enough to answer her.

James forced Clarinda to tell the story twice. Then, groaning, "You are ruined!" he buried his face in his hands, walking unsteadily to the window. Despite herself, Clarinda began to cry.

"What possessed you to outrage common notions of decency, you birdbrain?" Nancy kept her clenched fists by her sides, while they twitched as if they longed to box Clarinda's ears.

Clarinda didn't blame her. She felt like boxing them herself. She sniffed, having left her handkerchief at Venn's house. "I am so sorry. I was anxious about Venn's injuries, and thought to hand his care over to one of his servants, but the house was empty. After all, the Sermon on the Mount tells us –"

James threw down his hands. "Confound the Sermon on the Mount! – Well, I didn't mean that. But the injunctions of Christianity must be tempered with good sense, sister. You should never have set foot in the house of that man, even chaperoned. Why didn't you send your maid to tend to him? Women should cherish their reputation above anything. Now your wild notions of charity have lead to your ruin."

"But it's so absurd," sniffed Clarinda. "He was in no state to make improper advances."

"That is beside the point. The world will say, rightly, that you behaved improperly in entering his house."

James paced about in his excitement, "Now I must call on him, demanding he renew his proposals, which of course, the villain never will, after you humiliated him by that rejection. Then I can only consider myself insulted on your behalf, or be a laughing stock. I must challenge him. If he accepts, then we know what a fine shot he is."

Nancy let out a shriek.

Clarinda paled, but exclaimed, "You don't need to call on him. I'll retire to the country at once. Besides, we are not even gentry[20] for you to challenge him, and he should refuse for that reason."

"You wicked girl." Nancy turned on Clarinda. "See where you heedless ways have led us. If only you had accepted the murderous villain yesterday, then none of this would matter."

James squared his shoulders. "Whether you go back to the country or not, Clarinda, what of little Bella? You have ruined things for her. What chance of a respectable match for her now?"

"With the portion I will give her on her marriage –"

James cut in, "What sort of man would be tempted by a bribe into marrying into a family who live under the cloud of a disgraced sister?"

---

20   Not even gentry: An aristocrat would regard it as a loss of face to duel with a commoner.

If this went oddly with his recent attitude towards her noble suitors, Clarinda was too upset to see it.

As he handed her his handkerchief, she remembered the words that Harley Venn had spoken when he staggered into the hallway. Yet, he must have been confused, dazed by the blows to the head as he was. No doubt he had been seeking to excuse her presence to the doctor. Still, that didn't make sense: if there was no true engagement between them, her reputation was still ruined. It would be tarnished if there had been.

"Venn said something to the doctor about our being engaged," Clarinda muttered, "But I don't think he knew what he said."

Hope sparked in James' and Nancy's eyes. "I hope you confirmed that," said Nancy.

"I hardly know what I said," Clarinda muttered. "Then His Lordship began to vomit again, and the doctor sent us away."

James looked decisive. "Go and change those filthy clothes," he spoke as if Clarinda stayed in them from choice. "I must send a note to Lord Venn asking his intentions. I don't suppose he will be likely to admit me."

"Make it tactful, dear, and point out that he renewed his addresses and we are honoured to accept them... We'll never get those stains out, so there's an end of that dress. " In her shock, Nancy forgot that with Clarinda's new riches, the ruined dress was now the least of their problems.

In the hallway, Nancy surprised the footman near the door. He drew himself up, face wooden. "We are at home to no-one," she ordered. "Wicked girl!" she hissed after Clarinda as she went sniffing up the stairs.

Abigail was waiting for Clarinda with a bowl of hot water and a clean gown. She patted Clarinda as she unlaced her. "Excuse me, Miss, but it's more than I can endure to see you so meanly treated, when you acted for the best. I don't care what they say; you were right to help that wicked lord as a Christian should."

"Thank you, my dear. Perhaps you will join me in my exile?"

"That would suit me, Miss Clarinda. Can we take them kittens, too? It's a shame Lord Venn didn't fall down unconscious in the street, though. Then you'd have been spared all of this."

"If they didn't go for your watch or money then they'd been hired to set on you. Now it's you with the fine shiner," remarked Jack Molyneux to Harley Venn.

He had come with some news about the hooded figure and the curse, but decided to defer that until Venn was stronger.

Venn had a black eye half closed, and his gashed head was bandaged. "I'd say it was the Mad Major." He shifted, trying to find the least painful position.

Betsy appeared with a bowl of gruel. O'Hare's daughter Peg followed her. It had been sweltering in the afternoon, and she had insisted on standing by Venn's bed for hours, fanning him and only asking him if he felt any better every thirty minutes.

"That menace Seán sneaked out with a couple of other terrors armed with stones, looking for them bravoes," the maid said. "Of course, they didn't find them, but I'm betting they let fly at shop windows."

Venn gave a lopsided grin at this, but waved away the gruel in disgust. "That's enough to make me cast up my accounts[21] again. Some wine might revive me."

"O'Hare couldn't get credit from three wine merchants' the other day, and anyway, the doctor said only cordials and so," Betsy spoke briskly. Still, she had been nursing him kindly, and had even forgiven him his marital plans. She fussed about, straightening his sheets, with Peg helping.

"Are there only three wine merchants in Town? Take that miserable slop away."

"You can't have anything else until you've swallowed some." Betsy withdrew, swinging her hips and pulling Peg after her.

"A sneaking damned trick to play," Molyneux said between his teeth, taking another look at his friend's bruised face. "I see that pretty nose of yours has a charmed life yet, and escaped damage. I've a mind to call on him."

Harley Venn gave another painful grin. "It could be worse. Only now, I've had a note from James Greendale. He wants to know if the

---

21   Cast up my accounts: to vomit

covert engagement's still on. For all little Miss Greendale humiliated me with those hard words she spoke when she refused me, I'm going to be the gentleman and write back that it is."

"Are you raving, Harley? What's this about an engagement with her?"

Harley Venn looked as if he would have winked, had he been able. "By good luck, she saw them setting on me and weighed in with her parasol." He laughed delightedly, and then broke off, wincing. "She cracked it across the back of one of the bravoes. I do love spirit like that. And then fate helped me out." Molyneux saw the mischief sparkle in his eyes, for all that one of them was half closed.

"The foolish innocent, having helped me back here, was so ill advised as to come in with me, and under the eye of that old sourpuss next door. Old squaretoes Dr Spencer found us, *à deux*. The poor girl is compromised, so I'll forgive her ungracious response before, and gallantly come to the rescue. I tried to tell that damned hypocrite sawbones that we were secretly engaged, but was interrupted by another bout of puking. Romantic, eh?"

"I can't congratulate you, you rascal," Molyneux shook his head. "The girl's far too good for you. If the marriage goes ahead –"

"What sort of talk is that to your stricken and honourable friend? And what d'you mean, 'if'? She'll have to take me now, and I've always liked her body the best of 'em all. That will make getting heirs a pleasure. I couldn't take to the Trollope girl's hefty ankles. The more I tried not to look at them, the more they forced themselves on my notice."

'My dear Miss Greendale,

I hope this is the last time that I address you so.
Forgive my hand; I am still cross-eyed a trifle. I write for two
reasons. One is to thank you – more of that later.
The second is to renew my addresses. Finding myself unable
to rise from my sick bed, I am so eager, that I write hoping
that my written words will move you as my spoken ones did
not. But no more on that. I would speak much further of my
admiration, and my luck in having another chance for such an

angel for my wife. That must wait until we meet.

If any of the hard words you said to me before rankled, the courage you showed in tangling with those cowards earlier today, and the kindness with which you treated me have driven them from my memory. I hope that you will help me to be worthy of you.

Will you take me, Miss Greendale, so that when we meet next, I can salute you as my Clarinda?

I have ever admired spirit, as much in a woman as in a racehorse and a fighting dog, and I am all admiration of yours. Send me word and it will so raise my spirits, that I will be near cured.

I am your most devotedly indebted.

Harley Venn (and never mind the Lord).'

"Humph!" Clarinda put down the letter. "Had he chosen instead to insult and meet James, I think I would have threatened to meet him myself, provided parasols should be our chosen weapons."

"Then you're saved, Miss Clarinda! May I kiss you?" asked Abigail.

"Saved? Well, of course you may kiss me." Clarinda inclined her cheek.

The girl's soft lips caressed it. "I'm so happy for you! He's written to Master, too, renewing his proposals. I heard Mistress saying you're all to make out there's been a secret engagement all along. So you'll be Lady Venn and go and live in a castle?"

Clarinda sighed. "So it seems, my dear. I believe I am the only person in the household not delighted by this outcome. I should be, on my sister's account, and that is the only reason that I am going to marry the man. Truly, I would rather have withdrawn from so-called polite society and lived in seclusion with you and the kittens."

The girl's face fell. "Oh, Miss! Can't I come with you to the castle after all?"

Clarinda had to smile. "Yes, my dear, if you wish. I am sure Lord Venn will expect me to bring my lady's maid." Her face darkened. "Though I do begin to wonder if you knew all, if you would care to.

But, if there is a curse on the castle, then I'm sure it doesn't extend to the household."

The girl beamed. "Miss Clarinda, it wouldn't be a proper castle without a curse."

Clarinda glanced down at the letter in her lap. "True. I must write back when you have finished my hair. No doubt I should be grateful to Lord Venn for his magnanimity, given how I decidedly I rejected him before."

She bit her lip. "Remember this, my dear: for I can't say it again. As I am to marry the man, then it must be the last time that I speak against him. Lord Venn has many good qualities – generosity is clearly one – but even given the hypocrisy of society, it is not for nothing that he has become an outcast, while from a female point of view, his being a libertine is his worst fault."

Abigail gazed in admiration, thinking she sounded just like one of the heroines of Eliza Heywood or Fanny Burney[22].

Clarinda went on, "Seeing that when a woman marries, she loses her separate identity, it must be a foolish one who marries a man whose character she doubts, as I must with Lord Venn." She gave herself a shake. "Enough prosing from me, when my reputation will soon be as bad as his."

Abigail hastened to offer some comfort. "At least he's not old and worn out, like Sir Timothy. Lord Venn's a bit like a fallen angel, only more masculine – like the Count in *The Secret Closet* – that's such a good book, Miss; you must read it – and it isn't all Lord Venn's fault he's so bad."

Adding the finishing touches to Clarinda's hair, she continued, "His mother died early, and he never could agree with his father, who thought of nothing but them politics, which never does any good. He spent much of his boyhood over at the castle with his uncle, who was as bad as anything. Then, the old rake died and left him a fortune, which, his father casting him off, he threw away on gambling and wicked ladies and them worse things as immoral young gentlemen does."

---

22   Eliza Heywood and Fanny Burney: Eighteenth century writers of precursors of modern romance novels.

Clarinda had to laugh. "Abbey, truly, the servants know more of their masters than they do themselves. How did you find all this out?"

"It's common knowledge, Miss."

"Now for my writing materials. I'll kindly write my acceptance."

Clarinda wrote – chewing her pen:

'Dear Lord Venn,

I thank you for your offer. I accept it. I thank you for your kind words. I am sorry if before I seemed harsh and judgmental.

Clarinda Greendale.'

She hardly thought this satisfactory. Still, what answer, in these circumstances, was fitting? She could not join him in specious nonsense.

Abigail was in the dressing room, so when Clarinda caught a movement out of the corner of her eye, she thought that the girl had returned. Then, turning, she saw that she was alone in the room, and that the movement came from the oval mirror behind her to her right, which seemed to her unusually clouded.

She was dismissing it as a trick of the light when a figure materialised in the mirror's depths. She saw a seemingly distant, draped, bent figure, moving forward in the mirror. She felt a chill breeze.

A whisper sounded in her ears. Whether it was inside her head, she couldn't tell, though she sensed that the figure used another language, which she magically understood. "Beware: do not be drawn in –"

Then, she heard Nancy outside the door, calling her name. Such prosaic, everyday sounds made a visitation seem absurd. Seemingly the apparition thought so, too, for it vanished. Once again Clarinda found it hard to credit that she had seen it.

That was exactly as it had been, in the ballroom when she first saw a hooded form, though this one seemed different, and certainly smaller than that.

When that other figure had appeared after his proposal, Lord Venn insisted it was a stage trick, perhaps mesmerism. She could believe that he and his debauched friends and relatives could be mesmerised unawares; they were part drunk often enough. Yet, how had it been done to her?

"Clarinda." Nancy hurried in. As James' danger receded and a renewal of the Viscount's offer materialised, her anger with Clarinda abated. If her conduct could be defended as the natural anxiety of Lord Venn's secret *fiancée,* and she would have a title, then Nancy could forgive her.

She addressed Clarinda with only slightly more than her usual impatience. "You write your acceptance, of course?"

"I do, Nancy. I wonder: didn't that mirror come from our Uncle Greendale?"

"What a question at such a time: do get that acceptance written, my girl, before he changes his mind. Once we've got it in writing, he can't sneak out of it."

"I'll make up the envelope. But I would like to know about the mirror."

"For heaven's sake, I don't remember…Yes, I think it did. When we went to look over his things, something about it appealed to me. Now I cannot see why, as it's a plain enough mirror. I had it brought to Town on a whim. You are welcome to it."

Late the next morning, O'Hare, sniggering coarsely, admitted a female figure draped in veils. She had alighted from a hired carriage, emitting a heavy perfume and hoisting her skirts high as she gazed about the area, as if the litter on the pavements was the more offensive through having been cast out by tradesmen.

As she entered the room where a bored Harley Venn, still unable to rise without dizziness, lay on his daybed, dozing over a book, she drew in her breath as she saw his battered face. "The brutes."

"He'll do," said O'Hare. "Perking up fine he is, since he netted his heiress –" he broke off, pulling a discreet face.

Venn stirred, his eyes flickered open, and he grinned. "An anonymous lady visitor is just the thing to soothe away my ennui. What am I saying? I'm engaged, and by your height, you're not my betrothed."

"You may leave us, fellow." The woman threw back her veil as

O'Hare tramped out, grinning insolently. "Your poor face. What can I do for you?"

"I could think of a couple of things," murmured Venn. He didn't seem as touched as he might have been by her sympathy. Yet, her look as she ran her eyes over him was more that of someone assessing the damage done to a useful article, than that of genuine pity.

"Surely, you wicked creature, beaten as you are, you are not up to more than looks and talk, like to a rake three times your age?"

In her russet dress fitting closely over her magnificent curves, with her sultry eyes and mouth, she looked alluring enough to arouse one older than that. "Come and show your sympathy for Mr Harley," suggested Venn. "If anyone could get him to stand to attention, it will be you."

"Do you deserve it, having taken me into your confidence so little that I only heard of your engagement from my maid?"

"These servants are the Devil for knowing their master's affairs before they do themselves," said Venn. "The wonder is that I didn't hear of it myself from O'Hare."

She went over and ran a hand under the bedclothes, but Mr Harley was not as responsive to her caresses as usual. She went on to use other tricks, with little more effect. Venn cursed and they had to give up.

"I do believe Mr Harley is under your *fiancée's* control already," murmured Gabrielle. "I was going to ask you about this talk over the girl being seen going into your house, which quite shocked me. Ha, I see you're not going to divulge what she was about there."

He scowled. "The poor girl pitied me and has become a talking point by way of reward. Well, that's the way of the world, and damned hypocritical, but we both know that already."

She laughed, "I never expected such nobility in you, my dear, as to come to the foolish chit's rescue by renewing your offer of marriage. Her fortune has nothing to do with it, of course... There's Molyneux's voice at the door. I must be on my way, anyway. Oh, yes, do you still want that conjurer Lodovico Sharman's address? I have his card in my reticule."

Molyneux passed the two O'Hare children swinging on the curtains in the vestibule.

Jumping down, the girl smiled. "His Honour's much better."

The boy shook his head dolefully. "He's been knocked silly, as he's talking of getting wed."

Molyneux, though in a serious mood, had to smile himself. He stopped as he bowed to the visitor who came out of Venn's study. He recognised her figure and walk.

He found Venn lying back on his pillows looking sour. He scowled more on seeing Molyneux. "Why the mournful look, Jack? Lately, you've started to speak more like a conscience than a friend. If you're about to remind me of my proposed reform, I'll have you know, veiled visitors or no, Mr Harley's behaving like a dangling, useless conscience too."

Instead of laughing, Molyneux said, "Harley, you haven't heard, then? It's a grim enough story. Old Sir Timothy Carstairs was found dead, dangling from the gutter of his country house the other day."

10.
Ecstatic Fiancée

"**D**O YOU WANT ME TO propose again, now I am in a less squalid state than when you saw me last and you heard me renew my offers?" the Viscount took Clarinda's hands and squeezed them warmly, smiling roguishly at her. "That must go down as one of the most romantic proposals in history, with me asking for you in between spewing bouts."

Nancy had found something she must do out in the hallway.

Clarinda noted that Venn still managed to be handsome despite his black eye and bruised face. The wound on his head was largely hidden by his thick, waving light golden hair, and he was, as ever, dashingly dressed, the fashionably tight-fitting coat emphasizing his athletic build and a waist even more hollow than usual.

She wished to retort that she must be a fool indeed, to allow herself to be drawn into his pretence that this was anything but a marriage of convenience. "That isn't necessary, Lord Venn."

"Please call me Harley when we are alone from now on. I've longed to call you Clarinda for weeks."

And I've been longing to call you a fortune hunting villain.

"Your sister being out of the room, I want to say again how in your debt I am for what you did for me the other day. As like as not, those fellows would have beaten me far worse, or even done away with me altogether, without your coming to my aid, parasol in hand. And by way of thanks, I cast up my accounts on your gown. I own I had taken too much brandy that day, and you must have been disgusted to see it come up again."

"In the circumstances, that was scarce your fault, Sir – Harley. I shall now ever be renowned as a street brawler who does not scruple to enter a single man's house unchaperoned."

His lips twitched, but then his smile became grim. "If I hear that any man has spoken lightly of your conduct that day, I shall consider myself insulted, if he be a gentleman, so-called. If not, then I'll box his ears. I might do as much in either case. And if I hear a woman has spoken of you too freely, then I'll ask her husband or brother to bid her hold her tongue and he may take that as he pleases."

"But Sir – Harley –"

"You're misinformed, my dear. For all my faults of character, I'm indisputably a viscount, not Sir Harley."

She smiled. "You must give me time to get used to calling you by your first name."

"I hope I never give you cause to call me worse names." He kissed her cheek, and at the touch of his lips, she flinched.

It was not that he was unattractive as a man – far from it – and she must get used to rather more intimacy with him than that. Still, so degrading did she consider the sexual side of a marriage without love, that she would rather die an old maid. Now, she would be yet another conquest of this libertine, the only difference being that she had a ring on her finger, and he would expect her to give him heirs.

So much for her dreams of returning from this Town visit to Berkshire to lead an independent life with her own household, using her fortune to benefit the poor and oppressed.

No doubt she would have many opportunities to help the oppressed from now on - in various women who would turn up at her door, complaining that Venn had seduced them.

She thrust away these thoughts. She had wept over them for the last two nights, finally resolving to face the future with optimism. She must somehow try and love this man. She suspected that, with the exception of his sister, no woman had truly loved him in years, and that those women who thought that they did, probably mistook fascination with his looks, easy charm and reputation for wickedness for love.

She said, "Thank you for your gallantry. I was about to say, that if you were to duel with the male member of every family who have been talking about me, you will have too busy a schedule to attend the wedding. You must try to rise about the gossip."

He shook his head. "I am, of course, at your command. What I said before about your influence on me remains true. With your sweet guidance, you'll have me transformed apace from outcast to model citizen."

She forced a smile: "May I request rather than command you not to take too much brandy, or other stimulants, in the interests of your health?"

Resentment stirred in his eyes, but he bent and kissed her hand. "As you bid me, Clarinda."

"Thank you, Sir." Her younger sister Bella would have been disgusted at her restraint, but Clarinda saw she must use it with this wretch. His show of humility thinly masked unchanged arrogance and condescension. She glanced over to where Nancy fiddled with the grandfather clock in the hall, and said abruptly, "I've seen a wraith again."

He swore under his breath. "Where?"

"I saw a figure in the mirror; though hooded, it looked different. Yet, as before, it came and went so quickly, I can hardly describe it. You remember my uncle was formerly steward to your own uncle? That mirror came from him, according to Nancy. I don't know if that's relevant."

"What did the filthy thing do?" he asked between clenched teeth.

"It whispered – faintly – 'B*eware: Do not be drawn in* –' and then its voice faded."

"Did it seem threatening?"

"No. It seemed different, sadder; in fact –" she broke off.

He swore again. Catching hold of her hands, he squeezed them. "Whatever happens, I'll safeguard you from it. Now, my sweet, I have some disturbing news of my own. I wanted to enjoy a talk with you before telling you, if you hadn't heard. You haven't looked over the newspapers this morning?"

"James hasn't opened his yet."

"Clarinda, don't be alarmed or foolishly guilty: your former suitor, Sir Timothy Carstairs has been found dead."

Her eyes dilated as she drew in her breath. She said nothing.

He squeezed her hands again. "That's the way, my girl. You've got iron nerves. No vapours from you, and I do like that."

"What do they say of the circumstances?"

"I heard from Molyneux. Young Carstairs has gone out to Buckinghamshire for the formalities – he's the new Baronet now, after all – and we'll hear more of the damned business from him when he returns. It seems the old rascal went there, unaccountably for him in the season, and was found on his roof, dead of an apoplexy. That's not exactly where a man would go for a midnight stroll."

She bit her lip. "Too late, I feel sorry for my abrupt refusal."

His eyes sparkled wickedly. "Only thing to do, with an aging *roué* like that, seeing you're above caring for titles. If you must needs marry a no-good fellow, best marry a young one like me who'll at least give you some fun." He winked disgracefully.

Clarinda refused to smile. Fear for them all stroked her spine with icy fingers even as his warm, human ones caressed her own. More than ever she sensed that her uncle's grotesque end in France was a part of this sequence.

He still stroked her hands. She tried to withdraw them, but he kept them, his touch suggestive. "Your wide-eyed gaze makes me still more bitter against this damned malevolent trickster."

"Do you still believe it to be a series of tricks?"

"Of course, my sweet, what else could it be? I'm a sceptic, but you're devout, and believe in a Beneficent Deity, and surely that don't go with curses and murdering spectres and such a bag of moonshine?"

"In some ways, I am very heterodox," Clarinda sighed. "I don't discount such ideas. I'm not sure one should dismiss any explanation."

"Molyneux – there's a clever fellow – suggests we exhaust the rational explanations before we go on to credit such stuff as murderous ghosts."

She tried to take away her hands again, and still he retained them. "The older gentlemen were perhaps frightened to death, being in bad health through a lifetime's excesses."

He whistled and grimaced. Looking at him she noted once again on his youthful face – now rather eclipsed by the bruises, but ever present

– the fine lines traced by debauchery about the eyes and mouth. She knew that he routinely undermined his constitution, only deferring the ill effects through youth, strength, and exercise. Now, he stood before her perfectly toned and athletic. With passing years, he might come to look as unhealthy as the late Sir Timothy Carstairs.

"The thought of destroying my nerves through overdoing it is a good reason I should heed my good angel's strictures about drinking," he said. "But I will hunt down this trickster long before that. I put all these accidents, so-called, down to a conjuring trick such as a mass illusion, as I told you before."

He laughed. "I've found out the name of a tricky rogue who might know of such matters, one Lodovico Sharman, who's been away abroad, but who calls on me later today. He once did some entertainments at the Hoggs'. I didn't turn up, distracted by something else, I've forgotten what."

At that name, Clarinda stiffened. Their eyes met, hers sullen, his full of mock repentance, which could not hide the mischief behind.

She knew she shouldn't have reacted like that. No doubt he put it down to female vanity and jealousy. What had really overwhelmed her was the difficulty of the reality of 'trying to love him' according to the vows she must make. Of course, an aristocratic libertine would continue with his intrigues after marriage. She would be expected to look the other way.

"That was in my former, careless days," he smiled, ostensibly referring to the broken appointment at the Hoggs'. He gave her hands another squeeze, which she resented.

"Then any mass mesmerism which he may have done could not have included you." She gently moved her hands out of his grasp, and he surrendered them.

She went to the window – the one through which she had seen the being before – to gaze down into the square. A milkmaid led a cow with a jingling bell, crying her wares. A shouting little boy from further down bowled a hoop along, followed by his nursemaid.

These everyday sights seemed impossible to reconcile with hooded figures and a series of grotesque deaths.

Meanwhile, Lord Venn was tactful enough not to follow her. She could feel his eyes on her behind.

Clarinda turned about. "I am a hypocrite to feel badly about

Sir Timothy's coming to such an end, just after I turned him down so abruptly."

Now he did come over. He kissed her cheek, his lips sensuously tasting her skin. "I'm glad you did, and I'll say nothing of any previous rejections of yours. I'm only happy you'll be mine, now."

And now you will be nominally mine, save that I will very likely have to share your embraces with half of the Town.

"Did they search for Sir Timothy?"

"To be blunt, my sweet, they didn't have to look long. A gardener saw his body, which had rolled down to the gutters."

She repressed her shudder, while he said, "No point in dwelling on this dismal topic. I may even go up for the old sinner's funeral, to keep young Carstairs company. According to Molyneux, he was skittish over it: rather more given to vapours than you, my sweet. Let's have some music. Shall I give you a song, and then we can join in a duet? What would you like?"

She said without thinking, "*My Love is Like a Red, Red Rose.*"

He went over to the instrument and began. He played by ear, of course. In no time she was caught in the spell of his voice and playing.

Nancy came to the door to listen. James, coming from the study to suggest a game of chess, stopped.

Behind James and Nancy, the hallway mirror became opaque, taking in no more light. The depths stirred, a chill breeze invading the hall. The listeners were oblivious to it. Now the smaller cloaked figure appeared in the mirror, and its hands reached out, seemingly trying to break through the glass, and yet as the song went on, the apparition seemed to pause, and to listen too:

> *"As fair art thou, my bonnie lass,*
> *So deep in love am I:*
> *And I will love thee still, my dear,*
> *Till a' the seas gang dry."*

When Venn sang, it was impossible to doubt the sincerity of his words.

11.

The Showman

"**H**e's a giant: look out, he might eat you, Seán!"

"Why's he got such a red nose?"

The shrill voices of the children came from the passageway as O'Hare ushered in Lodovico Sharman, Professor of Magic, Markmanship, Swordsmanship, Languages and Subtle Influence.

O'Hare voice came through the door, "Get away with you, or I'll tan your hides," followed by the sound of scampering feet.

The showman did seem gigantic, standing some inches over six foot, and strongly made. As Lady Hogg recalled, he had been a magnificent creature when young. Now, his flesh was sallow, his features, and especially his nose, reddened and coarsened from drinking, his blue eyes were bleared, and his hair was dyed a brassy colour and styled to hide his receding hairline. His well-made but shabby clothes showed his decline in fortunes.

Reputed to be the love child of an Italian nobleman and an English rose, he now lived in rooms above a wine shop, to which he owed more money than he cared to remember.

Harley Venn winced at this reminder of how he might look himself if he went on with his excesses. Then, remembering how the abstemious Old Governor, once handsome himself, had when last seen, looked gaunt and haggard through mourning and bitterness, Venn felt better.

"Dr Sharman, it is good of you to spare me your time," he greeted his visitor in the unassuming way that made many excuse his wickedness, and – more usefully – to delay calling in their debts. "Forgive the insolence of those youngsters – they have no mother, and run wild. Brandy?"

"The honour is entirely mine, Your Lordship," Lodovico Sharman bowed. "Thank you, a small glass would be delightful."

As Harley Venn brought out the glasses, he swore at a knocking and voices at the front door below. It might even be an insolent tradesman hoping to force entrance that way. Then he recognised Molyneux's voice.

As O'Hare announced Molyneux, he shot a scornful glance at the Professor's neck cloth – tied to conceal a hole – as arrogantly as if he himself didn't every day run the gauntlet of tradesmen clamouring for payment.

After Harley Venn had introduced his two visitors, he said, "Molyneux, you can tell a grim tale better than me. You tell our story to Dr Sharman, while I pour the drinks. I don't know why I didn't let O'Hare hear it. Damn me, he knows it already. My housemaid Betsy bids me take care on the stairs, saying she don't want to be landed with paying for my funeral if my father won't foot the bill."

Molyneux nodded coolly. "Certainly, if you believe that Dr Sharman can advise us. After all, the story must be common knowledge."

Venn poured them all brandy in the fine old glasses. It was the first taste of anything stronger than boys' beer he had taken since what he called 'The Victory of the Parasol', and remembering how disgusting the brandy he had that day was on the way up again, he sipped it gingerly.

Finding it to his taste once more, he smiled, knowing himself to be on the mend, as he had proved with Betsy last night. Under her touch, Mr Harley had risen, engorged, swelling and eager, and he had delighted in her body several times.

He was untroubled by either his promises of reform to Clarinda or to the late Foyle. Those were for the future. She could hardly expect a lusty young fellow like himself to be faithful to her until they were married, and he thought he had done handsomely by her in renewing his offers.

Molyneux related in flat tones how ten years since, his father, having spent his last weeks in nervous torment, was found dead at the foot of the stairs with a broken neck, his favourite ring still clutched between his fingers.

As Molyneux went on to tell how Toby Venn was found dead at the foot of the shallow steps in the maze at Stoke Castle, with a look on his face that made the servants cover it quickly, the Professor plastered on his own a solemn look. This involved dilating his eyes and so lengthening his jaw, that his chin seemed to be trying to escape from the rest of his face.

Now the tale moved on to the death of their friend Foyle, and Venn clenched his fists and glowered. Having the details as they had of Sir Timothy's end on the roof of his country house, Molyneux turned to Venn. "Now for the part that involves your *fiancée*, Venn."

"Yes, Dr Sharman, I'm to marry the niece of my late uncle's former steward, and that wicked old rascal came to a grotesque enough end – squashed by a lightning strike to a wall over in France." Venn said.

"May I offer my congratulations, My Lord. That is happy news." Lodovico Sharman shook his head. "I refer, of course, to your engagement, not this other fatality."

"I don't know if it's connected with the other deaths, but the figure appeared to me when with Miss Greendale. She sees it, and says it's also appeared in her own mirror, which she had from her uncle."

Molyneux drew in his breath, and the Professor of Magic's puffy eyes widened.

Venn's eyes glinted as he recounted the story of the older Greendale's death and the vision Clarinda had seen.

Molyneux saw that for the first time, Venn associated the uncle's end with a possible threat to the niece. Molyneux was pleased at his look. True, Venn was always gentle to women after his own careless fashion, but this seemed to go beyond that. There might even be hope of some happiness for the girl in the union.

When Venn finished the story, he turned to Sharman, who sat, brow corrugated, crouched forward in his chair. "If Greendale's death was part of this, then it took another form, save for the thunderbolt. Now my fiancée is involved, whatever the explanation. You understand the arts of illusion, Dr Sharman. Molyneux believes that it is one, perhaps mass mesmerism."

He glared out of the window a moment, as if expecting to see the figure materialise outside. "Some trickster could have imposed on all of us when we were in our cups, and put the idea in our muddled heads – you must know the way it's done – but it makes no sense with Miss Greendale."

Lodovico Sharman said, "Mass mesmerism is easy to perform. I've done it myself: fleeting illusions for entertainments, visions of indoor snowstorms, and so on. Unfortunately, for a mesmerist to impose upon a subject, there is no need for that subject to be willing, or to listen. It can be done when his attention is wandering or when asleep."

"Like us, eh, Molyneux, on the rare occasions we attend church?" grinned Venn, draining his glass. "Clearly, we do well to keep away." He sobered. "The lady is forever at church. Still, she's devout, and don't doze or daydream."

"Miss Greendale is to be commended," said Sharman, "But there would be pauses in the service when her attention might wander. Besides, a skilled practitioner could catch her unawares at any number of social occasions when she was in a suitable state of mind: — say at a concert."

Venn whistled. "Fiend seize it, this becomes worse."

Molyneux nodded, grimly. "The timing follows no pattern. My father's death was ten years since, in July. Venn's uncle's, five years later, almost to the day. Then there is a long gap before Foyle's back in early May, and Sir Timothy's soon afterwards. Do you know the date of Greendale's death, Venn?"

Venn said, "Perhaps three months since. At that time, it meant nothing to me:"

Sharman wrinkled his brow again. "It would be the strongest mass illusion that ever I encountered, and beyond the skill of most mesmerists. I cannot give an immediate explanation for this series of catastrophes which Your Honours have been good enough to confide in me. I regret that need time to pursue researches."

Venn snorted impatiently: "Don't take too long. I want the matter cleared up before the wedding, which should be within the month at the latest. She wishes to delay, but that's a coy maid for you."

Now Lodovico Sharman pulled a sympathetic face. "I can only apologise to Your Lordship for the delay. This is a complex matter, and it would be misleading to promise an easy solution. That this vision appears to your *fiancée* is perturbing, though happily, it seems to warn rather than to threaten her. May I ask if it has ever warned either of you gentlemen?"

"I've only had the bogey talk like an opponent in a mill or duel, eh, Molyneux?"

Molyneux looked nearly as impatient as Venn. "But can the thing also be some other form of mass illusion visible to a group? How could it be done?"

Sharman looked, for the first time, abashed. "Through the transference of images created by thought from one mind to another."

Molyneux stared. Venn's eyebrows shot up. "Come, Professor! Let's not fall back on such tomfoolery as that."

"I regret arousing your incredulity, Sirs. While I know such a thing is possible, I cannot expect you to accept my word for it. Such a project could only be done by a powerful adept. Has anyone – apart from yourselves, the future Lady Venn, or the new Sir Frederick Carstairs – admitted to seeing such visions?"

The others scowled. "That's the damnable thing," said Venn, while Molyneux nodded. "None of the others in the Coconut Club would, saying it happened too quickly. Mind you, we were all half in our cups."

As Lodovico Sharman made to leave, he looked embarrassed again. "My Lord, you and Mr Molyneux honour me by your confidence, and I am happy to put my small talents at your disposal. Yet, to pursue my researches, I will need some funds, and finding myself financially distressed..."

"You and me both, Professor. Let me see if I can find a few guineas." Harley Venn grinned.

"No need; will this do, Dr Sharman?" Molyneux handed the Professor two gold pieces.

With bows, flowing speeches, and concern that the gentlemen safeguard themselves – for he would not have the impertinence to bid the Viscount take care of his charming betrothed – the Professor was on his way.

At the window, Venn watched him take his distinguished face, professional walk and mended coat across the road. "What a tricky rogue, eh, Jack? Ten to one, we won't see or hear of him again. Damn me, 'The transference of thought!'"

He winked at Molyneux, and they joined in a bout of laughter.

Venn wiped his eyes. "He's given us his money's worth in that laugh: we've not shared a proper one, since Foyle's death. How much did you give the villain? I'll repay you, when I wed and get my hands on the rest of good old Uncle Toby's tin, and I won't say what else out of due respect for my little bride. "

"Take it as part of my wedding present," smiled Molyneux, and then sobered. "For all that was as conniving a rogue as ever I've met, you ought to heed his words about taking care, and especially of your fiancée."

"None of the women in the case, your mother, old Toby's relic, or Foyle's either, came to any harm," said Venn. "Still, I urged her to turn that cursed mirror over to me, but she wouldn't, and so I told her to have it thrown in the cellar, or better still, smash the thing. I try and hurry the wedding along, so I can guard her night and day. Her family are all for that, but when I whisper to her between such kisses as I can snatch that I'll treat her like priceless china, she draws back with a face of vinegar."

He laughed indulgently. "This business of courting a coy maid is new to me, and I enjoy it. That the little thing is so devout makes it makes it even better."

Molyneux sighed. "I hope you'll break off matters with a certain voluptuous, red-haired lady?"

Venn frowned. "Why?"

"Your promise to Foyle, you rascal."

"I'll try when we're married. That I'm marrying at all's an improvement. That minds me, I must write to the Governor. We haven't spoken since he threw me out nigh on five years since."

He went to gaze earnestly in the mirror. However, his next words showed that no dark thoughts about spectres appearing there troubled him. "D'you think I look like our friend Professor Lodovico Sharman, Jack?"

Molyneux laughed. "No danger of that for some years yet; then you may get a glowing nose like his. But as a man of your word, you're set to stop the heavy drinking, my lad. Why?"

"Our voluptuous friend claimed to see a resemblance between me and the Professor. Damn me, if she says more such things, breaking it off would be a relief."

Molyneux frowned. "I wonder: in saying, 'Beware: do not be drawn in' was the thing speaking of you, or the whole crew of us?"

When Molyneux left, Venn put on his coat and walked briskly to the Major's house through the soiled streets, tossing a coin now and then to the beggars. The Major now lived in a small house in a road far less fashionable even than Venn's own, and it had taken all O'Hare's ingenuity and malice to track him down.

Arriving at the Major's, the Viscount met a couple of solemn-faced men taking away a sideboard. A slatternly serving maid flung open the door, shouting something obscene over her shoulder at someone behind her.

"Is your master there, my girl? If the coward fears to take off his coat and come round the back with me in the absence of his bravoes, pass on the message from me that he is a craven, diseased cur, and when next I see him, I will kick him down the road by his withered hind parts."

She dropped a curtsey. "You're Lord Venn, ain't you, Sir? No, he's taken himself off to France, and his creditors are all come like scavengers to fight over the furnishings." She glanced back into the house, and called: "Oi! I'm having that screen! I paid honest money for it."

Venn sighed. "Just my cursed luck. I suppose the dirty dish[23] served me an accidental good turn, as that drubbing he arranged for me led to my marriage to the lady of my choice." He saw no reason to admit that Clarinda Greendale had been his third choice.

Perhaps some thoughts of his own difficulty in paying his servants led him to ask, "I hope the coward paid you, my girl?"

"Not before I threatened him with the bed post, My Lord."

"You women are ever resourceful in your use of weapons," smiled Venn. "Take this for your trouble. I wish it was more, but until my wedding, I'm hard enough up myself."

---

23   Dirty dish: A dishonourable fellow.

There was, of course, a stir as Lord Venn's party entered his box at the opera. Some people bowed; some turned away hastily, while others stared. James and Nancy, for once delighted with everything, missed the insolence in some of those looks.

Harley Venn returned them as if he was in the prize ring. One by one each gentleman dropped his gaze.

He gave Clarinda a look of enquiry. She answered with a shake of the head. She had seen no more spectres since having that mirror wrapped in brown paper and taken to the lumber room.

The orchestra struck up the overture for *The Barber of Seville*[24], and Clarinda gloried in it. The musical Venn, who knew the opera well, was more interested in covertly fondling her knees. She thought that the singer who played Rosina looked meaningfully sometimes at him. Then Clarinda was distracted by Lady Barbara and Sir Hugh arriving and embracing her as a sister.

Barbara had been away at Brighton when newcomers from Town had brought news of the attack on her brother with scarcely hidden relish. Scribbling excuses for breaking her engagements, she ordered her horses tacked up, and set off at speed for London.

Her husband had been dismissive: "So that rascal's been brawling again, and this time he's got the worst of it. Depend upon it, there's nothing wrong with him that some days respite from fighting, tippling and worse won't remedy."

He had, as usual, been proved right. On Barbara's arrival at Venn's house she found him, not dying, but sitting up in bed, engaged, sipping small beer, and joking with O'Hare. He greeted her warmly but casually. On hearing of her dash to Town, he rebuked her for overworking the horses. She swallowed her indignation, supported Clarinda's actions, and planned a ball to celebrate the engagement.

"A month is too long, my sweet," Harley Venn now whispered in Clarinda's ear.

"A month is not long at all, Sir." Clarinda seized his fingers as they

---

24   The Barber of Seville: Opera (1816) by Rossini, premiered in London in 1818.

rested once more on her knee. His squeezes gave her stirrings she could do without.

"But I want you mine quickly, especially to protect you from these miserable tricks."

Harley Venn had written to her of Lodovico Sharman's visit and his theories – with a joke in every line. If the Hooded Phantom wished to strike terror into the hearts of Venn and Molyneux, then it had a weary task ahead.

"If you will keep calling me 'Sir', I'll start calling you 'Ma'am'," Venn threatened tenderly. "Would you care from some fruit or bonbons? I'll send my man." O'Hare was behind them in pugilistic stance, looking on the opera as if he had heard better.

"Not yet, I thank you." Clarinda caught Venn's fingers as they stalked up her thigh.

She supposed his financial situation was desperate. Still, as a peer he wasn't in danger of being taken to a spunging house[25].

"But I want to guard you, night and day."

And my moneybags.

"A shame that nobody guarded my unfortunate uncle and the others," murmured Clarinda, reflecting that if anybody had, none of this party would be here, and Nancy would be advising her to make cow's eyes at the local curate. "I am happy to hear Molyneux is gone to guard the new Sir Frederick Carstairs."

Venn gave a low laugh. "You should have read the letter the boy sent me on my engagement. He told me even if I devoted every waking minute to improvement for the rest of my days, I could never be good enough for you. He added that he was 'deeply wounded' that we'd had a secret engagement, thus prolonging his suspense, etcetera. Poor young fool, eh? And he is only one who resents my good fortune."

He indicated below. "See that piratical looking fellow with the dark whiskers? That's Tompkins, another boon companion of mine. When he heard of my coming marriage, he cursed me for an unmentionable traitor. But I'm a reformed man, and their chatter falls on deaf ears."

---

25   Spunging house: A private house to confine debtors; peers were exempt.

"Look, Sir!" Clarinda spoke in her silliest voice. "The villain of the piece."

"Here's a good song – and Ma'am yourself!" He turned his attention to the stage, taking her hand in his.

The next day, Clarinda winced over the letter from her sister Bella replying to her own explaining why she must marry Lord Venn.

Clarinda had been taking comfort in that through safeguarding Bella's chances by that marriage - or at least, not ruining them - she was acting disinterestedly. Bella disagreed with the outspokenness of fifteen. Her letter said in part:

> *'You always told me that any fate was better than wedding a man without principle. You described Venn as, 'The Villainous Viscount'. And yet you risked your reputation to care for him when he only had his just deserts in a beating. I think you must be infatuated. I never thought the sister I knew would betray her principles so easily.*
>
> *I'll go to Hades before I'll be a bridesmaid. I would rather we were two old maids together with the rheumatics and dowdy old bonnets...'*

"You say that now, my dear," sighed Clarinda. "But in time, you would have blamed me... Yes, Abbey?"

"The ladies with Mistress in her sitting room, Miss, are angling for an invitation to the castle – Oh dear, you weep! May I pat your shoulder?"

Clarinda blew her nose. "You may, my dear, and things might be a lot worse, after all."

They glanced across at where Nancy had insisted on hanging a picture of the monarch in his days as the Prince Regent. "Yes, indeed, Miss! Only think; besides being wicked, the Viscount might be as stout as King George."

12.
The Castle of Doom

June 1821

As Stoke Castle came into Harley Venn's sight, atop a hill and surrounded by beech woods, the stone walls warmed in sunshine, he grunted sourly, though he had been laughing and joking all the way.

Richard Welch laughed, showing his savage white teeth. "It's a sorry thing to come home to your own castle, eh, Venn?"

"The Castle of Doom looks a fine enough sight now," Venn admitted, "But of an evening, it can be gloomy enough. I was thinking that my father ought to live here. It would suit him well."

"Venn, should he come to your wedding, for the Lord's sake try and act contrite. It's the only way you're going to get the old man's pardon."

"If the Governor don't want to meet me halfway, then there's an end of it. I didn't like the tone of the note he scrawled me."

This letter said, among other things: – *'You write that without asking my permission, you have contracted an engagement with a female from the nouveau riche merchant class. Once, I would have been shamed; now I think it the best news I could have from you in your heedless rush to destruction…'*

"He can't help being dismal, any more than you can help being jolly.

It's all to do with the balance of humours in your body, I hear." Welch smiled as Venn scowled up at the castle. "Though now, you look Friday faced[26] enough yourself."

As a boy, Venn had never caught a first glimpse of Stoke Castle without a whoop of excitement, much preferring its gothic discomforts to his father's nearby Georgian hall. In those days, even at night, there had only been such stirring from ghosts suitable to its years.

In recent times, as the last glow of pink vanished from the clouds, while the chorus of the birds in the hills dwindled into silence, with only the blackbirds singing aloft, a melancholy seemed to steal over the building. He had started to call it 'The Castle of Doom'.

As the quiet of night came down, broken only by the odd cry of a night bird, and the grey walls darkened to black, the lights that appeared in the narrow windows seemed often to twinkle as isolated beacons of hope in a wasteland of despair. Even Venn felt it; it haunted his dreams.

On some nights in the banqueting hall, surrounded by roisterers up from Town, complete with wantons happy to befriend Mr Harley and his cohorts, Venn would pause in the middle of a song.

Then, an image haunted him. It was of a girl more alluring than any of the painted group with them, a girl in a simple old fashioned gown, whom he sensed had long lain underground far away. Then, if there was no pretty burden perched on his knee, fondling his side whiskers, he would bang down his glass: "Be damned to it, is some clumsy eavesdropper at the door? I hear the oafish whoreson shuffling!"

But silence would greet him as he flung open the door. Only the visor of a suit of arms standing in the passage would return his glare, axe in chain mail glove raised in frozen defiance.

He would go and flip a visor open, laughing: "Greetings, Cuthbert Venn! Do you care to join us? Here are some fine women who could even rouse a member dead and cold these three centuries and more."

Or perhaps a cat, slinking across the boards, would turn a glowing stare in at the door. Venn's friends would shout for Puss in Boots to join them, as he must have been to blame for the noise. Venn would close

---

26   Friday Faced: Gloomy.

the door softly on that gaze, and pause a minute before he went back to his song.

Welch laughed outright as Venn shook himself as if to throw off his thoughts. "You'd best get used to it, friend. Soon enough your wife will have you trapped here – with none of the wild parties we've enjoyed before. Not as if I'm casting aspersions on your bride: it's only female nature once they get their claws into you. Besides, you've told her she's got to make a respectable citizen out of you, so she's every excuse to play the tartar. You'll find it cursed slow here, and you'll have to live less the prodigal if you don't want to get through the lot you'll have on your wedding before you know it."

Venn looked stung as he urged the horses up the springy turf of the hill. "I won't have as much of the money from her as you might believe. Though I say it myself, I've been generous in drawing up the settlements with Greendale, by way of thanks to her for saving me from those bravoes."

He sighed, unable to dismiss his unusually thoughtful mood. "You know, I was the same age as young Carstairs when I started on what the Governor calls my 'downwards course' and the cards and the horses took most of it. It don't appeal now as it did. When I see young Frederick playing the fool with the betting, I tap him on the shoulder; the same when I see him knocking it back. I don't want him to go the same way as me."

They entered the forecourt, their horses' hooves loud on the cobblestones. Welch laughed as they reined in. "Watch out! You'll fast become a sober citizen. I call that tragic."

Venn laughed. "I'd call it farce. And depend on it, no wife of mine is going to act the tartar and forbid me from having my friends up for jollifications, even if, saving her presence, we have to leave out the light skirts."

He sprang down. "O'Hare, take the horses round to the stable. Where's the key? Go and find that old fellow. I hope he got my letter and there's food ready."

"Which do I do first...Your Honour?" drawled O'Hare.

Venn grinned. "Less of your insolence." An elderly man came up the basement steps. "Here comes Mann. Maybe he's been keeping company with those ghosts in the dungeons, eh, O'Hare?"

Welch laughed. O'Hare, who had insisted that the castle was haunted since first he set foot in it, looked grave. "Begging Your Honours' pardon, it don't do to jest about such matters."

He was no more given to worry than his master. He had left his infants with some coins for the pastry cooks' and the casual care of Betsy.

Mann grinned toothlessly, delighted to see them. Venn was moved to ask, "Is your wife well enough, Mann?" his query was not disinterested; Mrs Mann was the one who provided for his comforts on his visits, apart from the sensual ones.

Mann bowed and thanked him, his missing teeth making his speech hard to understand, though Venn knew it of old. Mann was former butler from the days of Toby Venn.

The man let them into the entrance hallway, where the floor was illuminated with patches of blue and red from the mullioned windows. To the right was the great hall, where the minstrel's gallery and the trophy stags' heads of yesteryear looked over the vast table.

Venn put the sadness the building now exuded down to the lack of a housekeeper's touch. "Sister Babs is looking out for more staff," he told Mann as he and Welch preceded him up the creaking stairs, past the suits of armour standing as sentinels at every turn, "More damned expense, Devil take it. Still, I've got to ready the place for my bride, and it's the only place where I can take her."

He had decided that his Lincolnshire estate was too isolated. Besides, a devout great aunt lived there and, whenever she saw Venn, berated him about his wicked ways. Stoke Castle was only a day's ride from Town, and the conjuring tricks could after all follow them anywhere.

"Be damned to those stairs: even a ghost would set 'em off," said Venn, as they turned off down the main corridor, and through habit, he paused to pull the nose of a bust of Julius Caesar. "You've got the best rooms, Welch – eh, what the Devil?"

He turned as a panel in the wall slid back, disclosing a gaping black hole, from which came an icy draught, incongruous for a summer's day, even on such a chilly June as this.

Mann jumped back as if a monster might leap out of it, while Venn and Welch burst out laughing. "I know these old castles are meant to have a secret passage, but yours showing them off takes that a touch too far," said Welch.

"Puts me in mind of a pantomime on Ali Baba I saw as a boy," said Venn. "The place is full of the things. I explored them all as a lad. I've never known one to open so obliging, all of its own."

He thrust his head and shoulders in the gap, staring upwards. "Most of 'em lead up to the roofs, and down to the basement and the dungeons. If you're agreeable, Welch, we'll have a look after we've taken some bread and meat, or whatever Mann's wife has laid on. We'd better watch out on those crumbling steps, eh?"

Mann muttered, "I don't like it. Of late, the things have done that more than once. They may have given you sport as a boy, Sir, but now them things ought to be sealed up. Encouragement for marauders, they are. One used to lead right to the village, and very likely still does."

O'Hare sauntered up the passageway, his eyes fixed on the gaping black hole. "There's another of them sliding panels to the passageways in that great room with the mirrors," he said. "The local girls set it off by accident. I've peeped in, and they said, 'You men never grow up'."

"They spoke true: that's why we have more fun," said Venn as they moved on, Mann frowning at O'Hare. "Welch, are you game for a grand tour of 'em this afternoon? With luck, like *Rinaldo Rinaldini*[27], we'll find a damsel kept prisoner. Weren't his henchman called Lodovico? Molyneux and I met one lately, who talked to me of 'thought transference'. I'll tell you all about that while we break bread."

"You did right to lend me these old rags of yours; it's damned filthy in here," said Welch, as he followed Venn into the chill darkness of the secret passage. Here the air was both stale and cold, and their covered lanterns cast moving shadows on the cobweb encrusted walls.

Venn grinned. "Never noticed it as a lad, though Uncle Toby cursed me for a dirty little brute when I came back from my travels. Now,

---

27   'Rinaldo Rinaldini': Christian Auguste Vulpius' renowned 1798 penny dreadful features a hooded figure who persecutes the hero, whose henchman is called 'Lodovico'.

about these steps, Welch: as I said, it seems that I am targeted by the hooded joker whose sudden appearance caused Foyle's death that night, and possibly that of some of our venerable late relatives. You didn't see anything but the lightning flash yourself that night, so as like as not if anyone follows his example on these stairs, it'll be me as a victim of mesmerism, or worse. Yet for all that, be careful. Don't scruple to go on all fours round the tricky bits."

"Prince Lucifer himself wouldn't make me crawl on these steps, decorated with rat dung as they are," Welch grunted. "If you believe that conjurer's likely to turn up here, the wonder is you're trotting up at all. How do you know he didn't open that panel by saying Abracadabra from afar, hey?"

"I was always a fool." Venn laughed as he set off up the unguarded steps, Welch following. "Anyway, I think our clumping up the stairs set it off." He was bent under the low ceiling, whistling cheerfully, the notes distorted by the encroaching stone. If the realisation that Timothy Carstairs had come to his end on his own roof – perhaps even lured there – struck him, it had no effect on his spirits.

Welch followed him round turn after turn of the crumbling staircase, trying to avoid the dusty cobwebs hanging all about. Venn warned now and then, "Watch out, Welch: a bit of stair gone here. I remember near toppling over that the last time I climbed up. That would have saved the world a lot of trouble, eh?"

"What did they use these things for? Was it an escape route in case of siege?" wondered Welch.

"Originally, and they came in useful during the Great Rebellion[28]," said Venn.

"It'll be a fine thing if our lights go out," said Welch, "Then we'd have to grope our way back, eh? Ah, there are some chinks of light above."

"That's the trapdoor," said Venn. It had jammed shut as tightly as when he first opened it years since. Balanced on the narrow stair, he dealt it a series of blows with his jemmy at short range.

Finally, it gave, some of the wood shattering and plunging down the

---

28   Great Rebellion: The war between royalists and parliamentarians of 1642-1651.

abyss by the steps. Light flooded the chamber and the sound of birdsong came to their ears.

"Damn me! Repair number one thousand on the list." Blinking in the light, Venn thrust open the cracked slab and sprang up onto the roof.

They walked about the ramparts, the early summer breeze in their faces a blessing after the foul air.

"Fine views," said Welch. "Did you say your little bride's an artist? There are enough fine views to keep her busy with her painting while you take some trips back to civilization. Ah, steps down. I suppose added after its days as a working castle were over."

"D'you fancy returning down that way, and –" Venn broke off as Welch's gaze fixed. He followed it to the maze.

In the sunken garden at centre of the maze, by the fountain, and foreshortened from this angle, stood a figure, shrouded in a dark hooded cloak, standing with arms outstretched.

"Standing there insolent as dammit," Venn spoke between his teeth, ducking out of view behind the parapet. Welch followed suit.

Venn's eyes sparked, and his fists were clenched. "A hundred to one the joker opened the panel. For a schoolboy jape I near took you into the trap, sure it was nothing but the vibration of our footsteps that set off the mechanism."

"The thing looks solid enough to be human," Welch spoke with a jauntiness that didn't quite come off as they made for the steps that circled the west tower.

"If only the sneaking coward stays put, I'll at last be able to rip the cadaverous head off its body," Venn's eyes yearned, while he placed a hand on Welch's arm. "But don't underestimate the filthy thing, Welch. I've never said as much before, but I begin to wonder if it is demonic, with all this tomfoolery. It's not your fight, it's mine: so don't feel you have to join me."

"Be damned to your rambling, Venn! Let's get down to the thing," was Welch's answer.

They went swiftly but carefully down the steps. For all that, Venn slipped on the moss, stumbled and leant in to the wall to regain his balance, swearing.

Welch followed Venn as he approached the maze through the shrubbery and the rose garden.

Cold though this summer had been, the roses were in bloom, varying from the deepest red to pure white. The tender scent of buds went unnoticed by Venn and Welch. If their nostrils dilated, it was with a longing to smell bloodshed. They moved as automatons of destruction as in the ring, deaf to the joyous birdsong all about.

They entered the maze. Now all was silent. The walks ending in high hedges hid all but a short view ahead and behind. They stalked as wary and soft footed as panthers, every nerve alert. At each rustle from the small creatures in the hedges they tensed, eyes glinting, yearning for the mystery assassin to show himself.

Venn led the way, springing about each corner, expecting to come on the enemy. As they came to the turn which led to the centre of the labyrinth, Venn touched Welch's arm.

Taking the turning, they came on the lawn and the shallow steps leading into the sunken rose garden, where the great fountain formed a centrepiece.

The tiered basins where Toby Venn had once sported with opera girls in the heat of summer noon were now dry and still. Instead, the shrouded figure loomed.

It showed no surprise at their sudden entrance. It raised its head to look at them. Its face was too shadowed by the hood for the features to be visible, though they had the impression of the skull-like head inside. Even in the second that they stared at each other, it seemed to grow in height. Venn was six feet, and now it topped him by many inches. It pointed one claw-like hand at them.

Its voice came hollow and echoing. "Filthy whoremongers. Disgusting progeny of diseased linage."

The Earl of Aylesbury would have drawn himself up in outrage at being included along with Toby Venn and Welch's own father, run through in a drunken fight when his son was still an infant.

Venn said, "Come and fight, then, filthy skeleton! Leave off your damned conjuring tricks: I'm no old fellow to scare into an apoplectic fit."

"So you face me at last," the creature's voice echoed in their heads, and they sensed they did not hear it with their ears.

Venn sneered, "You turned tail, cowardly assassin as you are. Come and fight me alone: throw off your conjuring outfit: I'll rip you in pieces. Stand back, Welch."

Instead, Welch moved to his side, his metal crow raised. The being made a grating sound which might have been a laugh.

"This is not your curse, wretch, worthless as you are. Your sorry weapon cannot touch me. Venn, a couple of blows from cudgels soon knocked the pride and fight out of your miserable carcase. Unlucky your latest female victim was fool enough to save 'Mr Harley's' worthless life to ruin more trusting innocents. Come and let me tear off your filthy member before you add more to your list."

"Damned liar!" Venn made a rush towards the steps leading down. Welch seized his arm with his left, dragging him back. "No, Venn: it is demonic!"

"I'll see the life fade from your eyes," the being's cracked voice shrieked in their heads, "You'll gasp for air as did that old lecher Toby Venn, his dirty heart stopped through fear alone, eyes pleading, fingers clutching at mine as I shook him as one of your terriers shakes a rat."

"You rave." Venn struggled to free himself from his friend's grasp. "Leave go, curse you, Welch."

"Get back to hell!" Welch shouted wildly at the being, holding on. But now, Venn wrenched free, leapt down the shallow steps, and rushed it. Welch followed.

As Venn snatched at the figure, his fingers plunged through as if it were made of a glutinous mist. He staggered. The thing a shrieked: "I will break you, dirty libertine: you cannot damage me."

Venn made a snatch at the being's hood, beneath which only the eyes, glowing holes alight with fury, were visible, and seemingly alive. Maddeningly, as he struggled to make good his threat of tearing it apart, he felt himself punch and rend at a jelly-like cloud.

A flash of lightning and a roar of thunder ripped the air. The thing was gone. They swore, ears ringing, eyes dazzled.

"They say I look like my bulldog, but you acted like one, you bloody fool." Welch gazed about. "Did you think to last a round with a demon?"

Venn's breath came fast. "It was that taunt about trusting innocents that made me see red, as much as it's sneering about how it did away with poor old Toby. I've never ruined a confiding girl, whatever else I've done. Yet, it must be a conjuring trick, Welch. I can't believe in demons, or in hooded spectres straight out of *Rinaldo Rinaldini.* "

Welch shook his head dubiously. "Venn, I've never said this before in my life, but that thing had me in a funk."

"We'd better hide behind my betrothed's skirts next time it comes, then," said Venn. "I never saw anyone as unmoved as was little Miss Greendale, that time it appeared outside her window."

On their way back to London, Venn had so reckless a race with another curricle that Welch, who sauntered into every fight with a smile, even when giving away half his weight, urged, "Go easy, Venn."

Arriving back at his house, Harley Venn had to drive off again, spotting his tailor waiting outside. Obviously, Betsy had barred the doors against him. Spying the viscount, the man gave chase with such speed that for a while he kept up with the tired horses, crying: "My Lord, have mercy on a poor man."

"You'll be paid in full soon, fine cabbage[29], never fear." Venn wondered if he might be able to use him, betting against his friends in a race. "You and I might be able to make something of your speed."

"Something on account, Your Lordship..." But now the phaeton drew away from the runner, leaving him gasping in the road.

Betsy glowered at Venn on his return. Her softness towards him after his beating had not lasted. Now she refused him her favours. She wanted him to install her as housekeeper in one of his properties. He held firm. "No, my girl; there'd be too much temptation. You and I must part. When my money comes in, I'll make you a handsome present by way of thanks for past services."

He thought this generous, but she didn't. While awaiting this payment, she had taken to banging doors.

Taking up a letter from the front hall, Venn muttered as he went up the stairs, "Were I much a villain as that ranting corpse has it, then I would persuade the wench with a couple of slaps in the face. But I

---

29   Cabbage: Term for a tailor.

never forced or bullied a woman yet, or seduced an innocent either, for all its chatter."

The letter was from Lady Hogg. She had recently suffered a public fainting fit, and retired for her health to the country. Venn had written that he hoped for her speedy recovery and return to Town, that they might enjoy each other again soon. He had not added that, having promised to reform, he must try and break things off before his wedding.

Whether or not Lady Hogg suspected this, her reply was uncivil.

'Lord Venn,

I wish both you and Mr Harley at the Devil.

GH.'

"These damned women: there's no understanding how their minds work," snorted Venn. "Yet, such bubbies as she had, and such a rear; I will never find such a body again."

He stood in silent and lascivious respect for her charms. Then, hearing O'Hare clump through the front door, whistling a jig, Venn yelled down the stairs for him to come to help him dress for dinner.

For dinner, Venn met at a club with Jack Molyneux and the new Sir Frederick Carstairs, now back in Town themselves.

The young Sir Frederick, lately Venn's acolyte, as much for his way of entering the prize ring with a quip, as for his mammalian mistresses, the cut of his coat, and his high spirits, was an apostate.

He could not forgive for Venn raising his hopes about Clarinda Greendale by saying that she had rejected him, only to dash them the next day in announcing their secret engagement.

Molyneux, knowing that lurid accounts of the background to the engagement were spreading like wildfire through Town anyway, had told the youth the truth.

This had made him more jealous than ever. That Venn had all the luck. Fancy having the good fortune to be set on by four armed men in

Clarinda Greendale's sight, and to be so savagely beaten about the head that she had rushed to his rescue, taking such pity on him that she had forgotten the proprieties. As for her being obliged to marry Venn to save her reputation – what better could a man wish?

"Perhaps to marry a woman who wants him," Molyneux had murmured. Carstairs had dismissed that with a wave of the hand.

When they called for wine, the new Sir Frederick, wearing light mourning and a sour look, insisted with more enthusiasm than tact that, "I only hope a good-for-nothing fellow like you, Venn, knows his good fortune in winning a noble girl like Miss Greendale."

Venn only laughed. "I hope a noble girl like Miss Greendale knows her good fortune in winning a good-for-nothing fellow like me."

Carstairs went scarlet. Molyneux put a hand on his shoulder. "He jokes, youngster; you know his way: he's the last person to admit he knows his luck."

Carstairs still scowled, but Welch, arriving late, began at once to tell them the story of the secret passage. His senses blunted by the excesses of lunchtime, he forgot about Sir Timothy's recent death on his own roof.

Carstairs lost his colour, and Venn nudged Welch.

Molyneux looked grave. "You pair of lunatics. What did you mean by walking into a trap like that?" He shot an uneasy glance at Carstairs.

"I was always a fool for a dare," Venn admitted, "Still, this was a while after that panel slid back so glib and inviting. We changed first into some old rags of mine my old valet rejected. I couldn't put Welch's magnificent calf clingers[30] at hazard, for fear he'd call me out. Sorry, Carstairs, I shouldn't jest over it with your uncle lately dead on his own roof."

"You came on the hooded figure on your roof?" Carstairs' eyes were wide.

"No, we saw it in the maze, just where Venn's own uncle met his end," the oblivious Welch took up his story again, "If it's the conjuring trick Venn says, it's a damned insolent one. It taunted us, and Venn would fight it."

---

30   Calf clingers: Pantaloons.

When Welch finished his story, Venn shrugged irritably. "My life becomes too like to a Gothic novel for my own liking: '*Revenge on the Rogue, Or the Phantom of Conscience.*' That dismal image talks like a tub thumper[31]."

"Can this bloody thing truly be some form of vision?" Welch wondered aloud.

"It's a family curse," Carstairs said bleakly, "Handed down from our seniors."

Venn said roughly, "Don't be a blasted fool, youngster: don't we live in the nineteenth century? It's a piece of tomfoolery for which I intend to make the joker pay dear. But first, like to our Professor of Magic, Swordsmanship and the rest, I must research the matter."

"Have you heard from that fellow?" asked Molyneux.

"No, and I don't expect to. But I surprised Welch by visiting the library at the castle, and guess what I found? A book on '*The Practice of Mesmerism*' by one A Folli. Avoid my eyes, Jack. "

"Is this a jape, Harley?" Molyneux wondered.

"No, it's real enough; and there's a chapter entitled, '*Subtle Influence on Gatherings of Persons.*' Did you know you just offered to foot the bill, without realising it?"

"It's no joking matter," muttered Carstairs.

"We must joke over this, my young friend, or whoever means mischief by us has us cowed," said Molyneux, "After you finish with that book, Venn, I'd like to read it myself."

"Are you going to lay the whole story before – before your betrothed, Venn?" asked Carstairs.

Venn's eyes sparkled. "D'you mean the adventure with the Hooded Spectre? She's seen it, scarcely turning a hair. That young girl has nerves of iron."

He had already told Welch and Molyneux of Clarinda's encounters. He now told Carstairs, who scowled. "You might have told me this before. It's shocking that she's been dragged into this."

"You've had your own family concerns," Venn said evasively.

---

31   Tub thumper: A Presbyterian preacher.

Carstairs objected, "They're from the same source, after all. You think I'm scared, and you're trying to keep things from me."

"Not a bit of it, I'm more scared than you and my bride to be." Venn showed uncharacteristic tact. "That minds me; I must warn her not to explore any of the secret passages. There's no telling what foolishness a woman of spirit might not be about, eh?"

Though he spoke lightly, he added, "Luckily, it seems the figure isn't interested in threatening her, only bidding her beware – of me, I suppose."

Molyneux said thoughtfully, "It might be an idea to take her on a continental tour. Keep her out of harm's way until we've somehow sorted things out. I'm going to do as Lodovico Sharman assured us he would, and pursue researches. I'll look in the library here. With luck, they'll have something like your tome on mesmerism."

Carstairs bit his lip.

Harley Venn shook his head. "I can't raise the funds to take her on a tour. I'm punting on River Tick[32] until the wedding day, and very likely for some time after, with those lawyers as slow as tortoises. You know, it's an odd thing that Uncle Toby made marriage a condition of my inheriting the other half of the legacy. It's as if my father had got to him. And speaking of my father, he writes that he wishes to meet my bride. She's honoured, eh?"

"If anyone could reconcile the stern father and the errant son, it would be She," pronounced Carstairs.

Venn grimaced. "Now Carstairs is making up the text for my fool titles for novels…Damn me, that looby has no more idea of how to play the fiddle than an ape." He leapt up and strode over to the raised dais where the musicians played.

Molyneux and Carstairs sighed, while Welch grinned, and everyone stared. They expected a quarrel, but instead of giving this entertainment, after some talk, Venn joined the musicians. Taking up the violin which was offered to him, he startled the audience with beguiling and soaring music.

At first, the diners talked on, preferring to ignore such behaviour

---

32   Punting on River Tick: In debt.

with a shrug: "Lord Venn, at it again." Yet, as he played on, they were drawn, all unwilling, into the spell. One by one, the voices hushed.

Now a chill draught blew in the hallway. The figure of an old woman, swathed in black robes like a peasant, appeared in the mirror that hung in the pillared ante room, visible through the double doors. She seemed to listen, head bowed. Then, she stretched out her hands and emerged.

She stood in the hallway, hunched, arms clasped tight across her chest, as in grief. She turned towards the platform where Harley Venn played with such casual grandeur, half-jokingly arousing in his audience a vision, a yearning which he did not share.

Harley Venn only knew that he played skilfully, just as he fought in the prize ring. He played as enticingly as he beguiled his way to a woman's bed, with smiles and teasing declarations, the shade of melancholy that sometimes darkened his merry blue eyes seeming to promise a passion beyond that of a rake's shallow lust.

The wraith clenched her fists, and then stretched out her arms in a seeming frenzy of rage. Oblivious, the musicians played on, with the careless Venn's notes leading and merging and emerging among them.

Now and then a serving man came out into the passage, hurrying, startled by the chill as he walked through the invisible figure.

"What does the villain mean by being able to play like that?" Molyneux – talented musician though he was – asked of the universe. He had no answer, and nobody heeded him any more than if he had been a ghost himself.

13.
Halcyon Days

A T THE BALL LADY BARBARA Davenport held in honour of her brother's engagement to Clarinda, she greeted her again as a sister. Doting on Harley, she was Clarinda's tireless champion: "Her actions that day show heart and courage. A curse on propriety. For once, he was in no state to lay a finger on her – not as if he would target an innocent anyway, whatever else can be said about his morals – and so everybody who tattles about it knows. I will be delighted to have her as a sister," she told everybody.

"I won't," Sir Hugh grumbled. "She behaved like a brawling hoyden at a fair. Low born she undeniably is, though she seemed the lady when we met before. Such a one will suit your scapegrace brother entirely. I hope I don't have to make a speech at their wedding? Whatever am I supposed to say?"

"Of course you must, or I shall be unhappy, Hugh."

She had been threatening him with unhappiness since long before their own wedding. Giving in as usual, he now greeted Clarinda warmly.

Harley Venn was magnificent and lithe as ever in his formal evening clothes, glowing and golden under the candlelight, seemingly lit with vigorous wickedness like an allegorical figure in modern clothes.

Clarinda knew that she could not equal his looks. She felt short, dumpy, and plain by his side, despite being beautified by another new ball gown.

This one was in pale peach silk, with intricate embroidery about the hem and so low in the bosom she blushed. With it she wore her hair dressed high on her head, knotted with ribbons and some family rubies Lady Barbara had given her on their engagement. The brilliance of the candelabras brought out its golden tints. She must be looking at her best, for Nancy, while applying her rogue, had said that she looked pretty.

Venn said, "You look delightful, Clarinda." He bent to kiss her hand, stealing a quick glance down her bosom. As ever, her skin tingled at the touch of his lips.

The villain hides something from me. Something happened at what he calls, 'The Castle of Doom'. I know him that much already. But I must not think of him as 'the villain'. I must somehow try to love him, without blinding myself to his faults. Otherwise, I must make vows that are a travesty – – apart from that foolish 'obey' one, that is – and end in detesting him.

Clarinda wondered what it could be that troubled him. He would not look uneasy after some debauchery with opera girls at the castle. She was sure his conscience was more elastic than that.

She told her inner voice to keep its sarcasm to itself from now on.

In that case, how will you retain any independent judgement? What your younger sister accuses you of will soon be all too true.

Be quiet: as if it isn't bad enough to sacrifice myself for my beloved younger sister, only to lose her good opinion.

Clarinda was so nervous at the thought of starting the ball that she had to relieve her tingling bladder. On her way to the closet, she passed a group which included Miss Trollope, dark, sultry and heftier in her cream gown than Clarinda had realised.

She was saying, "I find this story of a prior engagement queer. It was only days before that Lord Venn begged for my hand. I was sorry to disappoint him when he pleaded so. Yet, with such a reputation, I was shocked that he proposed. Whatever is this talk of the Greendale girl joining in the brawl when he was set upon, and going with him into his house?"

One of her friends tittered. "Perhaps she has a secret passion for him, and sacrificed her fair fame in the hope of entrapping him. I hear she chased after him from a ballroom once. Who would have thought it? She always seemed so proper."

Seeing Clarinda's approach, she cleared her throat and nudged Miss Trollope. One of the group giggled.

Clarinda walked by, pretending not to have heard, breathing heavily and reminding herself that such talk was certainly going on all over the ballroom. Some would say that she was lucky that her reputation had been salvaged to the extent that it had. Still, she hoped that Miss Trollope's dress burst.

For all Lady Barbara and Sir Hugh's efforts, Clarinda knew that there would be few respectable guests with fine names at this celebration of the questionable engagement of the scapegrace to a *nouveau riche* heiress. Now the Viscount was engaged, a number of families who had relented towards him when he searched for a wife, had rediscovered that he was an incorrigible rogue. Remembering his drunken street brawls, his habit of wearing rough clothes to keep the lowest company and his disgraceful household, they again avoided him.

Some of the minority of respectable society figures came to please Lady Barbara. Others came through curiosity, and others because they remembered the Earl of Aylesbury with respect, and would not snub his son, appalling though he was. Lady Hogg – and her husband – were absent. Clarinda wondered where she was.

Venn had asked some of his boon companions, fellow rakes and prize fighters. They moved through the ballroom seemingly unaware of the coldness of the respectable guests. Some of the rougher element walked as warily as if still in the prize ring.

The whole celebration was uneasy under the surface glitter, suiting Clarinda's own mood.

Now Harley led her to the top of the set to open the ball. She was nervous at all the eyes on them, and cast her own down. He smiled arrogantly. As the musicians struck up, he whispered to her, "Let them goggle like sapskulls; we'll enjoy ourselves and ignore 'em." He squeezed her hands.

As usual, it sent a thrill through her; as always, she resented it. Still, she should be grateful. To marry a man she didn't love and couldn't respect was bad enough; to marry one whom she found repellent as well would have been horrible.

They exchanged only the odd remark during their opening dance, while she concentrated on her steps. Then, the fierce looking Mr Welch came over with their former tutor in pugilism, Gentle Tom Higgins.

His face looked rubbery, as if the blows that had landed on it had changed the texture of his skin. With his flattened features, Clarinda was dismayed that Venn called him, 'The best defensive boxer I know.' Perhaps if Higgins' defence had been less, his face would have been knocked through the back of his head.

The man bowed, smiling enormously. "Charmed, Ma'am." He chuckled. "Forgive me my plain speech, but this rascal has told me all about your laying into those cowards with your parasol. I don't suppose you could give me a demonstration?"

Venn laughed. "The lady may, across your back, you insolent blackguard. Miss Greendale is no more likely to give away her strategies than you are yours."

The man gave a shout of laughter which turned heads. "Finely blocked, Venn. Keep him in order, Ma'am, and away from the whisky."

"I scarce touch the stuff these days," Venn said complacently.

Some more of the Fancy came to claim Higgins, and Clarinda couldn't resist asking Welch, "How did you enjoy your visit to Stoke Castle, Sir?" He, too, seemed uneasy beneath his smiles.

"Very well, Ma'am. Venn is planting rose bushes for you."

"That's right, Welch; give away my surprises. I remember your painting of roses, Clarinda."

It was typical of Harley Venn to address her informally in front of a new acquaintance. He had the assurance of the aristocrat, outraging etiquette whenever it suited him. She doubted he had remembered her love of roses, and few women disliked them.

Welch went to claim his partner for the next dance, and Clarinda could say, "I fear you both met with the hooded figure at the castle –Harley."

"You can tell, eh? You ladies see these things – beg pardon, that's an unlucky turn of phrase." Venn went on to recount the story with his usual light touch.

Seeing Clarinda pale as he mentioned the crumbling steps to the roof, a triumphant smile lit his eyes and twitched the corners of his lips. He quickly changed that look. "We were as careful as a couple of old valetudinarians," he assured her, laughing as he told her of the confrontation at the centre of the maze. "Its language wasn't fit for a lady's ears, but neither was mine as I charged it, enraged as any bull. Welch will have it that it was demonic, and other such absurdities. When I got free of him, it was no use. I passed straight through the thing, while it vanished with a shriek."

Clarinda bit her lip, and he smiled, again taking her hands in his own, somehow largely unmarked, unlike the knobbly paws of Gentle Tom Higgins.

As she thought of the brutal things that those hands – and the rest of him – had done, he smiled on her. "Don't look alarmed, Clarinda. It's all bamboozle. We see and hear what that trickster has put into our heads."

"I cannot believe it to be a trick," she said.

"There are difficulties with that explanation. As I've said before, it would be easy enough for some conjurer to foist some foolish vision on myself and the others when half drunk, but you are a stranger to that."

"As I hope you will be from now on," Clarinda said tartly.

"Of course, my angel monitress. I promised you, and ain't I selling my racehorses, and turning my back on betting? I fast become a respectable citizen. You see how your influence over me is like to some magic."

"I thought that any magic in the case was that of the trickster."

He gave his low laugh. "Your influence will last rather longer. But have you never seen a display of mesmerism or a magical performance?"

Clarinda felt like saying that she would soon, in his becoming a respectable citizen. Instead she said, "I am sure I have never seen mesmerism."

He nodded. "I will serve out this prankster for his insolence. Happily, the vision shows no animosity to you, instead mouthing warnings against me. You look serious, my dear; and no wonder, with these Gothic antics. But you mustn't let it make you superstitious. Come what may, I will keep you safe."

This was said with assurance. He added, as if presenting the final bouquet, "And if your feminine fancy leads you to believe it a vengeful spectre, then I must admire your iron nerves the more. It's a funny thing; when detailing the desirable qualities in a wife, every single one but 'courage' is mentioned. Yet I begin to think it indispensable."

"I am glad to hear it," said Clarinda, thinking that as married women had generally to undergo childbirth, courage was indeed needed not to quake when embarking on it even in normal circumstances.

He turned. "Here's Molyneux and young Sir Frederick, no doubt wanting a dance with you, and given how you look tonight, small wonder. The youngster's got a face as long as my fiddle. He'll get the better of his disappointment soon enough, and come visiting us at Stoke with news of your successor."

Carstairs, in light mourning for his uncle, did have a brooding and Byronic air. If his pimples detracted from it, Clarinda was happy for him that they were fading. He would be thought good looking, if he hadn't been in the company of the horribly glowing Harley Venn.

Since he became a baronet, several matrons had discovered that though he may have fallen in with a wicked set of rakes led by the ruffian Lord Venn, he only needed a wife to steady him.

As he danced with Clarinda, she supposed that he was as disillusioned with his old hero Harley Venn as her own younger sister was with herself. Perhaps she ought to introduce them; they had much in common.

"I hope that Venn behaves himself?" he asked coolly.

"So he tells me. And I hope, Sir, you are as strict in judging yourself as you are your friend?"

Far from being offended, he chuckled gleefully: "Upon my word, Ma'am, I'm quite the reformed character. It's not only Venn who wishes to change for the better."

He smiled throughout the rest of the dance, forgetting his heartbreak in this new view of himself. After he had returned Clarinda to Harley Venn, he stalked about the ballroom, adopting a look of self-conscious restraint whenever he passed a young lady. He went early.

He had only just left the ballroom when there was a crash, a splintering retort, and the floor shook among an outburst of screams and shouts.

The massive mirror on the northern wall had fallen from its fixtures and smashed to the floor, missing Harley Venn, Jack Molyneux and

Richard Welch by inches as it shattered, and covering them with shards of glass.

Nobody was seriously hurt. Only Venn, Molyneux and a retired Colonel nearby were even grazed. Molyneux bled from a shallow gash to his forehead. Welch was unhurt, but his carefully arranged stock had been cut into two pieces.

Venn, with minor grazes, his hair full of slivers of glass, laughed and gave a quick bow. "Ladies and Gentlemen: we only perform that stunt once a year for reasons of expense and hazard."

The pop-eyed Colonel, ruining his silk handkerchief as he mopped his bleeding head, burst out: "That damned rascal to play such tricks, by Gad!"

For once, Venn didn't notice that he had been insulted. His eyes, moving to the doors nearby, blazed as they fixed on something there. He was starting forwards, when a friend of Miss Trollope's screamed and swooned against him. Perhaps Miss Trollope had started a fashion for that.

Venn had to catch her. Meanwhile, Welch helped a large dowager, who leaned on his shoulder, moaning that her nerves were ruined, and Molyneux, mopping the blood from his forehead, was looking about to see if anyone was badly hurt.

Barbara and Hugh Davenport rushed over. One of the rakes, tottering over half drunk, skidded on a pool of spilt wine, and arms flailing, collided into a stout, honoured and corrupt member of the House of Lords, bringing him to the floor amid screams from his wife.

The prize fighters, thinking a fight had begun and acting on instinct, rushed them. Venn, trying to place the fainting girl to a chair, had to hold her up while he roared furiously at them to stop it or he'd make them. Molyneux, dripping blood onto the floor, sprinted over with Welch to restore order.

Clarinda, seeing the rascals had escaped serious injury, picked up her skirts and made for the door herself, having already glimpsed what she must find there. She was half way across the room, when Nancy seized her arm, pulling her up. "What are you about, Miss?"

"I saw something: do let go!" But Nancy's hold was as tight as that of the stricken maiden's about Venn's neck. Clarinda saw that girl was in danger of cutting herself from the tiny fragments of glass that gleamed about his head and shoulders, but she hung on anyway. Clarinda thought that it was lucky that she didn't love him, or she would be angry.

"For goodness sake, don't turn vapourish," snapped Nancy, and Clarinda felt as if she managed the impossible in thinking of several at once. Besides her horror at what she had seen and alarm at Venn and his friends' narrow escape, her indignation surged at being called vapourish. Somehow, at the same time, she saw all over again why she could not confide in Nancy about these recent horrors.

She broke Nancy's grasp by jerking her wrist downwards, noting the move for future use. "I thought I saw something odd. Never mind. Let us see if we can help anyone who has been cut."

James, who had been enjoying the ball by strolling about jingling his fobs, now came over. "Unlucky accident, that. A few inches nearer, and my sister would have been in mourning before she became a wife, eh?"

James would be more impossible to confide in than Nancy. He would ask a physician for a tonic for her nerves. Then he would cancel her membership of the circulating library, saying that the reading matter led to morbid ideas.

Venn placed the stricken maiden in a chair as her mother appeared. He rushed out through the doors. Clarinda could not follow him, for now she was stopped by Lady Barbara, who was urging the guests to go to the next room for refreshments. Sir Hugh having seen that the Colonel's cut was bathed, had sent him home in his own carriage.

"I'm so sorry that this should have happened at the ball for you, my dear. And when you are looking so charming in those family jewels, too. That mirror has hung there since our grandmother's day. So fortunate that no-one was badly hurt. The Colonel only had a graze to the back of his head, after all. One would expect him to be more battle-hardened. Harley, what were you doing? Do help me to urge our guests in for the refreshments while the servants clear away the broken glass, as Hugh is so long away with the Colonel."

Venn had strolled back into the ballroom, winking at Clarinda. When he came to hand Clarinda into the adjoining room, she asked, under her breath, "Well?"

"No need to ask what you mean by that. You always see what I do.

No sign by the time I had freed myself from the young lady, damn it. You shiver, Clarinda. "

Now the reaction was setting in, Clarinda's knees felt weak, and she was sure her hands shook, while his were steady. She saw he noted this too, and smiled. No doubt he put her concern down to hidden passion for himself and gloated over it.

She said, "Thankfully, though so near, you all escaped lightly, Sir, Mr Molyneux's cut forehead being the worst injury. But you saw how Mr Welch's neck cloth was torn. It could so easily have been his person."

He grinned, showing no annoyance that her concern was for them all. "I thought the knot improved, and so I shall tell him. Still, you are right to fear the possible loss of such upright citizens. Society would suffer as much as it has through those of Byron and Brummell.[33] A lucky thing young Carstairs left before the mirror fell, he nervous enough already. I'm happy that you're not the skittish type." He squeezed her arm. "We'll talk about it later, when we have more privacy. For now, try not to worry. I wanted to say how that is the most becoming dress in which I have seen you."

"Does it enhance my charms as much as my fortune? At this rate of improvement, soon I must be one of society's plainest beauties." Even as she spoke, Clarinda was ashamed of her words – however deserved – when he had just been in danger.

He gave his low, intimate laugh, and whispered, "You plain, my dear? You will soon discover how well I like your charms."

They came up to the table where James and Nancy already sat. As Venn drew out Clarinda's seat he said, "I do enjoy your wit."

"That is happy, Lord Venn," Nancy said. "My sister can be outspoken at times. Greendale is a great one for wit. Whenever our little one frets, he says, 'Milord calls for service.'"

Harley Venn surprised Clarinda by smiling warmly. "My youngest nephew tugs my side whiskers till the tears start to my eyes."

Clarinda reflected that within the year, she and this impossible rascal might well have a baby themselves. Assuming she survived childbirth – and she had a fine pair of childbearing hips – how would she bring up

---

33   Byron and Brummell: Byron had to leave England amid scandal in 1816, and Beau Brummell left due to debts during the same year.

a son to respect his father, while avoiding his example? The difficulties with a daughter would be different, though equally real.

These seemed impossible tasks.

The next night, Venn read his book on mesmerism in his lonely bed, sighing with boredom. There were many words in the volume, the information was thin, and he had much rather fight with the Hooded Spectre than learn such facts about 'The Gentle Practice of Influence on the Will' as A Folli, Practitioner of Medical Arts, supplied.

Now Betsy, seizing the moment a tacticians skill, appeared with her nightdress unfastened, showing the tops of her breasts. She placed her hand under the covers, squeezing gently.

"Housekeeper?" was all that she had said; but her fingers spoke for her.

"Damn me, that feels good," he closed his eyes. "At the Lincolnshire place, the housekeeping's getting beyond my ancient relative. You could go there."

She stopped, clutching his member. "Not the castle?"

He thought he showed heroic restraint. "Not the castle, my girl. That's unfair on my bride. I must set out properly, at least; and I couldn't trust Mr Harley to behave with you."

She thought. "It must do, I suppose," her fingers stroked, so that he stirred and sighed. "And I need more money, too."

"Haven't I ever been generous? But mind you're respectful to my aunt." Pushing back the covers, he drew her to him, kissing her, pulling up her nightdress, and running his hands down her body. "Mr Harley has missed you, you wicked wench."

14.
Skirmishes

June 1821

"**G**o to, it O'Hare!" yelled Harley Venn from his open first floor window. "Use your left."

Beneath, his man O'Hare was brawling with the pie man. Shockingly, this sordid fracas took place at the front, in view of the Viscount's neighbours, rather than at the back, where only the language and the reappearance of a battle-scarred tradesman supplied details.

Normally, the servants gave the rest, for as Clarinda had noticed, they knew everything about their masters. Lord Venn's household had given such entertainment to the street this season that they were legendary.

"He neglects his combinations," agreed Molyneux. Welch laughed too much to speak. Sir Frederick smiled uneasily; he began to see how Venn's japes must look to others. Besides, he was ever more worried by the threat closing in on them.

The burly pie-man was getting the best of it. "Left, I say!" Venn roared, leaning further out of the window.

"He's a fair go-er," conceded Molyneux, "Yet given how half your friends are hawkers and costermongers, why begrudge paying that fellow?"

"I gave O'Hare the money yesterday, but the milkmaid got to him first," said Venn.

Molyneux said, "Venn, at last I found a book on this mesmerism business, and not from the shelves at the club, at that. I had to buy the thing."

Harley Venn's neighbours to the right drew up in their carriage, just as they had on the day when he had been set on by the hired attackers.

Glaring at the miscreants, the groom jumped out.

"Ladies present," Lord Venn shouted down. "No blundering into them, you rascals!"

"They'll be safe enough," O'Hare called back without looking round, "There's for you, *gundiguts*![34]" He laughed as he thrust a knee in the large belly of the pie man, who wheezed and staggered back.

The groom handed down the lady of the house, and she turned her back, telling her son: "Disgraceful! Don't look upon them, child. Run in."

The boy – who planned to be like this wicked lord when he was grown – paused on the front steps, only to be swept in by his mother as O'Hare followed up his advantage with an elbow to the pie man's face.

Welch joined him at the window. "Why not put your man in the ring, Venn?"

"I need him to shine my boots, which he won't be able for, if he gets his brains scrambled in the prize fighting game," Venn returned, and bowed to the matron as she cast a disgusted glance backwards. "I bid you good day, Ma'am."

"Call him off, Venn," urged Carstairs. "We'll have the constable along in a moment. What would your bride say?"

Venn smiled. "You must allow me to enjoy my last days of freedom. Jack, the book I have on mesmerism has deuced too much fustian[35], with only the odd bit of practical value."

"The same with the tome I bought," said Molyneux. "Here's the O'Hare brats, not before time."

O'Hare's son and daughter rushed to join their father, only pausing

---

34 Gundiguts: A fat man.

35 Fustian: Nonsense.

to seize a pastry each from the pie man's unguarded tray. As Venn yelled, "Keep out of harm's way, youngsters!" O'Hare warned them to stand back in the stern tones of a responsible father.

He let himself to be pushed backwards towards the tray, while the red faced, wheezing pie-man struggled to seize him by hair, throat, or arms for one final, smashing blow to his face. O'Hare moved with the speed of a ferret, slipping from his grasp.

The pie-man lunged wildly. Borrowing a move from his master, O'Hare snatched his arm, using the force of the man's charge to speed him on his way. The man crashed head over heels onto his tray, smashing his wares with head and shoulders. He lay prone in the warm meat and gravy of a burst pie.

O'Hare, the children, and the audience above howled with laughter at slapstick straight from the pantomime.

"Give him time to get up," shouted Venn.

The pie-man did rise, but slowly. His fighting spirit had been ruined along with his wares. His shoulders slumped, and looking up to where the Corinthians[36] grinned at him, he shook his head. Despite the broken pastry and dripping gravy covering him, he spoke with a new dignity. "Lord Venn, I've heard tell you keep company with common men when the fancy takes you, so you know how things are with us. Yet you begrudge me my due. You should be ashamed."

He stooped to pick up his tray. O'Hare and his children went on laughing, but the men above frowned.

"Hell and damnation, he's right," said Venn. "Here, fellow, I meant to pay your due yesterday." He felt in his pockets, and aimed some coins to fall in the pie man's tray amongst his broken pastries.

The man showed no sign that he had seen his payment fall from above. With set face, he picked up his tray of ruined food and trudged away, followed by laughter and taunts from O'Hare's children.

For a moment, none of the friends spoke. None would admit to being ashamed, all owing debts to common traders themselves.

Molyneux summed up their feeling. "Nice little tussle, but the fellow had a point. It won't do, Venn. It's lucky enough that you're to be

---

36   Corinthian: A fashionable man-about-town and sportsman, as in 'Corinthian Tom' in Pierce Egan's 'Life in London' (1823).

wed and must turn your back on these pranks, at least when you're with your wife. It's time that you started living up to this vaunted reform of yours."

"That will happen soon enough." Venn turned impatiently from the window as the O'Hares trooped inside, the children munching on their stolen pastries and offering bites to their father. "This preachy way you've taken up of late don't suit you, Jack, when you are full as wicked as me."

"Beg pardon, Harley." Molyneux smiled blandly. "Telling you too often you're lucky in your bride will only make you refuse to admit it."

Venn laughed. "Jack, you know me better than I know myself."

Molyneux went on, "On this other matter, I ploughed through that blasted tome, and I don't see how mesmerism can explain it. It's only through luck that people weren't cut to ribbons with that great mirror splintering in a crowded ballroom. Thankfully, there weren't any women close by. It seemed to be aimed at us. And didn't the monster say it had no interest in attacking you, Welch? That old colonel got grazed, true. Ha! I hear he was lecher enough in his time."

The others nodded agreement as Molyneux went on, "I'm ashamed to say it, as I've said before, but my thoughts keep straying to the end of your late relative-to-be Greendale. Still, even if we troubled to travel to France, we'd find the truth evasive."

Welch said, "I'd swear that figure we saw was real."

"At the time, you called it demonic. Surely, you don't hold to that?" Venn refilled their glasses with more wine from a distant wine merchant's.

"Venn, you say you saw another figure at the ballroom doors, when the mirror smashed." Carstairs tried to speak casually.

"I couldn't swear to it, it came and went as quickly as with Foyle, but I had a sense that it was much smaller than that skeletal thing Welch and I saw in the maze. It was muffled in a hooded robe. It could even have been female."

Now a long, gaunt figure ascended the steps, its face almost hidden by a turned up collar. Despite the heat of the day, it was swathed in a greatcoat of old fashioned cut.

A minute later, O'Hare ushered Lodovico Sharman into the room. The children's' giggles followed him up the stairs.

"Dr Sharman, do take a seat." Venn turned to O'Hare. "Pour everyone a drink, fellow. By-the-by, that was a fine move of yours just now. Here's a crown for the performance."

"You can ill afford it…Your Honour. Still, I'll take it, as you'll soon be in clover." O'Hare pocketed the tip.

Venn made the introductions. "I don't know what conclusions you have made after your researches, but we've done some of our own, and were agreeing that our explanation of mesmerism don't fit what's happened."

Dr Sharman bowed. His hair glowed gold, but his face was even more inflamed than before. Venn, remembering how Lady Hogg had spoken of a resemblance between them, was almost glad that she had broken things off with him.

Besides, as he intended at least to try and act fairly by Clarinda Greendale on their marriage, his mistress had spared him the anguish of depriving himself of her flesh. A vision of her naked body came to his mind's eye, making him shift uncomfortably.

"I hope Your Lordship had my note? I apologise for the length of time I have presumed upon your patience," the Professor continued. "I hesitated to accept my conclusions, and tried to find some less outlandish explanation. May I ask Your Lordship if the spectre has been seen again?"

Venn told the man briefly of what had happened at Stoke Castle and the ball. Lodovico Sharman's rubbery features became grave, though he quaffed the wine eagerly.

"What conclusions have you come to?" Venn asked as soon as he had finished his story.

"My Lord, that the origins of this figure are supernatural."

Welch snorted. Venn and Molyneux's eyebrows shot up, but Carstairs nodded agreement, saying, "Of what nature, Sir?"

Lodovico Sharman replied without his normal air of threadbare bravado. "I would say, Sir Frederick, that it is one of two forms of spectre. The first is made by a practitioner of the forbidden arts to perform his will. The other is created haphazardly through a charge of energy, often connected with a violent death."

As his listeners stared, he adopted the tone of the lecturer, and paced about much as Venn himself did when thinking hard. "The second is known to the vulgar as a ghost. From the way in which this figure approaches you gentlemen, it may be the first. This has no name in our culture, but can be made by a process known to the monks of Tibet which has been used by practitioners elsewhere."

Welch whistled. Molyneux stared, while Venn said, "Damn me!"

Carstairs, trying to keep his voice steady, insisted, "Hear Dr Sharman out. We clung to rational explanations as long as we could."

Venn shook his head. "I don't believe in such foolishness, Dr Sharman. If that is the only explanation you can give, unhappily, you can help us no further."

Sharman bowed. "I regret that Your Lordship has no further use for me. Wild as these ideas must seem, evidence points to their validity. What troubles me is not that Your Lordship dismisses my conclusions, but that you face this danger unaware of the risks."

Venn said sourly, "I'd be a damned fool not to see 'em, this joker having killed off our friend and three of our seniors. Now he turns to me, besides trying to scare away my bride to be. Of course, I want the matter dealt with: that's why I hired you, Sharman. But instead of talking sense, you come out with cursed foolishness about spectres."

Lodovico Sharman drew himself up, his face arranging itself into many wrinkles denoting sorrow. "Will Your Lordship at least hear me on –"

Here Carstairs cut in, "'Cursed" is just the word, 'Venn! For the Lord's sake, we owe it to the gentleman to listen."

Molyneux and Welch nodded reluctantly. Venn snorted like one of his former racehorses, but muttered, "Beg pardon, Sir. I spoke too hastily. You have partly convinced my friends, and they are involved in this matter also. Do state your case."

Sharman bowed low. "Your Lordship is all graciousness."

The gracious Lord Venn strode over to the window. The air was sultry. Even here in the city, where so much of the weather was hidden by buildings and smoke, it was clear that a thunderstorm gathered.

The Professor made another speech, which Venn only made a half-hearted effort to follow. As his friends wanted to give this charlatan a try, he would go along with it. After all, he wouldn't pay the fellow for a long time, and certainly not for any footling attempts to lay ghosts with books and candles, or whatever he meant to do.

Venn was in a restless mood, partly through the weather. Mr Harley wanted to enter a woman – he would have liked to spend most of his waking existence in one – and his master – or slave – was eager to leave the room and urge Betsy to accommodate him.

Therefore, while Molyneux and Carstairs followed the whole of Sharman's arguments, and Welch frowned and looked confused, Venn only took in fragments. He watched two small urchins and a stray dog eating the mess of broken pastries outside his door. He felt in his pocket, and threw down some coins to the youngsters. As he watched them squabble over them, the sounds of their voices drifted up to the window to mix with that of Dr Lodovico Sharman.

'Gimme! I got it first, you whoreson, you!'

"A lingering image, fashioned through the will of the creator for a task…This often breaks free from its creator's command, to develop a will of its own…It may be the so in this case…"

"You lying bastard! Gerroff!"

"At Lord Venn's castle… With His Lordship's permission, I can carry out certain investigations –"

"What investigations?" Venn's mind snapped back into focus.

Neither he nor Welch liked the sound of 'certain investigations'. They had been forced to bribe magistrates to stop certain investigations. The Viscount, as a peer, was exempt from most legal action, but sometimes he took his contempt for the law too far, and had to pay an official here and there. Welch had to do so more often.

"I would like to question any staff remaining in Your Lordship's and Mr Molyneux's employ, who could remember what happened at the times of your late relatives' tragic deaths."

"Mann was the one who found old Uncle Toby," said Harley Venn. "You're welcome to talk to him."

"I will not impose on Your Lordship. I will stay at a local inn." Sharman cleared his throat. "On the matter of the expenses that I must incur there, which would not be above a couple of days –"

Dismayed at the thought of yet another bill, which must include the toper's daily intake of drink, Harley Venn said affably, "No need, Dr Sharman. You must stay at Stoke Castle."

Lodovico Sharman bowed. "My visit will be as short as I can make it, whilst doing further researches."

Venn sighed: "More researches, Dr Sharman?"

"Yes, Your Lordship, I must do the workings which I outlined. To recapitulate –"

"No, don't trouble," Venn cut in hastily, for Mr Harley's demands became urgent. His eyes twinkled with their normal mischief. "You'll be there a while, if you start old Mann talking. Frankly, Sir, while not questioning your own sincerity on this matter, I can't believe it myself. Unlike Sir Frederick here, I don't believe that we've exhausted rational explanations. But I am not the only one involved, and I could never forgive myself if I allowed my future wife to run into danger through my scepticism. Besides, my friends seem to take a different attitude, eh, young Fred?"

Sir Frederick Carstairs was solemn. "If you don't engage Dr Sharman, then I'll do it myself."

"It seems the matter is settled, Professor." Venn gave the man a smile, and hastily borrowed a few sovereigns from Jack Molyneux. These he discreetly passed to Lodovico Sharman, as one fellow with his pockets let out to the Devil[37] to another.

Then he rang the bell for O'Hare, and hurried out the Professor and his bowing speeches on his obligation. Making his excuses, Venn left his friends to rush in search of Betsy.

They guessed the urgent business that kept him from the room while they finished the wine. Carstairs, whose infatuation with Clarinda still resisted the prettier girls who were so friendly of late, was disgusted. When Venn joined them half an hour later, Carstairs glared at him. The Viscount, too cheerful to notice, twitted his friends on superstition.

As Venn's cronies left the house, the urchins had vanished. Only the dog crouched over the broken pastries. They agreed to meet at Molyneux's club later, and Carstairs stalked to his carriage.

"I must pay my respects to little Miss Greendale," gloated Lord Venn.

---

37   Pockets let out to the Devil: In debt.

"You jaded lechers have no idea how sweet is the novelty of courting an innocent. Sometimes she allows me a kiss."

Molyneux and Welch exchanged a wink: "You villainous hypocrite, Venn!" exclaimed Molyneux,

Having taken a wary look all about, in search of creditors – much in the way that his own ancestors might have scanned the horizon for enemies from Stoke Castle at the time of the Great Rebellion – Venn walked from his street to Russell Square.

The day was fine. Whenever he went on foot, Venn realised how much he enjoyed this innocent diversion. As he sauntered along, he thought how he would enjoy his equally innocent bride on their wedding night. It was his boast that he had never seduced a virgin. The Hooded Spectre's taunts suggesting otherwise had enraged him.

Likewise, he had never courted a respectable girl since he had been as callow as young Carstairs, and he truly did enjoy the novelty. He began singing the *Largo el Factotum* from the *Barber of Seville*.

Clarinda and her younger sister heard Venn's song as he came down the street. They were back from another fitting for the wedding dress which could then be another ball gown.[38] Clarinda hoped that Venn was sober. Had he known how little faith she placed in his promises of reform, he would have been outraged.

Clarinda said, "That's Lord Venn. He does have a wonderful singing voice."

Selina had relented to Clarinda's pleas to be bridesmaid, but was still sullen. "You would know it among thousands. I'll leave you lovebirds alone together. " She flung from the room.

"When you meet the Professor of Magic, Marksmanship, Swordsmanship, Languages and Subtle Influence, he will make you smile as much as he does me," Harley Venn told Clarinda some minutes later.

---

38   Which could then be another ball gown: Wedding gowns were not worn exclusively for the wedding in this era.

He had told of the meeting in the lightest way, she supposed to soothe her female terrors. They agreed that the figure which they had seen at the ballroom doors was different to the other, though in similar garb.

"I only saw it a moment, but it was like a small *beldame*. It could even be that the Tumbling Mirror was a prosaic accident. Yet, as mirrors play some part in this matter, very likely not. It fell when Molyneux and I were close, and Welch too, and any ladies out of harm's way. Our escaping save for a cut or two was a trick worthy of Dr Sharman himself. "

She forced a smile. "I am happy that you can joke over it, Sir."

"You've got spirit enough to join me in that. I'll be damned if I let this tomfoolery get the better of me; I'll find it out, or go to hell in a handcart. But no more on it for now."

Clarinda decided that she was going to do her own research. Venn's skepticism must limit his. Clearly, he failed to distinguish between such a man as this Dr Sharman and the serious investigators of such matters who surely must exist.

"Clarinda, you're at it again with that 'Sir'. Don't you like my first name? I've got enough of 'em, along with the Vernon imposed on all the male Venns. That's the old Governor's Christian name, not as if you can think of the old stick as having one. "

Clarinda murmured, "I like the name 'Harley' well. I yet need to become used to addressing you so."

Then, she dreaded that might encourage him to whisper hints that she must become used to greater familiarities with him than that – a fact about which she was all too aware.

He refrained. "You nicely brought up young ladies are raised all wrong," he shook his head, and resumed squeezing her hands and coaxing his arm about her waist.

In an effort to protect us from such gentlemen as yourself.

They were together on the *chaise longue* in the drawing room. Nancy, as usual, had found something urgent to do just outside the room.

If Clarinda had wanted this engagement, she would have welcomed the intimacy which this allowed. But she dreaded it; this not because she found the man unattractive, but because she didn't. She disliked the tingling that his touch aroused in her. She had overheard whispers about the horrors of the wedding night, but no-one mentioned these tinglings. She had heard one city wife giggle that she had, 'Screamed at the sight of the thing, and now I'm fond of it.'

She hoped that she would not scream at the sight of Harley Venn's. The only male organs she had seen – belonging to Greek statues, which after all Harley Venn resembled, save for his side whiskers – looked too insignificant to be alarming. Still, she knew from those whispers that 'in certain circumstances' they swelled and stood erect. She guessed that his was doing that now, and tried to edge away from him; but his tender grip upon her waist was firm.

He drew her closer. "Only another couple of weeks and you shall be mine," he murmured. "I'll find it easy enough to change my wicked ways, with my own domestic angel installed in my house – well, castle."

The man was too vain to credit that she might not relish becoming the 'angel monitress' to a pugilistic libertine whose name was mud for most of decent society. Clarinda had already experienced cuts or cold civility from such people on their outings, from their first drive out in Hyde Park.

Doubtless, he thought her rejection of his first offer was based on a denial of a passion for him, and that she was only too happy that it had became her duty to marry him.

He laughed, patting her cheek. "I've changed for the better already. You may have heard my name linked with that of one or more society ladies. I assure you, that is all past."

Clarinda kept herself from saying, 'Humph!' At a visit to the opera she had passed a group of ladies in the foyer discussing 'Lady Hogg' – she had caught the name, but nothing else – with giggles.

She said, "I must be blunt – Harley. I am happy that you wish to change your way of life for the better, though I must reject the undeserved title of 'domestic angel'. But on this news you give me, as evidence of your good intentions towards myself: I hope it wasn't upsetting to the lady in question?"

Perhaps she should have said 'ladies'.

He looked delighted instead of angry. "In your concern for my former mistresses, my sweet, you show yourself truly angelic even while rejecting such a claim. No other modest young lady would say as much.

But surely you don't rebuke me for severing a guilty connection?" His eyes twinkled, as at the greatest of jokes.

"No, Sir. But I would be sorry to think that you have hurt the feelings of any of these women to please me. We are all faulty beings; and I beg you not to set me above other women, because I have not faced the corruption of Town."

He laughed outright, and stroked her cheek again, shaking his head. "My dear innocent."

She swallowed her annoyance. "Harley – do be serious. I hope the honour with which you say you now regard me, you will try to extend to all females. It makes no sense to set one above others, making her responsible for your own spiritual welfare, while despising the rest save your sister."

He laughed again. "You are truly fitted for the role of my domestic angel." He brushed her cheek with his lips. "I don't despise women; they are the sex I love."

Clarinda was too vexed to speak. He released her and strode towards the instrument. "Now let's have a song, my dear. We'll soon have you singing and playing as well as well as me."

As he sang, '*My Love is Like a Red, Red, Rose*' Clarinda thought that what with his roguish self, the Hooded Spectre, and herself as Domestic Angel at what he called 'The Castle of Doom', they would make a strange household indeed.

15.
The Vows

Jume 1821

CLARINDA WAS INCREDULOUS AS SHE stood making the vows with Lord Harley Vernon Lucius Devereux de Clair Venn. Her voice was subdued. His rang out clear and melodious.

Her bridal gown was cream, cut low and lavishly decorated with silver embroidery and lace. Her hair was dressed with pink and white summer blooms.

James had marched her up the aisle to where Lord Venn, soberly but magnificently dressed in dark grey, stood with an equally fine Jack Molyneux. The cut on Molyneux's forehead was healed save for a slight line, mostly hidden by his tumbling the dark waves. He looked solemn.

By contrast, Venn, though steady and clear in his speech, looked as if he was keeping back his laughter. Clarinda suspected that he had primed himself with a fair bit of drink, or perhaps he was still under the influence of what he had taken the night before. His eyes had widened with pleasure at the sight of Clarinda, beautified in her finery.

James and Nancy were happier than Clarinda had seen them, even on their own wedding day. How could the groom being a social outcast matter, when the Greendale family had now married into the aristocracy? It was all thanks to that kind thunderbolt which had killed Uncle Greendale.

Selina made a sullen bridesmaid. Some young Venn relatives, including Lady Barbara's elder daughter, made up the rest.

When the bland divine asked if any knew of a reason why the bride and groom should not be so conjoined, Clarinda almost expected one of the spectres appearing in a thunderclap. The ceremony went on smoothly. In keeping away from the wedding, those visions after all emulated most of respectable society.

"Thank God that Hogg woman's still away from Town," murmured Sir Hugh.

"The less said of her, the better," said Lady Barbara.

"I'll hardly speak of her to the little bride. She looks well enough today. I've revised my opinion of her, but what are the chances of her keeping that scapegrace brother of yours in order, eh?"

"Do be silent, Hugh."

He nodded. "In other words, none. A shame your father didn't bother travelling down for the wedding. It would have been an ideal time for reconciliation."

"He wrote that he would send a present. I'm sure our new sister will charm him when they do meet," insisted Barbara.

Hugh glanced round at the guests. "We'll be lucky to get through the day without a few mills."

The congregation was made of the same uneasy mixture of guests as at their engagement ball. The respectable guests looked uncomfortable. The wilder ones were on their best behaviour.

Venn's tutor pugilist, Gentle Tom Higgins, looked sentimental, swaying slightly now and then. Young men dressed to perfection, though still befuddled from the night before, made up a fair portion of the guests.

Sir Frederick Carstairs sat towards the back of the church. His pimples had gone, and he enjoyed playing the part of the hero who sacrifices his own happiness for that of his friend.

"...For better, for worse, to love and to cherish..."

Venn placed the ring on Clarinda's finger, and calmly made his vows of, 'With my body I thee worship, and with all my worldly goods I thee endow.'

Now, there was no escape.

Clarinda felt numb as Venn kissed her lips. He had managed to snatch a couple of kisses during Nancy's absences. Then, his lips had gently kneaded and parted hers, and he breathed hard as she pulled away. Now his kiss was chaste.

He looked as pleased as befitted a man who had come into one and a half fortunes. The guests smiled too, apart from the Earl of Aylesbury's older friends and, of course, Bella.

Lady Barbara looked as pleased as James and Nancy. Perhaps she truly shared her brother's belief that Clarinda could make a respectable man out of him.

The wedding feast seemed to last for ages, with many toasts. Sir Hugh and the dark and dashing Jack Molyneux made suave and witty speeches. Venn made rejoinders. Clarinda was stared at, and blushed. There was fine feast, with soup, ham, fowl, tongue, pies and jellies, fruits, fine wines and other drinks, with of course, a magnificent cake. Clarinda ate little.

Venn clearly enjoyed his new role as Reformed Rake. Sometimes, he murmured to Clarinda, as if promising a treat, "We'll soon be alone, my sweet."

Sir Hugh's fear that there would be violence done proved wrong. Gentle Tom Higgins was invaluable. When a discussion between the more unruly guests became heated, he and a couple of his cronies moved towards them, and they calmed.

This made Venn, Molyneux, and a tipsy Welch grin. Clarinda saw it had been pre-arranged.

Clarinda suddenly remembered how Venn had told her – too casually – that Dr Lodovico Sharman had suffered from bruises and a hurt ankle through a fall down steps. "No need to look anxious, my sweet. The Prof's a toper, and most likely takes such tumbles half-a-dozen times a year. He can't remember a thing about it, but had he seen a skeletal apparition, you may be sure he would."

At one point, Jack Molyneux took Venn aside and seemed to urge something on his friend. Clarinda could not hear what was said, but Venn smiled reassuringly.

At last it was time for Clarinda to withdraw upstairs with her new sister Barbara, and a couple of maids, to change her dress to travel. Abbey had gone ahead to Stoke Castle, along with a basket with the cat she had adopted and her kittens. Much of Clarinda's baggage had also gone ahead, including the shrouded mirror from Uncle Greendale. Difficult as it was to imagine a ghost daring to show its face in Nancy's household, Clarinda thought it only fair for her to take on his ghosts as well as his fortune.

Another maid who would soon join their household was Abbey's friend Sally, the maid who Clarinda had visited on the unlucky day that she had compromised herself with Venn.

Now it was Clarinda's turn to be taken aside – by Barbara – who whispered, "I hope that your married friends have prepared you for the wedding night? It's nothing to fear, and Venn, wicked rascal as he is, does have a way with women."

"So I have heard," murmured Clarinda, "Thank you, Ma'am, I am prepared."

"Babs, now, please, and truly, there's no need to speak as if you are about to enter battle."

As they made their farewells to friends and family, Venn told Molyneux that they would come to check upon him. Molyneux nodded. "I hope I may be among the first of the guests to your castle, Lady Venn?"

"Of course, and Welch and Carstairs soon after," smiled Venn, "Else they won't believe in my turning into an upright country squire."

James saluted Clarinda, satisfied at a job well done. Nancy, as she kissed Clarinda, whispered in her ear, "If things become unbearable with him, come to us. Still, the settlements will safeguard your interests. As you know, he was generous about those."

Clarinda was astonished. She saw that now it was too late, Nancy had misgivings. For the first time, their eyes met in tenderness and understanding.

Gentle Tom Higgins squeezed his way to the top of the queue: "Lady Venn, they say there's spooks up at the castle, but I've no truck with such things. What with your way with your parasol, you'll be able to look after Venn here, eh, you rogue? But if not, I'll come up and give 'em a fair drubbing."

Venn laughed, "We must have this slugger up too, eh, my dear?"

Clarinda gave a laugh too. As with the rest of the day, she moved as in a dream: a bad one.

Harley Venn drove his bride to Stoke Castle through the sunshine following the earlier rain, at speed and in the highest spirits, singing. Perhaps this was a form of courtship. Certainly, he sang some of her favourite songs as he showed off his skill with the horses.

Besides Abbey, Venn's valet, whom Clarinda recognised as an incorrigible rogue himself, went on ahead, together with, 'Those little devils of his. Their mother's dead, and nobody else will have 'em, and I see why. Still, they're not bad hearted. Little Peg was sweet to me when I was beaten, and I can't forget that. What can you do, eh?'

Clarinda smiled, and then thought of something else. "Didn't you have a maid in London?" she wondered. "I suppose she didn't wish to leave Town?"

"She's gone to be housekeeper at the Lincolnshire house," said Venn easily. "It's getting beyond my great aunt. I'm not driving too fast for you, I hope, my dear? "

"I'm enjoying it," Clarinda was glad that the roads were so much better than in their parents' day. Then, they had still been frequented by highwaymen, despite the tollgates. Venn himself would probably have enjoyed travel then.

She was glad too, that Venn was not cruel to his horses. Though he urged them on, they seemed to rush as young, vigorous animals like him, rather than through dread of the whip.

Another being whose fate depended on him was the unfriendly kitchen cat. He had spoken casually to Clarinda of it as a fine hunter, saying that it had been a stray, and would survive well enough as one again, since the household was breaking up. She had asked if they could take it with them, and Venn had agreed, determined to please her. It had been sent to Stoke Castle with O'Hare.

Soon, the flatter countryside of Middlesex changed to the chalk hills and beech woods of Buckinghamshire.

"It is lovely countryside hereabouts – Harley." She had often admired it on trips over the county border from Berkshire.

"Here's the castle," said Venn, as they finished a series of sharp bends.

Stoke Castle, looked imposing on the loftiest hill, the ancient grey walls mellowed in the gold light. They drove through open gates on which lichen covered stone gargoyles crouched. The sun made gold bars on the tree lined drive curving through the park.

Despite Barbara's efforts, there was still only a few permanent staff living in. Some locals had been called in to serve as maids, grooms and gardeners. Now Venn would be able to pay them. Before, he had avoided hiring them. He would have been ashamed to delay paying them in the way he did the tradesmen.

They passed two youths working in the grounds, making gestures of respect. Venn shouted a greeting. They drew up by the great front entrance.

Clarinda was happy to see that there were bolts driven into the heavy doorway; she would have been disappointed, otherwise. Venn sprang down, gave over the reins to a bowlegged man who straddled forwards, hat in one hand, and turned to hand down Clarinda.

As she watched their vehicle taken round the side to the stables, she felt that with it went the last of her girlhood. It was incredible that she would ever feel at home here. She could not imagine strolling under the mullioned windows with thoughts of lunch on just such a summer's day in the future.

Venn greeted the butler, Mann, with some joke. Then Mann helped with the introductions of the staff. Everyone bowed to Clarinda, calling her 'My Lady'. She was too nervous properly to take in the names, and nearly glanced over her shoulder to look for who My Lady might be. She was pleased to see Abbey, and bent to the dogs which ran up.

Clarinda saw the dark haired and insolent O'Hare. She hated to think what he had seen in Venn's Town house, and what conclusions he drew from it.

Meanwhile, two bright eyed children, a boy of perhaps eight and a girl a little younger, jostled through the legs of the staff. Clarinda heard their comments as Venn gave her his arm up the steps.

"No, it's not her!" came the boy's piercing treble. "She's ain't got golden hair and blue eyes. Must be someone else, like that woman back in Town."

Ignoring the outburst of 'Shushes', the girl piped back. "Dafty, it's only in stories quality has golden locks."

"Master has yellow hair, ain't he? Ow - what was that for?" The two women nearest them pinched them into silence.

"Time to carry you over the threshold," the man Clarinda had married scooped her up in his arms. She was dismayed at the sense of helplessness; it reminded her of being little. The strength of a muscular young man was startling.

He carried her effortlessly up the steps and into the cool and dark of the hallway, joking with the servants. Absurdly, she was surprised by the warmth of his body through his clothes, as if she had expected him to be cold blooded, though his hands when they caressed her had always been warm. Also, once again she inhaled his personal scent, which she found appealing. That was one good thing, anyway. Those wearisome tingles boded well for tonight.

The servants laughed and cheered, led by O'Hare: "A fine sight, by God."

"There we are, Your Ladyship," Venn set Clarinda on her feet.

She gazed round at the great hall with the massive bare tables and raised dais for the quality, the blank metal gaze of the suits of armour standing along the walls, the high and narrow windows, the enormous fireplace, and the lofty minstrels' gallery and far away ceiling.

He laughed. "Don't worry, I don't spend time here. The rooms inside are more to my taste."

He was covered in reflected blue and red from the stained glass as he stood laughing in the sunlight. She wondered why he called it the Castle of Doom. She had better wait until they were out of hearing of the staff before she asked.

Abbey approached, and Venn said, "Tea for your mistress in her room, my girl. I know you females can't do without tea. Then, I'll show you about a bit, if you like, or play you some tunes in the second drawing room if you're too tired for that today."

Clarinda wondered if there was a third drawing room. Given the size of the place, it seemed possible.

The stairs creaked under their feet as Mrs Mann – looking sympathetic – showed Clarinda to the suite of rooms traditionally given to the mistress of the house. One of the serving men carried her baggage.

As Mrs Mann took her through a long wide gallery hung with portraits and full of antiques, Clarinda glanced at the walls, wondering if one of them would slide back. None did. No threat seemed to lurk in the passages speckled with afternoon sunshine.

"Such views." Clarinda paused to gaze out through the arched windows at the grounds sparkling in the late afternoon sunshine, with the backdrop of the rising meadows, fringed with beech woods, dotted with sheep or golden with ripening corn. Sheep and lambs called, as they must have done during the time of the siege during Great Rebellion.

"We have the best countryside in the world hereabouts," Mrs Mann said calmly. Then Clarinda noted the maze: Seemingly dozing under the sun's warmth, it had a sunken rose garden at the centre, with four sets of steps leading down. A fountain stood in the middle, and it seemed to her that by it she glimpsed a tall figure in dark robes.

Clarinda's heart lurched. Then she saw a tall man emerge from behind a rose-covered arch, and assumed it must be the same one. He was also tall, but prosaic. She remembered how Venn had spoken of calling in a man to mend the fountain. She resolved to explore the maze. Unravelling the mystery must start somewhere.

She stared at the grandeur of the bedroom into which she was shown. It was full of antiques, including a great bed hung with rich crimson drapes. Sunshine steamed in the windows built into the recessed walls, and fitted with window seats.

Mrs Mann left as Abbey came with the tray of tea things. "Wonderful!" Tea had never let Clarinda down during any crisis, and she trusted to it now.

"Miss Clarinda, you look fine in your travelling dress." The girl poured out the tea. "I've got your peach satin hung out for dinner. May I wish you joy?" She called on her own brand of logic. "It wouldn't be fair if all don't come out well, with you so kind a mistress. And I must call you 'Your Ladyship' now."

Clarinda smiled. "Of course you may kiss me, dear, and I'll always be Mistress Clarinda to you."

"Only think of living in a castle. It seems as if we will never know our way about, but if that simpleton who showed me up knows, then we will learn. They say that ghosts walk here, and that secret passages open of themselves. But I said Town folk don't hold with such foolishness. More tea, Mistress Clarinda? You must be tired from the journey, but now you shan't have to do anything except give orders and please His Lordship, as may have a reputation for wildness – begging your pardon again, as you said you would not speak against him when you swore yourself to him – and he does seem mightily good humoured."

Clarinda had to smile at Abbey's confidence that good humour did not go with a merited bad reputation. "If you see any ghosts, you must refer them to me. How are those cats and her kittens?"

"I put butter on their paws. The cook was cross, but I said it was the mistresses' pets. That man 0'Hare seems an idle fellow, and not at all handsome, not even for thirty. But I shall turn a deaf ear to any wicked things he says in the servants' hall."

"Quite the best thing to do, Abbey. Now you shall have some of this tea yourself, and then I must get dressed for dinner."

16.
Honeytrap

THE HUGE AND IMPOSSIBLY GRAND second drawing room, like so many of the rooms, was modernised, the windows enlarged. Harley Venn, dressed for dinner, with the sunshine glowing on his light gold hair, was by a side table, opening a letter.

He greeted Clarinda with a bow and an appreciative look, and kissed her hand. "You look ever nicer, my dear. My father has had a letter and parcel sent. Let's see with what words he honours us." He read aloud:

'Lord Venn,

I could not let your wedding day pass without a sign of acknowledgment to your bride. I hope that she will accept this trinket. I wish you both happiness. I hope and pray that you will take this opportunity to turn your back on your disgraceful lifestyle and dissolute companions, and on the sorry example of my late brother; that you may at last change your course towards becoming a respectable citizen and a worthy heir to our venerable title –'

He threw down the note with a curse. "It's the same sententious blather as ever. Open the package, Clarinda."

Clarinda, saddened that the possible reconciliation had come to nothing, opened the parcel to find a beautifully carved miniature wooden box containing a pearl necklace. "That is beautiful. That was so kind in your father, Sir. I hope you will write a gracious reply?"

"I'm glad he's given them to you, and I'll leave the response to you. I'm damned if I'll trouble to respond. I'm aware that he's disappointed in me. He's disappointed in the world. But let me help you put those on." He rose to fasten the string of pearls about her throat, caressing her skin.

She froze, too nervous for any of those tiresome inner throbbings. To escape from him, she took the opportunity of admiring the pearls in the mirror to move away from him.

She had no wish to hector him on their wedding day, when he was being so kind himself. Still, she had to say, "It would be such a pity to waste a chance to reconcile."

He shook his head, half smiling. "I see you begin on your role as my monitress betimes, Clarinda. But there's no such opportunity. My father and I never saw eye to eye. He's a joyless old stick. Uncle Toby, rascal though he was, had some *joie de vivre.* He was a bad influence on me as a boy – I can't deny it. Still, he would have had less if my father had some human warmth about him. He became still stiffer after my mother died some twelve years since."

"I'm sorry," said Clarinda. The sunshine fell on the faint lines of years of excess on his face. His youth seemed the stuff of tragedy to her, though acted out as farce in his life of brawling and worse in Town, during which he had wasted half of his uncle's inheritance.

She plodded on, "For all his position, the Earl's life sounds dismal. Perhaps he is lonely? Does your sister see him often?"

He waved dismissively. "Babs is a good girl, and does her duty by him. You'll have a nice sister in her."

"Very likely, your father and you were not made to rub along together. But it would be a happy thing to look back on, to have made some effort. He could have worded that note more graciously, but he may have seen himself as making an effort to meet you halfway."

"This day being a great occasion, I'll make an effort and sign my name to whatever you write to him. This shows faith in your judgement.

How will that be?" He smiled in delight at his own generosity. Clarinda, seeing that no more could be expected from him, agreed.

"Your own parents died early. You seem to have little in common with your brother and his wife, fond of them though no doubt you are, being one who does her family duty, unlike me. Were your parents more like you?"

"They were." Clarinda kept back a sigh, "But it was harder for my sister Bella, at twelve."

"Did you know your Uncle Greendale well? There was an old rascal for you." Venn's puzzled look made Clarinda laugh.

"I scarcely knew him. He called sometimes. Once, I suggested that if we are to pray for all creation, then surely that should include Lucifer himself. My uncle was delighted by that, mortifying my parents by referring to it ever after. But I think that was why he took the extraordinary step of leaving me his money, for he never did take to my brother."

Venn smiled. "He did right. I think your wishing to pray for the Prince of Darkness himself most sweet. Now you must make do with praying for one of minions in me, eh?"

Clarinda was relieved that they dined in the dining room, rather than the great hall. Even so, the oak panelled room was huge, the table massive. It was set out elaborately, with what seemed, as ever to her at formal dinners, too many dishes. The new cook had done well.

Harley Venn being at the top of the table and Clarinda at the foot, talk was difficult. Two locals stood to attention as footmen. Mann in his old post as butler looked as if carved out of stone.

Venn grinned as they entered. "In Town, I forget the size of these rooms. I should have ordered dinner in the little dining room."

They ate their soup and savoury amongst far away banter from him, while, as she had to raise her voice to be heard across the table, her replies were shy.

Venn exclaimed, "This won't do. I'll serve Lady Venn myself, thanks, Mann. Get a bottle or two from the cellar to toast us at the back."

When the footmen had gone, Venn laughed. "Damn me, I hate formal meals at home. Uncle Toby always would dine in state, even when alone. Let's place a chair by me, and I'll serve you myself, my sweet. D'you like chicken? Ladies generally do…Now we must toast ourselves."

Clarinda found that she had an appetite, and the dinner passed quickly. She remarked, "It is odd that this castle should have gone to the second son, not to the Earl."

"My grandfather lived here, but as my mother always preferred Aylesbury House, my father let Toby live in the castle in his lifetime and me after him, as he abhorred the place after Toby's death."

He asked about her life in Berkshire, and when she mentioned visiting in the village, said, "You must call on the villagers here too. It's fitting that you do good works on my behalf. I'll see that extra funds are ready the minute I have some pennies to hand."

He made her drink some toasts, and she saw that he was readying her for what she could only see as the coming ordeal. That fast approached. Close to midsummer as it was, the sky was still light, and the birds outside sang as if they would never tire. Still, the shadows lengthened.

As Clarinda finished a slice of tipsy cake, the heavy door swung open, letting in a chill draught. Nothing was there. Venn laughed. "These old buildings, eh?"

Clarinda made to withdraw. He bowed her out. "I shan't linger over my port." She should be honoured. Still, his only other company would be such family ghosts as stirred at dusk.

She felt the presence of these – or maybe, the Hooded Phantom – as she walked through corridors lit with evening sunshine on her way back to the second drawing room. There was a gaze on her back, admonitory rather than threatening, rather like that which the stern Earl must turn on his outcast son.

She had noted the turns on the way here. For all that, she managed to lose her way, coming into an ante room hung with pictures. Here she faced a full sized portrait of a youth so handsome, with so strong a resemblance to Harley Venn, that she drew back amazed.

Amongst the stylized portraits all about, this one stood out as lifelike. The youth seemed to have been caught and painted in an instant, in mid swagger, his clothes in the fashion of the late eighteenth century, his blue eyes insolent, bright fair hair unpowdered and tied carelessly back.

Tobias Marcus Vernon Devereux de Clair Venn.

More than ever Clarinda felt watched, so that she turned, but nothing was there apart from another portrait of the same man in middle age. This one was smaller, as if he took less pleasure in his appearance, and with reason. The hair was styled to hide its thinness, the features coarsened, the eyes had lost their lustre, the mouth its sculpted lines, the lithe, athletic figure of youth transformed into a man with a paunch and an unlucky taste for pantaloons.

The painter had tried to soften the effect. Emphasis had been placed on Tobias Venn's fine clothes, with the light falling on the castle behind him and the pink clouds in the sky. In the distance was the maze. Clarinda nearly expected a tall, dark, shrouded figure to be there, indicating his doom.

Then she saw a portrait of a handsome fair boy of perhaps twelve, with a look of mischief about the mouth and eyes. She didn't need to look at the title to know him.

This sight disturbed her more than ever. She retraced her steps to where she had taken a wrong turning by a walnut side table on which was a statue of Theseus, blade raised, battling the Minotaur. She had always felt sorry for the Minotaur. It couldn't help being a monster; it was just the way it had been made.

In the second drawing room, she went to the instrument and began a tune by Mozart. Lord Venn was right; the piano needed tuning.

Soon, the door swung open behind her. She knew, from that whiff of man's flesh, pleasant enough to hers, but somehow disturbing, that Harley Venn stood there.

She played on, taking glimpses of her groom as he came, smiling, to hear the rest of the song. He was so much more accomplished a musician than she, that his listening always made her diffident. She tried to remember the touches he had taught her in playing and singing.

She finished. He applauded. "You come on apace."

He was determined to be pleased with her today. He had reason to be. He had got his hands on his fortune, and while she was no beauty, he was looking forward to getting his hands on her by way of a temporary amusement. In a flash of irritation, she was tempted to tell him that there was no need to keep up pretence; he had married her for her money, not herself.

Yet, she guessed that if she did, he would pass it off with a compliment. 'But my sweet one, that was before I came to know you.'

Then he would turn on her his engaging smile, a twinkle in his eyes, as at some joke they shared, and as if the ruin of her dreams for a life of her own hardly mattered in the scheme of things. Nor would he understand how being married to him could spoil her life. After all, hadn't many women dreamed of him?

For a seemingly straightforward man of action and pugilist, at times he could be a slippery rogue.

She said, "That is praise from a master. Now your turn, Sir."

"Now whose turn?"

"Harley," she admitted. "And I do like the name. I always thought mine silly. It sounds like the heroine of one of Abbey's novels."

"As it's yours, I like it," he said, gallantly. "Now, I'll play your favourite songs."

He began with '*Verdi, Pratti*' from Handel. Clarinda remembered his singing this when he had still been courting Miss Trollope.

She had lately become engaged to a captain in a mediocre regiment. He was clearly an Adonis to her, for she went about glowing with happiness. Clarinda had overheard Venn muttering to Molyneux that, 'These women are unaccountable'. She had to smile over that now.

As the song went on, as ever she was drawn in by the spell of that melodious voice. As the colour faded from the fields and the western sky was lit with pink tinged clouds, this man she had married began, '*On Parting*'. The piano's being out of tune couldn't spoil his performance.

It came to her now that he sang the lyrics as a pretty sentiment. Perhaps as a youth he had been infatuated with some girl, but true love was a closed book to him.

Still, the music of his voice was thrilling as he sang:

> '*Thy parting glance, which fondly beams,*
> *An equal love may see:*
> *The tear that from thy eyelid streams*
> *Can weep no change in me.*'

She did not see how she could ever come to love this man if she had no respect for his character. It was true that he was brave; he was often generous minded. Still, he was mercenary enough to marry her for her fortune, and brutal enough to enjoy prize fighting, and unfeeling enough to lead the life of the libertine.

Yet she must try to love him, having sworn. Yet, the love song with which he beguiled her had no true meaning. True love would remain a closed book to them both.

That was no great matter. People of her own background, let alone his, hardly expected to make a love match. Clarinda and Bella, whose own parents had made one, were unusual in wanting that.

Still, things had turned out otherwise, and Clarinda believed that was part of a great pattern. Rising to meet Venn's spirits, she applauded him.

He bowed, and came over to her. "The kiss, dear maid?" He took her face in his long fingers – still, like his nose, oddly unmarked for a pugilist, and brought his lips down on hers, caressing and parting them. The moment had arrived.

He kissed her some more, beginning to stroke his hands up to her bosom, and down to her hips and bottom. Absurdly, she felt a stab of alarm, as if Nancy or James might walk in. His arms felt pleasantly strong as he gently held her. It was enjoyable to relax into them. Now, his member was hard against her belly, as she had known it before once or twice when he had kissed her. Absurdly, she was even more startled by the heat of his body against hers. It made the intimacy seem twice as intense.

He drew his lips away to say, his breath coming fast, "It's early, but I'd love to take you upstairs. Will you, my sweet?"

Seeing that as his wife, she must comply with his demands, it was nice of him to ask it of her as a favour. Besides, now she was starting to enjoy his caresses, though not yet enough to do away with her nervousness.

He said, "This won't be terrible, trust me. Now I'm going to show you something interesting. Put your arms about my neck."

She did, dreading for a moment that he was going to get his member out at once. Instead, he swept her up in his arms and carried her over to the wall and ran his fingers down it. A panel slid back. The secret passageway revealed was not pitch dark and sinister, but a narrow, winding iron staircase, with light filtering down from narrow apertures cut into the walls above.

Despite, perhaps because of her nervousness, she laughed. "That was a dramatic touch."

"Couldn't be bettered, eh?" Now he carried her inside and up the stairs, whistling a tune all the while. Though short, she was sturdy, with her hefty hips, bottom and thighs, but he carried her up the steep staircase as effortlessly as though she were a featherweight.

"How do I do as a mount, my sweet?"

She laughed uneasily now, thinking of Foyle, for the stairs were narrow and winding and she could see down the fall at the side.

He laughed. "Don't worry, I shan't slip or drop you, come what may."

That reference to the Hooded Spectre would have drawn her out of her sensuous mood, if he hadn't paused to kiss her again.

"Kiss me back," he murmured. She hadn't realised that she wasn't, so pleasant were those kisses. She responded herself, shyly. He pulled his lips away and set off again up the winding staircase.

On the narrow landing at the top, there was a rail of sorts. He held her with one arm while he worked the lever with the other. The panel slid back, and they stood in an ante room. Pushing the panel back into place, he carried her to her room. To her relief, there was no sign of Abbey.

He set her down gently on the bed. "Can you undress yourself?"

"Of course." He must have known some indolent women. Doubtless, he had happily served as their maid.

"Then I'll give you a moment to prepare for me. I'll be back betimes." Smiling, he went out through the door that adjoined his own dressing room.

Clarinda resolved to be brave and undressed quickly, putting on one of the lacy, half-sleeved nightgowns that formed part of her wedding trousseau.

He was back, wearing what Samuel Richardson's Pamela would have called 'a rich robe' in crimson – and naked underneath. He smiled at the sight of her perched on the bed, avoiding his gaze.

"You're a sweet sight, and you mustn't be frightened of me. I'll be as gentle as can be. You know me to be debauched, but this is new to me too, as I've always respected innocents. You've left your hair up. It's lovely hair. Let it loose."

She fumbled to release the clasps, and as it fell in heavy waves down to her waist, he took up a clump to let it run through his fingers. "Such lovely hair, full of gold lights."

He kissed her again. Soon the kisses became urgent. She kissed him back, as that seemed only fair, but alarm kept her cold.

He took his lips away to say, "I'm afraid of you as a maiden." For all that, as her gaze met his, his blue eyes sparkled with mischief as much as they stirred with lust. She had to smile then, and he patted her cheek with kind condescension. "That's better. I'll try to ensure this isn't an ordeal, my sweet."

Clarinda noticed again the clamour of evening birdsong through the part open window, and the breeze wafting through the scent of honeysuckle and cut grass. She was glad that it was still light; this would seem less natural in the dark, with the sounds of the rest of the animal kingdom stilled.

They kissed again. His touch was amazingly gentle for a savage pugilist. He urged her backwards on the bed and began to untie the ribbons at the neck of her the nightdress to ease it off her. Lowering her eyes, she sat up to help him. Perhaps he hadn't expected her to put it on, but it seemed brazen to await him stark naked.

She blushed under his gaze as he eased the nightdress over her head.

"Such pretty ones," he said, caressing one of her round breasts with one hand. She was proud of her breasts. He stroked down her hip to fondle her nether curves. "You've such a womanly shape, and your skin is like silk."

"Now, I must introduce you to Mr Harley." He drew her hand down to that strange organ. Unlike Nancy's friend, she had no urge to scream. As she explored it with her fingers, he sighed. "You do that so nicely."

Now he was pulling off his robe, to reveal his athlete's muscular, lean build and strong arms and chest, so pleasurable to run her hands over. He kissed and caressed and nibbled her all over, even burying his golden head between her thighs. The shocking thing was, that she loved it. Now she saw that there was something to be said for marrying a libertine after all.

She kissed and caressed him all over in turn, in a way she had never thought to do without choking with shame, and there was no reserve between them at all. They sensed each other's wants as perfectly as if they had been at this together for years.

Her tingling became an aching longing, so that when he made to enter her, saying, "I'll try to be gentle," she was all readiness.

Then he hesitated, feeling her wince. "Too painful?"

"Not at all…" She forgot about that brief pang as she was filled by an almost aching pleasure. They seemed to fit perfectly together. A shameless: "It's nice!" escaped her.

This delighted him: "I'll make it nicer."

He did, and she remembered little until they lay tangled together, their breath coming in gasps.

"You are a siren in disguise," he murmured, kissing the hollow at the base of her throat. "I knew I'd enjoy our wedding night, but I never guessed you'd have quite that effect on me."

She had no idea what to say to that, but he was murmuring, "Normally, I'm restless at this time of day, just livening up for the evening. Now, I could fall asleep, not stirring till dawn. I've never known anything like it."

Nor had she, but then she had rather less experience than he.

He lay down next to her, stroking her back. He fell asleep within a couple of minutes. She gazed at him for a few moments, startled at his handsomeness, and noting too, that even when he was relaxed in sleep, those slight lines of dissipation traced his face. She soon slept, herself.

When she awakened, it was dark. All was silent. For a moment, she had no idea where she was. Then she noticed the warmth and scent of the man lying close by her, asleep on his back, arms spread out, breathing deeply. The moonlight that came through the chink in the curtains turned the fair hair on his broad chest to silver.

The next moment she realised that she could see strange floating specks of colour in the air. She put this down to a trick of the eyes, or remnant of a dream, and blinked. The colours went on whirling.

She gasped, annoyed rather than alarmed. It was too bad that the visitations should intrude on them now. If anything materialised, she would tell it to be off as sharply as Nancy scolded beggars.

Venn stirred: "What?" The colours were gone. Now she could hear an owl calling outside.

"I thought I saw something – odd patterns."

"A dream," he murmured, drawing her close, and sniffing her skin appreciatively. "The trickster's Hooded Skeleton never changes that peal of thunder by way of an announcement, so there's no need to trouble it is that thing." He tightened his arms about her. "But should that trickster dare to snoop on us tonight, by hell, I'll tear the thing to pieces somehow, though my fists went through it before."

Clarinda thought of the other figure, but now he was stroking her again, and drawing her hand down. "Mr Harley would like another squeeze. You did it so beautifully before."

17.
The Crone

C LARINDA BLUSHED UNDER ABBEY'S SHY gaze as she took her morning chocolate from her. She glimpsed her own flushed, sated look in the mirror.

Just after the first, tentative chirp beginning the dawn chorus, the Villainous Viscount had staggered from her bed, giving her a kiss on the nose, and saying that she might laugh, but at this rate he'd be good for nothing but a sparring match with a fellow of ninety.

"What a lovely morning." She gazed out of the window as she sipped the chocolate.

Hooded figures and displays of coloured lights in the night seemed far away, with the fields bathed in sunshine and birdsong loud all about. Shattering mirrors and rakes toppling downstairs with their sins upon them seemed equally distant.

"What would you care to wear from your *trousseau*, Your Ladyship?"

"Abbey, you know there's no need to call me that in private. Perhaps I should wear one of my older dresses, to remind me my fortune came from Uncle Greendale, Lord Venn's uncle's ex-steward, industrious in villainies of all sorts, though generous in leaving it to me."

The girl's face fell. "But Mistress Clarinda, I was looking forward to dressing you in one of them new ones as I've hung up ready. My mother always says how the men don't like it, if you stop troubling to look smart after marriage, wearing old caps and turned over shoes. In '*Black Hearted Lord Wrath*' the heroine wears a gown of purest white silk." She looked thoughtful. "I don't see how she kept it clean earlier when she was held captive in the dungeon, praying most devout for deliverance and his heart of stone to be melted. I wonder what was done to launder it properly for the wedding."

Clarinda laughed. "I'll compromise, my dear, and I'll wear my peach."

"Them brats of O'Hare's is beasts," Abbey said as she laced Clarinda. "They stole the jam, jumped out most disrespectful from the pantry at Mr Mann, shouting they was headless ghosts. The boy pushed over a suit of armour, denting the helmet, as is precious old, and not to be treated so. Now they look for undiscovered secret passages, knocking on the walls most tiresome. Mrs Mann said there were some down the far ends of the castle, and they ran down there."

"That was sensible of her. I thought I heard that crash earlier," said Clarinda. "They are impossible, but we must make allowances, as they have no mother and a bad enough example in their father."

And his master.

Thinking of that passion with the rascal last night, Clarinda blushed, reminding herself that she must not allow herself to be duped by his beguiling ways in their bed. She must not become stupidly fond of him, or believe his empty promises of reform. She must be calmly, detachedly tender towards him. That must be the way to keep both her wedding vows and her self-respect, and avoid constant disappointment and bitterness.

He might enjoy you as a novelty now, but given your moderate charms, that shan't last. He'll get bored and make off for Town. Perhaps he will take up again with Lady Hogg. He'll probably start drinking heavily again soon.

Despite telling herself this, Clarinda couldn't stop smiling. That flushed and rosy look lingered, too.

Venn had scrawled a note for Clarinda: –

'Clarinda,

I will probably be late for breakfast. Been called away on a damned fool tedious errand. Don't wait for me.

Harley.
PS. You are most sweet.'

Breakfast was laid out in the morning room. Clarinda liked this light chamber across from the dining room, with its long windows and parquet floor. There was a mirror hanging next to the sideboard, and at first she didn't notice it flicker.

Humming, she made herself tea and helped herself to hot bread and ham. She was enjoying her breakfast when the flickering quickened, and a shrouded crone stepped out of the mirror.

What with blinking so violently, Clarinda was unsure if there had been a slight flash. She thought not. This ghost was definitely female, bent and wizened. From the folds of the hood of her cloak, dark eyes pierced Clarinda. The figure's outlines wavered, as if it might vanish at any moment.

Clarinda, though annoyed, tried to greet the ghost politely. It would be foolish to provoke her. "Good morning, Mistress. Can you tell me what you want from Lord Venn, his friends, and I?"

The crone's voice was shaking and seemingly distant, so that Clarinda wondered if she heard it or it was inside her head. Though she understood it, she knew that it did not speak English. "I come to warn you. Beware."

Clarinda replied tartly, "I don't like to be impertinent to my elders, even when they come out of mirrors. But you have already said so. Could you tell me rather, what we can do to stop your attacks on Lord Venn and others?"

The figure gestured impatiently. "Foolish girl. You sit gloating on a brutal libertine's caresses."

Clarinda almost chocked, thinking of this apparition spying on them, perhaps during that joyous consummation.

The Crone read, or guessed, her thoughts. "I have no interest in watching you. I am aware of him, and of you all. They, and you, are to me as figures glimpsed through a dim window – but I sense your thoughts. Do you spare none to other young women he has betrayed?"

Clarinda said heatedly, "I do think of them. I deplore the lifestyle of the libertine. Yet, he assures me he never debauched any innocents, and –"

"This is my final warning. Do not interfere. This does not concern you."

"But it must, now I am married to him. You strive to harm Venn and the others in league with that skeletal phantom."

"That is merely my instrument."

"As that is Venn's?" Clarinda gestured to a violin case that Venn had left lying on a high side table nearby. "I beg you to stop the attacks. I saw you at the door, when the mirror fell at the ball. That spectre destroyed the older men. They were bad enough; but they did not deserve such an end."

Her own voice and her lips shook, despite her urge to steady them. She was shuddering, her small aplomb deserting her. "There were grotesque rumours about my uncle's death. He had worked for Tobias Venn. Then, with Foyle, it began on the younger men."

The Crone clenched her bony and fists. "Those filthy libertines – once so arrogant – destroyed themselves through fear. They had no mercy to one who lit the world for me. Why should I show mercy to them and theirs?"

The dark eyes glowed with an inhuman thirst for revenge. Yet, behind the rage, Clarinda sensed a grief too deep for words, one that had turned a woman's spirit into this terrible wraith, trapped in a nightmare of revenge.

She sought for words. "I dread to think what they did to one you loved. But they could no more escape from being held to account for that when their time came, then they could make themselves immortal. If you turn yourself into an instrument for vengeance, you cut yourself off from mercy and destroy yourself even as you destroyed them. I implore you: it is never too late to draw back. There can be no justification for extending your revenge to the younger men."

The wraith's eyes blazed, fixing Clarinda's. "Do you imagine, after all I have done, that I will heed the feeble pleas of the latest fool of the younger Venn? That ruffian is fully debauched a wretch as was his uncle – or your own uncle – who was as much the tool of that *roué* of old as the spectre is mine."

Clarinda wrenched her gaze away. The figure wavered. Clarinda urged, "Wait! There must be something I can say to help Venn and the others."

Her mind whirled. She could not believe, whatever dread force this vengeful being could exert, that she was entirely cut off from the power that enlightened the darkness of the world.

"They were accomplices, all of them," the wraith raged, "That coward Earl left the room as the Honourable Tobias Venn's fellow rakes urged him on to ravish her."

"You forget, Mistress, I know nothing of this," Clarinda spoke as soothingly as she could. "It sounds as bad as can be; but now you have avenged yourself on them by sending them to their account. It is not the fault of the young men that they are related to a set of depraved *roués*, who doubtless encouraged them to follow their sorry example."

During her speech, the crone began to shake her head inexorably. It seemed to Clarinda that the figure wavered still more. "Mr Foyle is dead," she pleaded, "Please let it stop there. With that mirror, it was nearly Venn and Molyneux and –"

"I cannot stop what has been set in motion." The voice came fainter. "I did not begin this. I cannot end it. The being has taken strength from those killings. But you – Venn's wife – it is unbearable that you should remind of her, when you have none of her beauty..."

The figure dissolved. Only lightly coloured specks of dust circled, dissolving stars lit by the morning sunshine streaming through the windows.

Clarinda was struck by a sense of sorrow beyond words, which tore at her heart, and yet must find vent in words. Strangest of all, these words came to her as the cry from a man in a poem she knew: *'My daughter, O my daughter!'*[39]

---

39   My daughter, O my daughter: The poem by Thomas Campbell, 'Lord Ullin's Daughter'
(1818) contains the words:
'"Come back, come back!" he cried in grief
 "Across this stormy water;
 And I'll forgive your Highland chief,
 My daughter, O my daughter!"

Under its weight, she sat as in a trance, the tears flowing unheeded down her face.

The door opened. An athletic fair young man stood there, swinging a dead and bleeding rabbit by its ears, with the insolent O'Hare lurking behind.

The first man's handsome face, with its chiseled features and strong, long jaw, was glowing from exercise which lit up his eyes, as the sunlight lit up his bright hair. "Sorry I'm late, my sweet. We knocked down a rabbit. I don't like rabbit much myself, but O'Hare can take it for the staff. – Whatever's the matter?"

Clarinda fought to control her tears, but only broke down further. Venn thrust the dead rabbit on O'Hare and pushed the door to. With a quick glance to check that his hands and coat weren't bloodied, he hurried over to her.

"Whatever is it? Now O'Hare will have all the servants hall sniggering that my performance last night was so lamentable, you are still sobbing over the disappointment at breakfast."

"It's not funny: don't joke," bawled Clarinda. "It'll kill you, and it'll be my fault, because I didn't stop her; I couldn't find the words. But her anguish tore at me and those old rakehells destroyed her daughter."

He stared at a loss, while she continued to bawl. "Clarinda, you're vapourish; I'd never have thought of you. What's this foolishness about daughters? Steady on."

This did penetrate Clarinda's anguish, and she kicked out in exasperation, catching his booted ankle, so that he drew back, as from an angry mare. "You don't understand how awful it is. You'll never understand, because you're part of it."

He ruffled his hair. "Would you like some tea? Curse it, there's no more hot water. I can't ring for it or some wine with you in this state."

"No, it's not me who drinks in the morning: it was she, I tell you. Ah!"

"Who?" Venn gazed guiltily, as if he expected one of his former mistresses to step out from behind a curtain. "What's happened? You were happy enough when I left you."

"I'll never be able to make you see."

Her sobs moved him to put a hand on her shoulder. This not being repelled, he stroked it, and stirred by memories of comforting his sister, he drew her closer to him, and squeezed her head against his prize fighter's chest.

She stopped sobbing, and fumbled for her handkerchief. He supplied his own.

"I'll explain," she said, drawing away to dry her eyes and blow her nose. "I'm sorry for that outburst. Yes, I would like some more tea."

He rang for hot water, and she hid her red eyes from the footman by standing at the window. No doubt, though, the story of the new mistress's outburst was already going the rounds.

She told Venn of the ghostly crone's threats. "I pleaded with her, but nothing would move her: she said she could not stop things now."

Venn swore, as he had throughout Clarinda's story. "You are a brave girl to talk to what you think is a ghost, and I shouldn't have called you vapourish. I wish I had been here when the damned thing appeared. Where is it now?" He glanced round, as if now it was the ghost he expected to appear like a stage ghost, from the fireplace or a chest.

"Not in this world, or the next," said Clarinda. "That is the trouble. I believe she's suspended between two worlds, tied to this one by her obsession and by – what she has done. I have heard of such things. It seems your late uncle, Sir Timothy, and Molyneux senior and others were involved in something ugly with her daughter. I think your uncle forcefully abducted her, with the others' encouragement."

Even in her horror, Clarinda had to smile at Venn's look of bemusement, his bright blue eyes dilated. She felt a surge of fond concern for him in his unaware maleness. The Crone's taunts that she was infatuated with him, were surely wrong, or she would not feel this protective urge at his unawareness.

They were interrupted by the footman with the water.

"Are you recovered enough to make the tea? I never made any, myself." Venn said, as the man left.

"Of course, I am. Would you like a cup? But you must be hungry, not having had any breakfast, and I had little enough before that visitation myself."

"I've got some blood on my boots from that rabbit. When I looked in with O'Hare, it was to say I would join you betimes. Do you want to come upstairs while I change? I don't like leaving you, as that being – whatever it is, vision or spectre, might return."

"She won't be back in a while." Clarinda could sense this by the atmosphere in the room. "You go away and clean off that poor creature's blood, and I'll have some tea and we'll breakfast together."

He nodded approval. "You're back to yourself." He patted her cheek with enough condescension to bring a spark to her eyes.

He didn't notice that, being for once more occupied with thoughts than the external world. "I still don't credit that this is a ghost, though it must be a fine impostor to cozen you. Never mind, eh? We'll go into this more, and soon, we're to be honoured by a visit from the Professor of Magic. Let's have Molyneux up at the same time. Meanwhile, I'll see what I can get from Mann, who was with my uncle for years. For now, we shan't let these visions – whatever they are – spoil our breakfast. I've been looking forward to ham and eggs these last two hours."

She said after him, "Do be cautious, Harley,"

He winked over his shoulder. "A rogue as bad as me is indestructible, my sweet." He paused. "Faugh! It's an ugly enough business, if what that old beldame vision says is true, eh? But that other boggle maligned me enough, when Welch and I saw it, so who knows? No more of it for now, anyway."

O'Hare was in Venn's dressing room when Venn strode in. He said nothing, but raised his eyebrows.

"Less of the speaking looks. Help me off with these boots." Venn began to unbutton his waistcoat, "Pour out some water. I need a quick wash. I'll use cold, as I'm in a hurry for breakfast."

O'Hare moved to get it, complaining, "It's come to a pretty pass when a fellow can't have a normal look on his face without his master acting offended."

"Your face itself is enough to cause offence, whatever look you paste upon your sorry features." Venn grinned.

O'Hare nodded as he filled the basin from the jug. "You have your own orders…Your Honour. I know how 'tis."

"No you don't, you bloody fool." Venn dropped his shirt to the floor and began splashing.

O'Hare stood holding the towel and watching Venn's physique with detached admiration. "You are still in good condition…Your Honour. Lean as a greyhound, not an ounce of fat on you, and not one of these heavy toe-to-toe sluggers, no more than Mr Molyneux or myself. You'd have beat a couple of them fellows, shillelaghs[40] or not, but not four of them. And maybe then, your lady wouldn't have had to weigh in with her parasol, and you would still be fancy free."

Venn turned about, rubbing himself down briskly with a towel. "Stop prattling. I'm glad things turned out this way. I don't mind being married: I like my wife."

"Begging your pardon, so did I, in my early days with my old woman, God rest her. But them females is unaccountable hard to please. You never know what will set 'em off. Once, I said, 'Good morning' to mine, and she fetched me a clout in the face."

"Didn't I say, stop prattling? I'll be hard to please if you don't fetch me a clean shirt in a hurry."

Clarinda's found that she had an appetite, after all. Harley was hungry, and kept her laughing over nonsensical talk.

If it hadn't been for the previous drama, she would have disgusted herself by being like Samuel Richardson's Pamela in being shy at seeing her new husband after that first night of passion. As it was, the Crone's visit had done away with minor concerns such as bridal modesty.

Venn said, "And now I must show you the castle and grounds. It's just the weather for it. After that, I'll talk to Mann. I'll have to do that without you, man to man – sorry about the fool pun – as he'd be shocked to mention abductions before my wife. Come then, Clarinda, let's start with the grounds."

---

40   Shilelagh A heavy stick or club traditionally used in Ireland for walking or fighting.

She smiled. "Then, I suppose I must have my parasol, as unusually this summer, the sun's out again."

"You ladies and your dread of freckles. Have you had that broken shade mended yet?"

Clarinda' new parasol being still packed, she went out in only a bonnet, shocking Abbey, who asked for five minutes to find it.

Along with two spaniels, they spent an hour walking about the landscaped grounds. Everywhere, birds flew overhead and butterflies darted.

There was a great park, separated by a ha-ha[41] from the rolling meadows, on which sheep and cattle grazed. There was woodland skirted by paths, and a distant lake gleamed in the sunshine.

The grounds, though run down through years of neglect, still retained much of their grandeur, though the lawns were overgrown and the statues mottled with moss. They were set out with long vistas, and the natural and artificial skillfully blended.

In the sunshine, Clarinda's spirits rose, while it took more than the other rising spirits to subdue Harley Venn for long. He whistled as he showed her about.

They came to a rose garden to the west of the house, sheltered by high stone walls. It was a sun trap, full of the buzz of bees and the flitting of butterflies. Clarinda remembered Welch saying Harley had rose bushes planted in her honour. Then, as now, she had been startled at this gesture.

He smiled, guessing her thoughts. "The gardener said there were too many gaps, so as you like roses, I had more planted. Here they are. There's more – elsewhere."

She thanked him. However prosaic his motives for marrying her, it was nice to be honoured as a bride. By 'elsewhere' she guessed he meant the sunken rose garden in the maze.

Behind a high wall came voices: "Strawberries? Gimme some, meanie."

Clarinda and Harley exchanged a grin.

"Let's go down that yew walk," she said, and then she saw the maze at the end. "After what happened to your uncle and what you and Mr

41   Ha-Ha: A deep ditch to prevent cattle from wandering into the park from surrounding fields.

Welch saw in there, You cannot wish to go in." She felt a childish surge of disappointment; like her brother James, she loved mazes.

"I wouldn't let that filthy skeletal image keep me out," he said. "I would relish another chance to knock its head from its rotting shoulders, though last time, my fists beat against thin air. But I don't wish to take you in."

"I don't think that it should keep us out," she mused. "If those beings are the illusions you argue, then they cannot hurt us unless we lose our nerve, and I believe that still to be true if they are spectres. For all the crone's threats, that mirror missed you all. I think I will be more anxious for you, if we don't go in."

There seemed no threat as they walked through the gap in the tall hedge of yews that made a border to the maze. The dogs had chased off after a rabbit.

"Carstairs ridiculed an old ghost story about it," said Clarinda, remembering the painting at Lady Barbara and Sir Hugh's town house, and not wanting to mention Toby Venn's death in the maze.

Harley snorted. "There is one dating back to the Restoration, when our family got the Earldom. Old Cuthbert Venn supposedly came upon his mistress dallying with a young rustic. The story goes, he ran him through with his sword, killing him on the spot. Another story has it that the fellow later ran the local inn, dying aged eighty." He winked at Clarinda.

The heat fell on them like a physical presence. He strode briskly through the narrow, identical corridors, his hand supporting her arm, taking the turnings that led to the centre without a pause.

Only now did she remember her own painting, marvelling that she could have let it slip her mind. What had been her idea in painting it? She couldn't remember. It was as if she had been in a dream. The figures of the couple she had shown were blurred, though they were young. The hooded, cloaked figure which faced them, blocking the exit, was viewed from behind, and whether it was human or not was unclear, though it was unnaturally tall.

Suddenly, the song of the birds was faint in her ears. It was as if a cloud obscured the sun. Now the light breeze of the morning ceased, and thunder seemed near.

They were at the centre. Through an arch overgrown with climbing roses, she could see the small lawns, the four sets of steps leading down to the sunken garden, and the fountain in the middle, now working again, the water falling in a jewelled ray into the series of basins.

Clarinda's heart beat fast, and she felt Harley's grip on her arm tighten and heard his breath quicken as he glanced about, all his fighter's instincts on alert. She sensed a threat all about, but knew he would not flee, so she must stay herself.

"Fool that I was to bring you here! I'll get you out –" he began.

"We may as well face it now," Clarinda tried to keep her voice steady. "I don't believe it can do anything but frighten."

Then she saw the figure by the fountain. It was that of a young girl, slight, the red lights in her dark hair lit to a flame in the sunlight, in clothes with a somehow foreign look to Clarinda's eyes. She made a gesture of what might have been either resentment at their coming, or warning. Then they saw the flash. The crash came as they spun about.

The Hooded Spectre stood blocking the exit behind them, looming above Harley by a foot.

18.
Confrontation

Harley pushed Clarinda behind him and lunged forwards, only to be thrown back. Time seemed to stand still, so the song of the birds became a serious of droning, separate notes.

Clarinda felt her limbs to be leaden, her feet seemingly rooted. She felt as entrapped as a human spirit in a statue. Every breath became a gasping effort. She could not even cry out. Her tongue seemed bound.

Worse was the urge to destroy that invaded her mind. She longed to pull back the hood of the muffled figure that stood before them and rend its face with her nails. From his blazing eyes, she saw that Harley yearned to do worse, as his breath came laboured and he strained to move.

Clarinda fought her rage, telling herself that even this monster existed by the will of a beneficent Creator, who treasured all the living things of creation, so that a sparrow never fell alone.

The being's voice came echoing and distant, yet gloating.

Now you know the torment of your worthless elders. Venn, your sensualist uncle's arrogance turned to terror, and so, at last, I stopped his filthy heart.

With massive effort, Harley Venn brought out the words, "Let her go. She's an angel."

Clarinda was touched by that piece of gallantry, but thought it foolish. She could deal with the situation better than he. For one thing, this sense of being trapped inside a statue was only an exaggeration of the norm for a female. .

Harley felt the rage as a black wave of polluting longing, rather than the hot rush that fired him when challenged. That always left him sated and amiable when he had dealt out the necessary damage.

The creature glided forward, stretching long arms to seize him with gnarled fingers. Clarinda could feel how Harley strained, but could not stir. She struggled as fiercely: now she dreaded that the being would choke the life from him.

Deploring the hubris had led her to insist that this being could not hurt them except through fear, she made a silent prayer.

Suddenly, in her mind's eye, she surrounded them both by a silver blue glow. The idea came as something rediscovered. Now they could breathe more easily.

The monster staggered, as if it had run against an unseen barrier. Its eyes met hers from the depths of its hood. In that terrible gaze, she felt a pull on her senses, and she wrenched her gaze away.

"Do not try to pit your puny will against mine, you insolent piece of female flesh." It turned to Harley. "I see no angel. You brought this creature to be your consort slut and sentimental dupe in an alliance respectable in name only. She deserves no better fate than to suffer through you. She is tainted through that legacy from that depraved lackey Greendale. That money drew you and your fellow fortune hunters as carrion to a pack of jackals. As a debauched ruffian yourself, you are heir to Toby Venn's villainies."

Harley, eyes blazing, a cold sweat sticking the golden waves to his forehead, choked, "Slut? Give over your damned coward's tricks, let me move, and I'll rip your cadaver's head off your shoulders and stuff it down your rotting neck. That'll stop your blather."

"No: hating it feeds its power." Clarinda surrounded the being with light in turn.It hissed, drawing back. The weight that rooted her lightened.

Harley either could not, or would not, hear her. He vented his feelings in a torrent of threats and curses.

Clarinda said as calmly as she could, "Harley, let me speak. Ignore its taunts." She had discovered something. Even in her dread and loathing of the being, she saw it was as wretched, as driven, as a lunatic.

She said, "It is strange you despise females, when one created you as her tool."

The thing made a mirthless cawing. The noise must have sounded outside the maze, for Clarinda heard the prolonged notes of a dog's bark from outside.

"I have broken free from that hag's control," the being jeered, and Clarinda remembered the Crone's words that she could not stop the forces she had raised.

Yet she realised that in breaking away, this being had lost its original source of power. Now it must draw it from the loathing of others. Still, if it could succeed in that, its menace was real: that was how it had killed its latter victims.

Apart from her uncle, the older rakes had died through losing their nerve, as poor Foyle had done. If she knew anything about the scapegrace she had married, it was that he had iron nerves. She was less sure of her own. Still, unlike him, she would not allow the creature make her return its hatred. Yet, she feared that different killing in the case of her uncle. What did it mean?

"You poor creature, it is you who delude yourself," she said quickly. "You still pit yourself against the heirs of her enemies. If you have any independent will, then try to turn from the hatred that entraps you to ask for peace for yourself from the Creator of all things."

Harley rasped, "Don't waste your pity on that filthy damned ghoul."

"You play into its hands." Clarinda found it exhausting to play the part of a human lighthouse, striving to surround them both with rays of light and directing it towards the monster.

Finding that she could move, she took one of Harley's hands, squeezing it. He returned the pressure. She felt a charge of tenderness between them. It was tentative, but real, like that when he had comforted her before. Warmth seemed to spread from their joined hands, running down their arms to their hearts. An odd sense of peace fell on them both.

The being flinched back as if someone had flicked drops of scalding water in its face. Its shriek rang in their ears: "Save your cloying words for your murderous rough!"

Her lips twitched, but not with distress. Now, the absurdity of the being's speeches struck her. "You speak as a ghost in a Gothic novel, though perhaps you have no choice."

The spectre's form wavered.

Harley laughed scornfully. "True; this monster's attempts at conversation are hellish tedious."

The being reformed, looming over Harley by three feet. Still Clarinda's barrier of light kept it from coming closer. Its voice fading, it intoned, "It is not yet the time. Firstly, you must discover what a sorry bargain you have made in selling yourself for a title."

Harley tensed with renewed fury, and seemed about to spring on it in turn, so loosened were the bonds that held them. Clarinda held his hand fast, and pinned his will with her mind so strongly, that he paused as if he sensed it.

The being's voice came strident in their ears, "I will come to you again. That fool will betray you soon enough."

It was gone.

Once more the sun shone down on them and birdsong sounded in their ears. Again, she saw the butterflies flit among the blooms. They panted, not thinking of letting go of each other.

Their breathing calmed. Harley's taut muscles unclenched. He even smiled. "Round one to us." But for all his careless air, his voice was hoarse.

To me, you mean. You returning its rage and threats only made it stronger.

They heard the barking as the dogs chased through the maze in search of their master.

The exhaustion of that tussle swept over Clarinda, and her legs felt weak. She began to shudder, and he tightened his arms about her.

"You faced it bravely. Lean on me. D'you want to sit down?" He indicated a rustic seat near the closest set of steps. "I wish I had my flask. A nip of brandy would set you to rights in no time."

"I hope you're not in the habit of taking one out with you for a stroll? I'll soon get the better of this." She despised herself for having to lean against him, and he led her to the seat.

His eyes still flashed. "The insolence of the filthy creature, calling you a slut. I'll make it pay for that, if it's the last thing I do. You are less a slut than any other pretty woman I've known."

She noted the 'pretty', which he'd never called her before. Perhaps sensual pleasure played a large part in a man's opinion of a woman's beauty. A thought, outrageous and irrelevant, struck her, and she said without thinking, "Perhaps all women, or none, are sluts, any more than men."

He stared a moment. Then, dismissing such nonsense without bothering to dwell on it, he turned to greet and shout orders to the dogs which rushed upon them in a frenzy of wagging tails.

Clarinda absently patted the head of a spaniel as she gazed at the fountain. "Did you see the other figure? That must have been the crone's daughter. Can you still believe this is a series of conjuring tricks foisted on our minds?"

"I don't know what I think," he admitted, "Except that I want to force that hellish thing's taunts down its filthy neck more than I've wanted anything in my life, even more than my first violin or a draught of ale after a bout of fighting."

For some reason, the difference between those tastes struck her as ridiculous. Perhaps it was nervousness, as for a few moments, she could not stop giggling.

He looked down at her, frowning, so she said hastily, "No, I am not vapourish. It's provoking of you to suspect me. That was different to this morning, when the Crone's story upset me so."

He smiled. "You stood up to the horror bravely. I suppose I must have looked fool enough, rooted to the spot as I was, roaring hopeless threats; a sight fit to make anyone laugh when looking back on it. Let me get you back to the house. A dish of tea will be the thing, if you don't want a shot of brandy. You're in the same mood as a challenger whose come through the fight and can't stop laughing."

"I suppose it has been a wearing morning, with these dreary visitors," she said. "But Harley, I suspect it draws power from being hated in return. We must treat its taunts as we would the chattering of a monkey."

"But damn me, for that filthy creature – whatever it is – to insult you was beyond bearing."

"I don't think we will have to endure another visit from it a while.

That is as well, for we must be prepared when it does call again." She rose, and he came to take her arm. With the dogs scampering about, they walked back through the maze.

"You often came here as a boy," Clarinda mused. "Was nothing there then? After all, this girl's tragedy must have happened long before." Even though she supposed he must have been fairly oblivious as a boy, surely he would have noticed a ghostly maiden.

He shook his head. "Sometimes, in these old places, you feel as if someone else's there. But not as before, no."

All the while, the blue butterflies of the chalk meadows of Buckinghamshire danced about their heads.

"I am sure my guess is true," she urged him again, "It feeds off hatred. Maybe that is how it was brought about."

Those blue, beautiful and unreflective eyes dilated, the tapering dark brows shooting up. "Come, Clarinda. How can I not hate the damned thing? It's like this talk of forgiving your enemies. Can't be done, save you've knocked 'em down first."

"Think of it as a wretched, chained creature," she urged. "How can its existence be any less of a torment to it, than for us? The same must be true of its creator." When he made no response, she added, "I must come in here again."

"No!" he pulled her to a stop. "Promise me that you won't go in that place unprotected."

"I think I can promise that I shan't enter unprotected." She knew she was being evasive.

As they emerged, they came on O'Hare, looking solemn. There was normally something about his cast of feature, with high cheekbones and wide mouth, which gave them a subtly hilarious look, even when he was serious.

"What do you want, loitering here looking so sly?" Harley Venn greeted him.

"I'm glad to see you and your lady walk up looking so normal. "

"What d'you mean, you insolent rascal?"

"There's something wrong about the air here, though it comes and goes. So I told Your Honour before, but now it's stronger." He made a sweeping gesture. "I don't like it. I told the weans to take care."

This was the first time that his master had known him to do that. He looked startled, as O'Hare went on solemnly, "A fair demonic laugh came ringing out from that maze. Were you and your lady not after hearing it?"

Harley Venn said roughly, "Such ghosts as there are will more likely come after such wicked fellows as you and I, but do keep the youngsters out; they might get lost. Maybe a spectre was taunting you on the knot in your cravat. No more blather from you: my wife wants some tea. Where's Mann? I want to ask him something."

Mann gazed at Harley Venn as he lounged, long legs stretched out casually. "The old story of Master Toby – God rest him – and the other gentlemen over in France? Master Harley, you will know more of that than me, as your father wrote his account of it special as a warning to you, being wild – begging your pardon. It was in that letter he gave you to read the day you came of age."

"Curse it, I shoved it somewhere. If you remember, he threw me out the day afterwards," muttered Harley. "I was half sprung[42] when I was packing up my things, and somehow I lost that letter he gave me before I read it. Careless of me; I thought it was just another lecture from the old Governor, only this time in writing."

Mann shook his head mournfully, though whether over the family rupture, or the Viscount's actions that had led to it, was unclear.

Harley swore again. "It would be insolent to ask for a copy –supposing he had one – admitting I'd never read it. Mann, you know something of what went on in France with old Toby. I know you were close to the old rascal, working with him all those years, and drink must have loosened his tongue sometimes. You were the one who found him."

Mann stirred uneasily. "It was a shocking business. It was why your father was so fearful later on of your following your uncle's example."

"Tell me what you know," urged Harley.

"I only heard that old tale in pieces. The talk became wilder, as time went on, with those strange things happening to Master Toby and his

---

42   Half sprung: Half drunk.

friends. It all began over in France, before the wars. There only being eleven months between your father and your uncle, the old Earl sent them both on their Grand Tour[43] together.

'Over in France, they befriended Sir Francis Foyle, Sir Timothy Carstairs and the older Mr John Molyneux. One day, they rode out from Versailles into the countryside, where they stayed at an inn, where they saw the wench and all the trouble started.

'She was supposed to be so handsome they all vied for her favours, low born as she was. Something bad happened later, and it was whispered how there was an abduction. It was said that the girl died, as a result. But Master Toby never would speak of it, nor have any of his household talk of it on pain of being sent off.

'Master Toby had his servant Greendale with him, who was far worse than his master for wickedness, so that it was said he meddled in the black arts. He was involved in it, too."

"The Devil!" exclaimed Harley, appropriately. "Old Greendale? You jest."

Mann remained solemn. "Some say it was just folks' envious talk because starting off poor, he made money so easily, it seemed to fall into his hands."

Harley snorted: "That old scoundrel, in a long starred cloak and hat, waving a wand? If I'd known that was the way to get more tin before, I would have done as much myself, and it would have fallen into my pockets from the sky – or maybe, risen still molten from down in the other place. Tomfoolery, Mann."

"As you say, Master Harley," Mann closed his lips tightly.

"Don't pull that face, Mann. It minds me of when I was a boy, and you wouldn't tell me where my pet monkey had gone. I want your help."

"The Earl did keep a copy of that letter, to give to Lady Barbara's sons later on, just in case they should be drawn in, if you never had heirs yourself. You may mock, Master Harley; but he feared a family curse because of that bad business."

Harley shook his head. "Babs does have sons, and I'll be hanged if

---

43   The Grand Tour: The Grand Tour was a long tour of continental Europe traditional to young men from privileged backgrounds between 1660 and 1840, (excluding the years of the wars with France).

I don't get this mischief behind us before they're much older. I've seen some odd things of late, and so have Molyneux and the others, and if a hard headed fellow such as he gives such stuff credence, then – what's the matter?"

Mann's jaw had dropped, his eyes started, and his face blanched. "Then His Lordship was right; it's started on you youngsters."

"I thought you might suspect from stories of how poor Foyle went," said Venn, apologetically. "Never mind: before long we'll have Lodovico Sharman up here. He will mend matters betimes."

"You jest, Master Harley; you'd never trust a man with a silly name like that."

"Have you forgotten the Devereux and de Clair in mine? Molyneux and the others want to try him. Meanwhile, I must look for that letter of my father's again. Damn me, I hope I didn't leave it at Aylesbury House. I could have sworn I packed it up safely with something I wouldn't forget."

Mann asked gloomily, "Shall I help you look for it, Master Harley?"

"No, if it's anywhere, it's among my private papers." Harley grinned at the thought of Mann's face should he see some of those. "If I can't find it there, then I'll have to ask him, I suppose. Only fair to Lady Venn, seeing she's been dragged into this."

He jumped up and wandered over to the window to stare over to the distant hills. "Mind you, Mann, she got involved when that old wretch Greendale made her his heiress. He came to a sticky enough end, if the blather in France is to be credited. It would make me anxious for her, save she's so virtuous, and some other things I won't go into make me think there's no threat to her."

Mann frowned. "Whatever you have heard, Master Harley, and you may mock, they say Greendale's nasty end was due to his cheating his old ally."

"Who, Lucifer himself? What, is that the time? I must get changed to eat with Her Ladyship."

Afterwards, Harley spent half an hour sorting through old letters and documents which he had shoved carelessly away. There were bundles of unpaid bills dating back years. He whistled, wondering if they were still outstanding. He had tried to pay something to most of his debtors on coming into his inheritance, but with so many, he must have overlooked some.

There were letters from women with names long forgotten. Others were less affectionate. There were some from former seconds in duels, and an abusive one from a cabinet maker in Barnstaple, demanding fifty pounds. Venn had no memory even of visiting there; perhaps he had been in his altitudes at the time.

There were several stern ones from his father, though none with his birthday date. He avoided reading any of the brief notes sent after his coming of age. Even so, phrases such as 'disgraceful excesses' and 'dragging the family name through the mud' seemed to spring out from the pages at him. Swearing, he gave up the search.

"Mistress Clarinda, you're as pale as ghost yourself. You've never seen something bad? That nasty O'Hare said he heard someone laughing most demonic in the maze when you and Lord Venn was walking in there, but for sure that was His Lordship teasing? Shall I fetch you a glass of wine?"

Clarinda, who had thought that she had regained her calm, was dismayed. "Do I seem shaken yet? I can't deny it; the Viscount and I did sense unaccountable things in the maze. But most likely you will see nothing there. No wine, thank you, I'll have some with lunch."

She had no wish to alarm the girl, but it was wrong to lie. No doubt O'Hare had talked of the bride's earlier weeping, though with such a master, various inferences could be drawn from that.

Abbey tossed her head. "You wouldn't catch me wasting my time in there, Mistress Clarinda. I can't see the point of mazes, when you can get lost any day in London by going out of your way."

Clarinda giggled. "That is one way of looking at it. And I do hope, my dear, that the castle's reputation won't make you leave us."

"No, as I'd rather have a kind mistress and ghosts than a harsh one and none."

Clarinda and Harley Venn, their appetites unspoilt once more by their adventures, ate cold chicken, seasonal and exotic fruit and other foods in the light second dining room. Over the meal, he told her about the talk with Mann.

"So, I'm looking for that letter from the governor. I shoved it away somewhere, supposing it to be another written harangue. Lord knows I'd had enough of those." He grimaced.

"As luck would have it, my twenty-first was my last day in Aylesbury House. The next day he threw me out over my latest misdeed. Packing as fast as may be, I lost the thing. I did him the honour of putting it somewhere where I'd be bound to take it with me, but being half-cut[44] at the time, I forgot where."

"And you and your father have never spoken since?" Clarinda was appalled. "I'll be discreet, and not ask what caused the final rupture."

"I killed a man in a duel. Don't look at me so: it was an accident. I only winged him, but it festered, taking him off within days. He did his damndest to kill me, being heated over a quarrel over a lady. I was in two minds to fire into the air. I only wish I had."

Clarinda put down her fork, and could not stop herself from saying, "Heavens! You doubly wronged him."

He went on chewing. "Since then, I'm less fond of duels, and aim to miss if I can. His family swore revenge, but it came to nothing. Wrong as it is, I felt near as bad when I had to shoot my favourite horse after he broke his leg." He drained his third glass of fine wine, urging her to finish her first.

"One glass is enough for me at this time of day." No doubt she sounded priggish, but was determined to speak out against any heavy drinking even as he began on it.

"It takes a few to overset me," was his careless response. "If I can't find that letter, then as a last resort, I'll ask my father."

"Which reminds me, I must pen that note, thanking him for his generous present." Clarinda began to peel a peach. "I suppose if I am to be caught up in a Gothic adventure, I might as well make the most of

---

44   Half-cut: Half drunk.

it, though it is dreadful about that poor girl so long ago. Don't take any more wine, Harley. Have some of this fruit instead."

"Angel monitress, I'll do as you bid me. When you're ready, if you feel lively enough, I'll show you over the castle. But we'll avoid the secret passages, for fear of meeting the O'Hare brats."

As with the grounds, the interior of the castle was everything that Clarinda could have wished. Despite the modernising work that had been done over the last century, it still had many Gothic features, including turret stairs, long galleries flanked by rows of arched windows, bolt studded doors, ancient tapestries depicting hunting scenes or ones from classical mythology, and much else.

Harley was full of fun, making the idea of ghosts as incongruous as did the afternoon sun shining through those Gothic windows, which now alternated with showers. He pointed out where the secret passages were, making her laugh by ordering them to stay closed.

As she stood, admiring the views from a balcony, he slipped an arm about her waist. "I hope that doesn't turn you dizzy?"

"No, it's wonderful." Clarinda admired the distant views of the beech fringed hills, drawing in the country air, so different from that of the city she had breathed in recent weeks. She revelled in the calls of a distant rooster and of the lambs, and the birdsong near and far.

Harley caressed her waist with long fingers that seemed to have nothing to do with the distorted ones of his tutor pugilist Gentle Tom Higgins. He drew her back inside to kiss her, one hand entering her bosom, the other fondling her ample rear.

"I can't wait for tonight," he murmured, his breath coming quick. "This rear of yours; so many times I've ogled it, as you walked across a room."

"Mine among others," she murmured.

"Such is the nature of men. But I delighted in yours from the first." He pulled her against him, rubbing his hardness against her belly and drawing her hand down. "Mr Harley wants to kiss you."

In Clarinda's great bed, Mr Harley demanded to be kissed himself. Tactfully, her practiced lover hadn't asked this of her on that first night, though he had kissed her female parts tenderly and enthusiastically.

She was shocked all over again at her pleasure as they delighted in each other all over again. The spectre – or whatever motivated it – might seek to demean the natural joy they shared, to disgust her with them both, but it had failed. This felt right. Inhibition felt wrong.

She had married a man the opposite to everything she had wished for in a husband, except in looks (and courage, and perhaps good nature) and so it seemed only fair that they should enjoy each other in bed.

As last night, his touch was astonishingly gentle for a pugilist: that must be the musician coming out in him. He sought to please her as he caressed and stroked her, telling her how delicious he found her flesh.

All his talk was of her and his exaggerated view of her charms. She was glad of that. Before, she had wondered if he might speak of his former mistresses, and even make insensitive comparisons.

Yet, she resented a little how he had come by his knowledge of how to please a woman. This even made her resist his stroking and coaxing, until at last she had to give in to her desire. Soon, they lay spent, both astonished all over again.

When they had dozed a while, he roused to kiss her nose. "You are my private siren, but none would guess it. Such a prudish look you have sometimes. I can't wait to gloat over you in church, looking so respectable, as you did when first I saw you. You'll make a regular churchgoer of me yet."

"That is about as shocking a reason for attendance as I can imagine." Still, she had to smile.

"You are only a slut for me, my virtuous one," he smiled in a vain way she found provoking.

"I wish I could say the same of you."

He laughed condescendingly. "My sweet innocent, males and females are made differently, and that's all there is to it. You wouldn't have liked a man who didn't know which bit of your charming body was which. You should thank all those other women for teaching me so well."

"I hope that you thanked them yourself, instead of scorning them."

He pinched her nose. "Clarinda, you don't know the world or the women of the town. It's typical of you to worry about 'em, though. You're sorry for everyone, aren't you, ghostly visions and harlots and all? I'm glad I'm not. It must be hellish uncomfortable. Still, I'm happy you were sorry for me that day my friend the Major set his bravoes on me."

Later, Clarinda, wearing a negligee, and her hair tumbled down sluttishly about her shoulders, wrote a letter of thanks to the Earl, feeling guilty that she hadn't done so before, crones, hooded spectres, or no.

She expressed her thanks to him as warmly as she dared, given the icy relations between him and his son. When she handed the note to Harley, he barely glanced at it before scrawling his name. His face was closed, and he muttered something about 'miserable old sticks' as he threw down the pen.

19.
A Fool

THE NEXT THREE WEEKS FLASHED by for Clarinda. There was no sign of the Crone or the Hooded Spectre. All was still in the maze.

When not making love, Clarinda and Harley spent many hours together. When it was dry, they went out riding, she on the placid mare he bought her, and then he was her riding tutor. In the evenings, he joined her soon after she withdrew, and always seemed sober. He played pieces on the violin or piano, and often she played too, and then he was her music tutor.

She was happy to leave the housekeeping largely to Mistress Mann. As for the O'Hare children, they rioted about, only calming when forced to go to school. Here they got a name for fighting of which the Viscount himself would have been proud.

As promised, Harley went with Clarinda to church. If he took no notice of the sermon, he sang beautifully, and managed to keep his hands off her during the service.

Clarinda took up her artwork again. She also searched the shelves in the library for something on vengeful spirits and family curses. Unsurprisingly, she found nothing.

Clarinda was enjoying the taste of the home farm's butter on her hot bread at breakfast, when Harley swore and slapped down his pot of small beer[45], scowling at the letter he had just opened.

"What is it?"

Crumpling it up, he thrust it into his pocket. "Another moral lecture; this time, from Great Aunt Georgiana in Lincolnshire."

Clarinda couldn't help wondering if his older relatives and respectable society might long have done better to ignore his outrages. He might then have tired of them on his own, whereas their homilies brought out the willfulness that she knew to be part of his nature.

He gave her a forced smile. "Anyway, she sends you her compliments."

He had no intention of showing Clarinda the letter, which said, in part: –

'I congratulate you on your nuptials. Be so good as to pass on my felicitations to the new Lady Venn.

How dare you, Sir, impose your boldface of a discarded mistress upon me, assuming that I am doting[46] and unable to deal with household cares? I saw at once what she was. You were presumptuous, Sir, in assuming that your elders are so afflicted with years that you can so easily cozen them.

I will not send the bold creature to Stoke Castle, as you deserve; it would be injudicious to impose her on your wife. Instead I will return her to your sister Barbara, and she can make such arrangements for her future as she thinks best, as she may have some influence upon her. I understood she was misguided enough to teach the wench to read and so, no doubt, come by improper notions...'

Babs wouldn't tell tales, though he supposed that their great aunt had written a strongly worded letter to her. He must send money to Betsy quickly.

Meanwhile, he distracted Clarinda by asking if she had come upon any views that she wished to paint.

---

45   Pot of Small Beer: Weak beer was often taken with breakfast, water often being unsafe.

46   Doting: In one's dotage, ie, confused.

"The one I wish most to depict chews ham and eggs after his morning's ride."

Clarinda thought that he looked incredibly handsome, with the sunshine lighting up his bright fair hair and the sparkling blue of his eyes.

His vanity gratified, he smiled carelessly, "I've no patience with standing still, but if you have set your heart upon doing a likeness, I'll make an effort. How would you like to paint me?"

"I'll flatter you," Clarinda assured him. "I'll ensure the bloated face and bleary eyes you have come by from years of excess find no place on the canvas."

Even as she teased, she noted again those slight lines etched by those excesses on his youthful face. They had lessened since they had been here. Yet, they were still visible.

He laughed. "You mind me: on red noses, old Dr Lodovico Sharman, Professor of the Arts of Tomfoolery comes to us on Monday, courtesy of my friends' wish. Somebody once said there was a resemblance between us. Damned cheek, eh?"

Something about his tone made her guess that this somebody was one of his former (she hoped) mistresses, perhaps Lady Hogg herself. What had caused that lady's stay in the country which so fascinated the gossips in Town?

O'Hare, sneering at Lodovico Sharman's battered bandboxes and frayed cuffs, brought him straight to Clarinda as she sat at her easel on the terrace, painting the view over the rose garden towards the hills.

As she greeted the Professor, he gazed at her in admiration. She wondered if this was done to flatter, and if he was pretending to be overwhelmed by her beauty.

She saw that this astonishingly tall man – inches taller than Venn– must once have been an imposing figure, though now battered and humbled by misfortune. With his hair dyed an improbable gold and his bloodshot eyes still retaining some of their bright blue, just as his reddened nose had yet a hawk-like shape in profile, Clarinda could see that he had once been handsome.

"I am happy you could come, Dr Sharman. Lord Venn has gone to view a horse, but he should not be long. Can I offer you any refreshments? Would you care to step inside?"

"Lady Venn, that is most kind. I am delighted to accept your hospitality." the Professor bowed low over her hand. As O'Hare left with the order, the visitor directed covert, startled glances at her as he praised the castle.

"It is a delightful place, Sir. I come from nearby, and I am happy to live in the countryside again. Unhappily, we have already had two visitations, convincing me that they must be supernatural. Lord Venn remains the sceptic. Perhaps you would rather await his return, Sir, before we discuss it?" She said the last reluctantly, recalling how as a married woman, she must at least seem to defer to her misguided spouse.

Dr Sharman lengthened his jaw and deepened the creases between his eyebrows. "Lady Venn, I regret that during the delay caused by the minor injuries I came by from my fall, there have been further developments."

Clarinda expressed sympathy. He made no mention of how he had come by that fall, and it seemed rude to ask. Perhaps he had no memory of it. Whether this was through drunkenness or a more sinister cause she had no idea, as he went on, "I would be grateful to have Your Ladyship's own impressions, if I may."

"It will be a relief to speak of it," she admitted.

This man might be the trickster Harley thought him, but she sensed genuine talents shining through his trickery. Or had he subjected her to his 'Subtle Influence' already, as he gazed at her almost reverentially with those weary blue eyes?

She told the story of the meetings with the crone and what she called 'her instrument' – which insisted that it had broken free.

She kept back the wording of both, which brought a flush to her cheeks as she thought of it. The crone had said that she had no interest in spying on herself and Harley in the bedchamber, and she had never sensed a ghostly presence as they made love. Still, both she and the Hooded Figure seemed to know of their sensual delight in each other, and to seek to ruin it with their gibes. So far, they had failed in that at least.

Lodovico Sharman glanced away as she reddened, no doubt drawing his own conclusions about what she called the 'vile abuse'.

Clarinda felt foolish as she related her urge to surround herself and Harley with silvery blue light.

The Professor sighed. "Heaven be thanked. Your Ladyship will forgive me, but I see your aura. You have spiritual power. You instinctively knew how to combat the evil influence of that being."

Clarinda was sceptical. "My aura?"

"Practitioners of the forgotten arts tend to see them, as do persons of sensibility, unconsciously. Thus we say that a person strikes us as being sincere or otherwise, for instance. It is simple to train oneself to see them. Yours has the colours of enlightenment."

Clarinda, with a vision of him saying the same to Nancy, tested him. "And Lord Venn's?"

The Professor cleared his throat. "His Lordship is naturally good-natured. Meanness of spirit is contrary to his character. He has outstanding courage and loyalty, and is capable of great generosity. His aura reflects this. He is impulsive, and a man of action, enjoying youthful vigour and high spirits. These qualities have so far precluded him from giving thought to spiritual matters."

Clarinda's lips twitched. "You would make a fine courtier, Sir."

"I hope you won't think me impertinent, in saying that your own qualities will be invaluable in combating this evil. But perhaps Lord Venn does not wish you to be involved."

"He may not; still, I must."

"Your pardon, Ma'am. I cut in before you ended your story.'"

As she finished, the Professor bowed. "Lady Venn, I thank you for so lucid an account of these horrors. I explained to the gentlemen before, that I suspect this being to be what the monks of Tibet call a Tulpa[47], a wraith created through thought forms for a purpose, and then destroyed. Yet, such can break free of their creator's will, developing an independent existence."

Clarinda shuddered. "I never heard of such a thing, and wish I had

---

47   Tulpa: A being created by the use of thought forms, according to the magical practices of Tibetian monks, who taught that such a being would develop an independent will and break free from its creator's control.

not now. Still, however sinister the motives of the Hooded Spectre or the Crone who made it, they are part of a Divine plan. That plan being incomprehensible to our finite minds, we are left with the problem of how to deal with the wretched beings before they do more harm."

Lodovico Sharman nodded. "Your Ladyship is wise. I must firstly try banishing rituals."

They heard horse hooves in the courtyard, the barking of dogs, and Clarinda felt her skin tingle and her colour rise as Venn came up. She put it down to feeling uneasy under the Professor's gaze.

Harley grinned wickedly as he greeted their guest. "Sorry I was out, but I am sure my wife has explained matters to your satisfaction." There was a touch of sarcasm in his voice, and he shot a wicked glance at Clarinda.

She said mildly, "You are too much the sceptic, Sir."

Yet, Lodovico Sharman seemed delighted as he watched them. He asked his host if still believed that these visitations could be explained as conjuring tricks.

Harley gestured impatiently. "No damned idea. My wife claims that hooded thing thrives on hatred. Damn me, I never hated any of my opponents in the ring, but after what it has done and said, you might as well advise me not to breathe as not to hate it."

"Lady Venn is correct, My Lord. A being created through dark magic draws strength from fear and anger. It must have worn away the nervous energy of the older men, and perhaps, Mr Foyle. Forgive my seeming impertinence, but were the households of the older men congenial ones?"

"Fraught as dammit, in the case of poor Foyle and the older Molyneux," said Harley. "They didn't get on with their wives. My uncle was twice married, but the old rascal didn't let that interfere with his vocation as rake. Even so, the talk that his wives died of broken hearts was so much blather. Women have more sense. Old Carstairs got through two wives too, and wanted to take Lady Venn here for his third, but she turned him down flat, sensible girl as she is."

He gave a self-congratulatory smile, as if sure that Clarinda's rejection of Sir Timothy was because she had been pining for him, for all that she had rejected him too. She felt needled.

The Professor still appeared oddly satisfied, given that he had to deal with so impossible a client as Harley Venn. Perhaps he was looking forward to his few days' stay at the castle, safe from his creditors in Town.

They had some refreshments together[48] in the morning room, served by the youngest footman. Clarinda thought that he looked as if he should be playing marbles rather than working. Inspired by sending the O'Hare's to school, she began to plan education for the staff.

Harley said, "Welch, Carstairs and Tomkins won't come up until the shooting season begins. Molyneux will be here in a couple of days, though, while Mr Smythe, who's taken Langton House nearby, comes with his wife to dinner tonight. She's a fine looking woman."

Clarinda and Harley had now been married for three weeks. It was natural that so sociable a man should start to want other company. Yet the thought of Tomkins' visit made her nervous. He was the wildest of Harley's closest friends, and she feared that he would urge his old companion to return to heavy drinking and worse.

It was provoking the way that so many women seemed to encourage Harley's flirtatious ways. Mistress Smythe was pleasant, but she would make eyes at the rascal. Then, when last he had taken Clarinda out for a ride they had stopped at an inn for a rest. Here, the full mouthed serving wench had pouted on him as she leaned over to serve them.

Clarinda realised with dismay that she was jealous.

She had enjoyed their time alone together more than she could have believed as she trudged down the aisle on James' arm. Then, her great dread was being married to a man she couldn't approve, and must come to dislike.

Now she feared her tragedy might be to be married to a man she couldn't approve – and liked too well.

Clarinda, you begin to match your name for silliness. You will soon act like that heroine in that latest novel that Abbey devours in her bed at night – 'The Cursed Count and His Innocent Bride'. Of course, in that, only lurid symbolism signifies their marital embraces.

---

48   Refreshments together: Lunch was taken by middle and upper class females rather than males until early Victorian times.

If your Viscount runs through all Uncle Greendale's fortune, besides the remaining half he has from his own, will you be reduced to supporting him, yourself, and four or five heirs, by penning such tales? Perhaps he will help raise funds as a Professor of Pugilism, Marksmanship and Music.

She turned her mind to the immediate threat, and went with this man she had married as he showed Dr Sharman about the castle.

Dr Sharman lingered in some places, raising his eyebrows, dropping his jaw, and twitching his deep-cut nostrils. Whenever he did this, Harley winked at Clarinda and she pretended not to see.

"That is one of the secret passages, Professor," Harley said, as Sharman paused by part of the oak panelling in the library. He never came in here, unlike Abigail, who had found tempting reading material on the shelves, perhaps bought by Toby Venn's wives. Clarinda loved equally the massive room's elegant proportions and the collection of books.

Her heart lurched as she saw that a panel was open by an inch. Dr Sharman put his ear against it, and nodded solemnly. Now muffled wailing became audible to them all.

Harley swore. "It's those O'Hare' brats, and lost." Drawing back the panel to uncover a gaping dark hole out of which wafted an icy draught, he yelled up it.

Desperate howls came down: "We'll die here!"

"Seán's light went out!"

"Where are you, you confounded little devils? Hold fast: we'll get you, never fear. Don't try and move or you'll break your stupid necks. Mind that: I'll know if you shift an inch. Wait while I get a light." He pulled his head out and went to roar at the door for a covered light and quick about it.

Clarinda, with more energy than modesty, started to tie up her skirts to go in too. She sensed no threat in the secret passageway more sinister than its darkness and the narrowness of the steps. That, though, was bad enough; she dreaded the panicking youngsters would fall to their deaths.

"You'll only delay me up if you come, so I've got you to worry about, too. Leave your skirts down," Harley told her, and turned to Lodovico Sharman, who had thrust his head into the opening. "I won't impose on you as my guest, Sir."

"I sense no presence there," said Lodovico Sharman. "But I confess,

Lord Venn, that I abhor enclosed, dark spaces. I hope you will forgive my not joining you."

"Them ghosts is after us!" the boy's voice wailed.

"Of course, they're not." Harley shouted back. "They've got better things to do than waste their time on brats like you. Be a man and keep tight hold of your sister, or I won't let you ride on the new donkey."

Clarinda's lips twitched as Peg's voice floated down, "I'm the one holding *his* hand."

The footman came in with the light, and Harley climbed into the passageway, yelling again for the miscreants to keep still and wait for him. The sound of his ascent, echoing reassurances, and the lamentations of the youngsters drifted back to them.

"It is good of His Lordship to go in after them himself," Lodovico Sharman said to Clarinda. The footman nodded enthusiastically. Clarinda assented coldly. For some reason which she did not understand, she was in no mood to admire this.

With much shuffling, the sound of the voices approached, and Harley appeared, carrying the girl on his back and leading the boy by the hand.

They were all begrimed and covered with cobwebs. Some stuck to Harley's hair, while all O'Hare's work on the gloss of his boots had been in vain.

The filthy children howled. Clarinda moved to comfort them, but Harley took her arm. "I like you in that dress, and don't want it ruined."

Giving the youngsters a friendly pat, he pushed them over to the footman. "See they're cleaned up, Ned, and shut 'em up with cake. Mind, brats, if you ever play that trick again, we'll leave you in there all night. Curse it, I'm filthy. I'll have to change. Do you know your way about enough to show our visitor, My Lady?"

He pressed the lever which worked the mechanism, and the panel slid to. Then he walked off, whistling.

Clarinda stood dumbfounded.

This cannot be happening to a sensible, down-to-earth girl like me. Oh please, not with 'The Villainous Viscount'...

20.
'Pamela' and Tussles

July 1821

JACK MOLYNEUX CALLED ON LADY Barbara Davenport a couple of days before he was to leave for Stoke Castle. He was astonished to meet Betsy in the hallway. She lowered her eyes when she curtsied, just as if she had never met him, untroubled, naked on the attic stairs in Venn's town house.

"I see you've taken on Harley's maid," he remarked to Lady Barbara.

"Yes. To speak true, she was sent to me in disgrace by our Great Aunt Georgiana after he sent her up there to be housekeeper. She suspected them. Doubtless she was right. Still, I don't see why the woman in the case must always suffer the consequences, and never the man, and so I kept her on."

She smiled wickedly. "It's an absurd instance of like master, like servant, for the girl claims to be a reformed character. It all came of her helping herself to Aunt Georgiana's copy of Richardson's '*Pamela*' by way of revenge. I had helped her reading at my classes for the staff, you know, while she worked for Harley. Seemingly, she had never tried a novel before. Anyway, she was overcome by the tale, and has sworn to be another Pamela herself from now onwards."

"That is as ridiculous a story as ever I heard." Molyneux grinned.

"Besides, she is an excellent nurse. I saw how well she looked after Harley after that beating. She's been invaluable in easing the children through the measles. I only hope…Come in!" she cried, at a scratching at the door. "Yes, Betsy?"

The maid said, "We fear that Wilmot has the spots too, Ma'am."

"But he's not yet two," Barbara's lips trembled.

Molyneux flinched. The baby was a favourite of his uncle, who had introduced him to Molyneux. Too many babies sickened and died, which was why Molyneux avoided becoming attached to most. This infant had got past his guard.

As he told her, "He's young, but he's as hearty as his parents. He'll sail though this, you'll see," his tone rang false even to him.

Lady Barbara forced herself to sound cheerful as she showed Molyneux out. Though clearly desperate to go to the nursery, she asked if he had found any suitable heiresses.

"I don't have your rascal brother's title to tempt 'em," smiled Molyneux. "When you've a healthy household again, you must look out for one for me. Get off to the nursery to return the youngster back to health as soon as may be."

Molyneux went home thoughtful. He dined with Carstairs and the piratical looking Tomkins – so often Venn's companion for a wild night in the lowest company and dressed accordingly – and a couple of debauched cronies at the Coconut Club. He wished he hadn't.

Tomkins was determined to keep his circle of friends staunch rakes as long as he could. He had already been disappointed at Carstairs' drawing back from wild living before having more than a taste of it.

He laughed to scorn Venn's boasts of reform, while Molyneux's waning gusto for excess troubled him. Now Venn had wasted a three weeks in the country with an innocent bride, with the summer season over now George was crowned.[49] He shook his head more in sorrow than anger over their backsliding. To be debauched took conviction.

---

49   George was crowned: George IV's coronation was on 19 July 1821

"Have you heard from our rusticating friend?" he asked Molyneux.

"Not since last week's scrawl, saying he's delighted with his bride, and never thought he'd settle down so happily to married life."

Tomkins sneered. "Can't be that he's in love, eh, except with her moneybags. The rascal will be back in Town, maybe even before I leave. I heard today that Lady Hogg's got the better of her indisposition – wasn't poisoned[50] as some said – and after all, don't Venn use them skin sheaths? With those apple dumplings[51], that woman's a bloody tempting armful I'd love to tumble myself, unlike that whey-faced[52] Mistress Princum Prancum[53] he's wed. "

Carstairs flushed up red and stammered, while Molyneux said acidly, "You're half in your cups, Tomkins, but if Venn was by, you'd mind how you spoke about his wife. Beauty's a matter of opinion, and perhaps he finds her better company than us. You've never liked women, though."

"Yes, I do – opera girls and Covent Garden nuns[54] who'll raise their skirts for a consideration. But the respectable chits who hold out for marriage – Lord save me from the clutches of any of 'em till my beard parter[55] starts drooping."

Neither Molyneux nor Carstairs had been in a mood of late to endure Tomkins' talk. Swarthy face rouged and furrowed with concern, he begged them to take more drink. When they rose to leave, he and the others at the table abused them as traitors. They laughed and made off before as the others could stagger up to push them back into their seats. No sinister figure appeared to them as they went down the winding staircase.

They walked home through the littered and ill smelling midsummer

---

50   Poisoned: Pregnant.

51   Apple dumplings: Breasts.

52   Whey faced: Plain.

53   Mistress Princum Prancum: A stiff, proper women.

54   Covent Garden nuns: Prostitutes.

55   Beard parter: Penis.

streets, past vagrants and revellers, taking the same route that Molyneux had taken with Venn on the night of Foyle's death.

Carstairs cursed Tomkins. Molyneux, whose sense of melancholy had – aided by the drink he had taken – mellowed into a feeling of general goodwill, shrugged. "He can't help being low minded. Still, the old life starts to disgust me. I hope Venn keeps to his vows, though sadly for his wife I doubt it – but whatever he does, I want to change. In a way, it was our friend the Hooded Spectre, who started me thinking of it, and what poor Foyle said that night."

Carstairs tried to hide his shudder. "Don't speak of the thing, Jack; it seems to bring it closer. We're still no nearer to finding out what it is. Lord knows if that Professor fellow will do any good. I can't believe in his powers, but he's all we have got. And Venn insists still it is the work of a conjuror. I hope the thing hasn't appeared to him and his wife, as it did when he was with Welch. Welch is lucky; it said he wasn't involved."

"It's confounded tiresome, I know," Molyneux gripped his arm. "Remember not to let it play on your nerves as did our elders'. That's how it gets to you, I'll warrant. I'm due up at Stoke Castle tomorrow, and I'll see what goes on."

They parted near Molyneux's house, and he laughed as he watched the boy stride off. "His calf love must be wearing off, if he can call the former Miss Greendale, 'Venn's wife'."

This season, he had taken a house in an unfashionable street further north. Venn hadn't been the only one forced to cut back on his expenses. Having sent his man to bed, nobody was up to greet him. He let himself in with his own key.

Laughing, he mounted the stairs. Halfway up, he saw the being materialise at the top.

He sensed it detested him particularly now, because he tried to put his debauchery behind him, and so would be free of it. It dreaded their escape. As it existed to destroy them, it revelled in the degradation that gave it power over them.

It billowed towards him, arms outstretched. Despite the horrible mode of its approach, he felt resentment rather than fear. In the instant that he tensed to meet its attack, he sensed that it had lately been baulked, perhaps even drained of power. This could be the answer to how his friends at the castle had been.

He would not flinch. "So, you're back at your tricks. Why don't you say what you want?"

Now the thing paused, towering over him. "I must destroy you," its voice echoed in his mind. "Your fate was decided before you were born."

"Filthy monster!" Thinking of poor Foyle, and of his late father, Molyneux felt a surge of rage. A chill seemed to freeze him to the spot. He would fight, of course, and he sensed this must be a lethal combat. He would, like Harley Venn, fight anyone or anything, whatever the odds – that was one of the reasons they so valued each other – but the lust to destroy that swept over him was outside his experience.

Even as the monster closed in on him, he tried to resist this. But thoughts of his father tormented him. Molyneux senior's wrongdoings had been far worse than his own – he had trampled on his inferiors, ruined innocents, and betrayed friends. Yet, faulty as he had been, his son had loved him, and this thing had driven him to madness, and finally destroyed him. He must hate it for that.

Time seemed frozen as the thing loomed over him, skeletal arms raised to strike, and he battled to free himself from the icy weight to rend it into pieces.

"Come, wretch: your noble friend cowers behind his latest conquest's skirts, but there's no tender fool here to intercede for you. Meet the fate you deserve."

Though the ticking of the grandfather clock in the hall below was drawn out, that voice invading his mind was not.

There had been tender fools enough in Jack Molyneux's life. If it hadn't been for the disgust with debauchery that had lately come over him, one might be with him now.

"Your father was a coward. That ancient witch taunted him from mirrors, reducing his arrogance to craven terror. He even offered her that family ring on your finger."

Molyneux managed to stagger up one stair, groping for the phantom. One clear patch of his mind demanded: "Why?" He would like to know that, though he believed that he must die in this struggle.

If she will not come to you willing, then take the wench by force. She'll forgive you soon enough afterwards. Don't she like you well? She wants to come to you. Her commodity[56] *says yes, her scruples say no. What ails you to act so the booby? Play the man, and put you both out of misery.*

This speech from the being sounded in his head as something learned by rote until it had lost meaning. This, Molyneux sensed, was the force that had created this monster. It had been fashioned through hatred to pursue its maker's campaign of revenge, and knew nothing else. He understood this even as his reason seemed to give under the repulsive onslaught, and with a final effort he reached the monster, and grappled with it on the stairs.

Like Harley's before him, his fingers burst through the being's frame as through a glutinous membrane. For all its skeletal look, it was malleable. Groaning, he fought to tear it to pieces. Gurgling, its icy hands reached towards his neck. He smashed his fist repeatedly into that shrouded face, and it was as if he beat on jelly. He jabbed his fingers into its eyes, and gouged his fingers into it viscous flesh, trying to rip pieces off its face. The thing gurgled still, and its hands edged ever closer to his throat.

Balancing ever more carelessly on the stairs, he threw it. He kicked it. He pounded it. It dispersed and reformed. He smashed those hands that looked so bony, and they tore and reappeared. His breath came in gasps.

Then two voices came on him. One, incredibly, was Harley's, his tone mocking: 'My innocent even said, Jack, that we should pray for Lucifer himself.'

The other was from his mother, by contrast the most orthodox of believers: 'Vengeance is mine, sayeth the Lord'.

He discerned that these words were his door back to sanity and rescue. He stopped, wheezing, "No, you poor wretch, no…"

The thing's voice hissed and chanted in his mind. "Ignore that cant. Destroy… Destroy…"

The voice echoed in his ears. Now it had him by the throat and shook him like a rat. He burst free and felt himself losing balance at last, falling and rolling into searing pain and blackness.

---

56   Commodity: Vagina.

21.
𝕸irrors and 𝕻ortraits

"I BELIEVE THIS MAY BE THE focus of power," said Lodovico Sharman. He and Clarinda stood in the first drawing room, the one Harley never used. The dustsheets had been removed in honour of the new Lady Venn's arrival, but Clarinda had never explored the room.

Harley, who had taken her in when showing her about the castle, had said, "I suppose my grandfather had the Hall of Mirrors in Versailles in mind when he had the room panelled with these mirrors and decorated with gold leaf, and those murals painted on the ceiling. I don't like the place, myself."

Neither did Clarinda. Far more than in the picture gallery, she had the sense of being watched by the life sized portraits which hung on the walls, while the great mirrors everywhere gave a sense even of being watched by oneself. Besides, she was too critical of her looks to enjoy seeing herself from all angles.

She supposed that poor Dr Sharman liked seeing his ravaged looks reflected all about the room still less. As he spoke, almost to himself, she saw a blurring and shifting in the glass. She thought of the mirror from Uncle Greendale that she had brought up from London, and had placed in her dressing room.

Someone had removed its wrappings. She had draped it in a shawl, pushing it behind a chest. She had wondered if she should destroy it. Still, she had the intuition that she would regret it if she did, for if it was a focus for this evil, it was also a part of the solution. Perhaps though, it was not so significant. It was only one mirror among many.

She replied to the Professor now, "The focus of power, Sir?"

"Your pardon, Ma'am, I spoke without thinking. I believe that if the energies gather anywhere, it is here."

"Yet, we saw that Hooded Spectre in the sunken garden."

"Truly. Yet his mistress…" he broke off, fondling his cleft chin. "I think she needs mirrors. They must be dealt with separately. I sense that here, something gathers force."

Clarinda realised that she agreed, and flinched. He smiled. "Be assured that we will end this generational curse, and that you and Lord Venn have more protection through each other than you perceive."

"We have need of good angels," murmured Clarinda, "For I am little enough of one, myself."

The Professor smiled. "We each bear a spark of the divine. What separates the best of humans from the worst is allowing its influence."

"It was in a mirror that I have brought from London that I first saw the Crone," Clarinda told him. "It came from my Uncle Greendale. As you know, he was formerly Tobias Venn's steward. You know too, of his violent death in France."

Lodovico Sharman bowed, and moved on. Now Clarinda gazed with dissatisfaction at her image.

The afternoon sunshine turned her hair into a golden halo, and emphasized the youthful flawlessness of her skin and counters of her face and the clearness of her eyes, while it warmed the material of her peach coloured dress. But she thought herself short and dumpy.

It was unfair. How could any man fall in love with so prosaic looking a woman? Harley liked her best in this dress, so she must look worse in the others. She might have a fine, high bosom and a neat waist, but she was short-waited, with hips too full and her behind over ample, though he was forever praising it lasciviously. Her neck was short. As for her face, it had nothing particularly wrong with it and nothing particularly right with it either. Her wide set, lively brown eyes were her best feature.

"Here is Tobias Venn," her companion exclaimed, striding over to one of the life-sized portraits.

This likeness must have been taken between those of the youth and the one of the aging rake she had seen in the gallery. The young man was still arrogant and strikingly handsome, yet there was now a jaded look to his eyes and turn to his lips. There were no lines of debauchery. Clarinda could imagine the artist leaving them out, for she knew they would be etched on his face deeper than they were on his nephew's.

Glancing at the portrait next to it, she saw the name, "John Molyneux". The father was as dark as the son, his wide mouth smiling as recklessly. Those dark eyes had the same intelligence, but none of the kindness of the son's.

Clarinda turned, knowing whose painted eyes would return her stare next. Sir Timothy Carstairs in youth was scarcely much more appealing than he had been in old age, though he had more teeth and hair.

Finally, she came on Francis Foyle, the only one of the set still alive, also dark, tall and rangy. Clarinda wondered how he took the death of his son. She didn't like to ask Harley.

"There will be a secret passage," said Dr Sharman.

"Right enough, Professor: it leads up to the roofs," Harley Venn strode into the room, full of high spirits. "D'you want to see it? If those little brats are in it, I swear they can stay put till O'Hare shows his face."

The Professor looked almost alarmed. "I thank Your Lordship, but no."

At Venn's appearance, Clarinda's heart seemed to somersault. There was no doubting her feelings now.

The dinner party went well. Mistress Smythe smiled constantly, and had a pretty way of doing things. A wicked part of Clarinda's imagination pictured her smiling sweetly when using the closet.

The men were pleased with her, and Harley and Mr Smythe took it in turns to tell her tall stories to see how much she would swallow. Dr Sharman complimented everything and everybody. Sometimes he fell into a minute's reverie, but soon revived when Harley signed for the footman to refill his glass.

The men's glasses often needed refilling over dinner. When Mistress Smythe followed Clarinda to the second drawing room, she exclaimed, "Lud! It is always so, when my husband meets with the Viscount. Now they'll linger over their port and brandy for hours."

Clarinda smiled. Then we shall do very well without them."

They chatted for some while before the gentlemen joined them. They were all flushed, though Harley and the Professor were too well seasoned to show how much they had taken. Mr Smith was unsteady on his feet as he saluted his wife. "We've been saying how we want you to sing, dearest."

Clarinda made tea and coffee while Mistress Smythe sang for them. Clarinda, talking Dr Sharman his coffee, saw him start at her approach. "Excuse me, Lady Venn. I am troubled by a sense that something unfortunate has happened."

Clarinda thought from her own point of view it had, with her discovery that she was in love with the rascal who had married her for money. The Professor went on, "Forgive me. It is my role to give you reassurance, and as speedy a resolution to your troubles as I can. It is only because you are so evolved a soul that I confide this to you."

Harley broke off from assuring Mistress Smythe in between songs how as a boy he had taught his monkey to play the piano, to wink at Clarinda.

Ignoring him, and repressing a smile at the Professor's calling her 'evolved' Clarinda said, "But what is it you fear?"

He drew himself up in his seat. "Fear, Ma'am, is a sentiment unknown to Lodovico Sharman. Apprehension on behalf of others is another matter. I sense that one of the gentlemen in London may have come to harm."

"Gracious!" Now that Clarinda came to think of it, she had a sense of unease herself. She had thought it was part of her own concerns.

"All that we can do – and forgive me, Lady Venn, for imposing on you — is to surround us all, far and near, with a protective aura as you did for Lord Venn and yourself in the maze."

"I will be do my best," said Clarinda, as Mistress Smythe finished her last song, and they joined in the applause.

Now Harley insisted that Clarinda perform, and so she went to piano to sing *Barbara Allen* as he had taught her. Her audience was impressed and Harley looked smug.

After that he gave them a version of the factotum aria from *The Barber of Seville* that made even Lodovico Sharman laugh.

The hills rang with birdsong and pink tinged the sky as the Smythes' carriage rattled down the drive. A fresh evening breeze blew, and Clarinda shivered, thinking of the maze, out of sight from here, darkening under that roseate sky. It seemed to her that one must be brave indeed to venture there at dusk.

Harley put an arm about her. "You are chilly, my sweet. I have plans to warm you. An enjoyable and respectable evening. You must be delighted with my taking so little."

"It was a nice evening. But I would be even happier if you and your male guests drank still less."

He stared, and she saw the futility of arguing with a man slightly under the influence. "You joke, surely, or else have become a household tyrant. Next you will insist I take only Adam's Ale. You should have seen the amount I used to put away in Town."

"I am happy to have missed that marvel. I would not have you return gradually to your former drinking habits. You scowl, Harley. Only recently you wished to elevate me to the position of your 'Angel Monitress'. Now, it seems I am to be demoted to 'Domestic Tyrant' for performing the exact role you begged me to play."

For a second he stared wordlessly. He soon had a retort: "Humph! That comes of marrying a clever woman. Don't discourage me of making any effort, through being too hard to please." He nodded smugly. She was sure that from now on, he would regularly use this argument.

"I don't believe a woman has to be clever to object to either being elevated to a saint or demoted to a tartar. I don't doubt the charming but unthinking Mistress Smythe will let Smythe see her disapproval."

His gave a low laugh. "I see that this is down to female vanity, and you would be too angelic if you didn't have a bit of that. Own you are piqued, because I admire that little chit. Still, you mustn't take it amiss; I much prefer my own armful." He tickled her waist.

Many emotions surged through Clarinda. She replied as calmly as she could. "You are mistaken. It is merely that I do not want you to return to excessive drinking. As for your admiration of Mistress Smythe, I would be a great fool to object to that, when passion hardly dictated your choice in me."

She had no sooner spoken, than she cursed herself. What had led her to needle him, so that he might state truths that she must now find exquisitely painful? Did she imagine that, like the hero in one of Abbey's novels, he would suddenly discover a deep love for her, and they would walk off arm in arm into the sunset?

"It didn't dictate yours," he said, eyebrows raised.

She made no reply, and he smiled, patting her cheek. "We have only been married three weeks, but I become accustomed to you already. Life is so comfortable with you, it's like wearing my old Hessians.[57]"

"There is nothing like being compared to an old shoe or boot," said Clarinda. "I thank you for the compliment."

He pulled a comical face. "Damn it, you know I did not mean it like that: I've told you how I find you prettier every day."

"I thank you... Look at those bats." She gazed up at a great swarm passing overhead.

It was a wonderful sunset, setting the sky aflame, creating islands in the sky of brilliant yellow. It was a shame to waste it through not falling in love and walking off into it. But a man didn't tend to fall in love with his comfortable footwear.

That night, Clarinda was tired. Dismay at her discovery of her feelings for this villain had tired her far more than any dread of spectres.

She marvelled at her bad taste. He had killed a man in a duel; aristocrats – with the exception of the Earl of Aylesbury – might take a lenient view of that – but she did not.

Ironically, the thing that had most disgusted society with him – his way of keeping the lowest company dressed as a costermonger –worried her least.

---

57   Hessians: A fashionable form of boot.

What did trouble her, was that he was so savage, delighting in brawling, and that he went in for excesses of every sort, and had made use of any number of her sex for his heartless pleasure.

And this man was her love object! When she had sworn to love him, she had foreseen a calm, disinterested type of love. It was all too bad.

Yet, when he came through their adjoining dressing rooms, smiling teasingly, she still tingled. Most of the effects of his heavy drinking tonight had worn off, save perhaps for his being even more carefree than usual.

Now, merely to hold him in her arms was a joy. It was a sorry thing, to be in love with such a rascal, yet tonight she would be a coward. She wouldn't think of his past misdeeds, or the likelihood of future ones (assuming they could defeat the spectres, which she had to believe).

Tonight, she would not fret over the women who had held him likewise while he pleasured them. She had often done that before, when they lay talking together, sated for the moment. She must think of them again in the future, though it did no good, for he would not discuss them.

For tonight, though, she would allow herself to be selfish. For her this sensuous joy between them was unique; she was sure that with other lovers, however, desirable, she would not have it. As he had been her first she could not be certain; still, she sensed it. But she had no idea about whether this was so, for him. She didn't think it was vanity, or wishful thinking, that made her suspect that a special bond had grown between them.

Certainly, he had been astounded that first time by how effortlessly they could join in pleasure.

It was a joy to run her hands over him, delighting in those muscles. Yes; and how had he come by this spare and muscular physique? That was partly through training to fight savagely in a ring.

But she would no more think of that than of her predecessors, or of the future. She would revel unthinking tonight as the pleasure became sharper, a pulsing torment almost, and they both found shuddering release.

He soon enough fell asleep. She lay propped on one elbow, looking at him. At this time of year, especially on nights like this, it never seemed to become completely dark, even without the moon. The sky only turned into the deepest midnight blue.

Besides, a candle guttered on the mantelpiece, and by its darting light she gazed at him, noting the Grecian line of his nose, the candlelight glowing on the gold in his hair, side whiskers, and the hair on his chest. As never before, she moved forwards, and kissed his cheek.

The words of the skeletal spectre in the maze came back to haunt her. She had scarcely taken them in then, as her heart thudded with fear – not for herself. It had spoken of betrayal, and soon. Did it know the future, or did it merely seek to sow dissent between them?

Now she came back to the present. She thought of that mirror from London, shrouded in her dressing room. She should have the courage to uncover it, gaze into it, and confront the Crone.

She would have done so before, but dreaded raising something that she could not control. When the Professor said that she had spiritual strength, was that the truth? If he was the charlatan that Harley believed, what he said was of no account. Perhaps, though, he was only half a charlatan, and together they might succeed.

22.
My Daughter, Oh, My Daughter

"'Come back, come back," he cried in grief,
"Across the stormy water.
And I'll forgive your highland chief,
My daughter, oh, my daughter".

CLARINDA WOKE WITH THOSE WORDS in her head. They held a
key, she was sure.

She pulled a face as the memory that she had fallen stupidly
in love with her impossible rascal of a husband flooded over her. She was
hardly alone in that. It must happen even to the most sensible of wives.
It was a commonplace fate, probably, though most rakes were hardly as
outrageous as he.

At some point before dawn, Harley had left for his own bed. He
always did, though often he groaned, and asked how it was that she had
such an effect on him that it knocked him out for hours as the best of
his opponent's never had in the ring. Clearly, his knees were weak as he
stumbled from her bed.

She always laughed carelessly, to disguise her joy. He truly was
transported by his workaday looking wife as he never had been with his
society beauties. She had to gloat over that; but she rebuked herself; she
should not feel rivalry towards these women.

Yet, she wished that he would stay, too unguarded even to wake until Abbey tapped at the door. Somehow, that would confirm that this bond between them had an element not purely physical. But always, he climbed from her bed with the earliest tweet from the birds or cock crow from the home farm.

But now was no time to dwell on this. She had a sense that she must do something to defeat the threat that hung over them, and at once. She jumped out of bed, huddled on her dressing gown, and went through to the dressing room.

She peeped round at the wrapped mirror, pushed out of sight. What was the point of trying to summon the Crone? She remembered the wretched female's words – or thoughts, for Clarinda knew that she was not truly speaking fluent English – about not being able to stop what had been started.

On impulse, she hurried down the passage to the enlarged windows which looked over the western part of the grounds. Glistening with dew and still draped with long shadows, they lay before her in all the morning's renewal.

Her heart lurched as she saw a tall, cloaked figure moving towards the maze. Then she recognised it as the Professor. Turning, she darted lightly back to the bedroom to pull on a loose morning gown. She didn't trouble with her hair, leaving it free.

Sometimes Harley liked to enjoy her with it plaited, dressed in one of her modest nightdresses. He gloated that made her look yet more the innocent prude, as if looking for nothing more exciting by way of a night's entertainment than a chapter of some footling novel. Sweeping her up and carrying her to the bed, he assured her that he would give her some better amusement than that. Last night, though, he had freed her hair to fall in waves about her breasts.

The house was locked, but Clarinda met a sleepy-looking footman on the front stairs. She asked him to open the nearest door.

He blinked, perhaps finding it hard to recognise Lady Venn in this figure in a robe, with her hair swinging about her waist. "I must fetch the keys from Mann, Your Ladyship."

"Is there no other way?" Clarinda tapped her foot. "I must see to something betimes. I don't mind which door I use; I'll go out through the kitchens if necessary."

He bowed. "There's the side door, if Your Ladyship would please to follow me."

"Thank you. Please make haste."

Soon, she sped through the grounds towards the maze, holding up her skirts and soaking her slippers in the grass wet with dew. Lodovico Sharman had vanished inside.

Apprehension seized her as she entered, hoping that she knew the turns. She had memorised them when coming in with Harley here since their tussle with the being.

Turn left, turn right, go straight on...

Now she heard sounds, and her heart lurched again, for they came distorted. She began to murmur prayers for protection and guidance.

She heard a rhythmical chanting from the Professor. That was reassuring, but a distant rumbling, so low that she felt rather than heard it, was anything but.

"Poor foolish being, its voice will never rival Harley's," she quipped to keep up her spirits, as she trotted down the paths between the high hedges. Now she came to the centre.

By the fountain in the centre of the garden – where the spray sparkled, jewel-like, and the scent of water mingled with the perfume of the blooms in the beds all about, Lodovico Sharman stood, arms raised, hands grasping two smoking sticks of incense.

She could not make out his chant, and thought that he spoke in Latin. She supposed he worked a summoning ritual prior to one of banishment. Her heart lurched at the thought that he was calling up that hideous being from whatever plane in which it existed when not haunting people.

She comforted herself with another joke. "It is slow in answering. Perhaps it is fatigued."

Then a chill struck her as she guessed that it had exhausted itself in a recent destruction. Who had it attacked, Jack Molyneux or young Sir Frederick Carstairs? But it had not come for Harley since he left her bed. She would have sensed that, she was sure.

The Professor's voice rang in her ears. He was not now the humble suitor to patrons. He was strong in his role as practitioner of the arcane, where rank and worldly success counted for nothing. He threw out his chest and summoned the being as of right.

The rumbling increased. Clarinda saw the magician stiffen as he realised her presence. She repeated her prayers for them all – and especially the being. She sent out a wave of blue light, surrounding them all.

With a muted flash, and a roar that seemed to shake the ground under their feet, the being stood before Lodovico Sharman. A wind buffeted the sheltered garden.

Though summoned, the creature was as arrogant and threatening as the demons supposedly raised by the black arts. It loomed over the Professor, cloak billowing. "You dare to summon me, you besotted fool?" It moved as if to seize him.

Clarinda surrounded him with light. "You poor creature, is there nothing in the universe for you, but destruction?"

It pointed one skeletal arm at her. A hideous urge to destroy surged over her. She beat it back with brilliant light, and returned a blessing on it.

Its disembodied voice came sneering as ever. "Cease your mawkish blather. Go and look in the mirrors to test your charity."

Yet, it drew back, and then wavered at some force directed at it by Lodovico Sharman. "Do such as you seek to destroy me – a sottish, ne'er-do-well stage conjurer and a libertine's lawful slut?"

It sprang upon the Professor, fingers reaching for his throat. Something knocked it back. It threw out one arm, pointing a finger at him. She saw – or sensed – a charge of dark energy hit him like a charging beast, knocking him to his knees. The being's shriek of triumph rang in her ears.

Lord protect us! Yet, I know it cannot really harm us.

The ugly voice sneered: "Then why, dirty wallowing whore, did Tobias Venn die where we stand? Now this imposter can follow him and then Harley Venn soon afterwards."

Fighting to remain calm, Clarinda wound all about them all a brilliant light. The effort was immense; her breath came in gasps.

She saw the sunken garden changed to an oozing swamp. The stench of decay rose all about. She fought not to retch. An onslaught of hatred for the creature and its creator slapped her, almost driving all thought out of her mind. Staggering, wheezing, hair flying, choking in the miasma, she tried to block out the sounds of chaos sounding in her ears.

Somehow, she withstood it, struggling on with her light and benedictions.

The Professor of Magic staggered to his feet. His once handsome, bloated face, now set with purpose, was as near noble as she could have imagined. Throwing up his arms, he chanted in Latin.

In turn, a driving wind tore the cloak from the spectre like a giant hand. It was revealed as a cadaver, strings of muscle visible across its half dissolved flesh. Its lantern jaw fell open, and its mouth became cavernous with its howls.

All about, the sunken garden changed back and forth as in some mechanical magic display. At one instant the wasteland was before her eyes, at another the garden of roses.

"Look to the light... find peace..." Clarinda gasped.

With a final hiss, the being sank into the paving stones before them, giving off an oily smoke.

Clarinda heard running footfalls. Still concentrating on the light, not daring to turn her head, from the corner of her eye she saw Harley sprint into the maze, wild looking and dishevelled, just in time to see the being dissolve into the stones as a living thing might be sucked into a marsh.

He dashed towards it, and the skeletal hands clutched out towards his booted feet as it vanished.

Once again, the sunken garden was restored, the scent of the rose beds restored.

Then, Clarinda saw the figure of the maiden. She stood beside the fountain, transparent in her old-fashioned dress and cap of thirty years since. Again she seemed to give warning. Her face was impassive, as in a painting, while she pointed towards the castle roof.

The garden seemed to be moving back and forth; then Clarinda realised that it was she who swayed, as Harley caught hold of her, steadying her. She saw that he was in his shirtsleeves, his shirt gaping open at the throat, his hair tousled. His eyes sparked: she realised he was furious.

She had to lean on him, too breathless to speak, as he raged at the Professor: "What goes on, Sharman? What do you mean by involving my wife in your damned flummery?"

The Professor made no attempt to defend himself. Crouched and gasping like Clarinda, he was perhaps too breathless.

Clarinda wheezed, "He didn't...I did."

The blue of Harley's eyes blazed still more: "What d'you mean? You gave me your word."

"I did have protection, as I promised... from what I've learnt myself...I could not leave the Professor to fight alone..."

Clarinda saw her mistake as Harley turned on Lodovico Sharman. "Sharman protected you?" He made no effort to hide the contempt in his tone.

She saw that the rascal was angry that she had fought as part of a team with somebody else, and for saying that she could not leave another to fight alone. No doubt he didn't see that, but she could guess. The horror he had seen, with the being's disappearing into that stone, troubled him less.

"I protected myself throughout," Clarinda murmured. "I should have told you, but I came on impulse, when I saw Dr Sharman from the long gallery window. He did not willingly involve me."

"Lady Venn's help was invaluable," Lodovico Sharman said. "I must apologise for having been the cause of Your Lordship's concern for her safety. Yet, without her, I might not have withstood so powerful an entity. With it, it is possible my ritual has banished it."

Harley stared. "You think you've defeated whatever it is?"

"I hope so. But it is far easier for the creator of a Tulpa to dissolve it, than for an outsider to do so."

"Beg pardon, Sir," Harley said. "I did you an injustice in assuming you drew my wife into this, rather than that she acted impulsively, as so often." His tone was not, however, indulgent. Clearly, he was still angry with her.

The Professor of Magic said, "I can only admire the courage and determination Lady Venn showed throughout that tussle, and be thankful for the confidence with which you have both honoured me."

Whether he spoke with any irony, Clarinda could not guess. Harley said, "Humph."

He was still holding Clarinda – she assumed automatically – and now she was shivering in the morning chill. He added, "We'll talk of this later. Meanwhile, my wife needs tea, and no doubt too, Sir, you would like a glass of something stronger."

Now Harley's tone was certainly ironical, but the Professor of Magic looked eager as he bowed his thanks and hurried to pick up the extinguished sticks of incense. Clarinda wondered when they had gone out.

They walked back through the corridors formed by the high hedges, with Harley holding Clarinda's arm, for which she was grateful, as her legs still felt week. She said, "I saw that ghostly girl again. She pointed to the castle. If that spectre has been laid, then there is still the Crone."

Dr Sharman, pacing behind them, said, "I fear so, Ma'am."

The O'Hare children were at the entrance, wide eyed.

"Why ain't you at school?" Harley asked this whenever they annoyed him, even on Sundays. For all that, he patted the heads of both.

"Devil take it, Sir, it wants five and twenty to seven o' the clock." Seán pointed to the courtyard clock, proud of his new knowledge.

"Don't go in the maze, as I said. We may have seen some spooks inside, but if you pester me about it now, I'll ask your teacher to set you extra lessons."

The children gazed on them solemnly. "Them ghosts messed their hair," said the girl, "And the Professor's gone all chalky faced, with his nose only pink."

Clarinda said hastily, "It's rude for children to swear, or comment on people's looks. Run along and have your breakfast."

"But the master swears awful," the boy objected as the girl pulled him away, and Harley was overcome with a coughing fit.

"You've ruined your lovely slippers," mourned Abbey.

"I don't like to fall into extravagant ways, but I have a few pairs, after all," said Clarinda. "This is such lovely tea, dear. I hope the Professor enjoys a pot of ale[58] as much."

The girl sniffed. "More likely he swills down one of brandy, and I hope the Viscount don't join him. It's disgraceful to take strong drink early of a morning, though them foreigners is always at it, I hear, and he must be one, with that name. In *Black Hearted Lord Wrath* he 'quaffs a goblet of strong liquor on rising' before going to inspect the dungeons, where he comes on the heroine."

"I hope he offered her a cup of tea."

"No, he offered her riches to live as his mistress, but she proudly declined him. With a mirthless laugh he left her to the rats."

Clarinda fondled one of the kittens, which was playing about in the dressing room. "Then I hope some cats got the rats."

"It didn't say so. One of Lord Wrath's men as had a change of heart, freed her, having been won over by her beauty and noble mien. But begging your pardon, Mistress Clarinda, you must have seen something bad in the maze again, to come back so pale."

"The Professor works upon it. I tried to help a little. But there is more yet to do, and Lord Venn doesn't approve."

"I never thought of a wicked lord disapproving of anything save being said nay," marvelled Abigail, and before Clarinda could rebuke her, took the slippers through to the dressing room.

"Hell and the Devil, this is too much!" Harley threw down the letter he had just opened, swearing some more.

"What is it?" Clarinda, who had been eating breakfast with an appetite despite his sullen silence, was concerned.

"Babs writes that Molyneux's had an accident. Supposedly he fell down the stairs and is in a bad way. She also writes that young Wilmot is ill with the measles, which is dangerous, at his age."

---

58   Pot of ale: Beer was routinely served with breakfast, water often being unsafe.

The Professor was all attention as Clarinda murmured, "Oh no. Poor Molyneux and the poor baby. How awful for your sister."

Harley jumped up, draining his pot of beer as an afterthought. "I'm off to Town." He paused. "Damn it, you can't stay, Clarinda, with this spectre business. You'll have to come. I'll drop you off at your brother's, though. The house I took in Town this season is no place for a lady, and my other's rented still."

Clarinda was torn between concern for the baby and Molyneux, indignation that he spoke of her as if she were an animated parcel with no opinions about where she would stay, and curiosity. Perhaps his Town house had a seraglio in the attics, or a gaming hell in the basement.

Harley turned to Dr Sharman. "Beg pardon, Sir. I hope you'll be comfortable here. We may be away a while. Meanwhile, please regard this as your home."

He fidgeted through Lodovico Sharman's gracious reply, which ended, "Excuse my appearing to intrude at this distressing time, Lord Venn, but did your sister give any details of Mr Molyneux's accident?"

"She didn't write very coherent," said Harley. "But it must be part of this damned business."

"I shall do well enough at your Town house. It's my part to make it more comfortable," Clarinda told Harley. She knew she should not discuss any contentious domestic matters in front of their guest, but she also knew that if she must challenge being packed off to James' house. "Besides, my brother only remains in the city to finish some business matter. The others have left already."

Harley looked put upon, but made no reply. With a hasty, "We'll write!" to Dr Sharman, he went out, and Clarinda heard him roaring for O'Hare down the basement stairs.

"It is uncivil to leave you here alone, Sir, and I do not know when we will return. I must apologise," she said. "I hope you will not be too inconvenienced? As this must involve that monster, we weakened it too late to prevent Molyneux's fall. The baby's illness surely is not connected."

"It is heavy news. We can only hope that Mr Molyneux is not badly injured, and that both he and Lady Barbara's child make a speedy recovery. I may have made some small progress by the time that Your Ladyship and His Lordship return."

Harley was too distracted to make more than a cursory attempt at urging Clarinda to allow him to take her to her brother's, so she supposed that his Town house lacked a seraglio or a gaming hell. She said that she would go directly with him to Molyneux's house.

Here, they were shown upstairs by a grim-faced maid in middle age. She looked coldly at Harley as she made her curtsey, for all his amiable greeting, "So your mistress takes care of Molyneux? How does he do?"

"I'll leave it for the mistress to say, Your Lordship."

This added to their anxiety over Molyneux. Upstairs, they were greeted by Molyneux's cousin, Mistress Hart, whom Clarinda had met a couple of times before, when he had taken her out driving in the park. She was a sensible widow of perhaps thirty, with a plain face but a startlingly good figure.

She struck Clarinda as unlined and lively for one who seemed to her so afflicted with years, and she had admired the merry look in her eyes when brought into the company of one of her cousin's worst associates.

"How does Jack do?" Harley demanded as soon as he had made his bow.

"I believe he rallies, Your Lordship. I collect you have only this moment arrived in Town? Your coming at once through concern for your friend is kind. Lady Venn, you must be fatigued after your journey. Pray take a seat. Would you care for some refreshments?"

As before, Clarinda had the sense that the older woman pitied her.

"Thank you, Ma'am, some tea will soon put my wife to rights. Can Jack see me?" asked Harley.

"Certainly, Lord Venn, he is well enough now to see visitors. Our main concern is that his leg mends straight."

"Thank heaven for that." Clarinda joined with Harley's sincere but less elegant exclamation.

"What a Devil were you about, letting that hooded skeleton get the better of you, Jack?" Harley grinned. "I thought you'd have more sense than to go tumbling down the stairs at the sight of its ugly face. Does that leg pain you much?"

"I've had more fun," said Molyneux ruefully. "That was pure stupidity on my part. I lost my temper. That never does in a fight with a human, and least of all this cursed thing. Just at the last, I remembered something your wife said. I believe that saved me."

"Glad to hear it. She insisted on coming down with me when we heard the news. When I've wearied with you, we'll go straight to Babs, to see how the baby does." Harley could not keep his tone light when he spoke of that, so he added quickly, "Meanwhile, would you like to see my gaoler?"

"I'll be happy to see her, but I'm in no state to receive ladies at present. Sick rooms are distasteful places," said Molyneux, "Mary-Ann doesn't mind; we grew up together."

"Clarinda won't be alarmed by that, with those nerves of iron. At some unearthly hour this morning, she joined our friend the Professor in some damn fool scheme to dispel the skeletal spectre – I only knew of it through waking unaccountable early. I arrived in time to see the thing sink into the ground howling. I couldn't leave her up there, to be drawn into more of such pranks."

Molyneux started, then paled and bit his lips, while Harley waited, as he often had by colleagues in the ring, while the paroxysm of pain passed and he could say, "I never would have given the Professor that much credit. But that was hellish work for a woman."

"I was angry when I found out, but for all that, we're doing better than you did, so don't go fretting your stupid head over it." Harley placed a hand on Molyneux's shoulder. "But I see your cousin has you on the mend. Beware: these females are as scheming as they're tender. She'll have you yet."

"I recall you were the tricky one, announcing your engagement before that old doctor," retorted Molyneux. "Your act of gallantry worked most convenient for you. Like your wife, Mary-Ann revels in good works. She thinks me too debauched to face my maker yet: that's what it amounts to. I don't know why you will have it she's after me. Not all of us have a title and a fortune waiting for us to dazzle away our faults."

"Having lost my own freedom, it's only natural for me to want all my friends caught in the parsons' mousetrap[59] too," said Harley. "Will you see my domestic tyrant now?"

"Do, before this cursed leg of mine sets me off groaning again," said Molyneux.

Clarinda was deep in conversation with Mistress Hart – on herbal cures rather than marriage plans.

Clarinda was saying, "When Lord Venn was set upon, I should have sent him the poultice you say."

If Mistress Hart had heard talk of Clarinda's behaviour the day Venn was attacked, she gave no sign.

Clarinda was eager to speak to Molyneux – the more as she guessed that he had long been her champion – but when they reached him, he was writhing again. Harley went to ask Mistress Hart for something to ease the pain.

She said, looking at him compassionately, "I pitied the Thing before, Sir. But seeing you now, I feel for you rather more, and can only be bitter against it. So as I believe it feeds on anger, it is as well as I am away from it."

"You were right," he muttered, and though still writhing, he went on, "I thought of something Harley told me you'd said, when I was damned fool enough to try and battle that thing – and I'm sure that helped me. I think you wiser than I guessed – though I knew you to be wiser than we men. If you have faith in Dr Sharman, then we were right to urge Harley to try him. You must keep the rascal in order; he'd fight anyone or anything with his blood up."

"I think you are a fine one to speak," smiled Clarinda, adding ruefully, "And I've only recently discovered how lacking in wisdom I am. I'll try my utmost, though."

He winced and bit his lip a while. Clarinda looked about for something to ease him, and could only offer him cordial, which he refused. Then he said, "I want to say: I've come to see how wrong I have been, in my treatment of women. Meeting you taught me that, and if Harley's an ounce of sense, you should teach him still more. If I come through this, I'll never take the abandoned wretch's view again."

---

59   Parsons' mousetrap: Marriage.

Her eyes swam, and she patted his hand. "Thank you. I am so happy to hear that. Of course, you must come through this: you cannot let that skeletal thing make you its victim, too. Here they come with some medication. I do hope it helps."

Soon afterwards, Harley stood patting his sister's back, while she sobbed on his shoulder. "He'll get the better of it, you'll see, Babs," he muttered hoarsely. "He's a sturdy lad, and Clarinda was talking of some remedy that Mistress Hart swears by for fevers. It really helped Molyneux."

"She says it's safe for babies," said Clarinda. "She gave me some of the potion she has found best for measles, if you care to try it? But you may prefer to keep to the treatment of your doctors."

Barbara was so anxious about the fever that she would try anything, and called the housekeeper to have the remedy made up. Meanwhile, hoping that a visit from a favourite might rally Wilmot, Harley went up to see him, while Clarinda tried to cheer her sister-in-law.

As Harley went into the nursery, he had eyes only for the cot where the baby stirred uneasily, his face flushed. Hearing a gasp, he saw Betsy rise from a chair.

She made a curtsey, her mouth pursed up, and her eyes downcast. He would have thought her demure look absurd, had he the leisure to think about it. As it was, he grunted, "Good morning, my girl. How does the youngster?"

"Sadly feverish, Your Lordship."

He went to gaze on the baby, and not caring to disturb him, sat down by his cradle.

"I made a mistake in sending you up to my great aunt," he said, "I'm sorry for that. As in said in my note, I'll give you the means to set up on your own. It's only fair. I know I wasn't your first, but nobody knew of the others."

The girl's bosom heaved. "I cannot accept Your Lordship's generosity." She kept her gaze lowered. "I should return your presents. I was wrong to accept them. I blush to think that I lived as your mistress, and allowed you to enjoy me nigh on one thousand times."

He was startled that she had kept a tally, rather like an innkeeper. If it really had been that many times, given that he had made her a generous present every time, he began to see how, with other indulgences, he had got so much out of pocket. "I'm sorry you regret, it, my girl. As for the presents, I won't have 'em back. It's my fault you're out of a place, after all, so you should take something more. Anyhow, it don't feel right talking of it before the infant, though he's asleep."

Now the baby was making a painful version of the stirrings and murmurings he always made on waking. Seeing how anxiously Harley regarded him, the girl came and placed her hands on his shoulders.

"My Lord, I sense your sorrow and I feel it too." Her fingers gently stroked him.

That touch, and her breasts pressed against his back, belied her prim tone.

At that moment, the door opened, and Clarinda, whose footsteps were always soft, came in carrying the medication, and Barbara followed.

As the man and the woman inside the room glanced about, there seemed to be a sense of collusion between them, an awareness of being caught out.

Barbara calmly asked the maidservant to fetch tepid water to bathe the baby that sent her from the room. The girl made her curtsey with a prissy face that Clarinda would have found laughable at any other time. Meanwhile, the rascal Clarinda had married neither changed colour, nor avoided Clarinda's eyes. Instead, he said something about the medication.

That must be his ex-maid Betsy, though the last Clarinda had heard of her, she had been in Lincolnshire. Even from that glimpse of her touch, Clarinda could tell that they had been physically intimate, and that the girl knew the caresses he liked.

She had already suspected that this maid had been his mistress from his put on casual manner when she had asked about her. That was to be expected of a debauched master.

She had expected to meet with such willing women, besides ex-mistresses high in society. During their engagement, she had been lucky in that with him an outcast, and she a merchant's daughter not presented at Court, debarred from much of polite society, they had avoided the high born ladies whose favours he had enjoyed. She had been lucky too, in Lady Hogg's leaving Town.

It wasn't this confirmation that Harley had used his maidservant for his pleasure that upset Clarinda, though she must think it wrong; it was the intimacy of that touch and the united look they had turned on her. She had longed to comfort him all day herself, but he had seemed unapproachable, silently rejecting her sympathy.

This was wholly in character, after all. He would not admit to the need for tenderness from her – no doubt, he refused to see it in himself. Still, she had hoped that sense of closeness had sprung up between them, partly as a result of that joyful lovemaking, but also through their hazards, might have made him accept it from her.

How had that hard-faced maidservant got through his guard enough for him to allow her to touch him like that? When they had stopped for a meal at an inn, and to rest the horses, Clarinda had tried to speak to him. He had answered in grunts, refusing all sympathy.

She had patted Jack Molyneux's hand in her concern for him, which made resentment to that girl's squeezing Harley's shoulder seem unreasonable.

Yet, her own touch of Molyneux had been friendly. The girl Betsy's, she knew, had been enticing. Even as they watched Barbara persuade her infant to take the draught, Clarinda disgusted herself by brooding on Betsy and her statuesque figure, prim air and rather coarse face.

She knew these feelings were competitive and beneath her. If she blamed anyone, she should blame the libertine, not one of his former victims. He had all the power, after all.

The feverish baby continued to scream. They left, promising to call again tomorrow, while Harley urged his sister to send word if there was a marked change.

23.
Renegade

HARLEY CURSED FATE FLUENTLY IN the carriage. Clarinda put a hand on his arm. It was only as they came up to that house once pointed out by Abbey to Clarinda as a den of iniquity that she said, "Wasn't that girl who was sympathizing with you when we entered Betsy, your former maid? I thought she was at your great aunt's in Lincolnshire."

"She's with Babs, now. According to her, she's been useful in nursing the youngsters." He turned a cool glance on her. "You know how I lived, but there wasn't anything in her touching me."

"The girl was kind in offering her former master sympathy. I am sorry you did not think to accept it from me."

He muttered something unflattering about unreasonable, jealous women, and urged the horses past a lumbering dray cart. Clarinda cursed her weakness in speaking of the matter at all.

The day was wet, like so many that summer, and unlike in the country, none of the smells about them were pleasant. Yet this was a desirable part of the city. Clarinda saw why people with the means fled the Town at this time of year. The Coronation now being over, no doubt most of those with the means had already left for the country.

She felt more than ever sorry for those who had to live in squalor, and her mind turned again to a scheme to improve things for them. She must do something, and yet to provide a small patch of relief, adequate housing and some respite for a few of the poor was a drop in the ocean.

Harley handed her down and took the horses to the mews to arrange for their care. Clarinda went into the house where the Viscount had led so debauched an existence. The servants had not arrived yet, and she wandered pensively from room to room.

In here, it was so quiet that as she went down the passage towards the kitchen – where Betsy must have spent much time – she could hear the pump dripping. She glanced in at the drawing room, wincing as she came face to face with the life-sized portrait of Toby Venn. In her walk through the empty rooms she found none of the Earl. Had Harley put up that picture in defiance of the father who had cast him off?

In the study, the day bed on which she had tried to bathe his head with her handkerchief was still there. With how many women had he toyed on that couch? Prints of prize fighters decorated the walls, hung alongside heavily framed paintings.

In the drawing room, where O'Hare had once shown Clarinda and James when they had arrived early for an engagement, she looked again on the low table that must date back to the seventeenth century, defaced with scratches from the Viscount's boots, the upright piano, and a violin case still there.

Upstairs, she inspected the bedrooms. Here, there were no adjoining doors between the dressing rooms to the main bedrooms. She gazed at the bed, wondering again how many women he had entertained in it. Had he visited Betsy in her own bedroom under the attics?

Vulgar curiosity sent her up the attic stairs, to know something of Betsy's bedroom. O'Hare's she knew at once from the scent of cigars, no doubt filched from his master. The girl had left nothing of herself in hers save for the lingering aroma of perfume. As that was generally beyond the pocket of maidservants, Clarinda supposed that her master had paid for it.

Glancing out of the window, she started guiltily as she saw a fair, young buck, foreshortened from up here, striding towards the house with a bouncing athlete's walk. She hurried down to meet him.

"That young man from the pastry cooks' has renewed his offers," said Abbey, who saw no need to add that before, these had only taken the form of tooth sucking. "He has lost flesh, which he said was due to pining for me, but I think down to a bad pie. And he offered me pastries every day, but I would not be swayed in my aversion."

"Is that aversion, my dear, to the pastries or to the youth?" smiled Clarinda.

"I could almost like him thin, though he may gain weight again. But I was sorry that wicked O'Hare served out his workmate so savage, smashing the finest of beef pies, too…Such a pest that the Viscount's friends come to dinner today. I hope we have enough cutlery."

Welch and Tomkins, learning of the Viscount's arrival in Town through either supernatural means or O'Hare, had lost no time in calling and Harley had invited them to dinner. In the absence of a cook, this would have to be prepared at the pastry cook's. O'Hare had been reluctant to go to the local one, and now Clarinda saw why.

Abbey had called in at the nearest wine merchants, who far from being impressed by mention of Lord Venn, demanded cash.

Clarinda remembered Tomkins as the piratical looking man whom Harley had pointed out as the cohort most dismayed by his marriage and change of lifestyle. Certainly, she suspected that as a 'man's man' Tompkins was set to take a poor view of her, though he hid this under banter.

Welch seemed to like her well enough, in so far as he could take to any of his friends' wives, who were bars to the important business of life.

Of course, neither gentleman would think of being coarse in her presence; but she could imagine what their talk was like elsewhere.

She tried to be welcoming to both Tomkins and Welch, but found them uncongenial in her anxious mood. Harley clearly enjoyed their company. By tacit agreement none of them spoke of Jack Molyneux. They lingered over their port and brandy. Then they all left for a venue unsuitable for ladies.

Clarinda whispered to Harley, "I'm glad you have some diversion, but please don't take too much drink. I believe it may make things easier for the enemy forces."

His eyebrows shot up. "Yet you never said as much before, my dear."

He obviously thought that she had seized on this for her own purposes, while to her it made sense that any excess from the spectres' human targets must weaken their guard.

Clarinda went early to bed. She lay awake long, while the sounds of the Town night went by her window, with the occasional ringing of horses' hooves and the rattle of cart and carriage wheels, cries from late night street vendors, the distant shouts of revellers and of a night watchman.

She seemed to have been asleep for only five minutes when she heard Harley's step on the stairs, and his cheerful words to O'Hare, still up himself. As ever he came in to her.

He was not obviously part drunk, but he smelt of brandy and had taken enough for his sensibilities to be blunted. His approach to her was somehow impersonal. The effortless sensual understanding between them was missing. She tried, but whether it was fatigue, resentment over his attitude today, or jealousy, she could not respond to his caresses.

Finally, he said, one hand still caressing her breast, the other a handful of her ample behind, "Have you been sitting in an ice house?"

"I don't know what it is," she murmured.

"I always say that a man should pleasure a woman first, but…"

Reduced to only 'a woman' Clarinda felt the magic sensual link between them further frayed. She might be any of the others.

"Will you object to my concentrating on my own pleasure instead of yours, Madam?"

He was only joking; but now she felt the distance between them widening, to the point where they might address each other formally.

He did concentrate on his own pleasure. It was soon enough over. She hoped then that they might be able to talk. Instead, he fell asleep at once, and snored. She did not feel at all like kissing his sleeping face. She gave his shoulder a push and he turned about with a comfortable grunt to lie with his back to her.

For all his excess, Harley went out early to enquire after his nephew and Molyneux. The baby was improving: his fever had lessened. Molyneux had taken a turn for the worse, and his doctors an unhappy view of the case.

Mistress Hart, now worried, had sent for his widowed mother to come back from her trip to Scotland. Harley tried to rally Molyneux with talk of the upcoming fights he would miss, if he would insist on malingering, but Molyneux's wits were starting to wander. He answered at random.

Young Frederick Carstairs met Harley on the stairs. He was distraught. "I said how it would be, Venn!"

Harley adopted a *blasé* tone. "Stop talking rubbish, youngster. Come and do away with these jitters in a round with me at the Pugilist's. He'll get the better of this. His cousin won't allow otherwise." Though he spoke cheerfully, he felt far from sanguine himself.

Clarinda, alarmed, offered to help Mrs Hart nurse Molyneux. Harley snatched at this. "Not that I'd be happy about my wife nursing any other man but me save Jack, but as it's him… You are a fine nurse from what I remember, though I was half senseless at the time. Yet after all, these doctors are bound to take a dim view of a case; how else are they going to make money?"

Comforting himself in this way, he went off to work off his frustrations in the ring.

Clarinda spent the next few days divided between trying to impose order on chaos in this house, and helping Mrs Hart to nurse Molyneux.

He was already one of the long list of those for whom she prayed every night. Now she prayed for him and Baby Wilmot every hour. Back in Buckinghamshire, Harley had laughed when he had surprised her at her devotions, saying he hoped he was included. Now, coming into her room to ask her for something and catching on her knees, he made no jokes.

He called in every day to see how Molyneux did, and to tell him that if he would lie abed like this, he would be unable to be second for Harley's own planned fight with St Gilles Slasher, Molyneux rambled in reply. Mistress Hart, Clarinda and the night nurse now grappled with his fever as a deadly enemy, and the physicians were even beginning to fear mortification and to talk of taking off the leg, but Molyneux would not have it.

As Harley left the sick room, Clarinda said that she hoped that coming fight was fictitious. He merely smiled.

Now, Harley daily distracted himself by visits to the Pugilist's Amphitheatre. He got into several street brawls besides, his temper being worsened by his return to heavy drinking. As before, he went carousing with costermongers, dressed in rough clothes. This worried Clarinda not at all, though she had to laugh to see him in such clothes. This startled him.

"You look very nice as a working man," she said. Gratified, he kissed her nose. She was indifferent to the horror with which the neighbours looked on him as he lounged out on foot.

His heavy drinking was another matter.

The next day, Clarinda surprised a costermonger stretched fully clothed on the day bed in Harley's study.

She said, "Good morning. I'm sorry; I didn't know that there was anybody here, or I would have knocked."

The man, blinking, said, "Are you Venn's gentry mort[60]?"

"Perhaps. Would you care for some tea?"

Here, they were joined by Harley, in richly embroidered robe, and grinning. "What did I tell you? My wife is all good nature."

After that, they took an early breakfast together. The man could not believe that Harley was a lord, thinking it was all a hoax.

"It makes no matter, I'll be a plain 'Mister' with pleasure," Harley assured him.

Clarinda was sure that these drinking associates were no rougher company than some of the Viscount's noble associates. Over the next few days, as he rioted about Town, if he was never exactly drunk, he was never fully sober.

---

60   Gentry mort: An upper class woman.

Every morning, Clarinda pleaded with him not to drink too much. As he was still slightly under the influence of what he had taken the night before, this made it hard to reason with him. He either laughed at her, chucking her chin, assuring her that he was never drunk, unlike some of the brutes he knew, or suggested that she was a domestic tyrant.

"But my dear, remember what I said of the Hooded Spectre. Indeed, you mustn't let it through your guard."

He grinned: "Now, there speaks a pugilist's wife." He went off with his low laugh.

Yet, there was no point in trying to reason with him later in the day, as he wasn't there, and soon enough began to drink again.

There was no point either in trying a curtain lecture[61]. He came to her as a horribly attractive, slightly drunk ruffian. He was not rough as he demanded his marital rights. That was not his way with women; but he expected to get them, nevertheless. He had must always have been a gentle lover who sought to please a woman, and arousing one was part of his vanity. He put his lips and hands to work upon her. But it as if he was making love to any woman.

Since that first night in London, the special quality to their lovemaking had flown. Now she willed herself to feel again, and had perhaps half the pleasure she had relished before.

Afterwards, he would kiss her nose, mutter some sort of thanks and endearment and fall asleep at once. There was one night when he came to her more drunk than she had yet seen him, and Mr Harley hung his head as if in shame. His slave left, mortified. But with the dawn, he was back, taking her in his arms and lusty. Incredibly, he rose bright eyed every morning, and Mr Harley usually did the same.

It was a comfort to her that she sensed that wild as Harley's behaviour was, he had not yet been with other women. She didn't know how she could tell this. She preferred not to dwell on it.

Clarinda having found a chef, Carstairs, Welch and Tomkins came to dinner every day. This seemed to be some pact between them and Harley for the course of Jack Molyneux's illness. Neither they, nor Clarinda mentioned him. Still, he was always on their minds.

---

61   Curtain lecturer: A serious talking to in bed (these tending to be hung with curtains).

James, though asked, made excuses. He paid a couple of morning calls, stiffly inviting Harley to his club. He certainly noted that even at that time of day, the rogue was not entirely sober.

Carstairs was recovering from his infatuation with Clarinda as quickly as Harley had predicted. Now, Clarinda thought that he looked at her sympathetically. She wasn't surprised. No doubt everybody who was still in Town had heard about how That Villain Venn had gone back to his old ways. She felt sorry for herself, though it was all only to be expected. She could tell that Tomkins was gloating.

The day the costermonger breakfasted with them, they did not have a happy dinner. It was true that Barbara's team of physicians had at last agreed that baby Wilmot was on the mend, but Molyneux was no better. Besides, O'Hare, perhaps encouraged by his master's own excesses, had returned from an afternoon off not only with a black eye – the cause of hilarity from the men, though he refused to say how he came by it – but unsteady on his feet.

He was serving at table, along with the only other servant willing to come down to Town with them, a puzzled-looking young footman. O'Hare swayed as he served. He nearly dropped the fowl, while it was only through good luck that the wine he poured ended up in their glasses. Harley signed for the fellow footman to take over. O'Hare tottered out to collect the cheese.

"You must keep this rascal of yours in order, Lady Venn," Carstairs repeated.

For a moment, Clarinda wondered whether he meant Venn or his servant. "I must rely upon Venn himself to do that," she spoke more tartly than she intended.

Harley pulled a face, but was saved the trouble of reply by a crash as O'Hare toppled through the door.

He put up a fight not to overbalance and drop the cheese. He made flapping movements backwards, as if trying to take flight in reverse. This sent a large slice of cheddar into Tomkins' plate, which, befuddled himself, he stared at in dull surprise. Still, O'Hare's struggles only delayed his impulse forwards. To Clarinda, safely at the foot of the table, he seemed to topple over in a leisurely way, as if eager to show off his feat.

Harley had time to leap up, yelling, while the others turned their heads, before O'Hare plunged face forwards into the remains of a fruit tart, knocking over a decanter of wine and spraying Tomkins and Welch with food and drink.

Perhaps it was fate paying him back for his assault on the pie man. Forgetting Clarinda's presence, Welch and Tomkins' language was astounding.

"Hold your noise till the lady's withdrawn," said Harley, opening the door for Clarinda, and waiting until she was through it before jerking O'Hare to his feet by the collar and soundly boxing his sticky ears.

After this climatic end to their dinner, Carstairs took his leave. Tomkins – like Foyle before him, lean with excess – borrowed a clean shirt from Harley, while the stockier Welch went home to change in readiness to meet them at the Coconut Club.

"Please don't go out with them; I have a bad feeling about tonight," Clarinda urged him. A sense of foreboding was closing in on her.

"Damn it, stop scolding, My Lady. I want to take my mind of Molyneux."

"You know it doesn't, really; and it makes you vulnerable to –." But he was already moving away from her, eager to begin on his night's adventures. "I hope you will resist the temptations of opera girls and others," she said after him, trying to adopt a light tone.

"I tipped one of 'em off my knee the other night as she climbed on," he said with a wink, "Too tempting an armful."

Again Clarinda lay sleepless for hours, listening to the sounds of the Town at night, and tomcats caterwauling beneath her window. Now she felt that should have abandoned pride, run after Harley, and pleaded with him to stay home. At about one o'clock, with him still out, she drifted off to sleep.

She started awake in the grey light of dawn. When the shifting began in the mirror on the bureau across the room, she cursed herself for not covering it. She felt she could not face the Crone now.

It seemed that she must. The Crone emerged. "See your worthless wretch betray his empty vows, and hate him as he deserves."

A vision of Harley appeared in the mirror, kissing Lady Hogg. Clarinda took no notice of where they were, though later she realised that they must be in her rooms. Lady Hogg's chestnut hair tumbled about her shoulders, and her robe was falling open, revealing her opulent breasts.

Harley looked drunker than she had yet seen him. His shirt was half unbuttoned, his coat, waistcoat and cravat thrown carelessly on the chair. Now they drew apart, and gradually Clarinda heard phrases. As ever, she could not tell whether these were in her mind, or outside.

The pair did not look pleased, though they looked intense. Phrases sounded in her ear.

"…I warned you not to marry that insipid, dumpy little bourgeois…"

"…I like my wife well enough –" his voice sounded in her head. Then he broke off, looking struck. Some stray idea must have caught his befuddled mind. Clarinda's own reeled.

"Oh, stop!" She was addressing him, not the pitiless Crone.

She sobbed, missing their next words. The moving images froze and Clarinda, her hands over her ears, wrenched away her gaze and turned from the mirror. But she could not shut out the Crone's words or thoughts, spoken in French, yet translated in her mind with merciless clarity.

Yet, why was she outraged? The rogue had not married her for love. No doubt the sexual harmony that they could create, which was to her something tender, something extraordinary, was to him of no great account, and he was merely pleased to find pleasure with the woman with whom he had made a marriage of convenience, and with whom he must make heirs. In returning to his former mistress, he was doing what came naturally to a rake.

"I won't spy on him through your tricks, nor let myself hate them, though you strive to make me."

"So exemplary a wife! Your spiritual mentors would say that you must welcome him home, yes, even if he spends every night of your stay in London in that woman's bed or rolling with women of the town. That is the duty a proper wife owes her master. I wonder if you are so lacking in spirit. A little of hatred would be of use, but I seek to free you from the wretch. Me, I cursed him and the others before his birth."

Clarinda would not look at the reflection of the magnificent creatures behind her. Covering her ears failed to block out the Crone's gloating voice. That came as no surprise to Clarinda, who guessed that they communicated by thought, as in dreams.

She sobbed, "No: I won't hear! Your longing for revenge will never be satisfied, whatever pain you cause. Jack Molyneux told me how he wished to change: – your creature attacked him anyway."

"It is easy enough to swear to remedy your way of life, when that life seems behind you. No doubt Harley Venn will swear that again, as he faces his end."

Suddenly, Clarinda thought of the blue light. At once the Crone's taunts faded, and an idea came to her as the Crone's image wavered.

"I saw your daughter in the centre of the maze. You must long for re-union with her more than you wish to destroy the heirs to those who once wronged you both. The worse you do to them, the further you separate yourself from her."

The Crone stared at her wildly. Then, throwing up her arms, she shrieked and vanished.

Clarinda buried her face in her pillows.

When Abbey scratched at the door a little later, Clarinda was red eyed but calm. Abbey looked her concern as she set down a tray with a note besides her early morning chocolate.

"There's glad news from Mistress Hart. Mr Molyneux's new footman just delivered this," Abbey blushed as she mentioned the footman, but Clarinda was too busy tearing open the note to notice.

Molyneux had taken a turn for the better in the night. His fever had abated and his leg was on the mend.

"Thank goodness for that," Clarinda sighed. As she sipped the chocolate, she thought rapidly. "My brother returns home to Berkshire today. Could you deliver a note to him, my dear, asking him if I can have a place in his carriage? Now both invalids are on the mend, I would like to make a visit to my old family home."

Abbey nodded solemnly. "My lips are sealed on His Lordship's recent doings, but you must be grieved over it, Mistress Clarinda. Perhaps your withdrawal will be a silent reproach."

Clarinda smiled wanly, thinking that could be more ineffectual than her voiced ones. She scribbled a note to James, and sent Abbey off with it, assuring her that she could dress herself, as she wanted to make sure of her catching him.

Abbey was shocked at a viscount's lady dressing herself, but hurried off, remarking that she hoped Molyneux would soon be well enough to visit the castle – along with his footman.

Clarinda wrote:

'My dear Harley

Even though I write this in bitter resentment, you must know you have become so to me in the weeks we have been together. The Crone came to me from the mirror, and in it, showed me you kissing Lady Hogg. You have ever been straightforward with me; you never attempted to conceal your former relations with that lady, or your history as a rake. You had sworn that you meant to turn from your previous way of life, owing to your promise to your poor friend, Foyle.

This last week, under the strain of your concern for Mr Molyneux, you have been taking far too much strong drink and returned in part to your former way of life. But for that malevolent spectre to show me that you have renewed your relations with Lady Hogg, and to endure her taunts, was most painful to me nevertheless.

She sought, naturally, to turn me against you. Her creature foretold this in the maze when we faced the threat united.

I allowed myself to belief that we had a growing bond, and flattered myself that for all my moderate attractions and your long experience as a rake, you felt it too.

You are not a religious man, and to return to that liaison on our coming to Town may feel natural to you. Besides, it must be urged in mitigation, that in marrying me and giving up your mistress, you exchanged an outstandingly beautiful woman for a very mundane looking one. As an artist I cannot be blind to our relative attractions.

Yet, from things you have said, I cannot believe that the feelings of either of you ever were engaged. If they were, then though society and the church might condemn the liaison, I could not. Yet, as this is not a true love affair, then I beg you to end it with as much regard to the lady's feelings as you can, and to return to your previous resolve.

This last week, above everything, I have feared that through taking too much drink, you might draw in the Crone and her instrument. Now I fear it more than ever.

I would be a saint not to resent what has happened, and what I have seen, or to deny that I feel betrayed. But I am also bound to you by vows that have meaning for me. Yet resentful as I am, I might add strength to the malevolent presence at the castle.

Therefore, I will stay a few days with James at the Berkshire house, returning to the castle when I am more tranquil.

In the meantime, I beg you to take heed of my words, and not to put yourself at hazard by excess, or through fighting these malevolent spectres with hatred. I scarcely need urge you to avoid the castle, now that you are settled in Town.

Your wife, Clarinda.'

24.
Discoveries

WHEN HARLEY AND TOMKINS MET with Welch, Venn drank more than he had yet. His flare of anger with O'Hare had been more because he envied him his befuddled state, than at his serving at table in it.

Tomkins encouraged him. They went from one night venue to another. At one point they danced with women of the town near Covent Garden, at another they trooped up the treacherous winding stairs of the Coconut Club.

At some point, Welch left them to call on his mistress. Tomkins and Harley safely went down those stairs, and ended up in a gambling den. Somehow, cards had lost much of their allure for Harley. Besides, the creak of the waiter's shoes annoyed him. Gambling kept all its old appeal for Tomkins.

He jeered at Harley: "Come into two fortunes, and yet you begrudge a few guineas on the table. That wife of yours has got you truly under the thumb. I'd have believed it of some: I thought better of you."

"You forget Foyle," Harley stood up. As the waiter slopped by them in his cracked pumps, it became ludicrously important to him to see that he replace them, though it could do him no present good. He thrust some money on the man. "Get yourself some new shoes." The man left bowing his thanks.

Tomkins, bent low over the table, his voice slurred, doggedly returned to his argument. "It's twenty to one Foyle rambled, not knowing what he said. I hate to see a fine fellow brought low by a nagging female – and the best of 'em will try and tyrannize over you. Can't help it; it's the way they're made." Despite being in liquor, Tomkins kept his language clean in his eagerness to keep this member of the fraternity of rakehells from wavering from the cause.

Harley, drunk enough to be unsteady on his feet, bid Tomkins goodnight and made his way up the steps into the damp London night.

Harley was never quite sure how he came to be at the Hogg's town house. Yet, finding himself there, he followed custom, and went round to the back. He was admitted by a footman, who imagined what he would do to Lady Hogg's haughty body every night.

Harley was met in the back lobby by the confidential maid, high bosomed and cherry lipped, whom he was inclined to kiss. She drew back, saying that the master was out, and took the visitor up the back stairs to Lady Hogg's dressing room.

Lady Hogg was lovelier than ever in her state of *dishabille*, her robe falling open to reveal her magnificent bosom, her bright chestnut hair tumbling about her shoulders. Her eyes, nearly as blue as his, sparked at having her beauty sleep disturbed, but also with curiosity.

When she saw his state, her eyebrows drew together, but she never allowed herself a full frown, being nearly thirty, an age when most women were lined. "How now, you wretch? You're drunk; and I hear you're back to all your old tricks, brawling and rioting all about Town." Her full lips curled, showing teeth as white as his own.

He threw his coat on the chair. "And I hear you're not with child. You should've confided your worry to me, as I was involved. So that was the cause of that uncivil letter. I should have thought of that. But I've always used skin sheaths."

"I was in no mood to speak to you. Hogg and I go on most comfortably, and I had no wish to plant some cuckoo brat of yours on him. And now, you are a married man; how incongruous." She laughed, and he noted how hard her eyes were.

Unseen by either, the mirror behind them began to shimmer.

He paused, reluctant to reply, and then muttered, "I like my wife well enough." Unluckily, his eyes dropped to Lady Hogg's opulent white bosom. He began quickly to remove his waistcoat and cravat.

"You presumptuous creature." Still, she allowed him to take hold of her, and plant kisses on her lips.

There was a sudden sparkling of colour about them, and a muted flash, like that of distant lightning, in the glass. They paused. "What was that?" Lady Hogg, whose eyes were open, pulled away, stared about.

He stood back, too. "I needed that timely reminder."

She laughed scornfully. "Does your wife control you at a distance by conjuring tricks learnt from Dr Sharman? I am happy you like her 'well enough'. How exciting does that sound! Still, I warned you not to marry that insipid, dumpy bourgeois."

He hardly seemed to hear her. "I take about with me my own private weather," he muttered, then frowned. "I said that to Greendale, the day that I proposed. Yes, I do I like my wife well enough." He moved back, looking struck.

Lady Hogg supposed some passing thought had distracted his befuddled brain. He seemed astounded by whatever it was. "By heaven, that's it, and I never realized. What a cursed fool!"

"You're rambling," she said, "I've never seen you so drunk. You're still an appealing rascal, though. It's a shame that excess must spoil your looks."

He turned away, and began putting on his discarded clothing. "I must get back to the castle. We'll be a match for it together, now, if she'll only fight by my side again. I can't leave the Professor alone to face it: they were right about spectres."

Suddenly he turned, gazing at her. "I've just realised: Lodovico Sharman was your lover."

"He certainly was one of them," she smiled. "A decade since, he was, as I said, a magnificent creature. He was rather like you, though taller, and with a hawk nose, not Grecian. And with such an air! All the ladies fell for him like ninepins. That was before you came into society, let alone became an outcast from it. I liked him well, but he became a nuisance, wanting Hogg to divorce me, so we could marry.

When he spoke of shooting Hogg in a duel, I ended matters. Can you imagine? Did he flatter himself that I would throw away my title, to live as the wife of some glorified mountebank[62] or stage artist? But he was an entertaining rogue, just as you are a delightful savage."

Harley laughed without warmth. "To think that my wife feared that your heart might be involved in our antics, my beauty. Your what? The sweet innocent!"

She turned away. "You're too drunk to be civil. Whatever was the purpose of disturbing me? Go and blather at someone else; I've no patience with you."

He bowed. "Beg pardon, Ma'am. It won't happen again."

They left the dressing room through different doors.

The London day was new as Venn came out of the back door, the streets already bustling. He laughed to himself as he came out into it. Then, as he set off towards Molyneux's house, he sobered and walked along deep in thought.

He supposed he looked a disreputable enough sight in the rumpled clothing of last night as the youthful new footmen let him in, telling him that the master had been very bad in the night, and Mistress Hart had sat up with him. Biting his lips, Harley plunged up the stairs.

Mistress Hart, lit by the clear early morning sunlight after a sleepless night, struck Harley as looking even more wan and exhausted than yesterday. "How is he?" was his abrupt greeting.

"On the mend: that was the crises," she smiled wearily.

He sagged and swore in his relief. "Can he see me?"

Molyneux, even more pale and haggard than Harley expected, was sipping tea.

Harley shook his head. "What's all this I hear of your putting your cousin to yet more trouble? You look hellish bad. When are you going to stop this malingering and let me leave Town?"

"You look bad enough yourself, you villain," Molyneux shook his head, "And through the fever, I remember Welch telling me that you

---

62   Mountebank: A hawker of fake medicines who attracts customers with showmanship.

were up to all your old tricks again, curse you for an ingrate, with such a wife as you have. I can't thank her enough for what she's done for me, this last week, and so you must tell her."

"Not quite all of my old tricks." Harley grimaced. "But that's all over. I'll take my wife back to the castle, and behave. This time, I mean it. Besides, I want to settle the score with those entities before they cause any more trouble. Don't worry, I've been thinking it over just now, and understand more than you'd believe. From now on, I'll be as cool with 'em as I would another pugilist. I'll admit to it now; they are spectres. That minds me. I still can't find that deuced letter."

"What letter?" Molyneux began, but Harley patted his shoulder. "Never mind that, Jack, I'll tell you all about it on your visit to the castle. Get some rest: you still look sick."

"Mind you act right by your wife from now on. I've always said she was far too good for a wretch like you, but she cares for you more than you deserve. Give her my heartfelt thanks and eternal devotion," said Molyneux.

Harley dropped his gaze, and muttered, "This last hour, I've finally seen sense, and I don't need you to tell me that."

O'Hare opened the door to Harley, looking solemn.

Harley said affably, "Why the funereal face? Has there been more trouble with the pie man? I've happy news: Molyneux is on the mend. I suppose you've heard already, though, as Mistress Hart said she'd sent round a message. Is my wife up yet?"

"Up and gone…Your Honour. Left Town with her brother for a stay at his house, taking that saucy maid. She left you this letter."

Harley swore as he took the letter. "When did they go?" He tried to resist the dread that washed over him.

"Half an hour since."

"Get me some clean clothes. Then start packing. We'll be gone as soon as may be." Harley walked into his study, cursing his fumbling fingers as he tore open the letter.

After scanning a couple of paragraphs, he groaned, and swore some more. "That damned filthy scheming hell hag!" He took it up again, and tried to read the rest. It took him a couple of attempts before he got to the end. Then he dropped it on the desk, and paced about the study, lost in thought, face haggard with strain. Then he snatched up writing materials. He wrote swiftly, and without calculation: –

'Clarinda,

I have just read your letter. This is the first time in my wasted life that I have been misjudged. Before, when accused of something, I laughed aloud, knowing I had done far worse. That is the cursed irony.

Nothing more happened with Lady Hogg than those slobbering kisses from my drunken self that the Crone used to triumph over you.

Though I now see what I have stupidly denied – that she is a malevolent entity – still, I cannot believe that she could show you more than what truly happened. What you saw was bad enough: yet, if that spectre could have shown you worse, you know she would.

I went to my former mistress in my cups. That is no excuse. Luckily, those familiar fireworks brought me to my senses. Perhaps too late, I realised something I should have seen long since.

I shan't tell you of that now, in writing. I don't deserve that indulgence. Though I did not go back to Lady Hogg as her lover, I near enough did as the final piece of shabby excess after days of betraying my promises to you.

A couple of sharp exchanges ended that bathetic encounter. It dawned on my befuddled brain – so called – that I had been out all night. I returned – as I thought – back to you, only calling in to ask after Molyneux on the way.

I hear you already have news that he is on the mend. Here I pause to pass on his heartfelt thanks to you, and mine for helping to save one who has always been as a brother to me. He has been, like me, bad enough, but now we both wish to change. Though weakened, he took me to task. But there was scarce need for that. I already despised myself heartily.

You will raise those delicate brows of yours in that way you have, murmuring, 'specious promises'. I make none. I have broken too many of 'em already. You will find that now I'm sincere, I'm out of fine speeches, as this muddled letter shows.

I turned for home to beg your forgiveness, only to find that you had already left with your brother, finally disgusted with me.

During my encounter with Lady Hogg – whom I won't upset you further by abusing – the difference between how things were with her, and how I have ever found them with you, struck me like a bolt of lightning in itself.

I long to see you. But there some things I must do before I allow myself to come to you to say what I yearn to tell you, and to try to make amends.

I am happy that you are taking a holiday from me with your family. Please stay there a few days, and when I come to claim you, I hope it will be as a man slightly more deserving of such a prize as you than I have been.

Yours Ever My Angel,
Your Unworthy 'Lord and Master'.

This done, he yelled up the stairs for O'Hare to post it. O'Hare came sighing downstairs. "You don't want me to help you dress, then …Your Honour?"

"Get along, curse you, before I box your dense ears again," snorted Harley.

When O'Hare had gone, he went upstairs to put on the new clothes and try and resist the urge to go into Clarinda's room. He did anyway, turning away from the emptiness.

Normally, his superb constitution meant that he could go on an all-night spree and saunter out with bright eyes and a smile the next morning. Now, to his outrage, his gloom was made worse by the beginnings of a headache, while waves of mild nausea swept over him now and then.

Perhaps this feebleness over drink was due to his emotional turmoil, or it might be that prolonged anxiety over Molyneux.

Whatever the cause, it reminded him of his sufferings when he had been beaten about the head by the Major's bravoes. This in turn made him think of Clarinda's coming to his aid, and his many squandered opportunities with her. He cursed himself some more. O'Hare would have recommended the hair of the dog that bit him[63] for his morning head, but the thought sickened Harley.

As he came downstairs, the temporary cook, with a concern he thought undeserved, came out into the front hall with offers of breakfast.

He sipped from his coffee dish, forcing himself to nibble some bread in a manner that struck him as more fitting for a rodent than a human. "By hell, I am enough of a rat, after all. Not good enough to be a cur." He savagely pushed aside his plate, sending a stab of pain through his head as he yelled again for O'Hare.

He went in to his study just before he left to pick up some bills. The violin case on the piano caught his eye. This violin had been one of the Earl's twenty-first birthday presents to him. He had never opened it since they had quarrelled irreconcilably.

He took it wherever he lived, like his bad conscience, and whether as an act of defiance or penitence he could not say. Now he picked it up sourly. "You're disappointed in me. You ever were. That at least makes something we agree over."

A light rain fell during most of Harley's wild dash back to Stoke Castle. The horses' hooves sent up a spray that soaked the sides of his vehicle and splattered the sleeves of his coat.

By the time he saw the castle upon that hill, the sun was piercing the clouds, and a rainbow stretched across the luminous sky. Not wishing to think of how, the last time he had arrived, it had been with his bride, Harley urged the horses on to that last steep climb.

The cobblestones of the stable yard were drying as he reined in the

---

63   Hair of the dog; As in the use of the hair from the rabid dog to treat its bite, in the belief it would prevent rabies.

horses, and a groom came out to take the reins. He turned out of the yard, thinking it was a sad thing not to have a welcome back, though soon enough old Mann would hobble out to give him a formal greeting. Then the O'Hare children rushed up and flung themselves on him, hugging his booted legs.

He patted their heads. "D'you want to know when your father's back? He's not far behind me, and if you want sweetmeats from Town, he's got those too."

"No, Sir," said Peg, holding tight, "It's grand to have you back. It feels safer with you here, and you'll keep them nasty boggles away by laughing at 'em. We've missed you."

He had to swallow and clear his throat before he spoke. "Don't tell me you've let those fool things bother you?"

"That funny old Professor with the nose says they won't, but it's nice to have you here anyway," said Seán.

Harley took a hand of each, clearing his throat some more. "Let's see what's in the kitchen for you brats."

Now the dogs ran up, and it was a warm enough welcome. Then Peg, as Harley swung her along by his side, said, "Where's Mistress? We've missed her, too."

"She's taking a rest from the lot of us," said Harley, casually, "She'll be back soon enough."

The children accepted this, hauling him towards the kitchens. Still, it seemed to him that one of the dogs caught the forced brightness in his tone, and gave him a quizzical glance.

"I regret that in Your Lordship's absence I have failed to summon the female entity prior to banishing it," said Lodovico Sharman as they sat over their strong wines and brandy after dinner.

Harley had picked at the food. He had hoped a glass of strong wine might set him to rights. After a couple of sips, he set it down and swore. As the Professor – who had made up for his host's restraint – looked his surprise, he admitted, "I'm a confoundedly sorry host tonight, Professor; my apologies. I must have overdone it in Town, though that's never taken me this way before. Must be the years catching up with me, eh? After all, I'm twenty-six next birthday."

He thought it odd that looking at the ruined face of his Uncle Toby had never given him the dismal idea that he was viewing a version of his future self, as did gazing on the toper Lodovico Sharman. After all, he had far more physical resemblance to his toper uncle. Still, in those days Harley was too young ever to imagine aging.

As the Professor made a courteous reply, he went on, "Maybe it needs one of the heirs to this fun here, to conjure 'em up. Perhaps we should now have a try in that mirrored mausoleum of a first drawing room. Wasn't that where you said there's power building?"

Dr Sharman looked dubious. "I have not prepared myself. Still, I am at Your Lordship's command."

"I want to deal with the matter now, so I can go and tell my wife all is safe," said Harley. "She may be powerful with this mystical stuff, as you've said. But it's my fight. It shouldn't be hers."

"Well said, Sir," the Professor toasted his host. Though his tone was calm, Harley saw unease in those slightly bloodshot eyes. "If Your Lordship will permit me, I will firstly collect some materials useful for us."

Before the attack on Molyneux, the careless Harley Venn would have had to hide his smile. Now he nodded gloomily, pushing aside his nearly full glass. He hoped that tomorrow, he would have recovered enough to drink something alcoholic. It was bad enough to have this uncertainty about Clarinda. It was worse to have to face it unable even to drain a glass of wine. He may have sworn to avoid excess; still, his body seemed to want to make him a total abstainer.

He realised, as Lodovico Sharman followed him from the great dining room, that the man must have resented him as a successor in Gabrielle Hogg's bed. It was to the showman's credit that he had done his best to protect him against this curse. Perhaps, though, the Professor had long overcome his passion for his one-time mistress. He had provided entertainment for her daughter's birthday, after all. Truly, too often, poor men had to sacrifice their pride or starve.

While Dr Sharman collected his artifacts, Harley wandered into Clarinda's rooms. One of her robes was hanging by her bed. He picked it up, sniffed it, and threw it down, biting his lip and blinking savagely. As the mist in his aching eyes cleared, he turned to go, when something glittering through the open door of the dressing room caught his attention. It was a mirror draped in a fine shawl, mostly hidden behind a chest. The evening sun glinting on an exposed fraction of its surface had caught his notice.

He paused. People generally didn't cover mirrors – unless, like the older Molyneux, they were frightened by what they might see in them. He remembered how, on the night of Foyle's death, Jack Molyneux had spoken of his father draping and smashing mirrors in his last weeks. That was before either of them could see any significance in that.

This commonplace object might well be the one from that old rascal Greendale in which Clarinda had first seen the Crone. Harley had advised her to throw it in the cellar. She must have decided to bring it here. He went to pick it up, throwing the cloth down on a chair. This room also smelt of Clarinda, which disturbed him far more than a growing opacity in the glass. He left at speed.

The great mirrored first drawing room had all of the stillness of evening. Long shadows stretched across the floor, and motes of dust danced in the dark golden brilliance. As Harley came in, the Professor had lit some incense which already scented the room, and the mirrors seemed to cloud, the atmosphere to tense.

Dr Sharman laughed as he set the holders with the burning sticks of incense on the grand piano. "You say you you're your twenty-sixth birthday, Lord Venn? I would give much to be that age."

Harley absently set Greendale's mirror down on the grand piano, next to the violin in its case he had left unopened for nearly five years, carried about by him almost as sort of punishment. He supposed O'Hare must have dumped it there on his arrival earlier.

As the Professor of Magic's words fell on his ears, Harley suddenly froze, staring at it: "That's it!" He snapped open the case in a strong whiff of resin.

The long lost letter from his father lay under the violin, where he had put it as he had packed on the day after his coming of age, when he had left Aylesbury House forever.

"This is the letter from my father I had on my majority, which I told you I had lost. It might tell us about this curse." Harley's breath came quickly, though his fingers were steady, as he tore open the letter. He strode over to the window to get a better light. The still bright sunshine now hurt his eyes, but he blinked angrily and began to read.

When he came to the salutation, he bit his lip; now the print swam before his gaze for a different reason. He was astonished at himself. He, who never wept, on the verge of tears three times today: he must be turning into a milksop. Yet, even by his twenty-first birthday, his father had not addressed him so affectionately for years.

He read with his slanting eyebrows raised, his humorous mouth hardened into a line, and when he came to the last sentence, he cursed himself for a fool. Then he said hoarsely, as he handed the letter to Lodovico Sharman, "This gives the story of that business with the girl. I think you must read it."

The Professor of Magic joined the Villainous Viscount at the window, and read the letter in turn. It seemed to Harley that he took long enough about it, raising his eyebrows at some parts of the story, and clearing his throat at others.

Now the atmosphere in the room thickened, and the depths of the mirrors began to stir, while even the eyes in the portraits of the *roués* of yesteryear came to life. But over by the window, covered in the light of the closing day, the two men missed seeing how the wraiths from that old drama of which they read stirred into life before them.

25.
Death and the Maiden

'My Beloved Son

So I must call you, for so you are, for all the disgraces you have run into, and to which you have exposed me.

I must have seemed to you a harsh parent. As I told you, I wished to counteract the bad influence of my brother, and saw that you resembled him in your bold and reckless temperament. Yet I was also guilty of Lucifer's sin of pride, for I could not believe, though I allowed you to spend much time at the castle, his evil counsels could prevail over those of a father.

After your mother's death, this household became a mournful one. I knew I should bestir myself on your account, but could not. Your youthful spirits jarred on me, while Tobias, as careless at forty as at twenty, begged for your company; and thus you came under his influence.

For many years after the strange death of John Molyneux, my reason and religion could not permit me to believe in the whispers amongst the servants of an hereditary curse. Yet now, weeks after my brother's sinister end, I begin to fear for you, as I would not, were you less fitting as his heir. Even now, I can scarce credit that a Beneficent Deity would permit – but let me lay the whole tale before you, and then beg you to choose virtue over vice.

As you know, Tobias was scarce eleven months younger than me, and though so different in temperament, we enjoyed each other's company. By way of economy, your grandfather sent us on our Grand Tour together.

We were two years away. In Florence, we met with other young Englishmen, and took up with a wild set, as careless of their duty to their Maker as they were of that they owed their fellow man. Then, the urges of youth were strong in me too, and when young and lusty, one's account seems far away. These men were Sir Timothy Carstairs and Sir Francis Foyle and the older John Molyneux.

We travelled back through France as a group, and were content to linger in the environs of Paris. We had entry to Versailles, and enjoyed its splendours, unknowing that the sun would within two years forever set on its grandeur64. We lingered in the then thriving town.

We often rode out into the countryside, escaping the minimal control of our tutor or bear leader,65 and we came to a little village some miles distant from the town of Versailles and a world away in culture. Hungry and thirsty, we stopped to dine at a modest eating house or inn, run by a handsome peasant and his older wife, then about sixty, whom we were later to hear was feared as a witch. It was said that she could do wicked things with the magic mirror, and had initiated her nephew into these and other secret arts, her husband and daughter eschewing such practices.

Their daughter worked as serving maid. She was so lovely that as we entered, we ceased our loud swagger to stare open mouthed. She might have served as a model for

---

64   The sun would within two years forever set on its grandeur: The French Revolution broke out in July 1789.

65   Bear leader: A type of tutor or knowledgeable guide who accompanied young men on their tours of continental Europe. The frequently winked at debauched behaviour.

Samuel Richardson's Pamela. Ironically, the girl, who could read well for a rustic, indeed had a copy of that romance in translation, given her by some patron. I believe it influenced her behaviour. Yet John Molyneux, cynic though he was, would liken her to Clarissa66. At the time, I laughed.

We had planned to ride back to Paris the next day, but we were so enchanted that we stayed some days, vying for her favours.

We were all enamoured, but my brother was head over ears. After that, we came back often. We were delighted by the location and the humble eating house. The wench was coy, but she favoured Toby. We looked alike, but of the pair of us, he was the more handsome.

My brother had brought his lackey, Greendale, on tour. An immoral brute, he fascinated women, though a plain looking servant, while money fell into his hands. Some whispered that he worshipped the Devil, and his infernal master kept him well supplied with funds and conquests. Of course, we laughed such ideas to scorn – then.

And after all, it may only have been a family knack for business. His own brother, accounted a respectable man, so succeeded in trade that he was able to rise above his low origins, and purchase a country house and have his offspring brought up as gentlefolk.

The wretch, Greendale, served us well as a linguist, for he had lived before in France, and while we gentlemen had our Latin and Greek, he spoke French like a native.

This nephew of the crone I have mentioned, a sly looking fellow, had long been the girl's admirer. She scorned him, and the more when my brother began to court her. I remember Toby laughing that the rustic's interest in the magical arts did him little good, as it could not win her.

The nephew was obsessed with schemes for making

---

66   Pamela and Clarissa: While Samuel Richardson's Pamela is happy to marry her once would-be rapist, Clarissa is intransigent about Lovelace, who does succeed in drugging and raping her.

money besides, and he and Greendale became friendly during our visits, and I believe talked over mercenary schemes; and it was whispered, too, that for a consideration, he had shown Greendale how to use a mirror for magic. But I never spoke to either, except to give orders.

Toby often urged me to accompany him there, and sometimes, the others, when they welcomed a break from the town of Versailles. He courted the girl passionately, but she showed herself a Pamela indeed, and would have none of him outside marriage. He offered her bribes beyond the dreams of avarice for a peasant wench, but she would not give in, and he began to fret and lose flesh.

You may note that I do not give her name; truly, I cannot endure to write it, and I know not why, after all these years.

Then the beldame's favoured magical mirror went missing, but I cared little enough for such nonsense.

One day we all came to visit, and as ever, drank more than we should. The others fell to mocking my brother for pining away over a peasant wench, and now Sir Timothy, Sir Francis Foyle and John Molyneux all urged him, as she would not give herself freely, to abduct her.

Now Molyneux spoke up, saying: 'If she will not come to you willing, then take the wench by force. She'll forgive you soon enough afterwards. Don't she like you well? She wants to come to you. Her commodity67 says yes, her scruples say no. What ails you to act so the booby? Play the man, and put you both out of misery.'

When I heard those words, I jumped up to berate them, and Molyneux in particular, for abandoned wretches all. But they shouted me down. My brother had seemed undecided, but when I told them that I should warn the wench, he put his back against the door, and shouted that he would never call me brother again if I carried out my

---

67   Commodity: Vagina.

threat, while I said, that I would never do as much for him, did he carry out his.

While the others roared drunken cheers, we wrestled. He was stronger than I, but half drunk, and I got past him and righting my wig, went to the bar. I passed Greendale and the cousin leering in scorn, but gave no thought to it. The girl and her mother were out, but I warned the father in the strongest terms I could use in my schoolboy French. He nodded, agreeing with everything Monseigneur said.

Something went amiss. For the next day, the girl was loitering in the lanes on her way back from some errand, picking wild flowers, when a closed carriage bowled up to her, and my brother leapt out to sweep her up and carry her away. Then the villain Greendale whipped up the horses, and the carriage flew through the lanes to an isolated farmhouse which he had taken nearby, and which he had already offered to her as her home.

A local child found one of her little shoes, and brought it to the inn just as I prepared to leave, still not having spoken to any of the others. I saw my brother had gone missing, but refused to ask after him.

Then the distraught parents set up a search for her, in which I joined. But Molyneux, Carstairs and Foyle went back to Versailles, chuckling.

Meanwhile my brother carried her to her room and locked the door. Here he begged her to accept the monies, the house, all that he had offered her to be his mistress, saying that she might as well give in, as if she would not come to him willing, then he would take her by force. She would have none of him without marriage.

So then, he swore that he would leave her to think for an hour, then return, and ravish her if she still held firm, so she might as well comply. He left, pushing her back into the room as she tried to break out, and locking the door.

Instead, she climbed out of the window, using the vines that grew up the side of the wall. It was a high window, and though she was slight, the vines gave way and she fell and broke her neck on the cobblestones below.

My brother returning, discovered her body, and gathering her into his arms, broke into lamentations so loud that it brought the labourers from the nearby fields. He always swore that he did not mean his threats.

He was wild when I came to the farmhouse, hours later. I got him into the house, where like Lovelace68 before him, he had to be restrained and bled.

The locals were fierce in their hatred, and charges of abduction or attempted rape or some such, hung over my brother – but this was in the days of the Ancien Régime,69 our 'bear leader' came from Versailles to smooth things over, we were nobles and they were peasants, and the local justices winked at the outrage. Make no doubt it was such injustices, apart from mass starvation, that swelled the cry of Liberté, égalité et fraternité ou la mort'70 to a furious roar, that led to the reign of the guillotine and convulsed Europe in decades of bloody war.

I feared that we would be set upon, and went about armed in those days before he regained his senses.

The others were all dismayed at the girl's death, but protested that it was not their fault; they had never thought that she would go to such absurd lengths to protect her virtue from a noble she liked.

I had via Greendale that when the beldame back at the coaching house heard of her daughter's death, she stretched her arms towards the merciless July sky, and shrieked that she would be avenged on the English milord who had destroyed ma petite, though her soul never left the earth. Then she fell down of an apoplexy, and lay for weeks

---

68   Lovelace: The rapist villain of Samuel Richardson's 'Clarissa' (1752).

69   *Ancien Régime*: The old system in France, where the great majority of the population had no political representation at all.

70   *Liberté, égalité et fraternité ou la mort: The slogan of the French Republic.*

as a log, and ever after, dragged one leg, while one arm hung useless.

Yet, this enfeebled frame did not lessen her hatred of her daughter's abductor, or those who had urged him on. It was said that every night, she worked on her black arts in secret, and that the cousin now joined her, for he was now overcome with guilt and shame for turning against his beloved.

When Greendale went to the house, offering the stricken family money from his master, the cousin spat in his face, shouting for the return of the magic mirror he had stolen. Then they fought, rolling on the floor in hateful embrace among the broken pottery, until the locals separated them, and then the furious cousin raged that in due course, he would see Greendale flattened like a crépe.

Yet the wretch prospers still, so I heard from your uncle. He did not return to France until 1815 brought an end to the Revolutionary Wars. Then he made an armed pilgrimage to the churchyard where the maiden laid buried, and if rumour is to be believed, he abased himself before her grave until the Abbé remonstrated with him. The servants' tattle goes that a high wall nearby rocked as he passed, but we must discount such nonsense.

My brother seemed to forget our bitter quarrel, though he did know that I had warned the family of the outrage schemed with his friends. While always an unrepentant rake, as you know, he long prospered too. He soon regained his spirits, which he retained to the end of his days, save for the uneasiness of his last weeks, when perhaps he foresaw with the worsening of his health, his final account loom near. I pray for mercy for his errant spirit. He married two heiresses foolish enough to surrender to his outward charm, and squandered part of their fortunes. He remained childless, and became much attached to you.

As he had named you his heir to his private fortune besides the entail, it seemed only fair to let you be often with him, shocking old toper though he was. As he wished the family name to continue, he made your coming into the second half conditional on your marriage.

Now your beloved mother had died, and a shadow fell upon my own spirits, so that I could not much endure your youthful exuberance in the house, even in a mansion the size of ours.

When John Molyneux fell to his death, I made little of it. The man was a drunkard, diseased by his excesses that had affected his brain. I said it was co-incidence that led to his frenzied smashing of mirrors.

Your uncle, as you know, planted a rose garden in the middle of the maze. It was in sentimental memory of the rose among woman whom he had schemed to ravish; and now you can guess her name.

When I heard that he had died too of a fit, lying at the bottom of those shallow steps in that very garden, I began to tremble for you, though reason and the teaching of the church opposed my fears. Besides, you are no son to Tobias Venn, and your father tried to save the girl, though perhaps, he did not strive hard enough.

Sir Francis Foyle and Sir Timothy Carstairs are yet alive. The one, now reformed, is a friend of mine, though his son and heir has long been as wild as mine. The other is an abandoned wretch. I fear for you, Harley, if he goes the same way as the others; for while you are not Tobias Venn's son, in every way you are his heir. You lead a wild life. I pray my fears are groundless.

I lay the facts before you, and beg that you will not dismiss them as the superstitious fancies of an aging man. I hope that we can be reconciled after all the bitterness between us. But if you scorn what I have written here as so much nonsense, then do not speak of it, and neither shall I.

Your loving Father.'

26.
Shades and Returns

THE MIRRORS FLASHED INTO LIFE, and the scenes of that old drama back in the penultimate July of the *Ancien Régime* began to play out in each. One set off another, as in a staggered firework display.

In the first, the careless young bucks swaggered into the modest rural coaching house, astonishing the locals with their fine and foreign dress, their long powdered hair tied back – though Tobias Venn, vain of the gold of his, wore his unpowdered.

His older brother was quieter and darker, less handsome, though many must be awed by his title into believing him to be the finer. The young John Molyneux was as lively, dark and lean as his son would be. He led some jesting. The less striking Sir Timothy Carstairs and Sir Francis Foyle followed, guffawing at Molyneux's wit. They all – though already debauched – looked shockingly young to Harley Venn, who had only known them as older men.

The young serving man, Greendale, followed some way afterwards, insignificant and plain compared to his finely clothed master, but as alert as a pointer.

The girl served in the room, blooming and lithe. She was clearly a model of the style of beauty admired at the time, so that the *roués* fell silent, staring. A young man at a table, dressed in the style of a peasant with aspirations, scowled at them.

Only Greendale's attention was focused on him; he smiled in satisfaction, as if he had found something he had sought for years. Then his gaze moved on, not to the girl, but to the mother, who also served in the eating house, and he nodded.

This woman, though elderly, was scarcely recognisable as the gnarled and wizened crone, in whom hatred and a passion for vengeance seemed to have burnt up all flesh, so that only the flashing of her dark eyes retained the fire of youth. In this younger version, there lingered the remains of a beauty passed on to her daughter.

Sounds came now – a gabble of English and French, truncated phrases, thoughts, exclamations blended with the distant rhythm of approaching horses' hooves.

Lodovico Sharman rushed to seize the lighted stick of incense and, leaping next to Harley Venn, one arm outstretched, made a circle about them. The smoke glowed in the air.

The next mirror sprang into life. In it, Tobias Venn walked with the girl in the lanes, helping her to gather a posy of wild flowers, a strange amusement for so seasoned a rake. Sometimes, he sprang up to reach a high dog rose.

As they walked along, he urged something on her in halting speech, while she listened, eyes downcast, giving the odd reply, shaking her head. Sometimes, he snatched a kiss, and she did not always rebuff him.

The third mirror started into life. In it, the young Greendale, rough candle in hand, crept into a great room. It was a defunct dairy, full of strange artifacts, with bunches of herbs suspended from hooks, and piles of homespun candles placed amongst the old dairy implements. Several mirrors stood about.

Greendale looked about, his raised candle throwing shadows over the dark walls. Then, he snatched up a mirror Harley recognised, set on a small stand, wrapping it in a broad cloth. Quickly, he left with it under one arm.

Now all the mirrors in the great drawing room sprang into life, all at once enacting that past drama, each showing a succeeding scene. This was but one abuse of the rich and powerful of their social inferiors among innumerable through ages past. It was less ugly and squalid than many; but in intent, as sordid as any.

When the men whose images moved in the mirrors had walked the earth, young and vigorous, many of the principals of earlier abuses had been dead and buried for centuries. Now in their turn, the bodies of these visions had joined their predecessors underground. Yet in this glass, and in the hatred of the Crone and her unwitting slave, they lived on.

In a fourth mirror, Greendale and his now ally, the bitter cousin, conspired. In another, the girl and her anxious mother quarreled, and the cousin burst in, abusing her. In another, the young *roués* swaggered through Versailles. In another, Toby Venn rose from the bed of a woman he had bought, and groped swearing for his shirt, then as ever, unsatisfied.

Lodovico Sharman groaned. For once Harley Venn found nothing laughable about his grimace. In the mirror opposite, Toby Venn was back in a side room at the inn or eating house, arguing with the girl. He drew her on his knees; he kissed her, chucked her chin, and acted as Mr B,[71] thrusting his hand in her bosom and – as Mr B surely must – tried to pull up her skirts. Once again she struggled free, escaping through the door as it opened. The still handsome father stood there calling the enraged English noble to dinner and avoiding his eyes.

The murmur of voices grew louder, while the drumming of horse hooves beat a rising tattoo. The figures slipped through the mirrors, enacting their tableaux in the great room. The voices of years back mingled and broke apart in waves of French and English, but it was impossible to catch the sense of any, save one.

These were the words of the senior John Molyneux, echoing like an ugly mantra: *"If she will not come to you willing, then take the wench by force."*

"The glass from Greendale," muttered Harley Venn to himself, as the Crone emerged from that small mirror directly before them, her eyes blazing.

He made to break out of the protective circle, but Lodovico Sharman,

---

71   Mr B: The anti-hero of Samuel Richardson's *Pamela.*

beads of sweat standing out on his forehead, seized his arm. "For your life, no!"

The girl's wraith appeared in front of them, sauntering along through half visible lanes, picking an odd wildflower, oblivious to the beat of horses' hooves and rattling of carriage wheels loud about her. That coach and horses, cantering up the lanes in the mirror in front of them, broke through the surface. It was in the room with them, the scent of the sweating horses in their nostrils, the rattle of the wheels and the thud of the hooves beating like drums in their ears.

The driver – recognisably Greendale, with a hat pulled low over his face, as if that would somehow shelter him from disgrace - drew up the horses. Toby Venn jumped from the coach as it slowed, his handsome face set in ugly lines.

He made for the girl, and she shrieked and struggled, trying to tear at his face with her nails, but he caught her arm.

His nephew wrenched away from Lodovico Sharman and hurled himself on him.

Had that vision been made of flesh, it would have been floored. As it was, Harley burst through it and staggered, as he had with the hooded spectre. Now, he tried to bar the door to the coach. But that too was insubstantial, and he lunged through it.

The girl fought, but she was small, while like his nephew, Toby Venn was an athlete. He silenced her with a hand clamped over her mouth and nose, and as she bit his hand, he melted through his nephew, to pull her into the coach before she could do more than make a long scratch down one cheek.

Greendale whipped up the horses, and the coach plunged away, vanishing into an opposite mirror. Harley Venn turned, wild eyed and swearing, as the scenes at the farmhouse, with Toby Venn alternately cajoling and threatening the girl, slipped out of the mirrors. The older Venn's French was poor, and his frustration, as he cursed and threw up his hands as he ran out of words, might have been laughable in other circumstances.

The figures moved about the younger Venn, acting out further scenes, one after another, while the earlier ones played out within and without the mirrors at the end of the room.

The girl, tears running down her face, climbed from a high first floor window, skirts bundled up, gingerly stepping out onto the vines that grew up the wall, and slowly climbed downwards.

The tearing vines and her fall, her shriek cut short, came as the Hooded Spectre emerged from Greendale's stolen mirror as had his former mistress. Again, it started towards Harley.

Venn broke free of the charmed circle and darted towards the piano, snatching up the mirror. The Professor followed him and surrounded him with smoke from his stick. The being's movements slowed. It fought its way forward in a crouch.

The Crone raised one hand for the mirror, and with the other, gestured to the Hooded Spectre to stop. It still shambled forwards. She shrieked an order, extending one finger. There was a flash, a crash, and her rebellious slave was sucked back into the mirror, hissing. The Crone glared after it, and then melted into it also, while the images folded in on themselves and vanished.

The door burst open as Lodovico Sharman sagged at the knees, toppling to the floor like a felled tree. The O'Hare children stood wide eyed as the images disappeared.

Harley shouted, "No!" as he shoved the mirror on a side table, but the children dashed up to him. They scarcely spared a look for the unlucky Professor. The threat being past, whatever it had been, they were surprisingly calm.

"That was the bloody bad magic Father said we had to mind out for." Peg came up as Harley bent over Sharman, touching his face, which felt cold to him. "It couldn't hurt you, though. Is he dead? His nose ain't red now."

The Professor's chest rising and falling answered her question. "No, he's in a fit. Yes, that was bad magic, but Sharman didn't start it, for all his title as Professor of Magic. Run for Mistress Mann."

The boy ran off, while the girl glanced with more respect at the prone figure. "Has he a title, like you?"

The boy paused at the door. "I saw a ghost carriage. It won't come to get us at night, will it?"

"Not a bit of it. Go for Mistress Man quick now," Harley urged as he saw the Professor's eyelids flicker.

Mrs Mann came with her smelling bottle, and Lodovico Sharman partially revived, even taking some sips of brandy, though Harley thought he would have to be dead not to do that. Still, his eyes stayed glazed, and though he murmured, it was in Latin. They carried him to bed and sent for the physician.

Harley passed the time before the doctor's arrival in visiting the maze. Twilight was falling, but he had often gone in at that hour. Once he had been with Carstairs, which was how the youth could boast at the ball of there at dusk.

Now all was quiet. A chill breeze stirred the rose bushes. Harley felt befuddled, as if he had been drinking heavily. Also he, who usually lounged about in shirt sleeves on a chill autumn evening, was disgusted to find himself shivering, though it was not at least through fear.

Then, he saw the misty form of the maiden, standing again by the fountain. She made him a curtsy, and came towards him. After the recent events, he felt too drained for alarm, though now an icy hand caressed his cheek.

You tried to save me. I thank you.

As ever, when the vision had gone, he began to wonder if he had ever seen it at all.

Although Lodovico Sharman seemed half aware of what went on about him, he still spoke only in Latin. Harley, using his schoolboy knowledge, tried to answer him, but he made no response. The doctor tried the same thing, also to no effect.

Harley saw no point in trying to explain how the Professor had come to have a fit, while the doctor clearly put it down to excess without saying so. Undoubtedly, the Viscount and his guest had been up to no good, and there was no telling what years of that did to the brain.

The physician noted that the host looked pale and haggard enough himself, and lectured him on excess. "I take the liberty, My Lord, as one who has served both your grandfather and your uncle before you, to remind you of the damage done by over-indulgence…"

"I daresay," snapped Harley. "So you don't know what ails the Prof? Then leave those draughts, and I'll get a second opinion tomorrow."

The doctor also annoyed him by asking after Lady Venn in a pointed way. Harley wondered if he had already heard rumours about Clarinda's leaving him.

"You've got a fever…Your Honour," said O'Hare, as he helped Harley undress. "And the weans told me of them unholy boggles that Professor would annoy with conjuring tricks. He should leave them spooks alone. You've both done yourselves a mischief."

"Nothing to be done about it," grunted Harley. "I'll do you a mischief too, if you don't leave me be. Mind you keep the youngsters away from that room and the maze."

Harley passed the night restless, dreaming feverishly. Thoughts raced through his head unbidden, so that he began to wonder if he was going mad. By morning, he felt still more light-headed. Still, the Professor having been struck down, he must fight on alone.

The thing may have broken entirely from the Crone's control, as it had ignored that order she had shrieked at it just before they vanished. That might mean attacks from different sources.

"You women patch up the damage we men do, eh, Ma'am?" He told Mistress Mann as he stood in the doorway of Lodovico Sharman's room, watching her straighten his sheets.

The Professor was torpid, murmuring to himself. "Send for two more doctors," Harley told her, and went unsteadily down to the breakfast room.

Mistress Mann told her husband, "The master's not eaten a thing since he came back, and he looks ill himself. There's no reasoning with him, but I'll ask those doctors to have a look at him on the quiet."

"He's probably paying the price for going back to his wicked ways in Town as that wretch O'Hare talks of, bad enough for the mistress not to come back with him," Mann told her, breaking off as he realised that Peg was at the door.

"You don't think he's going to die, do you?" Peg broke in. "Still, that old Professor was after making a grand dinner yesterday, with two helpings of everything – which annoyed Father who likes a chicken pie above anything – and he was taken bad for all that."

Normally, Mistress Mann would have rebuked her for interrupting her elders. Now, seeing her anxiety, she said, "Nonsense, child. It took my cousin ten days of starving before it killed him."

Peg and Seán went to check unseen on the master in the breakfast room, silently opening the door. He sat alone at the grand table, his food untouched and pushed aside, his head resting on his hand. He looked so mournful that Peg supposed he was thinking. That never made people happy, and Lord Venn normally had more sense.

Sensing eyes on him, Harley turned about. "Morning, brats. Come and eat some of this for me. Then you should be on your way to school."

Closing the door in case Mistress Mann should see, the children helped themselves.

"I don't like school much," said Seán with his mouth full of ham. "Mistress Mann says that you'll die if you don't eat for ten days, and Peg's feared you ain't eaten for two already, so that's only eight to go."

Peg bit her lip, but Harley smiled at her. "Thank you, my dear; I'll make a point of eating before then, just for you. You learnt the sums to work that out at school, so school's good for something, besides fighting, though that's for you, my lad. Peg shouldn't do that as a girl."

"Father said the mistress did, that day when you was set on," objected Peg.

The Viscount sighed.

The Earl of Aylesbury was a man of regular habits, and took a dismal mid-afternoon meal. He had a poor appetite these days, and would rather spend the time doing something else. Still, the female dependants who lived with him were flattered that he joined them. Therefore, his sense of duty made him sit down with them.

Afterwards, he read for half an hour in his study. The butler rarely disturbed him, so when he announced, "A visitor, My Lord," the Earl stared.

"Who is it?"

The man cleared his throat. "It's Lord Venn, Sir."

The Earl's eyes dilated, but he spoke coolly. "Indeed? Show him in."

As he waited, he murmured, "I suppose the ruffian's very drunk to come here at all."

Although the Earl stayed seated in a calm pose, as his son appeared in the doorway, his eyes feasted on him. The young man looked almost haggard, certainly, as if he had been overdoing it, and he swayed slightly as he stood there, signs which the older man interpreted gloomily. But his shadowed eyes were darkened by emotion. The Earl saw that he held a letter.

"Sir – I have only just read the letter. I mislaid it for near on five years; I didn't know what you said in it, until I found it last night."

"You never read it?" the Earl made a movement, and then Harley was kneeling before him, clasping his hands, while the Earl embraced him. The tears of both brimmed over as they had not in many years. It was a while before either of them could speak.

Then Harley, blowing his nose, said, "I never saw those last lines. You must have had a sad view of me, when I said nothing of it, quite apart from all the other things. You were right to have a sorry view of me: I've got one of myself. I swore I was going to change for the better when I married, and I've got the best of wives. She's worth twenty of me, and I don't give a hang for birth."

Some of his old rebellious look came back as he said this, but the Earl nodded. "You are right to discount it, when there are so many low born people worth two of their betters. From what I hear, you are fortunate in her. I am eager to meet her."

Though Harley presently felt highly unfortunate, he smiled. "She's visiting her brother at the moment. She's not best pleased with me," he admitted, putting a brave face on matters. This was due to concern at the signs of aging that he had noted his once invulnerable seeming Governor rather than his pride not allowing him to voice his anxiety over Clarinda's absence.

"I went back to much of my old wild ways in Town," he admitted, "I made worry over Jack Molyneux and young Wilmot my excuse."

His father stiffened, but then conceded, "It is difficult enough to change. So, Lady Venn is not with you, now?"

"No, she worked hard at nursing Molyneux and the baby, and she went to her brother's to get the better of that, and her disappointment in me. I won't go back and beg her forgiveness until I've done something over at the castle. But I do beg yours, now."

"There's no need," said the father, "If you were a scapegrace, I should not have been so unbending. That only led to more wildness from you. Obduracy has ever been my fault as much as yours – that's what led to Tobias gaining such an influence over you to begin with, after all; and still I learned nothing from that. When we quarreled that day, over that young man's death after your duel –"

"You don't know how I regret that," said Harley, "I only winged him, but being in the wrong, I should have shot in the air, and not let his bungled attempt to kill me ruffle me into shooting back."

"No more on that. It was unlucky so shallow a wound festered, after all," said his father. "Regarding this matter you must undertake at the castle; it concerns that miserable curse, has it not?"

He looked outraged to have to admit to such a thing, and Harley didn't blame him. He felt outraged about it himself. The Earl flinched as Harley nodded. "Then I must be involved; I was at the beginning, after all."

Harley did not say that he was not only touched by the concern that his father had shown for him in that letter, he was also relived that in that drama of so long ago, he had not winked at the wrong done to the girl then, only to turn into a self-righteous hypocrite later. He had dreaded finding that out since that first talk with Mann, and dreading despising his father accordingly.

Now they looked at each other with mutual respect. Harley said, "No, Sir. It is good of you to offer. But I've an expert in these matters helping me," – he saw no need to admit that the expert in question was unconscious – "And we'll do well enough."

"Your hands are burning," the Earl touched Harley's forehead, "And your head too. You're ill."

"So everyone tells me," said Harley, "But I won't give in to it. It's only a fool cold."

"But what is this terrible thing that threw Foyle and Molyneux down the stairs? When I heard of their accidents, I half insisted on drunkenness by way of explanation, just as I put the deaths of the older men down to a lifetime's excess. To the deuce with this expert. I must face whatever it is with you."

Harley had to smile at the thought of the stiff look the Earl would turn on the foul abuse of the Hooded Spectre. "No, Sir. I thank you, but it would do no good. You weren't debauched, like Uncle Toby, me, Jack and the others."

He shook his head. "I hope young Carstairs will be safe until we can lay this ghost. But I think he must, because he's no more than a child. Your coming would only delay things until I was alone again, d'you see?"

"You've never lacked courage, whatever your other faults. But I dread to think of what you must face, though I also believe that this thing can only injure you, if you let it. You are the last person to be cowed by it. Yet, at least, stay here until you are better."

Harley shook his head. "No, it must be now. My wife would say it was all part of a great plan beyond our human understanding. You know what a godless wretch I am; but in a way, I do see that, too, and that I've brought this on myself." He grinned. "You won't be rid of me so easily, Sir. I'll live to plague you yet."

"It's all unjust – you aren't Toby's son, you are mine," his father spoke between clenched teeth, seemingly unaware of the implication of his words. This might have made Harley smile at another time. His late mother would have been as likely to dance nude about a maypole on the village green as commit adultery with her brother-in-law.

"I'm heir to his excesses, besides his wealth," said Harley. "And through Greendale's wealth my wife is drawn in too."

"If only she was with you, I'd be easier in my mind. Then, if anything happened..." the Earl's voice trailed off.

"I wouldn't be, though I'm sorry enough without her. I want to make her proud of me." Harley's voice was wistful, and he sighed.

So did his father. "What is this threat that you face? I would I knew the form it took. When my brother rambled about it once, I put it down to drink."

"It's foolish and Gothic enough," said Harley, carelessly, "And I think I know how to fight it now. I'll be back to tell you of it soon enough. And now it's time for me to go, as I must be back at the castle long before dusk."

The Earl shook his head. "If only we could have understood each other before. I know you too well to try and convince you to stay. It's pointless, my asking you to be careful. But somehow I know that you will win through. I'll send to enquire after you first thing in the morning." He forced a smile. "If you insist on going back, you must at least take some refreshment before you go. A glass of wine and some food?"

"Clarinda," Harley spoke the name as if he loved saying it, "Swears by tea, so just some for me, I thank you. It may do me good."

The Earl smiled his approval as he moved to the bell pull. Meanwhile, Harley felt that this malaise was sucking him of all vigour and pleasure. Wine nauseated him, and he had not even enjoyed looking at the rear of the new housemaid, Abbey's friend, as she walked down the corridor yesterday. At the time he had put that down to his dismay over Clarinda. Now he began to feel as if he was possibly dying.

He drew himself up. He was going to deal with the curse before he keeled over.

27.
The Kiss, Dear Maid – Once More

'*Nothing more happened with Lady Hogg than those slobbering kisses from my drunken self that the Crone used to triumph over you…if that spectre could have shown you worse, you know she would…I long to see you. But there some things I must do before I allow myself to come to you to say what I yearn to tell you, and to try to make amends.*'

CLARINDA'S HEART WHISPERED THAT THESE delicious hints of what the rascal would say would be the words that she longed to hear. She told it to be quiet; he might only want to say that he had become mildly fond of her and that they must try and pull together. Still, her heart went on glowing whatever she told it.

Yet, this was overshadowed by her sense of foreboding for Harley, even more than by indignation over his late treatment of her. Last night, she had put her feeling of dread down to unhappiness over Lady Hogg. She saw that it was due to what must be happening at the castle.

The letter had been delayed. Harley had ignored her pleas – well, he didn't believe in obeying a wife, after all – and been at the castle overnight. She called for Abbey.

"My dear, I must go to Stoke Castle immediately. You pack my things and I'll have you picked up tomorrow."

The girl smiled. "It's nice to see you happy again, Mistress Clarinda. Has the repentant lord summoned you, remorseful for his former misbehavior, as in – but beg pardon, that's impertinent."

Clarinda dimpled. "It is, Abbey, but you may as well finish your sentence."

"I was going to say, as you'll remember as happened with the squire in 'Pamela', Mistress Clarinda, though she was only a lady's maid, when that happened. To be sure you read that one, anyway?"

"I did, and tried my best to forget it. He had tried to ravish her, and while she was right to forgive him, she should never have gone back to marry him."

"Mistress Clarinda, you shouldn't ride back alone. I'll come with you. Ah, I see you have made your mind up, as with them kittens."

Nancy, Bella and James were less understanding. "But you only came yesterday, my dear, and we know how the Viscount went on in Town," said Nancy. "It will do him good to wait. Besides, we can't spare the carriage this evening, as we dine at the Hope's."

Clarinda saw that Nancy, having successfully married her off to the Viscount, took that connection for granted, and even missed her. Meanwhile, Bella, though she had softened towards Harley Venn since talking to him at the wedding, nodded. "It would be too weak." As she had already accused her sister of complete weakness in marrying such a villain, Clarinda had to smile.

James frowned. "It's too late in the day now to think of setting off. I'll take you in the carriage tomorrow. Then, Nancy and Bella can come, and you can show us round the house and gardens, and I'll have a try at that maze."

Clarinda could only hope that Harley had not already had a different sort of try at the maze himself. "You must do that very soon, but I have good reason to go there at once. I'll take my old horse and be back long before dusk."

Selena and Nancy said that it was bound to rain. James doubted that he could answer for her life, perhaps thinking back to the days of his childhood, when highwaymen had been abroad. Clarinda laughed, kissed them goodbye and set off.

The sky had clouded over again, and it was sultry. As Clarinda rode on through the country roads, the clouds turned livid, and she thought that it would be just her luck to be struck by lightning.

She passed an occasional farm cart, and the people working in the fields made obeisance as she rode by. That was a servile custom with which she would love to do away. As always, she greeted them.

She sighed with relief as she sighted Stoke Castle on its hill, surrounded by thunder clouds.

"Gothic enough; no wonder Harley calls it 'The Castle of Doom," she murmured. "Those wretched spectres: I'm sick of them."

At last she rode through the gates, which were opened for her by a boy working in the garden nearby. In answer to her anxious queries on how everyone fared, he was talkative.

"Those O'Hare brats hooted shocking at the Curate when he called, taking him for a 'creditor', whatever that is – but what would you expect from heathens? The Professor had a fit after some funny goings on – The Master? He is well enough – Ah, thank you, My Lady!'"

Clarinda thrust some coins on him and urged the horse into a canter to the stables. Handing the horse over to the head groom and hoisting her skirts, she rushed to the front of the house.

She could hear music. The windows of the first drawing room were open, and Harley was singing, 'The Kiss, Dear Maid.' She thought that his voice sounded hoarse, though still melodious. She whispered, "Ah, you rascal. You shall not return the kiss untainted back to mine, quite. But then, neither am I quite a maiden." She nipped round to enter unseen through a side door.

He didn't hear her footsteps. He was at the piano, in his shirtsleeves, and even as he played and sang, there was something sad about him. She moved towards him. Now it seemed to her that he sang the words with a feeling he had not before: -

> *'By day or night, in weal or woe,*
> *That heart, no longer free,*
> *Must bear the love it cannot show,*
> *And silent ache for thee.'*

As he stopped playing, he turned, sensing her gaze. He blinked, as if doubting his eyes, and as if they hurt. "Clarinda?"

She smiled. He leapt up, knocking over the piano stool, and crushed her in his arms, kissing her again and again, only breaking off to gaze at her as adoringly as she could wish. "You're back – you shouldn't be – but I'll never let you go again!" He went back to kissing her.

She had to pull away from those delicious kisses. "Ow! Not so tight."

He loosened his hold a little. "Sorry, my darling; I'm a brute."

She was alarmed by his body heat. His skin felt as hot as had Molyneux's and young Wilmot's. "Why, you are burning."

He gave a wild laugh. "Probably a taste of things to come, eh? Tell me you forgive me for being so damnably stupid."

"I might," she gave a happy laugh, lips against his skin, "But you were going to tell me something. And I hope you don't quote the lines you did when first you proposed."

His face was already too flushed for him to colour any more, but he winced. "Arrogant fool that I was, to blather that cant, thinking it was a fine thing to draw you in. But though it never was only your money for me, that was part of it, and you were right to despise me for a fortune hunting dog. Now I feel all that I said then, but I can't put it into words."

She laughed, stroking his face. "For a plain and serviceable girl such as me, three words will do, if only you mean them. Then you must tell me what ails you."

"Clarinda, I don't know what ails me, but I must tell you what you have come to mean to me before it lays me out: then I'll go happy, though you can't feel the same way. When I didn't care, I even flattered myself that you had fallen for me. But how could you care for a scoundrel like me? Still, I'll say those three words. I…"

As if on cue, that Gothic flash of lighting lit the room, and thunder seemed to shake the floor. The mirrors split across, and the portraits jumped from the walls.

The Crone stood before them, her voice needle sharp in their ears: "No - he lies!"

Harley tightened his arms about Clarinda, while all about them, the spectres spilled out in tableaux to enact the later details of that sorry drama of the *Ancien Régime.*

The translucent form of the girl, Rose, lay dead on the cobblestones, fallen vines draped over her like a wreath. Toby Venn stood over her, shaking his fists at the blue vault of the sky reflected in the shattered mirrors behind.

Nearby, the younger form of the Crone appeared, raving too, swearing vengeance, her fists also stretched to heaven, passion distorting her face, so that none of the blurred figures grouped about dare approach her.

The steward and his ally, the cousin, Rose's former admirer, grappled on a rough floor visible through the boards of this one, cursing each other.

Clarinda clamped her lips tight as the shade of the older figure of her uncle Greendale appeared, standing by some steps, eyes dilated, rooted to the spot as the wall above him toppled and fell. The stones broke him as if he were an insect, squashing his head in a burst of crimson. Then mercifully, they buried him from sight as carefully as if poured over him by a playful giant. The women and children nearby remained untouched.

Gasping, she remembered to send out those waves of silver blue light, and the menace in the atmosphere seemed to lighten.

"I don't lie now," Harley said calmly. He reached behind him to the piano, "This is yours, *Madame.* Though I can't change the past, and save your daughter, I can return it to you."

The Crone snatched the mirror, as if suspecting he would take it back. She signalled to him, gliding over to the wall. "Come, as you think yourself brave, young man."

"You stay here, my love," Harley told Clarinda. "Don't try and interfere."

"Who said only now he'd never let me go?" Clarinda caught his hand.

Together, they followed the Crone. A panel slid open in the wall, revealing the foot of a flight of curved, crumbling steps in a dark recess the size of a cupboard. Clarinda's heart jolted. She went on surrounding them by light and whispered a prayer.

The drawing room doors burst open. Lodovico Sharman rushed in, his hair disordered, his clothes pulled on anyhow. Like Harley, he was in his shirtsleeves. He looked recovered as he approached, holding a smoking stick of incense in one hand, and a lit candle in the other. He shouted an abjuration, pointing at the being. It wavered. Then, snarling, it reformed and glided after Clarinda and Harley.

Clarinda may have spoken bravely of their being strong together, but now, as they made their way up the dark, winding steps, belief in her strength seemed an empty boast. She had never liked the idea of climbing crumbling, unlit steps with a great drop to the open side. Harley obviously had as a boy, which she thought showed his often poor taste in entertainment.

Only a dim light filtered down from above. Harley guided Clarinda, holding her on the inside against the wall, and keeping a wary eye on the Hooded Spectre as it billowed behind them.

She knew that he was ready to jump on it, risking falling to his death if it raised a threatening hand to her, and she feared this as much as she loved him for it. As her heart surged, the being hissed, and fell back.

Poor creature; I pity you.

She thought of her loved ones, living and departed, of Bella, and of the misguided but loved James and Nancy. She sensed, too, that Molyneux was with them in spirit, though very much alive. Perhaps he was asleep, and watched them in a dream. The thing hissed and wavered. Still it returned to dog them up these endless steps.

Harley's night vision was excellent, or perhaps he remembered the climb from his boyhood. He knew each crumbling step, warning her. Once he had to halt and pull her up a missing one. He burned with fever: she could feel the heat in his fingers. Every now and again she squeezed them.

Always the Crone glided ahead of them, her footfalls silent, oblivious to their thoughts. The closeness of these beings in the tunnel was hideous, and Clarinda had to fight back waves of panic, exhaling and whispering prayers.

At last, the light above brightened, and the worn steps became visible. Unlike the other passages, this one was open to the sky, the cover hurled aside as if by force.

The Crone had perhaps opened it from below. She was on the roof, her mirror in her gnarled hands. Harley handed Clarinda up, and the Hooded Spectre came close behind.

They stood on flat leads between the towers. Above them, the lowering clouds flickered with lightning. The gardens spread out as flat as a table beneath them, the crowns of trees below them. No bird sang. Clarinda knew this to be more than the gathering storm. No bird would sing, until this final scene was over.

A threatening murmur started, the hum of voices caught in a rising wind. Once more, the spectral figures moved in front of them, enacting their ends in ghostly surroundings.

Old Timothy Carstairs lurched towards them on his misty roof, clutching his chest, while a duplicate of the figure that glowered beside them taunted him, drawing him on.

The older John Molyneux staggered down a flight of phantom stairs, proffering a ring, whispering pleas lost on the monster which seized him, grappled with him, and hurled him down the last flight.

Far below in the grounds, a phantom carriage sped through a mirage of the rural lanes of France towards the maze, the drumming of the horses' hooves loud in their ears.

In the middle of the sunken garden, Toby Venn closed with another image of the hooded phantom, hitting it in frenzy. It reformed after every blow, finally seizing him to shake him as a terrier with a rat, hurling him down the steps.

At each ghostly re-enactment, the image of the being before them gurgled exultingly. All the time the gale gained power, and Clarinda saw what a threat this must be to the humans up here.

The Crone pointed with a fleshless hand. A phantasm of the winding staircase at the Coconut Club appeared before their eyes, with the group of revellers surging towards them, the younger Foyle leading, a shadowy Lord Venn himself close behind. In a flash, the spectre appeared, and Foyle went over the railings.

Clarinda did not see young Frederick Carstairs. She hoped that meant that he was to be spared, young and relatively innocent as he was. Whereas, Harley and the others…Unable to finish that thought, she threw a protective glow about Harley.

The Crone, still holding the mirror, and her creature turned upon

Clarinda and Harley as they stood, hands joined. Clarinda saw how Harley fought to subdue his savagery. His chest heaved with the effort.

"Tiresome spectres," she mustered a calm tone.

"You waver; you confuse her with your daughter," the being's howl mingled with the sound of the wind buffeting about the towers. Had Clarinda not lost her sense of fun on the steps, she might have found it absurd. "Give the rakehell to me, as you did Foyle. Then we both can be free."

"Do you order me, insolent one?" The Crone's voice came sharp, but as ever, as a voice in dreams. She paused, gazing at the leads as if looking through the roof, while the rising gale whipped at her cloak. Perhaps she could even see Lodovico Sharman far below.

"You rave of escape from me," she returned, "You failed with Molyneux and the parlour magician downstairs, who even now mumbles his incantations."

Clarinda supposed that was one good thing. Still, she was bitterly disappointed in the Professor of Magic for keeping below.

The Hooded Spectre intoned, "The libertine's lawful slut hinders me, oozing tenderness. You'll no longer keep me from destroying her. I am stronger than you now, you shrunken hag!"

It rushed towards Clarinda, and Harley thrust her behind him.

The Crone pointed one finger, directing an invisible charge of power at the monster. It hissed as its form wavered and smoked, and its cloak dissolved. It solidified again, resembling once more an unusually lively cadaver, made of glutinous half rotted flesh, and dressed only in windswept rags.

The Crone moved her finger in a circle about Clarinda, who found herself rooted to the spot. She felt like hissing herself at this injustice.

The Crone's cracked voice was less hostile as she addressed Harley. "Young man, you tried to stop your uncle's shade; you return my mirror. I give you what you would call a fighting chance. Destroy the being, if you can, now it has substance. If you love this girl, then fight to the death for her."

Harley and the monster circled each other, looking for an opening.

Clarinda fought to move: pleading with the Crone seemed ridiculous, but that didn't stop her. "If you relent, I beg you to stop this!"

"I tell you it has taken too much male energy from its victims. I must destroy my own in trying. Even after your magician's banishing, it returns to destroy. You weaken it still, by your passion for this savage young brute."

"But he's ill; let me fight too," gasped Clarinda, desperately trying to picture the force binding her dissolving.

A gust of wind swayed them all like saplings. Lightning ripped the sky overhead. The Crone's voice sounded in Clarinda's ears, undimmed by simultaneous thunder: "Let the male aggression run to its end. There is no other way. He brought this on himself. He threw away your love. He near betrayed you, and must yet."

"You tricked me in showing me that image. He did nothing to your daughter, or any innocent. I've seen her; she is beyond this –"

"Silence! You lie yourself!" the voice was a shriek.

"No; she comes to the maze..." Clarinda turned to surround Harley with light even as the being lunged at him. He threw it, smashing it to the leads. Lying prone, it tried to trip him, but he twisted free to kick its head, bursting its nose in a spray of dark, oily fluid.

Even as she acted as a human lighthouse, a part of Clarinda's mind noted that to be surely against those Broughton Rules Harley had talked of.

Leaping up, the creature got in a brutal blow to Harley's ribs. He jumped back, avoiding much of the impact; still, it rocked him and the monster tripped him in turn. Gurgling, it raised one foot to stamp on his face, black liquid trickling over him. He seized its foot and rolled, hurling it sideways on to the roof and wrenching the leg so that it tore half off in another gush of dark fluid.

Clarinda had heard of people screaming without knowing it. She realised that the moaning in her ears came from herself as much as from the gale.

He stumbled up, and the monster was up too. Somehow balancing on the half-severed, buckled and leaking leg, the thing aimed a kick to his groin. Harley whirled back, but the blow got him in the thigh. The creature hurled itself on him, teeth bared, only to be met by combination punches to the head that knocked it off its feet to spin it over backwards.

It rose at once. Now its head, oddly dented, lolled grotesquely to one side. That seemed only a minor inconvenience to it. It rushed him, stumbling on its torn limbs, able to focus on him despite its dangling head, hissing and splattering black liquid, closing in.

Clarinda remembered overhearing Harley saying to Molyneux something about how a well-covered man could take body blows far better than lean fellows like themselves. She saw how they rocked him, surround him with protective light though she did. Again the monster tried to attack his groin. Perhaps it targeted his male parts as its own decaying ones were of no use to it or others.

Damp gusts battered them, and lightning split the gloom as Harley punched, kicked, threw and gouged the monster and it strove to do the same to him. He avoided its return attacks, landing far more blows than it did, literally tearing it apart. Clarinda thanked Heaven that skeletal as it looked, it was made of glutinous matter.

Besides its lolling, dented head and torn leg, one of its arms hung by strings of matter; still, feverish as he was, Clarinda could see how Harley tired. Her own breath came in gasps as she strained to break her bonds.

Shrieks came from below. The O'Hare children, attracted to trouble as to a magnet, saw the fight. A human enemy would have pleased them. One like a half-decayed corpse made even Peg doubt the result.

Now the monster hurled itself on Harley, sinking its teeth – which were far from glutinous – into his shoulder to tear off a chunk of flesh. He thrust his fingers into one of its eyes, gouging downwards. Oblivious to pain though it was, it loosened its bite to wrench its head away. Yet more of its black blood dripped onto the red drops of his own that stained his shirt.

"It pushes you to the edge!" Clarinda could see how the monster forced him ever backwards towards the chasm. Now she noticed something beyond.

The girl Rose stood once more by the fountain in the sunken garden, her arms outstretched towards her mother. The spectre of Toby Venn and the carriage had vanished.

"Your daughter." Clarinda somehow found a moment of calm.

The Crone raised her head. Even under the shawl, Clarinda saw her eyes dilate. She stretched out her arms also, her wail piercing in their ears. Then, whirling about, she aimed her finger again at her former slave, hurling an invocation.

Its flesh seemed to boil and it howled. Still it was there, seizing Harley's throat, forcing him towards the drop now only six foot away, while he gouged its remaining eye and the howling wind buffeted them.

Clarinda was free. She leapt to seize and wrench back the monster's head, twisting and swinging on it.

Though she felt its neck tear yet more, it flung her off, hurling her towards the edge. Even that touch sent a thrill of revulsion through her. Pain wrenched through her foot and ankle as she hit the leads, while her stomach rose as she rolled near to the drop. Harley, released from the thing's grasp, thrust her backwards with one leg, stumbling.

A voice from across the roof sounded, shouting some magical words. Lodovico Sharman was behind them at the trapdoor, hurling Latin at the monster. It fizzed and began at last to shriek.

The Crone glided forwards, raising the mirror, which sparked into a light as bright as the lightning flickering above. Her voice now calm, she spoke one command.

The being was dragged, keening, across the leads towards the mirror, dissolving as it went into a boiling cyclone of smoke, the sound now blended with that of the wind. With a flash it melted into the glass.

As she staggered to her feet, Clarinda could only think, "Good riddance." If things only turned out well, she might later be able to pray for the monster.

"It ends," the Crone, the edges of her form now dissolving, offered the mirror to her. "I must go. Hold up the mirror without fear; then break it."

Harley stood, bleeding, bruised and panting, knuckles split, hair wild, smeared with the spectre's gore. The Professor watched too as Clarinda held up the mirror. The Crone stretched up her knotted arms to the pulsing sky. With a long sigh, she vanished into a spiral of dust curling into the mirror. Clarinda, glancing across to the sunken garden, saw that the image of the girl had vanished.

The shades of the young and old John Molyneux and Timothy Carstairs were now drawn across the roof to be sucked into the mirror also. They looked neither to left nor right, and disappeared, drawn into the mirror with only a vague murmur of distant voices from that other July day so long ago.

The older Toby Venn followed. His debauched face was turned on his nephew. Harley watched him, eyes wide and chest heaving. The aging *roué*'s lips moved. The sound wafted distantly to their minds might have been, 'Forgive me'.

His nephew's look answered him. Whether this wisp of a plea was equally addressed to the vanished Rose and her mother, Clarinda had no idea.

Now her Uncle Greendale came up. He avoided her eyes, and it was only as he finally dissolved that a whisper about 'Pray for me,' came to Clarinda's ears. Clarinda bit her lip and murmured one for them all.

As he, too, turned into swirling particles that vanished into the mirror, the younger Foyle came up behind. He seemed more aware than the others as he swept towards them.

He paused by his old friend, smiling. His voice came teasing and human, and his transparent hand squeezed Harley's shoulder. "Game fight, Venn. You found the right one, though you took long enough to see sense." With a bow to Clarinda – who insanely, found herself smiling acknowledgment – he was gone.

Clarinda hobbled as she moved towards the edge, holding the mirror aloft, and Harley seized her waist. Glancing down, she became aware again of the murmur of voices from the staff transfixed below, staring up at the roof.

Harley joined her in a breathless shout of "Stand back! Heads below!" as she hurled the mirror to the ground yards from the group.

It seemed to hover in the air a long time. Turning, it burst into fragments, the frame splintering into sawdust. The inevitable blinding flash and crash came, and nothing hit the ground.

"Jesus, Mary and Joseph!" said O'Hare.

Harley, still breathless, yelled down, "Don't come up!" Ignoring the shouts drifting up, he drew Clarinda back from the edge. "Foolish girl, I told you to keep safe."

"As always. Are you much hurt?" Clarinda stroked his face. Though the foul black blood that had smeared him had vanished, he was stained with his own, and perhaps it was this which gave his skin a blotchy look.

"I've had worse from a mill with a journeyman." Even so, his smile was rueful, and his blue gaze dazed.

Clarinda realised that the wind had calmed into a breeze. The storm had passed, incredibly without rain. The clouds above were pierced by sunshine. One by one, the birds began to sing.

Lodovico Sharman said, "A brave fight. Together we have triumphed. The spectres are banished. I worked upon that, while my body lay torpid. I knew from the first that your mutual love must protect you."

Harley's voice held no mockery. "I'm happy you joined us, Professor. I thank you for all that you have done."

"Forgive my delay. It took me some while to overcome my dread of enclosed spaces and heights." He smiled proudly. "But now they have left me, and I shall descend happily. I fear Lady Venn has hurt her foot, and you look ill besides battered from that fight, Sir. "

Harley tightened his arms about Clarinda. "I'll carry my wife down. There's a better way, with a rail, by the west tower. We'll follow you. There's something I want to say to her."

With a courtly bow, the Professor was gone.

Clarinda and Harley's lips met in a kiss. The heat in his made her drawn back in alarm. "You are truly ill, my dear. You mustn't carry me."

"I'd noticed. I feel worse by the minute, now that rush from the fight's gone. Damn me, when I asked for you – the second time, I mean – I spewed most disgusting, and I don't feel far from that now. I might even be dying – but here are those three words: I love you."

She had never thought that hackneyed phrase would sound so perfect. "I believe you do." She frowned. "But thinking about it, you have behaved so badly, and are not at all the sort of man I hoped to marry. Sadly, I think it must take me a long time to give you even a lukewarm return. Yet, I will try very hard to force myself to like you a little."

His face fell. "When you wrote that I had become dear to you, I hoped that it was more than that. Well, I am justly served. Before, I flattered myself that you had fallen for me, vain fool that I was. But why would you love a villain like me? I find you more desirable and lovely than any woman, now, and only you will do for me. If you were to try hard, though, my darling, couldn't you love me a little in return, wicked though I am?"

She dimpled, melting. "I've loved you for weeks. But I see as you have chosen the incongruous role of domestic angel for me, that I must be a strict one."

He sighed. "Ah!" They kissed again, and he said, "You had me rattled, Clarinda. I'll do my best to change, but I'm going to let you down again and again."

She smiled. "Then I'll remember today. Especially if you will only change your attitude towards all women, not just me – and help me to use much of the money we have from those wrongdoers to put right some of the injustices all about."

He shook his head. "I can only try. Ah, you are so adorable." He drew her to him again.

Again, she was alarmed at his body heat, and how he swayed. She pulled away. "You need a doctor. You are much too dizzy to carry me down those steps. You'll launch us both into space. We'll both totter down together. "

"I carry you over the roof, anyway." Staggering, he picked her up and lurched over the roofs with her. After some steps, he paused. "Damn me, I think I truly am dying, at that!"

Gazing at his face, she suddenly laughed. He looked outraged. "You find that amusing?"

She slipped out of his hold, and squeezed his arm. "I don't think you're at all likely to die yet, my love, though you will feel you are for some days, and I'll show you every devotion, and so, no doubt will Peg. You're covered in spots. You have the measles."

The End

Futher Reading

If you have enjoyed this book by the author, you might enjoy:
That Scoundrel Emile Dubois
Or, The Light of Other Days
available now.

'Ravensdale'
available now.

and also
'Where Worlds Meet'
available now.

'Alex Sager's Demon'
available now.

Lucinda Elliots's blog on writing and literary criticism is on
http://sophieandemile.wordpress.com

About The Author

Lucinda Elliot was born in Buckinghamshire, England, and brought up in spacious great houses in isolated areas which her parents were renovating before it became fashionable. As these would have made fine settings for Gothic novels, that is perhaps why she writes Gothic.

www.ingramcontent.com/pod-product-compliance
Lightning Source LLC
Chambersburg PA
CBHW071120170626
46809CB00002B/441